PRAISE FOR J[

"An original romantic read that starts out light and plunges you into a powerfully emotional journey, spanning several well-plotted years."
—Tome Tender

"There are parts that will pull at your heartstrings and others that will have you blushing and breathing a little heavy."
—Lustful Literature

"K. A. Linde may be crowned by some as the 'Queen of Angst,' but Jewel is certainly giving her a run for her money."
—After Dark Book Lovers

"Absolutely awesome deliverance. Her humor is completely on my level, and so are her trauma and anxiety and emotionally driven plots."
—The Romance Vault

"I'm thrilled that I picked this book back up. It has become one of my favorites!"
—One Click Bliss

"Like all things JEA, this love story is mesmerizing, smart, and sexy as hell. Everything she writes is shimmery, soulful wizardry. I can't praise this book enough. JUST READ IT."
—Pam Godwin, *New York Times* bestselling author

"Beautifully and poetically written. Enthralling me from the very first page, Jewel E. Ann's book is exceptional. It's one of those stories that lasts with you well after you read the last page."
—Jenika Snow, *USA Today* bestselling author

"What a compelling read; we were hooked—furiously turning the pages yet never wanting this brilliant story to end."

—TotallyBooked

"Ms. Ann's words are like a soothing balm to my reader soul one minute and then a raging heat wave the next. She takes every emotion and plays them perfectly through her words."

—Dawn, Two Unruly Girls with a Romance Book Buzz

"Brilliant, captivating, and beautiful. The words within the pages hurt me and healed me. This book is another fascinating and fleshed out reminder of why Jewel is one of my favorite storytellers."

—Kate Stewart, international bestselling author

"I do not have enough words to adequately express how much I loved this book. Brilliant. Hilarious. Utterly breathtaking. *Fortuity* left me speechless with an addictive blend of wit, steam, and emotion. Five stars is not enough!"

—Aly Martinez, *USA Today* bestselling author

"Poignant, sexy, and so moving, *When Life Happened* will tear a hole in your heart and fill it back in piece by piece. I'm still thinking about it days later. Five stars all the way from beginning to end. Just bring the tissues!"

—Lex Martin, *USA Today* bestselling author

FROM
AIR

FROM AIR

JEWEL E. ANN

 Montlake

Text copyright © 2024 by Jewel E. Ann
All rights reserved.

Published by Montlake, Seattle

www.apub.com

Amazon, the Amazon logo, and Montlake are trademarks of Amazon.com, Inc., or its affiliates.

ISBN-13: 9781662523670 (paperback)
ISBN-13: 9781662523687 (digital)

Cover design by Hang Le
Cover photography by Regina Wamba of ReginaWamba.com
Cover image: © Bernulius, © Miresan Ciprian, © PAVLO SVITLO, © Vitalii Stock / Shutterstock; © Regina Wamba

Printed in the United States of America

For Georgana, this is just the beginning.

Chapter One

JAYMES

"You should get a gun and a vibrator." Melissa crosses her arms, rocking back and forth on her flip-flop-clad feet. She's angry that I'm leaving her. We've been best friends for as long as I can remember. And, according to her, best friends never leave. She's a total Cancerian.

With a laugh, I inspect the three things in the back of my Jeep—a suitcase, my skateboard, and a box.

That stupid box. For the record, I don't want to know if I'm dying. Preparation is overrated, along with dying wishes. My mom had six months to live—six months to prepare for her death. She died in three.

Three months to rethink her life.

Three months to sort through her belongings and specify which boxes I should keep "forever." She was a hoarder; I am a minimalist. Out of fifteen keep-forever boxes, I only lug around the one containing the contents of her fire safe—some jewelry, her passport, miscellaneous certificates, photos, and a dozen or so manila envelopes. I believe they are tax returns. The rest of the boxes reside in Melissa's parents' storage unit. They're confident I'll want everything when I'm old enough to appreciate the sentimentality of it.

Mom lived up to her zodiac sign—she was a Cancerian like Melissa, who also keeps everything.

On point with minimalism, I am a Virgo.

"A gun and a vibrator? Interesting combination. There's a high probability of a self-inflicted injury with either one." I close the back of my Jeep and turn toward Melissa and her pouty rosebud lips and piercing hazel eyes beneath her perfectly arched brows.

"Everyone in Montana owns a gun," she says, flipping out her hip while the thick Miami humidity wreaks havoc on her long chocolate-cherry hair, curling her recently chopped bangs. A regrettable decision.

"And a vibrator?" I raise an eyebrow that's less than perfectly arched.

"You're not a people person." She smirks, smoothing her hands down my shoulder-length black hair like a mother fussing over a child before taking family photos.

Suppressing my eye roll, I lift onto my toes and hug her. "You're a person, and I like you. And I'm going to miss you."

"I've heard Montana's cold in January. Have you ever seen snow? Have you driven in it?" She changes the subject while wiping the corners of her eyes.

I take a step back, adjusting the waistband of my Lululemon leggings and tugging my white crew neck tee away from my sweaty chest. "I'm leaving Miami. I think it's safe to say every place north of us is colder in January. Winter won't last forever. And I *have* seen snow— once. I'm sure Fiona is great in the snow." I give the side of my Jeep two confident slaps.

"Fiona is only as good as her driver." Melissa sniffles while checking her reflection in the back window. She scowls and corrals her frizzy hair with one hand while her other keeps the wind from blowing up her cotton skirt for a peep show.

I can't look at her red-rimmed eyes. If she makes me cry, I swear I will strangle her.

"Also"—she continues her futile case—"your mom would not be okay with you having a male roommate you've never met. Stranger danger."

"Good thing she's—"

Melissa gasps, releasing her hair and pressing her fingers to my lips. "Jaymes Lanette Andrews! Don't you dare say it."

I crank my neck and bat away her hand. "Stop. It's been two years. I love her. I will always love her. But I will not live like she's looking over my shoulder."

Melissa deflates with a sigh.

"Listen, Mel, one of the other nurses knows Will. She said he's as good as they get. She's the one who gave me this rental listing. I'm not worried. You need not worry either. And my mom is"—I quickly inspect the alleyway behind our three-story apartment building, littered with bikes, trash bins, and a handful of cars, before lowering my voice—"dead. So she's no longer worrying about me."

"I'm serious about the gun, Jamie."

I open the driver's side door. "I don't know how to use a gun. I'd only shoot myself in the foot or accidentally kill someone. Love you! I'll call you when I make it to my first stop."

It takes six days, multiple near fender benders, and white-knuckle driving in the snow, but Fiona and I arrive in Missoula—thankfully, in one piece. Icicles hang from the gutters of my temporary home, a simple gray two-story with a steeply pitched roof, white shutters, a dilapidated porch, and a tiny balcony on the second floor. It's perfect.

The driveway's been cleared of snow, so I pull behind an old red Bronco cloaked in dirt and salt residue.

When I open my car door, a gust of frigid air bites my face, a sure sign this Miami girl will freeze her tits off.

I hop down. *"Shit!"* My boots find no traction, and I nearly do the splits, saving myself by planting my hands on the slippery driveway.

"Whoa! Easy there. Are you okay?"

I gingerly slide my feet closer together. It's what I imagine ice-skating is like if you're bad at it. "Yes. I'm great. Just stretching. It's been a long drive." Standing upright, I brush the snow off my hands.

A sandy blond with a thick mustache gives me a winning grin. "You must be Jaymes."

I accept his proffered hand. "Jamie."

"I'm Will. And I apologize. I meant to throw down a little ice melt."

"It's fine. I need better boots. I opted for warmth, not traction. Both would be good."

Will chuckles. "Traction's good. What can I get for you?"

"I just have a suitcase, my skateboard"—I open the back of my Jeep and frown—"and a box."

"Got it." He hauls my suitcase and box toward the house. "You just focus on staying vertical."

"Thank you." I follow with cautious steps and my skateboard hugged to my chest.

A faint piney scent, maybe a furniture polish, greets me when I step inside, wiping my boots on the blue-and-metal-gray braided rug. On my left, a half-dozen cast-iron hooks hold coats, hats, and scarves. Stairs covered in worn beige carpet make a steep incline to the second floor.

"Leave your boots on," Will instructs me, nodding toward the stairs. "There are two bathrooms upstairs. You'll share the one with the blue shower curtain." The narrow strip of wood flooring creaks under his boots while he leads me to the sliding glass door at the back of the house.

"With you?"

"No, with Maren. You don't want to share the other with Fitz and me. The toilet seat will always be up, and we don't clean it as often as we should."

We pass the living room on the right. There's not much wiggle room around the oversize brown leather sofa and matching recliner facing the bone-colored wall behind a TV—a buck's head on one side and a collage of black-framed photos on the other. A repurposed tree trunk on casters serves as a rugged coffee table atop the *very* worn beige carpet.

The mahogany blinds covering the bay window could use a dusting, but everything's tidy and welcoming, including the open kitchen between the living room and the back door.

Will opens the sliding door to the covered deck.

"Uh . . . who are Maren and Fitz?" I ask as he nods to the left at the laundry room before stepping outside.

"My other roommates." Will treads through nearly a foot of icy snow.

I skip and jump to land my feet in his boot tracks.

He stops at a red shed in the corner of the yard, nestled between two groupings of evergreens sagging from the heavy blanket of snow. "It's my house, but they rent rooms as well."

"What are we—" My question dies the second Will opens the door to the shed. I take a hesitant step inside, where there's a daybed with a white-and-blue checked comforter, floral decorative pillows, a light-blue velvet chair, and a weathered white dresser with a mirror.

Leaving my boots on the shaggy gray rug, I step onto the navy-painted hard-surface floor that's curiously warm. A row of plants sits on a window ledge surrounded by white shiplap walls. It's a lovely room, just like in the photos.

However, that it's in a shed in the backyard wasn't in the photos or the description. The listing said it was a four-bedroom, two-bathroom house with a shared living room, kitchen, and laundry.

"The *feminine* decor is all Maren's taste. But since you're a girl, I'm sure you won't mind it." Will deposits my suitcase and box on the floor. "Here's a key to the house." He hands me a fire hydrant key chain with a dangling silver key.

I glance over my shoulder at the house.

"Everything good?"

I turn back toward him. "I, uh . . ." I set my skateboard on the floor and toss my purse on the bed before taking the key from him.

"Shit. You thought it was in the house?"

"Kinda, sorta . . . yeah."

With a sigh, he scrubs his face. "Maren was right. I thought the 'private room' made it clear. Is this going to be a problem?"

"Not per se." I offer Will an earnest smile. "I had a picture in mind, a room in a house. It will take a bit to adjust for the discrepancy between reality and my expectations." My incessant nodding gains momentum as I adapt in real time. "As long as I drink nothing after eight p.m., I should be good. Fine. Yep. No problem."

"Cool. Well, the floor's heated, and the walls are well insulated. You shouldn't need anything else, but feel free to buy an extra blanket. Things around here are laid back. Spend as much time in the house as you want. We cleared a shelf in the fridge for you, and you have a kitchen cabinet."

"Thank you." I turn in a slow circle while finger combing my staticky rat's nest of hair.

"So you're a nurse. Correct?" Will removes his beanie and scratches his head before pulling his hat back over his shaggy hair.

I stare at the tiny mole beneath his left eye for a second, the same eye that has a slight twitch when he smiles. "Yes. A travel nurse. I lucked out and found a six-month position here in a mental health clinic."

"Oh." He returns a sheepish grin. "I think you mentioned that in one of our messages. Sounds stressful."

"I worked in the ER, which was way more stressful."

"You'll fit right in with this first responder crew."

"Oh?"

He briefly glances out the window, blue eyes squinting at a bird feeder hanging from a steel shepherd's hook. "I'm an engine chief for the Missoula Fire Department. Fitz is a smoke jumper, and Maren is an air tanker pilot."

"Smoke jumper?"

"Yes. They're wildland firefighters who parachute into remote areas to suppress fires. They can get there quickly. Some call them elite, but I don't feed Fitz's ego, and neither should you."

I chuckle. "Sheesh. I feel boring in comparison."

"Don't." He rubs his jaw. "You'll be a breath of fresh air around here. Egos get out of control in a houseful of firefighters."

"Good thing I'm not in the house." I give him a toothy grin.

"Damn." He shakes his head. "I messed up that listing. I'm sorry."

I wave him off. "I'm kidding. Don't be sorry. This is perfect."

"I hope so." He steps toward the door. "Well, I'll let you get settled."

"Thanks."

"Oh, fair warning." Will turns back to me. "Maren will hunt you down when she gets home. Be prepared. She's"—he twists his lips—"a lot."

"I left a roommate who is *a lot*, so we'll be good."

"And try to ignore Fitz if you do happen to run into him. He's a loner and an asshole. I don't want to use the word *sanctimonious*, but I just did. However, he pays rent on time, and he's gone more than he's here, so we put up with his stellar personality. But I'm sure you're used to dealing with mentally ill people."

Biting my lower lip, I nod several times. "Got it. Leave Fitz alone."

"Exactly." Will winks and shuts the door.

Chapter Two

CALVIN

A white Jeep with Florida plates occupies my parking spot. I grumble and pull my truck onto the street. I like order and routine when I can have it, but I live with two people who are routinely out of order.

When I push open the squeaky door, Will's perched in his usual spot on the sofa's edge, remote in hand, zoned in on his PlayStation game. The brown leather is worn to a little bit of nothing on that side. He barely turns his head in acknowledgment; it's more like a flinch that doesn't require more than 1 percent of his attention.

"Why is there a Jeep in my spot? Is there a naked girl from Florida in your bed while you're playing games?" I drop a K-Cup into my life support machine. It's almost five o'clock—which happens to be my coffee cutoff time in the winter.

"I forgot to tell her where to park. And she's not in my bed." When his avatar dies, he hurls his remote across the room with a few expletives.

It's hard to believe he's thirty-seven and not seventeen.

"Then where is she?" I snatch my blue YETI Rambler mug from the shelf. "Finishing the job in the shower?"

"Fuck you, Fitz. I get the job done." He ambles into the kitchen, snags a bottle of lager from the fridge, and twists off the top. "The

Jeep belongs to our new roommate. She's nice. She's normal. Don't piss her off."

Pressing my hands against the counter's edge, I arch my back and roll my stiff neck. "How would I do that?"

The sliding door opens, and a woman in light-gray leggings and a white sweater that engulfs her body steps inside. Big brown eyes land on me, and she curls her dark, pin-straight hair behind her ear on one side. It doesn't tame the static, as clumps and strands still cling to her face and stand out in all directions. Her glossed lips rub together before she offers me a shy smile beneath a butterfly of freckles along her nose and sun-kissed cheeks.

As soon as I realize I'm focusing on freckles and thinking the words *sun-kissed cheeks*, I avert my gaze and clear my throat. "You're parked in my spot."

Will slaps my shoulder. "Just like that, Fitz. Good job."

"Yes. Sorry." She holds up a key. "I was just going to move it. Where do you want me to park?"

"Anywhere but in my spot." I offer the most direct and helpful solution—the most obvious one.

Will coughs the word *asshole*. Then he snags her key. "I'll get you parked on the street. When Maren moves out and Fitz's parachute fails him, you can park in the driveway beside me."

"I have a backup chute," I inform Captain Dumbass before sipping my coffee. Will's a blowhard disguised as a suck-up.

There's a reason he's still single. And it has nothing to do with his job, unlike me. I'm happily married to mine.

"Fitz, just stop talking. Go read a book." Will shoves his feet into his black boots and exits the front door.

"I'm Jaymes Andrews. You can call me Jamie or Wretched Woman Who Parks in the Wrong Spot. Whatever works." Her hand floats in the air between us along with the hint of something sweet, like a fruity body spray or perfume.

I don't think I've ever shaken hands with Will or Maren. But I'm not the asshole they think I am, so I shake her hand. If only my other roommates were here to witness my cordialness, it might earn me a little reprieve from their whininess about my disregard for human contact.

Jamie has small hands, or maybe that oversize sweater makes everything about her seem dainty.

"I'm Calvin."

Her eyebrows lift a fraction. "Not Fitz?"

"Calvin Fitzgerald."

"Do you prefer Calvin or Fitz?"

I shrug, tucking one hand into my back pocket. "Doesn't matter."

"Well . . ." She points toward the stairs. "I just came inside to use the bathroom. I'll try to keep my hydration to a minimum so as not to disturb you." Her lips twitch.

Is she mocking me? I'm well versed in childish mockery, thanks to those other two.

"I can get you a five-gallon bucket if you tire of trekking through the snow." I hide my grin behind my YETI mug.

Jamie ascends the stairs. "Before I left Florida five days ago, I'd only seen snow once. It will be a while before I tire of trekking through it."

Once?

"Did you scare her off already?" Will kicks off his boots and brushes the snow from his hair.

"Scared the piss out of her. She scurried up the stairs to the bathroom. You really should add a toilet and sink in the laundry room." Suddenly, I'm concerned about the new girl climbing stairs to use the toilet. What is wrong with me?

Will retrieves the remote he threw across the room. "She looks like she's lived on the beach in a bikini for the past two decades."

"Yes. She's tan." Eyeing Will, I wait for him to look at me. "And young."

He smirks. "She's twenty-five."

I lift my brows.

"What?" He puffs out his chest.

"Don't fuck the new roommate. House rules."

It's the rule that *he* made because he let his dick ruin a good situation in the past.

"*Pfft.*" He sips his beer. "Twenty-five. That's twelve years younger than me and ten younger than you, Fitz. Damn, that makes me feel old."

"Are you talking about me?" Jamie skips down the stairs with the confidence of someone who's lived here for years—like Maren.

Great. Just what we need: another spitfire woman.

"We were talking about your tan." Will smiles. "Can I get you something to drink?"

"I'm good. I'll run to the store soon." Her lips corkscrew while she's tapping her fingers on the back of the sofa. "Once I search up the nearest store on my map app."

"Go with Fitz." Will gestures at me with his beer.

I shake my head. "I'm not going."

Will tries to call me out with a knowing smirk. My eyes narrow in his direction. He mirrors my expression. He's dense, with the subtlety of an elephant.

"Fitz, you go every Wednesday at six thirty if you're home. You're so predictable it's nauseating." Pleasure bleeds from Will's words. I'm his favorite target.

And he's mine.

I peek at my watch. "Don't you have your ballet class soon?"

"Tai chi, asshole," Will corrects me. "And yeah, I need to get going." He tosses his empty bottle in the bin. "Maren should be home soon. If I were you, I'd stay in the shed until then. But then again, you're used to the mentally unstable. Maybe you can fix Fitz for us." He winks at Jamie before jogging up the stairs.

Jamie leans against the back of the sofa, arms crossed. "Fix Fitz? Are you broken, Calvin Fitzgerald?"

"Do I look broken?"

Her head tilts to the side. "Not the kind of broken I'm used to seeing. So I won't judge you *yet*." She grins.

It's a pleasant grin, and I berate myself for thinking that the second it pops into my head.

Freckles.

Pleasant grins.

Jesus, I need sleep.

"I've lived a sheltered life, so you might be perfectly normal for someone who jumps out of planes to fight wildfires with a big axe."

"Yes." I rub my neck. "I gathered that from the snow revelation. And that *big axe* is called a Pulaski."

"Oh, the snow." She sighs. "I'm in love with snow. Who knew? I'm in love with the mountains. I've lived in Florida my whole life. And I was homeschooled until I attended college. So, yeah"—her nose scrunches—"sheltered."

"Homeschooled?" Will's silvery voice rides my nerves as he reaches the bottom of the stairs. "Holy shit, Fitz. She's your soulmate."

Jamie regards me with twisted lips and expectant eyes.

"Fitz was homeschooled. I've always assumed that's why he's socially awkward." Will retrieves a bottle of water from the fridge. "But now I must develop a new theory, since you're perfectly normal, Jamie." He slides on a black hoodie and grabs his keys. "Be good, kids."

"Bye," Jamie says, because she doesn't know that acknowledging Will on any level only encourages his obnoxious behavior. Her attention returns to me while I dump the last few sips of my coffee into the sink and rinse my mug.

"You're a fixer?" I ask.

"What?"

I peer over my shoulder. "Will suggested you could fix me, even though I'm not broken."

"Oh." She nods, climbing onto a barstool. "I'm a nurse. I took a temporary job here at a psychiatric clinic. The doctors fix people. I just help keep people alive, comfortable, and medicated. And working with psych patients is extra rewarding. So many of them have been abandoned by friends and loved ones. I feel like I'm their advocate, the one person who sees them regularly and cares for them."

"I see." I dry the mug and hang the towel over the dishwasher handle. "Well, I have to run to the store—"

Shit. I can't walk that back. Now she knows I'm a liar.

Jamie hops off the barstool and eyes me with a tiny grin while fiddling with her gold pendant necklace. "I get it. You like alone time. Grocery shopping isn't exactly a team sport. I'm not a social butterfly either. What's your sign?"

"Sign?"

"Zodiac sign."

Is she serious? Do I seem like the kind of guy who knows my sign?

"Smoke jumper. Loner. Grouchy." Her finger taps her bottom lip.

Grouchy? *What the fuck?*

"Capricorn?"

"Again, I'm standing here not knowing what you're talking about. And I feel like a dick after the grocery store comment. So help me not be a dick by just getting to the point."

Her eyes widen. "Total Capricorn. Did you just have a birthday? Or is your birthday coming up in the next week or so?"

What is she? A psychic?

"December 28."

She doesn't even act surprised that she made a lucky guess. "I'm a Virgo, so I respect solitude too. Later, Calvin."

"If you want to go to the store with me—"

"Nope." She putters to the sliding door and lobs a grin in my direction. "I don't want to go with you. Maybe because I don't want you judging me for my food choices, or maybe you *are* a dick. It's too soon to say."

Chapter Three

JAYMES

"Estrogen!"

My head snaps to attention at the piercing squeal when I enter the house with two bags of groceries and catch an immediate whiff of buttery popcorn.

A long-haired blonde, several inches taller than me, surges in my direction with gregarious energy, a glint in her blue eyes, and her arms spread like an eagle approaching its prey. "I'm Maren." She hugs me. "Do you love my old room? I already miss it." Holding me at arm's length, she gives me a slow assessment. "You're cute as a button. And so tan. Damn, I need to get to the beach more often."

"Down, girl," Will calls from the floor behind the sofa with a foam roller at his back.

"Jamie." I return a nervous smile. "I'm delighted to meet you."

She carries my bags to the kitchen while I remove my coat and boots.

"Oh, that bag is—"

Too late.

Maren has my box of tampons on the counter next to my toothpaste and deodorant.

"That goes to my room." I clear my throat and conceal my embarrassment with an overkill smile.

"I'll put them in our bathroom. There's no need to haul your toiletries in and out of the house. If you don't like my shed, just let me know. We can swap rooms. Traditionally, the shed is for the newbie—the house rookie. But I remodeled it when I moved here, and honestly, it's the best room in the house because it's not in the house with these disgusting men." Maren disappears upstairs with my toiletries.

"Told you she's a lot." Will lumbers to standing in his gray low-hanging sweatpants and black T-shirt and joins me in the kitchen to unpack my non-tampon bag of groceries.

I have two bonus roommates and more help than I need.

"This one's yours." He organizes my nonperishable items in the empty, faded oak cabinet below the beige-and-green granite counter. And I use the word "organize" lightly.

I'll redo it later.

"Your shelf in the fridge is the empty one, and we share condiments. If you use the last of something shared, you have eight hours to replace it."

I laugh.

"I'm not joking." Will tips his chin toward the stairs. "Fitz will lose his shit if we run out of Dijon. He's such a mustard snob—puts it on everything."

"You only have to put up with us for a few months," Maren notes, popping around the corner while tucking the front of her red-and-white flannel shirt into her black skinny jeans. "When fire season starts, Fitz and I will be nonexistent. And Will spends his days off trying to impregnate half of Montana."

"Lies. All lies." Will looks askance at Maren.

I giggle, folding my paper bags. "It's fine. It sounds like I'd better not get attached to any of you, since you're leaving me in a few months."

Will and Maren share somber expressions.

"I said something wrong." My gaze ping-pongs between them.

They continue to inspect each other for a few more seconds. Then Maren musters a sad smile. "We might as well give you full disclosure." She swallows hard.

Will starts to stroll past her but stops and kisses the crown of her head before finding his spot on the sofa.

The temperature of the room drops ten degrees in five seconds.

Maren pulls in a shaky breath. "We have a room available for you because my brother, Brandon, died last summer. A firefighter—a hotshot."

"I'm sorry." I squeeze her hand, hoping my presence won't be a reminder that he's no longer here, the way that box in the shed is a reminder that my mom is gone.

She nods, blinking back the tears. "Thank you. It took me a while to feel okay about sleeping in his room. But it's oddly comforting now. And go ahead and get attached to us." Her sadness turns into something resembling hope. "Isn't that the point of life?"

"Except Fitz. Don't waste your time on him," Will adds.

Maren smirks and releases my hand to blot the corners of her eyes. "Definitely don't waste your time on Fitz. It's not that he's a pariah, but he's not far off."

"Poor Fitz." I snicker, retrieving the bag of trail mix from my cabinet. "Maren, what do you do when it's not fire season?"

She fiddles with the edges of my grocery bags. "I—"

"She transports Professor Gray Balls to his conferences." Will cackles.

"William, should I be concerned that you seem to know his balls are gray?" Maren asks.

Will ignores her.

With an exaggerated eye roll, Maren returns her attention to me. "Ted is my dad's best friend and a professor of environmental physics. He travels all over the world to conferences. He's brilliant. Sought after. And . . ." Her nose wrinkles.

"Old?" I question before filling a glass with water from the filtered jug in the fridge.

"Eighty-two," Maren confesses.

"Maren's waiting for him to die," Will says. "Fitz and I firmly believe he's leaving her all his assets when he dies."

"Why is that?" I take a sip of cold water.

Maren slides the folded bags under the sink next to the garbage. "Ted never married. No kids. No family other than a sister in Portugal who's not doing well. And he's *not* leaving his money to me."

"Maren, you massage his anal glands." Will tosses the game remote aside and grabs a handful of popcorn from the stainless steel bowl on the tree-trunk coffee table.

"Stop." She snorts. "You're such a dumbass, Will. It was his dog. And it was only once."

I bite back my smile when she looks at me. "I'm, uh . . ." I jab my thumb over my shoulder toward the back door. "I'm going to go call my friend before it gets any later." My jaw stretches in a long yawn. "She's on eastern time, and so is my body. Are you showering? I need to wash off the day's drive before I pass out."

"Nope. It's all yours."

"Maren never showers." Will's relentless.

She flips him the bird without taking her eyes off me. "I don't wash my hair more than twice a week, hence the shower cap, *William*."

This is more than I ever expected. I have a great place to stay and three new friends. Well, two new friends and Calvin Fitzgerald.

Back in my shed, I FaceTime Melissa.

She answers right away, wrapped in a fuzzy pink robe, hair piled in a bun on top of her head, and face covered in a gray clay mask. "Tell me it was a huge mistake, and you're coming home immediately."

An irresistible smile creeps along my face while I retrieve sweatpants from my dresser drawer for after my shower. There won't be any scurrying off to my bedroom in nothing but a towel. "Don't be mad, but I think I love it here."

"What? No! You just got there. What can you possibly love already?"

"The snow. The mountains. My room. It's a shed—a she shed. But look!" I turn my phone in a slow circle.

"That's super cute."

"It is." I plop onto the bed. "The downside is I must trek through the yard and snow to use the bathroom."

"That seems like an important piece of information to withhold when advertising a room for rent." Melissa wrinkles her nose, causing the face mask to crack.

"Agreed. But I think I'm going to love my private space. And I have the nicest roommates."

She clears her throat, giving me the stink eye.

"I'd like to retract that last statement."

"You'd better."

I blow her a kiss. "You know I love you the most."

"You said 'roommates.' Is there more than just the guy?"

"Will owns the house. But he has two friends living with him. Another guy and a girl. They're all firefighters and older. I'm definitely the youngest in the house. Will is an engine chief with the Missoula Fire Department. Maren is a tanker pilot. How badass is that? And Calvin, who they call Fitz, is a smoke jumper. Mel, he jumps out of planes to fight wildfires!"

Her eyes bug out. "That's . . ."

"Mind blowing."

"Is he single? Is Will? What's the situation there? I hate cold weather, but if a guy's hot enough, I think I could relocate."

"I don't know. I haven't asked. I don't want to sound interested."

"Well, I'm interested. So, say you're asking for a friend."

"That's code for 'I'm asking for myself.'"

"Sometimes. But sometimes you're actually asking for a friend."

"I need to get showered. I'm exhausted."

"Don't leave me hanging, Jaymes!"

With a giggle, I shake my head. "I miss you already."

"Aw . . . I miss you too. But seriously, if those guys are single, I'll be there by this weekend."

"Muah! Night, hon."

"Night."

I'm sure this will get old, but tonight, I don't mind throwing on my puffy white jacket and black boots to make my way to the house in the snow.

Maren's at the kitchen island with her head bowed over her phone, and Will's stretched out on the sofa watching football. I give Maren a quick smile before jogging up the stairs, feeling ecstatic because my wings have spread wide, and I'm on a new adventure.

"Oof!" I grunt, body slamming into shirtless Calvin and his woodsy scent of bodywash, aftershave, or maybe just rugged Montana masculinity.

He grips my arms and guides me to his side. "In a hurry?"

God took a little extra time sculpting Calvin Fitzgerald—high cheekbones, strong jaw, thick brown hair, and just enough natural body to land him a shampoo commercial if the smoke jumper thing doesn't work out. It's unfair to every other man. Don't even get me started on his intense blue eyes.

There's a burn scar above his right pec and another peeking out just above the waistband of his sweatpants. He's fit, to put it mildly. Melissa will never be allowed to visit me.

"I officially feel violated," Fitz says.

Peeling my gaze from his bare chest, I swallow and smile. My lips tremble, so I press them together. "I have a friend. An herbalist. She makes oils and salves that help scars fade. Good ingredients like, uh . . ." I hug my clothes tighter as Fitz lifts an eyebrow. "Calendula, lavender, salvia . . . I think some sort of nut oil."

"A nut oil?"

My cheeks burn. "I think it's a European filbert or hazelnut." I stare at my feet, briefly closing my eyes.

Shut up, Jaymes!

"For my scars, not my nuts. Correct?"

Will and Maren were right—Calvin Fitzgerald is an asshole. He's feasting on my embarrassment.

"I can ask my friend if there's anything in the salve that might help you grow a pair, but no guarantees." I lift my chin and smirk, enjoying this triumphant feeling.

"Sucks being homeschooled."

"Why?" I ask.

He cinches the tie on his sweatpants. "Because you're given a copious amount of information—*Jeopardy!*-level miscellaneous information. And while it might make you the most interesting person in the room, it's not usually in a good way. What starts as an herbal salve recommendation becomes an awkward conversation about testicles."

"I'm a nurse, *Fitz*. I can talk testicles all day. What do you want to know? Need me to see if yours have dropped yet?" I mentally air punch—the right words at the right time. I can tell Montana is a perfect fit for me.

Fitz confirms this by rubbing his fingers over his lips to hide his grin. "Welcome to Missoula, Jaymes Andrews."

Shoulders back. Chin up. This feels amazing.

I wink at Fitz before continuing to the bathroom.

Chapter Four

The first day at a new job is the worst. It's as if I have no formal training. I'm not a real nurse. And everyone, including the employees in the café serving lunch, knows more than I do.

"Don't feel overwhelmed," Cecilia reassures me on our way to Dr. Reichart's office. Cee's the office manager. She's worked at the clinic longer than anyone else. But when she flicks her tousled ash-blond bangs away from her face and adjusts her black-framed glasses with a conspiratorial grin revealing her coffee-stained teeth, I decide her words lack comfort.

"I'm not overwhelmed," I lie. If only I could borrow her confident smile and introduce such a lively chirp to my words.

"Was Dr. Reichart part of your interviews?" Cee hastens down one hallway of short red-and-gray speckled carpet, takes a sharp turn, and blasts through the next hallway, which looks just like the first. I'm already lost and three steps behind, standing at five feet four. She has at least six inches on me, all in the legs, not to mention the extra inch in the soles of her pink-and-blue HOKA shoes.

"No. She was on vacation." I jog to keep up.

"Act indifferent. She doesn't like it when people try to impress her."

"Don't impress my new boss. Got it."

Cee glances back at me, lowering her chin to eye me over the rims of her glasses. "It's hard to explain. You just have to experience her. Then you'll know what I'm talking about. If she didn't wear a white coat, you might be unable to distinguish her from the patients." Cee knocks on the door.

"Yes?"

"Jaymes Andrews is here. She's been brought up to speed on everything."

I'm not sure I'm up to speed on anything—definitely not on the long-legged office manager. Crossing the threshold, I prepare to be surrounded by sophistication, modern decor, an abstract painting by some artist I've never heard of, and maybe some Beethoven and rare plants.

Instead, I'm surrounded by bare white walls. There's nothing on her desk except a computer and an M&M'S dispenser, and she's turning circles in the middle of the room while wearing a VR headset.

"Just a sec . . ." She makes a swiping motion with the controller in her right hand like she's swinging a sword.

When she peels off the headset, I blink hard several times. Dr. Everleigh Reichart looks underage. She blows a few strands of amber hair away from her face before slicking them back toward her ponytail. A few pimples reside along her hairline, which makes sense because she must be fifteen. I do the math in my head. This is a joke. There's no way she has a medical degree, let alone a specialty in psychiatry.

"Do you play?" She holds up the headset, revealing her short purple-painted fingernails.

I shake my head. "I was homeschooled. And I'm not saying that to impress you. My access to technology before graduating high school was limited. But I hear VR is pretty cool."

She snorts, revealing polished teeth that would look fairly perfect sans a little crowding on the bottom. "Don't worry about impressing me with your homeschooling. I bet you're still a virgin."

"I don't think so." *Can she ask me that?*

Dr. Reichart tosses her headset on the desk, hazel eyes narrowed a fraction at me.

When I offer my version of a conspiratorial smile, she laughs.

"Let's just get it out of the way." She dismissively waves her hand in the air. "I was a freshman in college by age twelve. Undergraduate degree three years later. Med school . . . you get the gist. Too smart for my own good, according to my parents." She dispenses a handful of M&M candies and shoves them into her mouth, leaving a lingering sweet aroma of chocolate in the air. "My dad is a physician in India. My mom paints pictures of naked couples, and she lives in New York. Any more questions?"

"No. That answers all the questions I didn't think to ask. I look forward to working with you. Cecilia said patients love you."

She drops her chin, dramatically rolling her eyes. "Aw, shucks."

I gesture toward the door because I'm way out of my league on every level, so it's time to leave. "If there's nothing else, I'll get to work."

"Stop by my office again over your lunch. I'll teach you how to play *Beat Saber*."

"Okay. That's . . . kind of you." And weird. I back out of her office. Cecilia was right. There are no words to describe Dr. Everleigh Reichart.

"You're going to get towed," Fitz announces, stomping on the rug before removing his brown boots.

I pluck a spoon from the drawer for my potato-leek soup, which has one more minute in the microwave. "I'm parked where Will told me to park."

"It's snowing. You can't park on the street." He deposits his green Carhartt jacket on a coat hook.

I can't get enough of Calvin in cargo pants and snug-fitting, long-sleeved T-shirts, but I'll never tell him that. His ego runneth over all on its own.

"Help me out, Fitz. Offer the new girl more than doom and gloom. Try suggesting a way to keep me from getting towed. I believe the word is a *solution*."

He retrieves a black cherry iced tea from the fridge. "Why are you talking like that?"

I blow at the garlic-and-thyme-filled steam while carrying my soup to the table. "Like what?"

He tips back the bottle of tea, eyeing me the whole time. "Slowly. Softly. Like you're talking to a child."

I grin just before cautiously sipping my soup. "I think Will and Maren expect me to fix you."

His lips droop into a frown. It's hard to keep my composure. Calvin Fitzgerald is the epitome of a brooding man. Taking him on as my pet project should be fun.

"Park in the driveway." He gives me a toothy grin that's a little frightening. "See? I just fixed myself. But if you want to take credit for it, go ahead." Fitz sets his tea on the counter and pulls a white paper bag out of the fridge along with a jar of hot sauce. He peels back the paper around the half-eaten burrito, shakes sauce onto it, and shoves a bite into his mouth.

"I'm not *allowed* to park in the driveway." I'm tempted to end my sentence with a "duh" instead of a period, but my mom would disapprove. Dead or alive.

"Will's on shift until Wednesday, and Maren's taking Professor Gray Balls to New York," he mumbles over a mouthful of the burrito.

I slurp another sip of my hot soup before grabbing my keys and tucking my feet into my boots. "So we'll be alone. That's good. You can share your deepest secrets with me." I slide my arms into my jacket.

"Fuck that." Fitz saunters up the stairs with his burrito and hot sauce in one hand and his tea in the other as I head out into the cold.

Will said Missoula rarely receives this much snow all at once. There's a mountain of it that's already been plowed. It engulfs my legs past my knees, sucking my boot right off my leg when I open the door and climb into the driver's seat.

"Oh, come on!" Holding the steering wheel for support, I lean sideways to fish my boot from the drift.

Shoving my foot back into it, I start my Jeep and press on the gas. Nothing.

I switch to reverse.

Nothing.

It's four-wheel drive. What's the problem?

After several failed attempts, I trek toward the garage, curling my toes to keep from walking out of my boots. Four different shovels hang on the wall. I grab two that might work well.

I bail snow, fall on my ass twice, and come dangerously close to losing my fingers to frostbite. My toes are total goners. Yet, I'm sweating through my clothes.

After unearthing my Jeep and pulling it into the driveway, I drag the shovels back to the garage. My gaze snags on the upstairs window at the corner of the house.

Calvin's watching me with his arms crossed. Has he been watching me the whole time?

"Asshole," I mumble.

He grins as if he can read my lips.

Minutes later, Fitz descends the stairs while I tug at my boots and peel off my jacket in the entry. "You needed to pull a little farther to the right. I won't be able to get past you in the morning."

I huff, blowing my sweaty bangs out of my face. "What time do you leave?"

"Five." He plops onto the sofa and kicks his bare feet onto the coffee table.

"Five? Why so early? Isn't it offseason for you?" I stick my finger into the soup and lick it. It's lukewarm.

"My body doesn't get an offseason. PT every day."

"Yeah, me too. I always get my ten thousand steps in." I pop the bowl of soup back into the microwave.

"Wow, ten thousand. What is that . . . four? Five miles?"

"Something like that. I have short legs."

"Yeah, speaking of your legs. You should lift with them when you shovel. Your back's going to hurt like a motherfucker in the morning."

"Oh? Did you make that observation while you watched me dig out my Jeep?"

He opens the book he brought down. "I did."

"You could have helped." I stir my reheated soup.

"And I probably would have, but rumor has it I'm broken. Maybe you can fix that, and then I'll have the mental and emotional capacity to recognize when a damsel is in distress."

"Did I look like a damsel in distress?" I glare at him.

He focuses on his book. "I don't know what you looked like. I just know it was painful to watch."

I absentmindedly tap the spoon on the edge of my bowl.

Calvin clears his throat, scowling at me.

"Sorry." I stop tapping.

Minutes later, he clears his throat again and shoots me another scowl.

"What?"

"The chair creaks every time you bounce your leg. Stop bouncing your leg. Can you hold still?"

"No. I'm a fidgeter. I always have been. Did you know—"

"Stop." He holds out a flat hand in my direction. "If you don't want to sound like a nerd wearing a 'homeschooled' neon sign, then don't ever start a sentence with 'Did you know.'"

"Fidgeting is good for your health. It increases blood flow, reduces artery disease, and calms anxiety."

"*Did you know* that it has the opposite effect on those in the same room as the fidgeter?" Calvin eyes me with displeasure.

"That's not true," I scoff.

He smirks, refocusing on his book. It's a book on the *Titanic*. And *I'm* the nerd?

After studying him over my soup bowl for a good five minutes while focusing on not fidgeting, I clear my throat. Fitz seems to speak that language.

His head swivels in my direction.

"Why jump out of planes?"

"To get to the fire. Any more questions?" His uncompromised grin is as fake as mine but not nearly as playful.

"Hotshots don't jump out of planes."

"Yes, *Encyclopedia Britannica*. I used to be a hotshot, so I can confirm that you are correct. But we smoke jumpers *jump*. It's in our name."

I take my bowl and spoon to the sink to wash them. "I bet you have a lot of first dates but not many second dates. Can you confirm that as well?" I roll up the sleeves of my pink-and-white-striped button-down.

"Roommates don't have to talk. It's not a requirement. It's a lot different than dating. No one has to speak. No one cares what anyone else is wearing. And it's no big deal if you want to walk away without an explanation."

I chuckle, rinsing the bowl. "Sometimes roommates can be friends who do, in fact, talk. I've gathered that Will and Maren aren't interested in letting you into their friendship circle, so I'm offering to be your friend."

When he doesn't respond, I peek over my shoulder, surveying the room. The empty room. Fitz left. He vanished without any explanation.

"Or roommates works," I murmur to myself. "I have other friends. Like . . . me, myself, and I because I'm talking to myself." I shake my head while drying my hands.

I'm unsure if I despise Calvin Fitzgerald or if he's officially my newest obsession.

Chapter Five

Betty O'Neil runs late every day. She's thirty-seven, has five kids from four men, and has never been married. Betty works with the mentally ill to feel normal—at least, that's my best assessment of her situation.

There's a lot to assess with Betty, such as her light-pink bob with freakishly short bangs. Did she wash her platinum hair with a red sock? Are the bangs a new style or a trim gone terribly wrong? Is she worried that one of her offspring might yank that silver septum piercing out of her nose?

"What's on your shirt?" I nod while she slips on a scrubs top over her white turtleneck.

"Hell if I know. After I wash my clothes, they're dirtier than before I washed them because I live with little monsters who keep crayons, markers, and bite-size candy bars in their pockets. Don't tell anyone I said this, but I might have too many kids."

"At least your scrubs top hides it."

Betty taps her tablet. "Has Lewis Cron arrived? His wife couldn't get him out of bed yesterday to make his appointment."

"Not yet." I lift my coffee to take a sip, and Betty snags it.

"I need this more than you." Her brown eyes roll back in her head when she takes a slow sip. She shoves it back into my hand, and I frown at the red lipstick stamped on the lid.

"How's it going at your new place? Isn't Will the best?" She digs through her purse and pops a piece of spearmint gum into her mouth.

"He's great. I never asked how you two know each other." I follow her toward the reception desk.

"I hooked up with one of his friends a few times."

"Oh?"

"Is it terrible I don't remember his name?" She peers over her shoulder and cringes. "It was ten years ago. A smoke jumper, I think."

"Calvin?"

"Maybe." She pushes through the door and calls her patient.

Why on earth does she not keep track of the men who impregnate her? And what about birth control? I have so many questions. But for now, I have to get to work. I pivot and hurry in the opposite direction, pressing my lips together like I have a secret I can't wait to share.

Did Fitz hook up with Betty O'Neil? Come to think of it, I'm pretty sure Betty said one of her kids is eight or nine.

A miniature Calvin Fitzgerald? That would be something.

When I arrive home after an enlightening day with Dr. Reichart (including a fifteen-minute *Beat Saber* tutorial between patients), Fitz's truck is in the driveway. He's been in Arizona for the past two weeks. I've been spoiled with just Maren and Will. Fitz is emotionally exhausting. I need my other roommates to take some pressure off me, but they're not home.

"I shoveled a path from the driveway to your shed," Fitz says with his back to me while stirring something on the stove that smells savory, garlicky, and delicious. "So you don't have to track snow through the house or remove your boots only to take ten steps and have to put them back on."

"Then you wouldn't get to see my lovely face." I slip off my boots and tug at my scarf.

"I'd get by."

"Would you really? Don't lie. You've missed me. How was Arizona?"

He doesn't respond. Typical.

"I, uh . . . work with Betty O'Neil. Does that name ring a bell?" I fill a glass with water just to get a glimpse of his face.

"No. Should it?" He offers a quick sidelong glance.

"She thinks she might have hooked up with you ten years ago."

"And why does she think that?" He sets a lid on his pot of chili and retrieves a bowl.

I finish my glass of water. "Because Will fixed her up with a friend who's a smoke jumper."

"This might surprise you, but I'm not the only smoke jumper in town."

"But you're Will's friend." I lean against the counter.

Fitz crumples half a sleeve of saltine crackers and dumps them into a bowl while smirking. "I can see why you might think I'm Will's only friend, but I'm not. However, it's weird that you're talking about my sex life at work."

"Because you don't have one?"

He chuckles. "Wouldn't you like to know?"

"Not really. I'm more concerned about Betty. She has five kids, and—"

"Five kids is a legitimate concern." He whistles while ladling chili into his bowl.

"Is it possible that you dated Betty, and you just don't remember? After all, it was ten years ago."

"Absolutely not. I keep a scrapbook of all my dates. Photos, cocktail napkins from bars, bullet-pointed details, and a few locks of hair." Fitz takes a seat at the counter and blows at the swirling steam.

He's a freak. I thought Will and Maren were joking, as friends do, about Fitz needing a minor fixing.

He glances up from his soup. "Christ, Jaymes. You can't think I'm serious."

"You're an asshole." I tug the fridge door, fetching my half bottle of wine.

He lifts an eyebrow just before taking a cautious bite of chili, chewing slowly for several seconds. "What does Betty need? Are you coming to me for money?"

I allow myself a generous glass of wine since I'm stuck here alone with Fitz. "Depends." I take a healthy gulp of the riesling. "If one of her kids is yours, I think you should pay child support and offer to take your kid for a few nights a week."

Fitz's lips part, and a small drop of chili dribbles from them. He doesn't blink. I'm not sure he's breathing.

"She has five kids from four men. Perhaps you're one of them."

Finally, he blinks and wipes his hand across his messy chin. "Jaymes, did you hit your head?"

I set my wineglass on the counter across from his bowl and rest my arms beside it. "You mean to tell me that you've never had a one-night stand with a woman? There's *no* chance that you've unknowingly impregnated someone? Do you keep condom wrappers in your scrapbook as well?"

"As a matter of fact, I do. I keep the whole goddamn condom—sperm and all. I count each one of those little fuckers to make sure one didn't get away."

"Stop." I snort, covering my nose and mouth to keep from spewing my wine.

Fitz does his best to hide his grin while he shovels more chili past his lips. I retrieve the remaining quarter of a baguette from my designated pantry. It's stale. I break off a chunk, dip it into the pot of chili, and pop it into my mouth.

"Did you seriously just dip your bread into *my* chili?"

I glance over my shoulder and shrug, quickly chewing. "Will said we share condiments."

His nose wrinkles. It's kind of cute. "Chili's not a condiment."

"It is if you dip bread into it." I shamelessly dunk a second chunk of bread into the pot. "Or if you pour it over a baked potato or hot dog."

"You're never going to make it past the thirty-day trial."

I tear off another piece of bread. "Thirty-day trial?"

"It's in your rental contract. It's in *all* of our contracts. The six-month lease is contingent on a no-fault thirty-day trial. If you don't like it here, you can leave in the first thirty days without forfeiting your security deposit. And if any of your roommates don't feel like you're a good fit, the six-month contract ends on day thirty."

Shit.

I read the agreement—sort of. It seemed pretty standard. If I read about a thirty-day trial, it didn't stand out to me because why wouldn't my roommates like me?

While chewing on this new information, I ease the lid onto the pot of chili and clear my throat. "I'll replace your chili."

"How will you do that when you don't know my secret ingredients? It's a family recipe, and I'm not sharing it."

I find a ten in my purse and toss it on the counter beside his bowl. "Are we good?"

"Ten dollars? Really?" Fitz grunts before tipping his bowl and scraping the last soggy crackers into his spoon.

"I didn't eat even a dollar's worth of your chili." I cross my arms.

He licks his lips after the last bite. "If you truly believe that, what are the other nine dollars for? Are you trying to bribe me into not voting to kick you out? It's going to take more than nine dollars." Fitz carries his bowl to the sink.

By the time he rinses it and turns, I'm in his personal space, eyes narrowed at him. "If I find out there's no thirty-day trial in my rental agreement, I'm going to tell Betty that you remember her, and you specifically remember not wearing a condom. And ever since that night, you've secretly pined for her."

He tucks his fingers in his back pockets. "You're going to lie to your friend?"

"I don't know, Calvin. Am I going to find anything about a thirty-day trial in my rental agreement, or did you lie to me?" My head tilts to the side.

He scratches his scruffy jaw. "What does Betty look like?"

"Oh my god! You're such a shit. You probably did sleep with her. What are you going to do if you have a nine-year-old child?"

He blinks several times before lifting his hand to my face and brushing a few stray hairs away from my eyes. I stiffen. It's . . . he's . . . well, he's close. And it's an intimate gesture. For a few seconds, I swear he's going to kiss me.

We can't kiss. We're roommates. I know *that's* in Will's bylaws for this rental situation.

"I'd say it's no fun because you're too easy, but that would be a lie. It's still pretty fucking fun."

The need for revenge simmers deep in my belly because I know the answer to this question before I ask it. "You don't know Betty, do you?"

He slowly shakes his head.

"And there's no thirty-day clause."

Fitz continues to shake his head.

"Watch out, *Calvin*." I stab my finger into his chest. "Payback's going to be a bitch for this one."

A world of possibilities dances in his glimmering eyes, but I will wipe that grin off his face. I don't know how or when, but it will be epic.

Chapter Six

"To my next midlife crisis." Cee raises her shot glass with one hand and straightens her rhinestone birthday crown with her other while most everyone from the office celebrates at a bar by the river in downtown Missoula.

Two days earlier, Cee got her first tattoo, her Yorkie's head on her forearm, to celebrate forty-five. Nobody knew it was her birthday until she showed off her ink. So Betty wasted no time arranging an outing— any excuse to escape her kids for a few more hours.

Now, we're crammed around two high-top tables by the door, and every time someone comes in or out, the acrid stench of cigarette smoke and vaping aerosol makes its way to us, and a gust of cold air bites my exposed skin. The black strapless dress was a bad idea, but I wanted to wear something special for my first official night out with my new friends.

"Are your teeth chattering?" Betty asks, pausing her wineglass at her lips.

Said teeth chatter while I nod several times.

She chuckles. "Then put your coat on."

"Then it looks like I'm leaving."

Betty offers me an eye roll just as the door opens again.

"Be r-right b-back," I say, grabbing my clutch and navigating toward the back of the bar as if I'm using the ladies' room instead of searching for heat.

"Could you be more underdressed?"

I turn toward the bar, where Calvin Fitzgerald is perched on a stool with a mug of whatever beer's on tap in his hand. He makes an agonizingly slow inspection of my dress while wetting his lips.

I had fewer goose bumps standing by the door.

"It's the only dress I brought with me, and I didn't have time to shop for a new one." I hug myself, rubbing my bare arms.

"It's, uh . . ." Fitz's gaze lingers on my bare legs and red heels.

My heart races, and my fingernails scratch at my skin because I'm a fidgeter, and I think I like how he's looking at me. And that's wrong.

It's against the rules.

I know he's just toying with me, so I drop my arms and pull my shoulders back as if I'm ready for the paparazzi to take my picture. "See something you like?" I'm not letting him have the upper hand. I'm still planning my revenge.

What is it? I have no idea, but it's still on course to be epic.

His gaze flicks to mine, and his eyes are a little bloodshot. A slow grin works its way up his face. "I don't *not* like it."

Oh my god!

I'm not drunk. I've had three sips of wine. He's the one with impaired . . . everything. It's a game. Unfortunately, I like this game a little too much.

I like when he looks at me as if I could be his dinner. That's messed up. Right?

His gaze abandons mine again, and it takes me a few seconds to register his new point of focus. *Points* of focus.

My erect nipples.

Damn Missoula weather!

Crossing my arms, I clear the frog from my throat. "I gotta get back to my friends. Do you need a ride home?"

He finds my face again. "I'm good. Thanks."

"Good." I nod. "That's good."

Fitz sets his beer mug on the bar and steps down from the stool, putting us so close I can feel his body heat. As he reaches for my neck, I turn to stone—a stone with a racing pulse. Sliding my gold chain between his fingers, he inspects the round pendant with a sand dollar in the middle. It belonged to my mom. And I would tell him that if I could speak.

"I have to use the men's room." He releases my necklace and brushes past me.

Whoosh!

I expel a huge breath and regain my composure before rejoining the birthday party.

For the rest of the night, my gaze wanders to the bar. Fitz buys another beer and plays pool with a guy he seems to know, from the way they're laughing and chatting.

He leaves the bar around midnight with his friend, whom I didn't see drinking. I hope he's the DD.

"Happy birthday, Cee. I'm heading home." I give her a big hug, and she mumbles something incoherent. "Who's driving her?" I look around at my coworkers.

Dr. Reichart raises her hand. "I am." She shrugs. "I don't drink."

"Thanks for doing that. I'll see everyone Monday."

By the time I make it home, the house is dark except for the porch light. The squeaky front door doesn't care that I'm trying not to wake anyone. Hopefully, Maren and Will are heavy sleepers.

What about Fitz? Did he make it home?

I listen for any sign of him upstairs. What if something happened and his friend took a different route and that friend wasn't fit to drive?

Removing my heels to keep them from clicking along the wood, I pad toward the back door, but my brain won't stop worrying about Fitz. Spinning around, I decide to ease my mind by checking on him. I tiptoe up the stairs, stopping when I hit the squeaky one. After listening for a moment, I continue to the top and creep toward Fitz's room.

His open door sends my nerves into panic mode. If he were home, it would be closed.

Before waking Will and Maren, I make sure Fitz isn't passed out on the floor, choking on his vomit.

As I approach his bed, the knot in my stomach tightens. It's still made. He's not home.

I turn, running into a dark, monstrous figure. The bogeyman in the flesh. My heels fall from my hands as I gulp down one breath after another to hold back my scream. Adrenaline hijacks my heart; it might explode. If I were eighty, I'd be a goner.

"Booty call?" Fitz asks while I breathe behind my cupped hand.

A sliver of streetlight finds his bare chest, and my gaze slides south a few inches to his unbuttoned and unzipped jeans.

Panic turns into rage, and I shove him. "What are you doing?" I whisper yell.

"Me?" He chuckles in a hushed tone.

"You about scared—"

"The piss out of you?"

"I was making sure you made it home alive."

"That's sweet of you."

I can't read his tone, probably because everything is muffled by my raging pulse.

"How can I repay you?" He looms over me, lips curled into a smile that's as ambiguous as his tone. "Are you staying?" He nods to the bed.

My eyes begin to flare, but I temper my reaction by forcing a slow, calming breath through my nose. "I'm pretty good at taking care of things myself. Nobody knows me like . . . me." It bears repeating: I'm not drunk, but I sound like it. Did I really just tell Fitz that I'm an expert at masturbating?

His grin swells. "Well, damn, Jaymes. I've never gotten that response before."

I roll my eyes before plucking my shoes off the floor. "You're so drunk."

He pops his lips several times. "I could be."

I try not to giggle, knowing he won't be like this in the morning. He'll eat me for breakfast with one look, and that look will give him the upper hand again.

A creak sounds from the hallway. Fitz pulls me into his chest, walking us several steps to the left so we're not in the line of sight.

One of the bathroom doors closes.

At first, we don't move, despite my hands, cheek, and torso being pressed to his half-naked body. I don't know about him, but I'm a tinderbox. If he tried to kiss me, I wouldn't stop him.

Warmth floods my body, reaching my toes and the tips of my tingling fingers that ache to curl into his flesh. If he lets go of me, I might pass out from this lightheadedness.

The toilet flushes, and thirty seconds later, Will or Maren exits the bathroom. When we hear the distant click of a shutting door, Fitz releases me.

"Thanks for worrying about me," he murmurs.

I take a step back and pump my fists to get a little feeling back into my hands, but I don't look at him. "Of course," I say with my sweetest voice, too sweet.

I need him to question my sincerity the way he makes me question his.

I need to get a grip and shut this shit down.

I need . . . an orgasm.

"Nighty night, Fitz." I scrounge every last bit of confidence in my body and blow him an exaggerated kiss.

His lips part in the dim light, brow tight. And that's how I know he feels it (whatever it is) too.

This *cannot* happen.

Chapter Seven

CALVIN

I can't relax in my own home.

Am I to blame? Sure. But this is getting ridiculous. Jamie's taking "revenge is best served cold" to a new level, and she's using her body and my attraction to her as new weapons.

It's been a month since she threw down the gauntlet in the kitchen and two weeks since the bedroom incident. I'm mentally wiped from sleeping with one eye open. Is she going to deflate my tires? Short-sheet my bed? Put plastic over the toilet? Remove all the labels from my cans in the pantry? Or seduce me so we get kicked out of the house?

"Fitz, here are your clothes from the dryer. I've folded them for you. I'll set them on your bed and hang your shirts so they won't need to be ironed," Jamie announces in a honeyed voice while toting a laundry basket up the stairs in her usual weekend leggings, pink fuzzy socks, and oversize sweater.

"Dude . . ." Will drags out the word without taking his eyes off his game. "Are you sleeping with her? You'd better stay out of her pants, or Maren and I will fight over who's going to kill you. It's a rule. A hard line that can't be crossed."

I keep my head bowed to my phone. "Why would you ask me that?"

"Because she's been cordial to you—dare I say flat-out thoughtful? If you're not giving her regular orgasms, then it makes no sense."

"Sometimes I do push-ups in the kitchen and let her watch."

"You're an idiot." Will laughs.

"Maybe she's more magnanimous than we give her credit for."

Will grunts his skepticism.

He's not wrong about Jamie. Not only has she failed to retaliate, she's been outright generous to me. It's disturbing. My distrust grows exponentially every day.

"Fitz, I noticed one of your shirts has a missing button," Jamie chirps, skipping down the stairs. She has entirely too much bounce in her step for a Sunday afternoon. It's unnatural. "I can find a button and mend it for you."

Will snorts. "Jamie, Fitz spends most of the winter at a sewing machine when he's not down south. I'm sure he can sew on a button."

"I'm not following." Jamie stops behind my chair and tucks in my tag.

I stiffen when her warm, delicate fingers brush my nape. What the fuck? She's softening me up for the kill.

I despise her method of revenge. She makes me *hard* and soft at the same time.

"Smoke jumpers make their gear and repair their parachutes," Will informs her before tossing his remote aside and grumbling about the game.

"Seriously?" Jamie rummages through the kitchen on a scavenger hunt for ingredients to bake something. It's her weekend MO, along with wearing a light-pink apron that matches her socks and looks like something from 1960. She wears her hair braided down both sides when she bakes.

Goddammit! I need to stop noticing so much shit about her.

"No joke. If you need something repaired, just send it to work with Fitz." Will heads up the stairs.

"That's some sexy stuff, Fitz." Flour puffs into the air when she plops the bag onto the counter beside her mixing bowl.

"Sewing is sexy?" I navigate to the barstool at the counter. It's weird, I know, but I enjoy watching her work in the kitchen. Also, I have to make sure she doesn't put something in the baked goods to poison me.

"In and of itself, no." She measures the dry ingredients on the scale she bought a few weeks ago. "But sewing your gear, then jumping out of a plane to fight a fire . . . *that's* sexy."

"So we agree I'm sexy." I can't hide my wry grin.

She keeps her focus on the scale. "No. Smoke jumpers are sexy. You're my roommate—a brother of sorts. You're disqualified from ever being sexy in my mind. Separation of church and state."

"So much for Will thinking we're sleeping together."

Clunk!

She drops the measuring cup onto the floor. "W-what?" Fumbling to pick it up, she then rinses it off and dries it.

"He thinks I'm giving you orgasms, and that's why you're being so nice to me."

"Pfft . . . " She tries to blow off my comment, but her cheeks flush, and she can't focus on me for more than a second.

"We both know you're being nice to throw me off."

She clears her throat and wipes her forehead with her arm. "Throw you off?"

Is she sweating?

"Don't think I've forgotten about your threat."

"My threat?" She cuts the stick of butter into cubes.

"Payback's going to be a bitch. Sound familiar?"

"Not really." Vanilla fills the room while she pours it into a measuring spoon. "I'm a nice person." She twists the lid onto the bottle.

"Nice people never have to say they're nice people. They're too humble to feel the need to put themselves on a pedestal by saying they're nice."

Jamie crinkles her nose like she has an itch before rubbing it with her arm. She mixes, scrapes, and lines the baking sheets with parchment paper. By now, she has streaks of flour on her face and hair.

I can't turn away. I want to crawl onto the counter with a pillow and fall asleep while watching her. She could make a visual meditation app. This shit's my crack.

"So you've been sewing this winter? Is that what you do in Arizona? Do they fly you all over the country to sew?" She ignores my previous comment.

She's good. Too good.

"It's not all I do. And no. We do prescribed fires in Arizona."

An airy smile touches her lips as she stirs the ingredients. She's up to something. "Don't tell Will I let you lick the spoon." She offers the spatula.

"Nope." I hop off the stool. "I don't want to lick the spoon." Blowing out a breath, I shove my hands into my back pockets.

Jamie's eyebrows lift into dubious peaks.

"Just do it. Whatever you're going to do to me, just fucking do it, and be done." I hate that she's brought me to my knees on this, but I need some sound sleep again.

She wets her lips and saunters toward me, invading every inch of my personal space with her tempting body and sweet smell. I need a one-night stand. Hell, I need a string of them to get my goddamn roommate out of my head.

Her teeth scrape along her bottom lip while she ogles her prey, her gaze stretching from my feet to the top of my head. She runs her hand along my shoulder while her lips quirk into a sadistic grin. "I'd say it's no fun because you're too easy. But that would be a lie. It's still pretty fucking fun."

With my hand, I encircle her wrist, removing it from my shoulder. She has batter on her fingers, and I bet it's now on my shirt. Her breath hitches, giving me a renewed sense of control, if only for a brief moment. A blush fills her cheeks again, revealing her weakness, which I believe is me.

With two quick steps, I pin her to the fridge door. Her eyes flare. Yep, I'm back in control. Guess who's getting his first good night's sleep in a month?

My grip tightens on her wrist as I suck on one of her fingers. Her lips part, and a tiny moan escapes. I have a game plan, and it's all about control. That's where my enjoyment lies. That and the promise of peaceful sleep.

Do I like sucking her dainty finger? It doesn't matter.

Do I like her reaction to me doing it? I mean . . . I'm a straight male in my prime, so yeah, it's mildly satisfying but entirely beside the point.

The front door opens just as I prepare to lay down the law. My fake seduction screeches to a halt, and I lurch to the other side of the kitchen. Jamie hugs her hand to her chest as though I bit off her finger.

Maren's gaze ping-pongs between us, hemorrhaging a fatal amount of distrust as she slides off her scarf. "What's going on? It better not be—"

"It's not." I dismiss her absurd assumption. "I'm just taking back the upper hand because she won't hurry the fuck up and poison me." I'm a bona fide imbecile. I need to jump out of a plane and screw someone *stat* with no strings attached. Nurse Andrews is messing with my psyche. I bet she's a pro at her job.

"Poison?" Maren echoes her skepticism.

Jamie peels herself off the fridge door and takes a few wobbly steps to the sink, where she surgically scrubs her hands. "Fitz is suffering from persecutory delusion. It's more prevalent in men, and sadly, it's treatment resistant. However, cognitive behavioral therapy and medication are worth a try. It's definitely better than hospitalization."

Maren kicks off her boots and shoots me the stink eye.

Resting a hand on my hip, I drop my chin for a brief second before lifting my stern gaze so she can see how *uninterested* I am in Jamie.

Maren points up the stairs. "I need to shower because I have a date. Yes or no? Have you two hooked up?"

While I say, "Christ, no," Jamie dries her hands and says, "Never."

Maren nods. "Cool. Then stop being an asshole to her."

I don't get in one word of my rebuttal before she's halfway up the stairs.

My attention redirects to Jamie as she throws the towel onto the counter and crosses her arms. "Calvin Fitzgerald, if you think for a single minute that you can make me go weak in the knees and manipulate me into forgetting about what you did and what you have coming, then you *are* delusional."

Walk away.

Nope. I can't.

Instead, I grin, but I don't speak. I step closer to her, but I don't touch her. Her chin inches upward in defiance.

"If you're so immune to me, so steady in the knees, then why did you moan when I sucked your finger?"

Her nose wrinkles. "I did not."

"You did."

Just when I think I have her, she takes the last step between us and uses the same finger I sucked to jab into my chest, reminiscent of the thing that started all this. "If I made a noise, it was a groan, not a moan."

"Is there a difference?"

"Yes. A moan indicates pleasure. A groan indicates distress or suffering. Fitz, you could never make me moan."

"You blushed."

She shakes her head. "It was anger . . . distress and suffering. You can suck all of my fingers and all ten toes if that's what does it for you, but it won't ever make me weak in the knees."

"I bet there's somewhere I could put my mouth that *would* make you weak in the knees."

Why THE FUCK did I say that?

A plume of embarrassment spreads from her neck to the tips of her ears.

Oh, yeah. That's why I said it.

"Look." I run my knuckles along her neck, and she shudders. Although I'm sure it's a frightened shiver. "You're red again. I'd better leave you alone before you get any more hot and bothered. I mean . . . angry and distressed."

She wets her lips, eyes set in an indignant scowl, before whispering, "You're going to pay."

And just like that . . . I'm back in the same sinking boat. Only this time, I didn't merely poke the bear. I kicked her in the teeth and stole one of her cubs.

Chapter Eight

JAYMES

The smoke jumper base is a quick drive from the hospital. Since Fitz escaped to his room for the rest of the night after our standoff, I've decided to pay him a visit today with a container of chocolate chip cookies.

The sewing revelation has piqued my curiosity. Do these jumpers really sew their gear?

And I'd be lying if I said I didn't want to mess with him.

I tap the light dusting of snow off my boots before stepping into the entry. A nutty caramel coffee aroma greets me along with country music. Displays with pictures and historical details about smoke jumping cover the walls. A mannequin wearing a tan jumpsuit snags my attention because the high rounded collar looks Elvis inspired.

A young blonde with curls turns down the music on her phone behind the counter and offers a welcoming smile. "Hi. Are you here for a tour?"

"I'm here to see Calvin Fitzgerald. I'm Jamie, his roommate." I open the container and hold out the cookies. "I baked them yesterday."

She smiles. "Oh, wow. Thanks! They smell amazing."

I point to the mannequin. "What's the deal with the funky collar?"

She takes a bite and hums her approval. "It protects the neck when falling through trees. The suit is made of a protective Kevlar material and lots of padding. Smoke jumpers get dropped into some pretty harsh terrain. It's a badass job. But I'm sure Calvin's told you all about it."

I try to imagine Fitz in that getup. "He's rather selective with his sharing." I give her a wry grin.

She laughs. "I'm Bailey, by the way. Come with me. Let's find Calvin. He might be eating lunch."

I follow her past a room with industrial sewing machines, all idle. We end up in an open space resembling an oversize garage with crates and boxes stacked along the perimeter, workout equipment on one side, and a picnic table with Fitz and two other guys eating lunch on the other.

When he catches a glimpse of me, he stops midchew. I'm instantly rewarded with his obvious shock. It's fair to assume he's caught off guard by my presence because there's nothing sexy about my purple scrubs and puffy white jacket.

Perfect.

"Fitzy, I brought cookies for you and your friends." I plaster on my best smile. "Aren't you going to introduce me?" I slide the container of cookies on the table.

I can tell by his narrowed eyes and how he slowly sets his sandwich on the paper bag that he's not offering any introductions. His buddies must be used to his stellar manners because they don't hesitate to introduce themselves.

"Gary." He adjusts his snowboarding-moose baseball hat, sharing a glimpse of his bald head, before offering me his hand.

I shake it. "Jamie. It's nice to meet you. I'm Fitzy's newest roommate."

The grin on Gary's salt-and-pepper scruffy face brings me so much satisfaction. He likes me, my nickname for Calvin, or the cookies. Perhaps all three.

"Todd." The other guy offers a friendly nod. He looks closer to Calvin's age. Maybe early to midthirties with what appears to be a dark-blond mullet under his solid-navy ball cap. Todd is the guy who drove Fitz home from the bar, but I don't mention it because Fitz doesn't need to know I spent the rest of the evening with one eye trained on him.

"A pleasure." I scoot the cookies toward him.

The sugary aroma mixes with Todd's open bag of cheesy Doritos for a rather interesting combination. He snags one and stares at it while grinning. "*Fitzy*, you never mentioned your new roommate is a baker. You also never mentioned she's beautiful."

"Aw, shucks, Todd." I tuck my chin and twist my body. "You're the sweetest."

He puffs out his already broad chest, clad in a green Missoula Smoke Jumpers T-shirt, and winks at Fitz, who rolls his eyes. "Well, are you going to give her the tour, or am I?" Todd addresses Fitz with a grin.

"I really should get back to work." I peek at my watch.

"It won't take that long," Todd promises, grabbing another cookie and shoving half of it into his mouth.

"Well"—I corkscrew my lips—"I suppose I have time for a quickie."

Gary covers his mouth and coughs a laugh while Todd perks up with a face-splitting grin.

"Christ," Fitz mumbles, stuffing the last part of his sandwich into his bag.

"A quickie it is." Todd begins to stand.

Fitz grabs his shoulder. "Just sit your ass down." He jerks his head in the direction from which I came. "Let's go, Jaymes."

"Bye, guys. Nice meeting you. Make sure Fitzy brings that container home to me." I give them a wiggly-fingered goodbye.

"Stop by anytime." Todd delivers his invite with a flirty smile.

"Oh, you can count on it." I skip to catch up to Fitz and his sexy ass in gray cargo pants.

Of course, he's wearing a red smoke jumper shirt that's accentuating every muscle beneath it. And I've decided I'm mildly obsessed with him wearing brown leather boots that are rarely tied. He might as well be my celebrity crush. I'm never going to tell him, and he's off limits.

"We're even now. Understood?" He shoots me a hawkish expression.

"Even? Whatever do you mean? I brought you and your friends cookies."

"And I'm giving you the *quickie* you suggested. We're even." He nods to the room with sewing machines. "That's where we sew shit." We parade a few more feet, and he points to the right. "That's the ready room. And over there is the loft, and the rigging room is beyond that." He turns abruptly, and I bump into him.

When I take a step back, he gives me a tight grin. "There was your quickie. Thanks for coming by."

I snicker, offering him an easy nod while wetting my lips. "Was it good for you? I'm not gonna lie—I didn't climax this time. Perhaps Todd would have been more effective." I peer toward the rooms we didn't visit. "You barely gave me the tip. Maybe that's all you have to give. A dickhead of sorts."

He crosses his sinewy arms. "Are you done?"

I bounce my head noncommittally. "Are you?"

He blinks several times before he surveys the entire length of my body. I hold stone still and think of gross things like vomit and nasty flatulence, anything to keep from blushing. Fitz feeds off my uncontrolled vulnerability.

"How deep do you want it?" he asks in a throaty voice, reaching for my hand and pulling me toward the tall room with hooks hanging from the ceiling. I try to focus on the surroundings since I've never seen a room like this one. However, all my focus goes to my hand in his.

Mine's cold but soft.

His is calloused but warm.

And despite our size difference, my hand fits nicely in his.

That notion sends me down another rabbit hole. Would other parts of our bodies fit this well?

In the next breath, he drags me through another door, leading to a room with lengthy tables and walls of cubbies with packs. He drags me to the far end at a vicious pace and stops, releasing my hand and spreading his arms like the Christ the Redeemer statue. "We went all the way. Did that do it for you?"

I hold his gaze, and we have a stare-off. Then I mutter, "I could use a cigarette."

Fitz's facade cracks, and he grins. "Get the fuck out of here."

I bite my lower lip and pivot, retracing my steps to the exit. *Best I've ever had,* I mouth as I peek over my shoulder.

After work, I grab a workout at the twenty-four-hour fitness center that I joined a few weeks ago. Then I pick up a pizza to make up for my burned calories.

When I don't see Fitz's truck in the driveway, a pang of disappointment hits me, and I quickly reprimand myself for having that sentiment. Maren's home. She and Will are my favorites anyway. Or so I tell myself.

"Ugh! You're killing me." Maren slams the fridge door when I enter the house. "I'm starving. I need to buy groceries, and you brought pizza I have to smell?"

I toe off my boots and set the box on the counter. "Good thing I'm thoughtful and like to share." I open the lid, releasing that woodsy, tangy, sweet oregano aroma. "Help yourself. But if the guys show up, hide the box. I think they eat ten thousand calories a day."

She gathers her wavy hair and pulls it over one shoulder with a grin before nabbing a slice of pizza. "Jaymes, you're my favorite person."

"How was your trip?" I ask, washing my hands.

"Boring." She tugs at the neck of her white hoodie.

"How's your inheritance looking?"

Maren laughs. "Not you too."

"Just kidding."

She plucks a mushroom off the pizza and pops it in her mouth. "How was your day?"

"Never boring." I lean my hip against the counter and take a bite of pizza. It's still hot and *so* good.

"How have things been around here? Have you seen the *boys* much?"

I laugh at her reference. "I don't see Will that often, but I see Fitz in the evenings when he's in town. He's . . ."

"Fitz?"

I nod. "He's so intense."

"Mmm . . ." She sets her slice onto the box lid and takes a swig of her Razz-Cranberry LaCroix. "That's just him. He likes his space. Spends a lot of time alone. He's a voracious reader. Antisocial. Laser focused on things that are important to him. Controlling. And yes, intense."

"His job. That's what's important to him. He's a total Capricorn." I take another bite of pizza and chew it slowly. "I respect that."

Maren fists her hand at her mouth for a few seconds and swallows. "Yes, well, I don't know much about zodiac signs. But he loves his job."

"And he's never been married?"

"Fitz?" She coughs a laugh. "No. That would require him to pursue a woman beyond"—Maren's lips twist while she contemplatively gazes at the ceiling—"the bedroom. He can get women to sleep with him. I mean, look at him." Maren grins. "But he either has no desire for anything beyond that, or he's emotionally dead, because I've never met a single woman in his life. I suspect he's not a virgin since he sometimes doesn't come home at night. But who knows? Maybe he is." She tosses the last bite of crust into her mouth.

"He's never brought anyone here for the night?"

She shakes her head, bending the tab of her LaCroix can. "Have you seen *Lars and the Real Girl* with Ryan Gosling?"

"No." I tear off a paper towel to wipe my hands.

"Well, he plays a character in love with a life-size doll named Bianca. Will's waiting to meet Fitz's Bianca doll."

I snort into my napkin. "Stop . . ." I shake my head. "Poor Fitz. I think you and Will are awfully hard on him."

"No. No. No. There is no 'poor Fitz.' In case you haven't figured it out yet, he can give it just as good as he can take it."

"Oh, I'm aware. We're currently in the middle of something he started over a month ago. I'm waiting for the perfect moment to get revenge, but if I'm being honest, I feel like the revenge is the torture he's experiencing waiting for me to get my payback."

Maren holds up a finger. "Watch your back. Fitz is ruthless."

I hum while sipping my water. "I might be more ruthless. Actually, he can be charming."

Sexy. Downright irresistible.

Maren inspects me through narrowed eyes like I'm speaking a different language.

The front door creaks open.

"Speaking of," she whispers.

I peer over my shoulder at Fitz. He eyes me and then Maren. "Talking about me?"

"Well, I'm going to shower. Thanks for the pizza, Jamie." Maren saunters past Calvin and playfully nudges him.

He squints at her, but he also relinquishes a tiny grin. When his attention shifts to me on his way to the kitchen, I scramble. After tossing my napkin in the trash and emptying my water glass, I nod to the pizza box. "There's two slices left, if you want them."

He lifts the lid and inspects them before eyeing me. "What did you do to them?" He sets the empty cookie container on the counter.

"Do to them?"

"Yes. What did you do to them?" He steps past me, snatching a kombucha from the fridge. "Poison? Pubes?"

"Pubes?" I suppress my laughter. "I've spent my life in a bikini, Fitz. I don't have pubes to spare for your pizza."

Fitz turns, removing the lid. He doesn't make the slightest effort to hide where his eyes are pointed or the wolfish grin taking up residency on his face.

"I feel thoroughly violated." I find a toothy grin.

In its own sweet time, his gaze crawls up my body.

Fuck him. Really. Could he be more obvious? Is this payback for my visit to his work?

Is this a test?

He's toying with me, causing me to overheat just to make me blush so he can reveal his victorious smirk. I reject his smirk—no victory for him.

"Were you abandoned?" I blurt out before he can focus on my red cheeks.

"Excuse me?" His brow knits tightly.

"I heard you're dating a blow-up doll. That screams abandonment. Are your parents still alive? Did you get dumped by your one true love? Did your family dog get hit by a car?"

There's a pregnant pause.

No words.

Not even a blink.

It's just me and Fitz's unreadable expression.

Finally, he blows out a slow breath and stares at his feet. "She's not inflatable. Her name is Mrs. Wilke, after my parents' old neighbor who touched me inappropriately the summer I turned fourteen. She invited me over to discuss payment for mowing her yard. She told me to sit on the sofa while she fetched her purse. When she returned, she asked me if I liked her dress. I shrugged. Then she said it was made of the softest cotton her skin had ever felt. And she asked me if I wanted to feel it.

"I shrugged again. In the next breath, she grabbed my hand and guided it up her arm and then down the inside for some serious sideboob action, holding it *there*. And she said, 'How does that feel, Calvin?'"

I can't move. Can't breathe. And Calvin's frown deepens with each word as his eyes narrow at the floor between us.

"I'm sorry."

He shrugs one shoulder and sighs. "So I named my sex doll Mrs. Wilke. And when I fuck her, I say, 'How does that feel, Mrs. Wilke?'"

What the hell?

Calvin finally glances up at me and scratches his chin beneath his barely restrained grin. And that says it all—everything is a lie.

"Sucks being homeschooled." I wink and saunter toward the door for my boots and coat. "Fitz, if you and Mrs. Wilke are ever open to a threesome, let me know. It's been a fantasy of mine for years."

Chapter Nine

CALVIN

Maren hums while scrubbing her and Jamie's toilet, hair corralled like a hay bale on top of her head. She's still in her nightshirt, boxer shorts, and brown teddy bear slippers. It's our biweekly cleaning day—the easiest biweekly cleaning ever because our new roommate is a perfectionist. Jamie's always organizing, washing laundry, and cleaning shit.

She bakes.

She has a great job.

She's sexy as fuck.

I'm not marrying her, but some guy should.

"Maren, do you want to be my date to Gary's birthday party this weekend?" I ask.

"Oh man, I wish, Fitz. Gary has the best parties. But I can't. I'm going home this weekend."

When I don't respond, she eyes me over her shoulder. "Ask Will."

"He's working."

"It's okay for you to go alone."

I cross my arms. "I know."

Maren chuckles, returning her attention to the toilet. "Order a ride if you drink too much, and have a condom in your pocket if you don't want to be some third-grade teacher's baby daddy."

"Are you sure you have to go home this weekend?" I stop short of begging, but I'm sure she can hear my groveling undertone. Crowds make me uneasy. When I get uneasy, I drink. When I drink, my dick wanders.

"Ask Jamie."

"There's no way I'm asking Jamie."

"Ask me what?"

I suppress a sigh at Jamie's stealthy way of sneaking up on me. She needs more weight to her steps or a few creaks in her joints.

Maren flushes the toilet just as Jamie makes it to the top of the stairs. "Fitz needs a chaperone to Gary's birthday party this weekend."

"I don't need a chaperone because I'm not attending the party." I brush past Jamie to the stairs just as she flips a dusting rag over her shoulder.

"I think we have a mouse in the house," Will declares with the refrigerator pulled out of its spot, inspecting the area behind it. "Are those traps still in the garage?"

I mumble a "yeah" on my way to the laundry room.

After I knock down a few cobwebs in the corners and empty the lint filter, Jamie appears in the doorway. "I'll be your date."

"I don't need one." I dump the clean sheets into a laundry basket.

"Then why did you ask Maren?"

"Because she knows Gary."

"I know Gary." She steps closer, plucks a sheet from the basket, and folds it.

"No. You've met Gary. You don't *know* him." I fold the pillowcases and set them on the dryer.

"Well, what better way to get to know him than at a party?"

"I'm not going."

"Why don't you take Mrs. Wilke?"

I don't acknowledge her, but I know she's grinning.

"Stop!" She takes the sheet from me. "Didn't your mom teach you how to fold a fitted sheet?"

Her question knocks the wind out of me, but I disguise it with a shrug and a murmured "apparently not." However, I do remember how easy my mom made it look, despite the fact that memories are not my friends.

Jamie makes it look easy too.

"Tuck the corners into each other. Then fold the flap like this." She glances up at me with a quick grin. "Voilà. Now, it's a rectangle; you can fold it like a flat sheet. How does a professional parachute packer not know this?" She hands me the folded sheet laced with a floral fabric softener. "Now, when is the party? Do you want me to drive so you can drink? Maren said it would also be my responsibility to keep you from impregnating anyone. Clearly, she doesn't know about your scrapbook of carefully counted sperm."

"Christ!" I drop the folded sheets into the laundry basket, then rake my fingers through my hair. "I'm not a child. I don't need a chaperone."

"Then why did you ask Maren to go to the party with you?" Jamie lifts onto her toes, invading my space to fix my hair. I've never felt this on edge. "Because she likes Gary's parties," I murmur, losing some of my fight because I've decided her hands in my hair and breasts pressed to my chest beat watching her bake, but just barely.

"Maybe I'll like them too." Her fingernails gently scrape my scalp, and I shudder, jumping back a few feet.

We have a brief stare-off while the washing machine gurgles. She blinks first. I'm not sure if that means she's won or lost. But then she grins because she did that on purpose.

"You're taking me to the party." She flicks a resolute nod at me before spinning on her heels and strolling out of the laundry room.

"Why would I do that?" I follow her.

She glances over her shoulder and grins while curling her hair behind her ear. "Because I'm the best *you've* ever had, Fitz."

"The best what?"

"You'll see."

The last time Gary hosted a party, a fire started in the kitchen. His wife called 911. Sixteen firefighters attended, and she called 911 for a small stove fire. I hope this party is less eventful, but I have an uneasy feeling about it because Jamie is anything but predictable. And she's sure as fuck not punctual. We were supposed to leave a half hour ago.

I knock on her shed door.

"Come in."

Jamie's floral scent and a Taylor Swift song from her Alexa greet me.

She eyes my reflection in her mirror while applying lip gloss. "Are we fake dating or just best buds? How much alcohol are you allowed to have? And do I prevent you from having sex or just make sure you're properly fitted with a condom?"

"You're already proving to be an inferior plus-one. *Not* the best I've ever had. I've never needed to tell Maren any of that information. She just gets me."

"Oh, I get you, Fitz." Jamie rubs her lips together and caps her lip gloss. "The alpha personality that allows you to jump out of planes and fight fires is struggling. You *need* it. And an idle winter feels like torture. I've rattled the structure on which you thrive—the new roommate shifting the dynamics around here."

I scoff, surveying the tiny space. "Nice try."

Jamie shoves her feet into chunky black boots that look too big for her body. She's jaw dropping in black tights, a short denim skirt, a low-cut black top, and silver hoop earrings peeking out beneath her straight black hair. Her tan and freckles have faded a few shades lighter. She's fucking gorgeous, but I'll never say those words to anyone.

"How do I look?" She threads her arms through her puffy white jacket.

"Late." I glance at my watch. "You look thirty minutes late."

"It's a party. Can you really be late for a party?" She squeezes past me, opening the door.

"If they run out of Gary's famous ribs, then yes. We'll be too late to the party, and it will be your fault."

Jamie navigates around the house to her Jeep like a prancing antelope taking its favorite path to avoid areas of slushy snow, mud, and muck.

I give her directions to Gary's house, but I don't know why she's driving. There's a slim chance I'll drink enough to need a driver. I don't trust her. Okay, I don't trust myself with her unless I'm in my right mind.

When we arrive, Jamie steps out of the Jeep, wearing her signature smart-ass grin. "Do you have a girlfriend pet name for me or just a best-bud name? I'm not a fan of 'princess,' but 'queen' is fine."

"Just get the fuck inside."

That grin doubles. She's *a lot.*

"This is a great house." She stops halfway up their steep driveway, gawking at the cream-and-redbrick two-story Queen Anne–style house, complete with an asymmetrical front facade hugged by a wraparound porch and a conical roof over the polygonal front corner tower.

"It's fine," I mumble, pressing my hand to her back, encouraging her to keep walking.

When she slides her gaze to me, I keep my eyes straight ahead of us, despite my grin. Yes, it's a great house.

"Whoa, whoa, whoa . . ." Gary appears before we get the door shut behind us. He squeezes my shoulder with one hand and hands me a beer with his other. "Did you bring a real girlfriend to my party?"

"You've met Jamie. She's my roommate. Maren couldn't make it."

Jamie pays no attention to us as her bug eyes survey the entry that's technically the parlor. Gary's wife, Evette, insisted they keep the character of the home. The rooms are small, but the ceilings are tall, and each space has an abundance of embellishments, such as elaborate dark woodwork, colorful stained glass windows, and embossed botanical wallpaper in muted green-and-gold tones. For a good time, I could mention the burgundy velvet drapes just to see Gary lose his shit.

"Uh . . ." Jamie shakes her head. "Nice to see you again. Happy birthday." She whips out a bubbly voice and face-splitting grin while giving him a quick hug.

Jamie's rousing personality shines for everyone but me. I bring out something in her; I'm not sure what that is yet.

"You have a stunning home." She digs into her purse. "I brought you this." She hands him an envelope.

Is she showing me up? It's a no-gift party.

"You shouldn't have." Gary winks. "But thank you. Grab something to eat, and enjoy the party."

"Sounds great," she replies with too much enthusiasm.

When Gary heads in the opposite direction, I slip a hand into my front jeans pocket and glare at her, again catching her floral scent. "You bought *my* friend a card?"

"I bought *our* friend a card and a gift card for coffee."

"You're making me look bad."

She messes with the collar of my gray flannel shirt. "I put your name on the card too." Her gaze flits to mine when she's done with my collar. "I make you look *better*."

"You're full of shit. Now go eat." I gesture with my chin before taking a swig of my beer.

"Bossy."

I shake my head, but not before grinning.

"The ribs. Dude, make sure you get the ribs." Todd sidles up to me while wiping sauce from his lips.

With an easy hum, I shift my attention to the spread of food on the dining room table.

"What, uh . . . is going on with you and my girlfriend?" Todd stuffs half a brownie into his mouth.

"Girlfriend?"

He eyes Jamie, filling her plate with food. "It's not official yet, but we shared a moment when she brought those cookies. Are you cool with me asking her out?"

"Is your wife cool with it?"

"Soon-to-be ex-wife. I'll message her and ask."

"Make sure you get your balls back in the divorce settlement."

"Fuck you, Fitz." He finger combs his mullet.

My nose wrinkles. "What's that smell?"

Todd sniffs his fingers. "Oh, that's my tea tree hair oil. Keeps everything in the back soft and smooth." He chuckles before making his way back to the food.

As with all of Gary's parties, there's music, enough food to satisfy all of Missoula, and a well-run bar, courtesy of Evette churning out drink after drink; her tight red chin-length curls spring in all directions when she shakes a cocktail. Evette's a gifted mixologist when she's not teaching first grade.

I fetch some food and chat with my buddies while keeping one eye on Jamie. For a designated driver, she's consuming too many mixed drinks. She doesn't have enough body weight to handle that much alcohol.

"Another beer?" Gary finds me again and holds out another bottle.

I shake him off. "I think I'm driving home."

"But you brought a driver."

For the past hour, Jamie's been chatting it up with a group of teachers from Evette's school, head tipped back in laughter and a new drink in her right hand every fifteen minutes. "I brought my roommate. I think this is her first party."

Gary's gaze follows mine, and he smirks. "What is she? A buck ten? This won't end well. Maybe you should show her the bathroom, so she doesn't lose it all over my floor."

I barely register his words because my shitty DD is too entertaining. I have no idea what she's saying to everyone huddled around her, but they seem to hang on her every word. I bet she's, once again, sharing embarrassing *Jeopardy!*-level information. Perhaps she's telling them about her friend's nut oil.

I can't focus or relax because I can't take my eyes off Jamie. She makes me lose a game of darts, and I come in last playing pool.

I meet Deana, Rachel, Gabby, and Jocelyn. At least, I think those are their names. Four single women. Four possible chances to get laid. Yet I let my poor dick down because I brought the wrong roommate to Gary's party.

"Hey, Evette. Have you seen Jamie?" I yell above the music, leaning over the bar while she shakes a drink.

"I'm not sure. But I can tell you, she's a keeper." Evette waggles her eyebrows at me.

I return a toothy grin. "Well, at the moment, I'm just trying to *keep her* from emptying the contents of her stomach onto your furniture or carpet."

Evette gives me a funny look.

I check upstairs when I don't find Jamie on the main floor. "Jaymes?" I knock on the bathroom door.

It eases open, and she jumps, glancing up at me. "Shit. Fitz. Sorry. Um . . . are you good?"

My hands rest against the thick doorframe, blocking her from exiting the bathroom. "I'm drunk as fuck. And I think I just impregnated the music teacher from Evette's school."

Her eyes widen, lips parted.

"And I want to go home, so I've been looking for my designated driver."

She swallows hard and salutes me with a shaky hand to her forehead. "At your service."

"You're drunk."

She narrows her eyes. "I am?"

I cast my gaze to the ceiling. "I'm glad we brought your Jeep and not my truck. Let's go."

"Do you think you should at least exchange numbers with the music teacher before we go?" She follows me to the stairs.

I ignore her.

Gary's bushy eyebrows slide up his forehead when I reach the main level. I nod and give him a tight grin. This is the earliest I've left one of his parties.

"Oof!"

I turn, and Jamie's on the floor.

"Oh my god. I'm so sorry." Travis, another smoke jumper, cringes. "I didn't mean to back into you."

"It's fine." I scoop her off the ground and into my arms. "She drank too much."

"My jacket," she mutters while squirming.

"It's by the door." I tighten my grip on her wiggly body. When we reach the entry, Gary's waiting for us. "It's the white one." I nod to her jacket.

"Thanks for coming." He drapes the jacket over her.

"You're going to drop me," Jamie whines when I step onto the porch.

"I carry a hundred and fifty pounds of equipment for miles in the heat of summer. I think I can manage to carry your drunk ass to the street without dropping you. Where are the keys?"

"Oh, look. A full moon." She tips her head back and grins in the crisp air of the windless night as I descend the driveway to the desolate street. "Did you know that a white moon cycle results in higher rates of boy babies? That's when you're ovulating during a full moon."

"I haven't ovulated during a full moon, but sometimes I turn into a werewolf."

She giggles. "I would love that so much. Calvin the werewolf."

"Get your keys out so I can drive."

"You're drunk. I'm your driver."

I laugh. "Cute. But no. Tonight's not my night to die or kill anyone else." I set her on her feet at the Jeep and hold out my hand.

"No. You've had too much to drink."

"No. *You've* had too much to drink."

A slow grin creeps up her face before she clenches my shirt and rests her forehead on my chest. Her body shakes with laughter.

"You're *so* wasted," I say under my breath.

"Why won't you believe me?" She laughs. It's more like a cackle.

I cup her face and kiss her—*not* because I want to kiss her. It's to prove a point.

When her warm lips start to move against mine, I nearly forget the point.

I nearly forget I shouldn't want to kiss her.

So I end it before it ends something in me, like all my common sense. Her hands fly to my wrists, eyes flared.

"See? If you were sober, you wouldn't have let me kiss you," I say.

Shock continues to paralyze her expression. Is she breathing?

A car drives past us, its musty exhaust lingering while the brakes squeak as it slows down to pull into the driveway.

"Give me the key," I say.

After a few more seconds, she releases my wrists and slips a hand into her purse to retrieve her keys. As I reach for them, she pulls them away. "If *you* were sober, you would not have done that. Get in the Jeep. We never speak of this again because I'm not letting you get me kicked out of the house." She marches around the front of the Jeep to the driver's side.

How can a nurse be so irresponsible?

I jog after her. "The fun's over. There's no fucking way I'm letting you drive."

When I reach for the keys, she hugs them and angles her chest away from me. "Calvin Fitzgerald, get your stubborn, controlling ass in my Jeep. I am not drunk."

"I watched you down over six cocktails in less than ninety minutes." I bear-hug her from behind and slide my hand between her chest and crossed arms to steal the keys.

"Calvin, stop!" She wriggles. "I'm not drunk! They were mocktails. Virgin drinks."

I halt my pursuit of the keys. She stumbles a few feet from the door, breathing heavily. Cheeks and nose colored pink from the air.

Fuck.

She blows her hair out of her face. "I'm your person. I know you ate two plates of food. You lost a game of darts and two games of pool. You talked to a dozen guys and four women. I know you drank one bottle of beer. And you didn't impregnate the elementary school music teacher because I met *him*. His name is Mitch, and his wife is six months pregnant with their first child."

I manage a few blinks before I find a weak voice. "You let me think you were drunk."

"I did no such thing. You made an assumption, and I laughingly played along. But I thought you knew the truth, the way *I* knew the truth about you. Then you"—she stabs her hands in the air between us—"*kissed* me. If Will and Maren find out, it's on you. I'm not moving out. You did this. A controlling Capricorn."

This woman and her moons. There are so many things I could say. An apology. An explanation for my behavior. A promise that Will and Maren will never find out. *So* many good options. Yet, I go with the most reckless response.

"We didn't have sex," I murmur.

Jamie squints. "What?"

"We didn't have sex. That's breaking the rules. We can't have sex with other housemates. That's the rule. But if you orgasmed, I'll keep it between us." It's not the right time to smirk or taunt her, but I can't help it. I live for getting a reaction out of her.

She balls up her hands. "Get. In. The. Jeep."

Chapter Ten

JAYMES

Calvin kissed me.

CALVIN KISSED ME!

I loved it because I wanted it. I hated it because I shouldn't have wanted it.

What was he thinking? What was *I* thinking? I started to kiss him back. The only upside to the kiss is Fitz's guilt.

It's been two weeks since the party, and he's not said anything about it. It's like it didn't happen, except for his random acts of kindness.

He folded my clothes last week. After it snowed, he cleared a path from the house to my Jeep and dusted the snow from my roof and windows. A few days ago, he made his famous chili and put some in a thermos for me to take to work for lunch. Yesterday, I made a torte, and he washed all the dishes.

If he's not careful, I might marry him.

Conversely, I don't get more than a few words from him, the occasional glance, and a polite smile.

He thought I was drunk, so he kissed me to make a point. So what? It was just a kiss.

A kiss I can't forget.

"Is there something going on between you and Fitz?" Will shoots me a questioning glance while tossing a bag of popcorn into the microwave just as I slip on my boots to head to bed.

Shit!

I clear my throat. "Going on?"

"Maren mentioned it. She thinks he's doing nice things for you."

I stiffen while trying to slide my hands casually into my pockets. "Is being considerate a crime?"

"No." Will turns, leaning against the counter and crossing his arms. "But sleeping with a housemate is a crime. It's a hard rule."

I cough a laugh. "No. Rest assured—I'm not sleeping with Calvin. Honestly, I think he's trying to butter me up so I don't retaliate. I have yet to get proper revenge for some of the shenanigans he pulled on me."

Will offers me a sheepish grin. "Sorry. I'm not trying to be a dick. I'm just trying to keep the peace around here."

"You're not a dick. You're one of my three favorite people in this house." I blow him a kiss before opening the door.

He chuckles. "Night, Jamie."

"Returning to Miami yet?" Melissa asks the second I answer the phone on my way home from work the next day.

"Not yet. But I miss you like crazy. How are you?"

"Lonely."

"Stop guilting me."

"Fine," she huffs. "I'm good. There's a new PA in our department. He's my future husband. I just don't know how to break it to his wife."

"You're not a home-wrecker."

"I would have said that, too, but he's funny and smart. And kind. Gah! A nice guy. Jamie, do you have any idea how rare that is?"

"I do. And I'm sure his wife does too." I pull into the Good Food Store's parking lot to grab a few items.

"I'm not *really* going to steal him, but he's going to star in all of my sex dreams, and I'm not even going to feel guilty about it."

"I'll allow that." I giggle while unbuckling.

"What about you? Are you still a Montana virgin?"

I adjust my earbuds and head into the store. "What exactly is that?"

"If you haven't had sex in Montana, then you're a Montana virgin."

"Who told you that?" I pluck a basket from the stack and hook it over my arm.

"I have original material. *I* came up with that."

"Then yes, I still have my Montana v-card."

"Nooo! Say it isn't so. Why be a travel nurse if you're not going to take advantage of meaningless sex in all fifty states?"

I inspect the apples before sliding several into a bag. "If you must know, Calvin kissed me after a party. He thought I was drunk, and he tried to make his point by kissing me."

"Oh my god. How is that making a point?"

"He said I wouldn't have let him kiss me if I were sober."

"But you did?"

I smile at the guy next to me who grabs a mango. When he turns and heads back to his cart, I lower my voice. "It's not like I had a choice. He didn't ask me. One minute, my head was on his chest, and the next, my face was in his hands, and his lips were on mine."

"Wait. Why was your head on his chest?"

"Just . . . it's not what you think. The point is, I didn't let him do anything."

"Was it good?"

"What?" I stroll toward the bulk aisle for trail mix.

"Was the kiss good?"

"It was quick and unexpected. It was . . . weird and awkward."

"But you think he's hot."

"I think this conversation has gone off the rails."

"You're saying he's *not* sexy?"

"You're not listening to me."

"I am. But you're not making sense. Just answer the question."

"I'm not answering the question." I fill a bag with trail mix.

"Why?"

"Because it's irrelevant. We're roommates. It's a hard rule—no sleeping with your roommate. We'd get booted out. And I like my setup. I'd rather not have to leave before I move on to my next job."

"Yada yada. Is he hot?"

"Stop." I set the bag in my basket.

"Have you had a sex dream about Calvin Fitzgerald?"

I giggle. This is absurd. I shouldn't have told her about the kiss.

"It's okay if you have. That makes you normal. Who am I going to tell?"

"I have to go."

"No. You're not ending this call until you just tell me. Have you had a sex dream about Calvin Fitzgerald? Huh? Huh? Huh—"

"Yes. I've had a sex dream about Calvin Fitzgerald. Are you happy now?" I huff and turn the corner. "Oof!" And I run right into *Calvin Fitzgerald*. "Shit. Sorry. I . . . I have to go." I pluck out my earbuds and toss them in my bag.

He didn't hear me. *Please, God, say he didn't hear me.*

"Watch where you're going," he warns with a taut voice, a jar of mustard in one hand and something wrapped in butcher paper in the other.

It's the most we've said to each other since the kiss. I can't think of Fitz or look at him without thinking about the kiss. Who am I kidding? I can't do anything without thinking about the stupid kiss.

"Hey. How was your day?" I ask in singsong, clinging to small talk like Rose clung to the door after the *Titanic* sank.

He doesn't speak. And I can't decipher his expression. This sucks. Did he hear me?

Fitz's gaze makes its usual inspection of me. Nothing to see. I'm in my not-so-sexy purple scrubs, and I'm already flushed. Why must he toy with me?

I clear my throat to get his attention. "Will's been talking about either re-siding the house or a kitchen remodel. I think I will get an electric kettle for my room and eat ramen or order takeout. How about you?" I hold my breath and offer a constipated smile.

"SPAM."

What?

One word? I'm freaking the hell out as to whether or not he heard me, and all I get is SPAM?

"You eat SPAM?"

"I do," he says with a confident smile—too confident.

"Yum." I roll my lips between my teeth. "Well, uh . . . I'll let you finish your shopping. See you at home."

"I have another stop to make, so if you're nestled in your shed by the time I get home, have *sweet dreams*."

I freeze—as in, I stop breathing. My lungs stop oxygenating my blood—death by embarrassment.

My brain scrambles, body sweats. The sooner I can come up with an explanation that's not the obvious one, the sooner I can breathe again. "Don't look so smug. You heard one side of the conversation and took it out of context."

His mouth purses into duck lips while his eyes narrow. "Can a sex dream be taken out of context?"

I survey our surroundings, replying in a hushed voice, "I'm on the verge of saying whatever it takes to shut you up, the way I was willing to say *anything* to shut up Melissa. So what's it going to be, Fitz? How many times do I need to lick your ego before you let this go?"

His eyebrows make a slow ascent up his forehead. "I wouldn't have taken you for a licker."

"I'm not a licker."

"No?" He cocks his head.

I groan. Not moan. *Groan.* "If you let this go and promise never to say another word about it, then we can be even."

"Even?"

"Yes. Even. I still owe you for the bullshit about the thirty-day trial in the rental contract and your assery about Betty."

"Assery? Is that a word? Is it like cantankerous?"

My eyes narrow. "Take it or leave it."

He beams victoriously. "We're even."

He's good. I'll give him that. After a long day, I'm tired and not feeling up to the challenge. Nevertheless, there's no way I'm rolling over on this and admitting defeat by letting him manipulate the conversation.

I can tell from the gleam in his eyes and his puffed-out chest that I will *never* live this down. Melissa is on my shit list, right next to Fitz. For that matter, I'm upset with Will and Maren, too, for thinking something's going on when it's not. If everyone stopped pestering me about Calvin Fitzgerald, maybe my brain would find more appropriate dreams.

Chapter Eleven

My mom used to say that humans are good. Our natural inclination is to do the right thing. Show kindness. Express love. Be pure in thought.

Pure in thought . . .

I'm struggling with that one.

Sipping hot chocolate on the sofa in my loose-fitting jeans and pink hoodie, I set up my profile on a dating app. I need a distraction from a certain someone. As soon as that thought enters my mind, that certain someone opens the door. It's been over a week since the grocery store incident.

"Hey," I murmur without taking my gaze off my phone.

"Hey." Fitz carries a bag of take-out food into the kitchen.

"Did you have a good day?"

"Training. Procedural review. We'll be jumping again in no time." He sets his sandwich and a pile of fries on a plate.

"How do your parents feel about your job?" I glance at him as he sits at the counter.

He inspects his sandwich before taking a bite and chewing it slowly. "It's fair to say they're probably indifferent."

"I doubt that. I can't imagine a mother feeling indifferent about her child jumping out of a plane just to trek to an out-of-control fire."

He appraises me for a few silent seconds without offering a comment.

"Where do they live?"

"California."

"Is that where you grew up?"

Fitz nods before taking a drink of water.

"Siblings?"

"You're full of questions tonight."

"Just making conversation."

"I have a sister."

"Older or younger?"

When he gives me another look, I return a tiny cringe. "Sorry. It's a natural follow-up question."

"Younger."

I nod several times. There's a line he doesn't want me to cross. I can't see it, but I feel it. But I also feel his patience with me. "Do you want to ask me anything?"

"Where's Maren?"

That's not what I meant. "She has a date. And Will's working."

"And you're drinking hot chocolate and playing on your phone." He pops a wad of fries into his mouth.

"I'm working on my profile for this dating app. What would you say are my best qualities?"

He stops midchew and lifts a brow at me.

"Fine. I'll go first. If I were helping you with a dating profile, I'd say you're adventurous, funny, and loyal."

"Sounds like a profile for a dog," he murmurs behind a brown paper napkin.

"News flash. Most women love dogs. If you could channel your inner canine, you'd be an immediate swipe right."

He slides his plate aside and rests his arms on the counter. "You're a good baker. You have straight teeth. And you're inquisitive."

I bite back my smile. "I see. Those are good things, right?" I type them into my profile. "Maybe I can add some hobbies that will be better clickbait. Like . . . surfing. Diving. Fishing. Skateboarding. Stargazing. Concerts." When I peer up at Fitz, he has a pleasant smile.

It's not his normal expression around me, which makes it a little creepy yet still satisfying.

"What?"

"Nothing." He rubs his hand over his mouth as if he can wipe the smile from his scruffy face.

I stand and mosey toward the sink with my mug. "That look isn't nothing."

"I didn't know your hobbies, except for skateboarding." He turns, resting his backside against the counter, hands on either side.

"Well, unlike me, you're not that inquisitive." I wash out the mug.

"Not true. I read two to three books a week."

"Then you don't care enough about people to ask about them." I dry my mug and lift onto my toes to put it back in the cabinet. "Maybe you only like fictional people."

"Not true."

I laugh. "You're killing me, Fitz. If that's not true, the only expla-nation is that you don't like *me* enough to ask me about myself. My family. My hobbies." I tuck my fingers in the back pockets of my jeans and position myself a foot from him. "When Maren and Will speak unfavorably of you, I defend you. I've never visited them at work with cookies. I don't bake their favorite brownies. I haven't accompanied them to any parties. I'm your person, but you're not mine. And that's okay."

Tiny wrinkles line his forehead.

I force a smile for him because I don't want to make him feel bad. "Maren and Will are nice to—"

My words die, trapping my next breath in my chest because Fitz's hand slides behind my head, and he kisses me. All thoughts dissolve into a mushy mess. Thinking isn't an option. All I can do is feel. And I love the feel of his hand cradling my head and his lips moving against mine. *This* is a real kiss. It's not hard like the first time he kissed me. It's slower and deeper. I feel it everywhere.

Why? What? How? The questions fire in every direction, but they spin out of control, unanswered. I'm terrified of what comes next.

"I'm not drunk," I murmur when he releases my lips.

That's not entirely true. My blood alcohol level is under the legal limit, but I'm intoxicated. Drunk from that kiss.

"You're generous. Distractingly mesmerizing. Quirky in a brilliant way. And ineffably beautiful." Keeping his hand on the back of my head, he deposits one last kiss on my cheek, letting his lips linger until we hear a car door shut.

Maren.

He's halfway up the stairs before I can breathe or formulate a thought with a prayer of materializing as actual words. When Maren opens the front door, I touch my fingers to my lips.

"Worst. Date. Ever." She tosses her burnt orange tote bag onto the sofa before collapsing beside it and tugging at her black knit scarf like it's strangling her.

I clear my throat, but it does little to clear my head. And my knees are embarrassingly shaky, just like my voice. "Um . . . w-what happened?" There's no way I'm not at least ten shades of red in the face, so I busy myself in the kitchen, making my lunch for tomorrow.

"He took me to the restaurant where his ex-girlfriend is the chef. And she comes out to see if we're enjoying our dinner. Then, he goes on and on about me being a pilot, and when she seems unimpressed, he ignores me for the rest of dinner. So before dessert was served, I excused myself to use the ladies' room and left."

"Uh-huh." I store my salad for tomorrow in the fridge.

"Jamie, did you hear a word I said?"

"Um . . . yeah, of course. That's a bummer. Sorry to hear it didn't go well." I rest my hip against the counter and cross my arms.

Maren studies me for a second. "Thanks. You okay?"

"Me?" My head jerks backward. "Yeah. Of course. Why wouldn't I be?"

"You're acting weird."

"I'm just . . ." I shrug. "It was a long day. I'm tired. I probably should have stuck to half a glass of wine instead of a full glass." I lie, faking a yawn. "I'll grab a quick shower and head to bed unless you need in the bathroom first."

"It's all yours." She snags the remote. "I'm going to sulk for a bit. Maybe watch a love story, since I think they only exist in movies and books."

"Ha! Probably." I slide on my black boots and slip out the back door, pausing for a second. Then I grin and press my fingers to my lips all the way to the shed. On autopilot, I collect my clothes and return to the house. Maren's watching *What's Your Number?* and Fitz's bedroom door is shut when I reach the top of the stairs. While I shower, I wonder if he's asleep. Is he thinking of me and that kiss? Is he touching his lips the way I touched mine? Is he touching himself differently?

Are we going to get kicked out of the house?

What am I supposed to say when I see him again?

After my shower, I slip into my sweatpants and hoodie and wrap a towel around my head. I've never hurried from the bathroom to my shed as fast as I do tonight. Desperate, I start to text Melissa, but it's late in Florida. And what would I say anyway? How do I explain something I don't understand myself?

My heart races, chasing feelings that are sprinting out of control. I lock my shed door and remove the towel from my head. When I reach for my brush, there's a note tucked beneath it on the dresser. It's an envelope ripped in half—junk mail.

It's just a kiss. X

"Just a kiss," I whisper, tracing the letters with my finger.

Just a kiss at Gary's party.

Just a kiss in the kitchen.

Will there be more? I hope so. An unavoidable grin steals across my lips.

You're generous. Distractingly mesmerizing. Quirky in a brilliant way. And ineffably beautiful.

I'm in trouble.

Chapter Twelve

It's a busy morning in the kitchen as Maren makes an omelet and Will grabs a glass of water and a handful of vitamins after getting home from his shift. Then there's Fitz, filling a reusable mug with coffee.

As for me . . . well, I'm trying to keep from shitting my pants, vomiting, or making eye contact with Fitz.

Just a kiss. *Pfft.* It was just a kiss at Gary's—a singular kiss after a misunderstanding. Last night was *the kiss*. And there was no misunderstanding. So *kiss* is now *kisses*. Plural.

"Later," Will mumbles, heading up the stairs.

"Later," Maren echoes while scuffing her teddy bear slippers to the table.

I shove my lunch in a canvas bag, sling it and my purse over my shoulder, and bolt out the door with a quick mumbled "Bye." The lazy sun finds my face as I reach the end of the drive, giving me hope for spring. When I climb inside my Jeep, I take my first real breath of the morning.

However, that breath dies when my Jeep won't start. Not a sound.

"Shit." I grip the steering wheel and close my eyes. After a few deep breaths, I slide out, deflating a little more with every step back to the house.

Maren glances up from her plate as I shut the door behind me.

"My Jeep won't start." My nose wrinkles.

"That sucks. Fitz?" I cringe when she yells his name.

He jogs down the stairs and grabs his jacket. "Yes?" Pulling up the zipper, he glances at Maren and then at me.

"Jamie's Jeep won't start. Can you jump her?"

Jesus . . .

He tips his chin to focus on his gloves. "Yeah, I can jump her," he says with a grin that Maren can't see. Thank god.

I've got nothing. I'm too busy ping-ponging my gaze between the two of them. Does Maren suspect something?

"Let's go, Jaymes," Fitz says, opening the door.

I scurry after him. "I don't know what's wrong with it. It started just fine yesterday. And I didn't leave on any lights."

And you kissed me last night!

"When's the last time you put a new battery in it?" He opens the driver's side door and pops the hood.

I rub my hands together and blow on them. "I have to say never."

He chuckles. "You need a new battery. I might start it for you, but it probably won't start when you leave work later. If it were me, I'd go to the gas station this morning and see if they have time to slip a new battery in it." He treks to his truck and positions it in front of my Jeep.

"What do you need me to do?" I ask.

"Didn't your dad teach you how to jump a car?" He rests the jumper cables over his shoulder while opening the hood of his truck.

"He died when I was five."

Fitz eyes me for a second and offers an apologetic smile. "Red goes to the positive. Black is negative." He holds up both cables. "Connect them to the dead battery first."

I pay close attention because I have a feeling this might not be the last time I need to jump my Jeep.

"I'll start my truck, then you'll start your Jeep."

After my Jeep starts, Fitz shows me how to disconnect everything in reverse order. "Drive around for a bit before you stop at the station, and leave your Jeep running while you ask them if they can fit you in. If they can't, then call me."

I climb into my Jeep, and he stands at my open door.

"Thank you," I murmur before scraping my teeth along my lower lip and averting my gaze.

"Anything for my person."

My heart doesn't simply stop; it explodes into pieces so tiny I'll never put them back in order.

I clear my throat. "Calvin Fitzgerald, there are rules in our household."

"I'm aware."

"I'm not getting evicted."

"Neither am I." He's so confident.

Me? Not so much. "My job in Missoula is temporary."

He nods.

"You'll be nonexistent when fire season starts."

Again, he nods.

I can't look at him and say the words, but I also can't dance around them any longer, so I grip the steering wheel to steady my nervous hands, gazing at his truck in front of me. "You kissed me, Fitz. Twice. Why did you kiss me?"

"Because *not* kissing you became too exhausting."

A man has never broken my heart. Homeschooling helped by reducing the size of my dating pool. Casual dating has helped too. So it doesn't make sense that I *know* Calvin Fitzgerald is on his way to obliterating my heart. Yet, I do. I know it with absolute certainty.

I slowly turn toward him.

Fitz bites the inside of his cheek with a downcast expression. I've never seen anything sexier than this man at this moment showing me a sliver of vulnerability.

He rubs the back of his neck. "And I have impeccable endurance, which means I have a complicated relationship with my feelings toward you," he says, lifting his gaze with a tense brow. "So I need to be consumed by work. And I need to know that you're temporary in my life."

My heart digs through its emergency kit and pulls out the tools to construct a fortress around it.

I manage to say the opposite of what I feel. "It was just a kiss."

Fitz's gaze washes across my face before he relinquishes a tiny smile. "Yes."

◆ ◆ ◆

"Sorry, I'm late. Thanks for being so understanding. Stupid battery." I sigh when Dr. Reichart meets me in the hallway while I slide my stethoscope around my neck.

"No problem." She blows at the steam from her coffee. Already, half her hair has fallen out of her ponytail. "Did you get a new battery?"

"I did."

"It's come to my attention that you're living with Will Landry."

My brain trips for a few seconds. "Um . . . Will? Yes. He's my roommate. One of three."

"Are you two dating?" She's moseying toward her office while she sips her coffee, her thumb sliding down her phone screen.

"No. It's a house rule. No dating your roommates."

Technically, it's "no sexual relationships," which I think has been fine-tuned by Calvin to mean kissing is apparently okay because it's not sex?

"Is he dating anyone?"

"Not to my knowledge."

She smiles when we reach her office, slipping her phone into her coat pocket. "Tell him I said hi."

"You know Will?" Duh. She brought him up. I shake my head. "I mean, how do you know Will?"

"He popped my cherry, then ripped my heart out, threw it on the ground, and crushed it to smithereens with his mammoth black boot." She stomps her foot to the floor and twists it like she's extinguishing a cigarette instead of her proverbial heart.

"Oh. Whoa! I had no idea—"

Dr. Reichart pins a scary smile on her face. "The past is the past. I don't hold grudges."

That smile is not a no-grudges-held smile.

"I'll let him know you said hi."

"Great. Tell him I'd love to get coffee with him."

Pressing my lips together, I nod a half-dozen times. As soon as she's behind her office door, I'll text Will and tell him to pack a bag and leave Missoula *stat*.

"*Beat Saber* during lunch?" She lifts her sculpted brows in question.

"Sure," I squeak.

The door clicks, and I turn, smacking into Betty. "Oof! Sorry."

"Mrs. Edie requested you. I guess you were 'nicer' to her last week." Betty gives me a cheesy grin.

"Did you know Dr. Reichart lost her virginity to Will?" I follow Betty in her new green sneakers to the break room.

"That's impressive." She messes with her pink micro bangs.

"That she lost her virginity to Will or that Will took it?"

"Neither. I meant it's impressive that she remembers who took her virginity."

"You don't?"

She peers over her shoulder at me. "Is that even a real question?"

Betty's a slut. I love her. She's kind and funny, with years of nursing experience that she shares with the other nurses. A true role model at work. But her legs spread like my spring-loaded kitchen shears. I don't need a full hand to count my sexual partners. Betty needs a spreadsheet.

Spread-sheet.

"Have you gotten some lately?" Betty asks, snagging a stale donut.

"Some what?"

"Oh my god. If you have to ask, then I know the answer." Betty's face sours when she discovers how long that glazed donut has been in the pink box.

"Sex?" I glance up from my tablet.

"Yes. That's when a guy puts his penis—"

"Stop." I laugh. "It's been a hot minute. But I've recently been kissed."

"Oh, tell me where."

"In my kitchen and by my Jeep after a party."

"No. Where did he kiss you?"

"Um . . ." I glance over her shoulder to the nursing student waiting for Mentor Betty. "The lips," I murmur.

"Which lips?" Betty waggles her eyebrows. "Do you know what I mean?"

She must think I'm still a virgin and not just a Montana virgin.

"Wouldn't you like to know?" I wink and toss her a conspiratorial grin while brushing past her to get to Mrs. Edie.

"You little hussy."

I cringe, and my face flushes when the *male* nursing student eyes me. He heard her. Now I'm Nurse Hussy because I let Betty think my labia was recently serviced.

It's going to be a long day.

Chapter Thirteen

CALVIN

During my years as a firefighter, I've heard my fair share of bloodcurdling screams. However, as I get out of my truck, I don't expect to hear one coming from my house.

I sprint through the door, resisting the urge to kick it down. When I race past the entry, I find Jamie standing on the kitchen counter, one hand gripping the top of the fridge and her other hand cupped over her mouth.

Eyes wide.

Legs shaking.

I don't smell smoke. Is someone in the house? I can't get a read on the situation other than that she's paralyzed with panic.

"Run!" She points toward me.

A mouse runs past my boot and hides under the sofa.

I follow the mouse's path, inspecting every kitchen corner before glancing at Jamie. "Where is it?"

Her brow lines with as much confusion as I have in mine. "You just watched it run under the sofa."

"No. Where is the rattlesnake? The bear? The mountain lion? The escaped convict? Where is the scary thing that was chasing the mouse?"

She scowls.

"Tell me you're not on the counter screaming your lungs out at a measly little mouse."

"Did you see it? All"—she wiggles her fingers—"fast and twitchy. Beady little eyes. A horrifying critter spreading disease, stealing food, and chewing through the furniture."

"Get down." I hold out my hand.

She shakes her head, pulling down the long sleeves of her fitted white T-shirt to hide her hands. "It's under the sofa. Get it."

I try not to laugh, but she's quite the sight. "Maybe I need to get on the counter too. Will might show up soon. He was looking for it the other day. Why should I risk my life if you're unwilling to risk yours?"

Her frown deepens. "I'm irrationally scared of a mouse. I need you to be my hero today and get rid of it. Is that what you need to hear?"

My lips corkscrew, and I nod several times. "That works. Be right back. Keep an eye on Mickey."

"Where are you going?" she shrieks.

"He won't come when called, so I must entice him." I jog to the garage and retrieve the right tool for the job.

When I return and open the fridge, she gasps. "What are you doing with that?"

I spread peanut butter on the mousetrap and set it.

"No. Nooo way."

I place the trap by the sofa.

"Fitz, no. You can't kill it."

"Sorry, Jaymes. We don't have a choice. When bears attack humans, they have to be put down because they've tasted human blood, which means they're more likely to attack humans again. Mice are no different." I return the peanut butter to the fridge. "That mouse has heard your terrified screams. Now it craves that reaction and will dedicate its life to scaring the shit out of you. If I don't eliminate the mouse, it will hunt you down, run across your bare feet, and burrow into your shed."

She slowly hunches, lowering her butt to the counter and letting her legs dangle off the side. "Calvin Fitzgerald."

"Jaymes Andrews." I stuff my hands into my pockets but can't hide my impish grin.

She bites her lip, partially disguising her smile. "You are the most intense person I have ever known. But at the same time, you don't have a serious bone in your body. That makes you an enigma. Most days, I can't decide if you like me or can't stand me." Her lips turn into a pouty frown.

I rest my hands next to hers on the edge of the counter. "I like you too much."

"I'm not having sex with you, Fitz," she whispers when my gaze drifts to her neck and lower to the outline of her nipples beneath her tight shirt.

"If I had a dime for every time I heard that"—I lean in until my nose touches her neck, inhaling her floral scent while my lips skate along her collarbone—"I'd have zero dimes."

Her body vibrates with laughter, and I wish it would shake me out of this. Whatever *this* is.

Am I bored?

Lonely?

Having an early midlife crisis?

I don't want a girlfriend or a wife because I'm happily married to my job. Kids? Hell no. I don't need anyone to leave behind. Being left behind is fucking awful.

Still, my hands slide up her arms, and I kiss her neck. Something's overriding common sense. This is headed for a self-preservation debacle. Will I destroy her to protect her from my past? My biggest fear. Or will I lose myself in whatever this is between us and resent her for being my weakness?

Jamie draws in a shaky breath that silences her laughter while her head lolls to the side.

I'm a dumb fuck. There's no denying that.

Self-torture? Check.

Risking my current residence? Check.

Disregarding Will's nonnegotiable house rule? Double check.

Maybe that's okay, since I have no plans to let it go past this. I'm technically not breaking any rules. I'll keep my lips above her shoulders and my hands in neutral territory.

Our lips fuse, and I fight my mind's urge to make sense of this.

Does this have to make sense?

I've dined on SPAM marinated in Kool-Aid. To the average person, that doesn't make sense. And it doesn't have to.

Her hands rest on my chest and slide south. I grab her wrists. "Nope," I say between kisses.

She bites my lower lip, and I'm forced to suppress a moan, which channels all the tension straight into my dick. We might need our own set of rules.

SNAP!

"Ahh!" She leaps off the counter, wrapping her arms and legs around my torso.

"What's going on?" Maren's accusatory tone is the cherry on top of this clusterfuck as the front door clicks shut behind her.

Fuck. That was close. Too close.

Jamie's gaping eyes fill with distrust.

I peel her arms and legs off me.

"Yuck. Yuck. Yuck!" Jamie runs out the back door—no shoes and no explanation to Maren.

I retrieve the trapped mouse and hold it in the air.

Maren doesn't flinch. "Will's going to be thrilled."

"Unlike Jamie." I smirk.

Maren laughs, shrugging off her brown wool coat. "That did look suspect for a moment. Is that why she was holding on to you for dear life?"

"No. She suddenly felt really horny. I tried to push her away, but—"

Maren snorts. "I'm not buying that one." She collapses onto the sofa and checks her phone.

Good. I don't want her to buy it.

"I'm going to toss Mickey in the trash and make sure our new roomie isn't stuck in the corner of the shed in the fetal position."

"I love that about her. She's not like the rest of us. It's refreshing."

"It's something," I mumble before heading outside to dispose of the mouse. Once that's done, I knock on the shed door.

"Come in," Jamie calls in a muffled tone.

When I open the door, she glances up from the bed, where she's dangling upside down off the side, looking underneath it.

"Seeing if Mickey has a family?"

She flips her head up, kneeling on the bed, and flicks the hair out of her eyes. "Fitz, you killed that mouse. I swear I heard it scream. Did you hear it? And, oh my god." She covers her mouth for a second, eyes wide. "We. Almost. Got. Caught."

I acknowledge her with an easy nod. "We should stop."

I 1,000 percent don't mean it.

After a long pause, lips slightly parted, she nods. "Probably."

Well, shit.

"No pouting."

Her nose scrunches. "What? I don't pout."

I cross my arms and widen my stance. "It's easy to say that now because I just gave you what you wanted. But in a few days, when you're having withdrawal, I bet the pout comes out."

"Um . . . no. If anything, you'll be sulking because the only woman in the world who gets you has now banned you from kissing her. And that's going to suck for you. Maybe try to avoid Will and Maren until you can get a grip on your sulkiness."

"I can take it or leave it, baby." I shrug.

Baby? I don't say that shit. I *need* to jump. I need to ride the adrenaline high. I'm bored. That's the only explanation for my taking the bait. She's distracting only because I'm not focused. In another month, I'll look back and laugh at this ridiculousness.

Jamie smiles, but it looks forced. "Well, there you have it. You'll have more time for Mrs. Wilke now that you're not kissing me." She stands at her mirror and brushes her hair. "I hope I haven't driven a wedge between you. If you need me to apologize for my behavior, I'd happily help get you out of the doghouse."

It's impossible to hide my grin. "I'll handle her. I'm quite good at it."

Jamie's cheeks turn red, but she giggles and throws my favorite line back at me. "Get the fuck out of here."

Chapter Fourteen

JAYMES

I miss Fitz's lips. It's only been a week, but they're missable lips, and that's indisputable—a fact.

However, I've found a good distraction. Melissa's parents are celebrating their fortieth wedding anniversary, and I'm flying down to Miami for the party.

After buttering her up with pizza and wine, I share my fabulous idea with Maren. "How do you feel about a girls' trip to Miami with me?"

"Really?" She washes our glasses in the sink. "Just say when."

"Fantastic. This weekend."

"Noooo. Say anything but this weekend. That's in five days. I have to work. Have you heard of a little thing called prior notice?"

"Dang it. I know." I deflate. "Melissa didn't give me much notice. It's her parents' fortieth wedding anniversary. They debated on having a party and decided at the last minute to do it. I don't want to miss it."

"Sorry. I'd love to go, but . . ." Her smile bleeds with genuine disappointment.

I fold the empty pizza box. "I understand."

"Besides, you'll be there with your friends. I doubt you'll need me there."

I nod several times, but then I cringe. "Full disclosure?"

"Of course."

"It's my first time flying. I'm a little nervous."

Her eyes widen. "For real? You've never been on a plane?"

I shake my head, hugging the empty pizza box.

"Oh, you'll *love* it."

"Says the pilot."

"Well, I'm bummed. Had you given me more notice, I would have flown us down to Miami."

"It's fine. I'll survive. If I can dive in the ocean and swim with sharks, I can survive a plane."

"For sure." She dries her hands and winks.

"Survive what?" Will saunters into the kitchen in his black active-wear for his tai chi class.

"Jamie's flying for the first time this weekend."

"Seriously?" He narrows his eyes at me before opening the fridge.

"Yes. Seriously. Let's just state the obvious—I've lived a sheltered life. I have a lot of firsts left to experience."

"You'll love it," Will assures me.

"See?" Maren grins, brushing past me. "Fitz will say the same thing too."

"Fitz jumps out of planes. I don't think he's qualified to rate flying when you stay in the aircraft."

Will and Maren laugh while I fish my phone out of my purse.

I message Melissa to let her know I'll book my ticket before I go to bed, and then I head upstairs to shower, but Maren beats me to it. As I turn, Fitz exits his bedroom, pulling on a blue-and-orange Marmot hoodie over a white T-shirt.

"Hey," I say in an unavoidably breathy voice while giving him a tight smile.

"Hey." His gaze slides down my body.

I clear my throat. "Are you in for the night?"

He shakes his head, taking his sweet time, returning his gaze to mine. "Bowling with Gary and Evette."

"Bowling?"

"It's a heavy ball with finger holes, ten pins—"

"Fitz, I'm going to knock out your pretty teeth if you don't stop mocking me like I was born yesterday."

He gives me a shit-eating grin. "You think my teeth are pretty?"

"Have fun bowling."

The bathroom door opens. "It's all yours." Maren adjusts her robe's sash.

"Thanks." I step toward the door.

"Fitz, did Jamie tell you she's flying for the first time this weekend? She asked me to go, but I can't. I told her she'd do just fine."

I close my eyes. *Thanks, Maren.*

"Is that so? What were you . . . born yesterday?"

"Be nice," Maren scolds on her way to her room. "If I lived in Miami, I probably wouldn't have any desire to leave either." She shuts her bedroom door.

"Where ya going?" Fitz's eyebrows slide up his head while he rests his shoulder against the wall, hands in the pocket of his hoodie. Freshly showered Fitz with damp, messy hair is too much for my ovaries. His face has a little more dark scruff than usual today, and his playful gaze makes me squirm.

I cross my arms. Then fold my hands. Then lace them behind my back. God, he makes me crazy with a need to touch him. "Miami. It's Melissa's parents' anniversary. It's just for two nights. And Maren's right. I'll be fine. No big deal. It's not like I haven't wanted to fly. I've just never needed to before now."

"You asked Maren to go?"

I nod.

"Is she your person now?" He's baiting me with a giant, fat worm.

"I thought we ended the you-being-my-person thing."

"I thought we ended something else. I was unaware that the two were mutually exclusive."

"They're not." I tip my chin up as if I know where this is going. I don't.

"Then I'm hurt you didn't ask me."

I narrow my eyes. Hurt? He's not hurt. He's, once again, messing with me.

"I'm hurt you didn't invite me bowling. You know I like Gary and Evette."

He pushes off the wall and glances at his watch. "Hurry up. We leave in twenty minutes."

"I . . ." My words die when he gives me a challenging expression. "Twenty." I smile and shoot into the bathroom.

"You're late," he scolds when I hop in his truck.

"Two minutes."

"If you're two minutes late for your plane, it will leave without you." He pulls onto the street.

"So why didn't you leave without me?" I stare at the side of his head. His lips twitch.

"You knew I'd be worth the wait."

Fitz gives me a sidelong glance. "Yeah. You're worth a two-minute wait." He returns his attention to the road.

"Five minutes?"

He bobs his head in contemplation.

"Ten?"

"No."

I laugh. "Yet another reason you're still single."

"You think that's it?" His brow furrows.

"Perhaps."

He hums. "Then what explains why *you're* still single?"

"That's easy. I'm ten years younger than you. I'm hotter than you, which makes me intimidating. And I chose to be a travel nurse because I don't want to stay in one place for too long, which makes me inaccessible."

"You're not hotter than me."

I *love* that he latched on to that. "We'll ask Gary and Evette."

"*Pfft.* Then you lose for sure. Despite what you think, they're my friends."

"Speaking of hot people, did you know that Dr. Reichart lost her virginity to Will?"

Fitz shoots me a glance with a sour face. "No."

"Yes. And he broke her heart too."

Fitz focuses on the road. "Fucker never told me that."

I giggle. "Well, I wish I didn't know. I don't know if I'm comfortable hearing personal details about my boss. Don't tell him I said anything. I need to convey a message. I just haven't yet. It's a weird topic to discuss with him."

"Why are *we* discussing it?"

"Because I wanted to distract you from obsessing over my superior hotness."

He grunts, and I grin victoriously.

When we arrive at the bowling alley, Fitz pays for our games and shoes.

"I could have paid."

He struts toward the lanes, several steps in front of me. "You're paying me back in other ways."

I nearly trip over my own feet. "W-what?"

He stops, causing me to bump into him. "You're paying for my plane ticket."

"Plane ticket?"

"To Miami. I invited you to go bowling, so I'm paying. You invited me to be your emotional-support person this weekend, so you're paying for my plane ticket."

"I didn't invite you."

His gaze shifts to the side for a beat before he grunts a laugh and continues toward the lanes. "You did."

I can't take Fitz to Miami. That would be a disaster.

"Hey! You brought Jamie. I'm so glad," Evette gushes, hugging Fitz and then pulling me in for a tight embrace, her wiry curls brushing my cheek.

"Do you have my back?" I murmur next to her ear.

"What?" She begins to pull away.

I grip her shoulders. "We don't have much time. Just say you have my back."

When I release her, she narrows her eyes and nods while straightening her camel-brown crisscross sweater that barely touches the top of her shapely hips.

I grin. "Can you two settle something for us?"

Gary sets his beer on the table and adjusts his black ball cap. "What's that?"

"Who's hotter? Fitz or me?" I pull back my shoulders and smile.

Gary sniggers, reaching for his bowling ball. "My wife's here. I can't answer that, even if she says Fitz, which she will."

"No. I think Jamie is hotter," Evette declares, eyeing me carefully to confirm she's *having my back*.

I wink. "Thanks." I blow her a kiss.

"Then I second that." Gary gives me a resolute nod.

"Traitors," Fitz grumbles.

I follow him to pick out a ball. "Well, that's settled."

"Don't think I didn't see you whispering in her ear." He shoves his fingers into a ball and picks it up.

"That's a little too much ball for you. Size down," I say, picking out a pretty six-pound green ball with sparkles.

"I don't know how to handle anything but big balls."

"Stop," I snort, returning to Gary and Evette.

"You started it," he mutters behind me.

Gary and Fitz show their ultracompetitive sides for three rounds while Evette and I sip cheap wine and see who can have the longest streak of gutter balls.

"He's pretty smitten." Evette leans into me as the guys hover around the ball return.

"Who?"

She nudges me with her elbow. "Calvin, of course. Gary and I have never seen him like this."

I squint. "Like what?"

"He can't take his eyes off you. He couldn't the night of the party, and . . ." She nudges me again to make sure I see Fitz making a glance in my direction as we speak. "We've never seen this side of Calvin. What have you done?"

It was just a kiss.

"I think you're mistaking his distrust of me for something else."

"Hon, I'm not mistaken about anything. If you both are too blind to see it, Lord help us all. This kind of chemical reaction will be explosive."

I return a nervous laugh and shake it off with an exaggerated eye roll. But for the rest of the evening, I can't stop noticing Fitz stealing glances at me so often it makes me sweat.

"Thank you so much for coming." Gary hugs me after the last round.

Fitz watches.

Evette hugs me again too.

Fitz watches.

It's a little chilly when we emerge from the building into the late-night air glowing from the full moon.

"Brr . . ." I rub my hands together. "Isn't spring supposed to be here soon?"

"It's in the fifties, Beach Babe." He chuckles, opening my door.

I raise an eyebrow. "This feels too special. What's the catch?" I climb into his truck.

"Catch? To opening a door?"

"You watched me dig my Jeep out of the snow shortly after I moved here. You're not the guy who opens doors for a lady."

His lips pull into a lazy, lopsided grin. "I didn't know you were a lady at the time."

I open my mouth to respond, but he closes my door and circles around the front of his truck. He starts it and turns on the heat. When he moves to put the truck into gear, I rest my hand on his.

"Let it warm up a bit," I say because we're parked at the far end of the lot with no one around us, and when we get home, Will and Maren will know we pulled into the driveway.

He eyes me with a neutral expression for a few seconds before nodding.

I take a gander out the window. "I'm booking my flight before I go to bed. Are you serious about going to Miami with me? Because you don't have to—"

"I'm serious."

"Is it"—I slide my hands between my thighs to warm them—"a good idea?"

Fitz draws in a long breath and releases it just as slowly. "Depends on who you ask."

"I'm asking you."

"I think . . ." He's full of sighs, but no two are the same, and I can't distinguish what each one means. "I think Miami sounds like a great getaway before I jump into a long summer."

"Have you been to Miami?"

"Of course," he says.

I'm sure many people in their midthirties have been to Miami or somewhere in Florida. A twenty-five-year-old who has never been on a plane is a much rarer phenomenon.

"Why were you homeschooled?"

He doesn't say anything. He doesn't move.

I angle my body toward his. "I was homeschooled because my mom thought raising me without a father would make me more susceptible to the influence of boys in school, which I'm pretty sure was code for teenage pregnancy." I grin.

Fitz finds a tiny one, too, when he glances over at me. "So you're still a virgin?"

"Ha ha. Real funny."

Fitz studies me during a long pause. "My parents homeschooled me for the same reason."

"I see." I bite my lip to hide my grin. That's not why he was homeschooled. He's so full of shit. But I play along. "Love comes in all forms. I'm sure what seemed extreme caution at the time was not meant to be anything more than love. Just before my mom died of cancer, I began to realize how incredibly different a mother's love is compared to any other kind of love." As the words slide past my lips, I feel a pang of guilt. "I wish I would have seen it years ago. My dad died when I was five. She raised me by herself. I have to wonder if his death made her extra protective of me. Like I was all she had left."

He nods, gaze softening into something unreadable while we stare silently at each other. I wonder if he's on the verge of sharing more of his past with me.

"I've noticed you've been rather pouty lately. I predicted it," he says, *not* on the verge of sharing anything personal with me. He's a labyrinth.

I don't push it. Instead, I roll my eyes because I've not been pouty, and he knows it. "I've noticed you've been sulking lately. I predicted it."

He grins.

"My friend Melissa will assume something is going on between us if you go with me to Miami."

"That's because you confessed you were having sex dreams about me."

"Stop. No." I shake my head. "It wasn't a confession. She was pestering me, so I told her what she wanted to hear to shut her up."

"Liar."

I shove his arm. "I'm not lying."

He laughs.

"Stop laughing."

"I can't." He laughs more.

I unbuckle my seat belt and lean over the console to cover his mouth with my hand. "Enough with the mocking."

He pulls my hand away, exposing a massive grin on his face that's mere inches from mine.

I know it's going to happen.

He knows it's going to happen.

The only unanswered question is who's going to cave first.

I think it's me because I lean in closer, but he leans toward me simultaneously, and we meet in the middle.

The kiss is unhurried.

His hand skates along my neck. I grip a fistful of his hoodie while my mouth opens wide for his tongue to tease mine. It's a heady mix of forbidden desire and utter weakness.

"No one's getting evicted," I murmur when he breaks the kiss to suck the sensitive skin below my ear.

"No one," he whispers, gently tugging my hair so I'll give him more access to my neck.

I have a painful need to rub up against him. I'd give anything to feel any part of his body brush along my breast or slide between my legs. My breaths fall from my lips in tiny puffs. I'm panting.

Showing zero control, I start to crawl over the console.

"Jaymes," he mumbles, grabbing my hips to stop me.

"I'll move out," I say, without an ounce of blood circulating to my brain.

He chuckles. "You don't mean that."

I win. Wedging myself between him and the steering wheel, I thread my fingers through his hair and kiss him. Whatever's been going on between us has been the slowest torture of my life.

I break the kiss and rest my forehead on his. "You can't go to Miami with me."

"Why?" His hand slides up my side under my jacket, stopping at my breast. His thumb brushes over my shirt, teasing my nipple.

"Fuck you, Fitz." I breathe heavily, rocking my pelvis, longing to feel him *everywhere*. "You know why."

"You don't trust me?" His other hand does the same thing, making my breath hitch. He's hard between my legs, thumbs slowly circling my nipples.

I'm ready to snap.

"I . . ." Again, I rock my hips.

And again.

And again.

"I hate you," I whisper over his lips.

He kisses me.

I moan. Not groan. It's embarrassing but unavoidable, like the way I grind against him. Every cell in my body feels heavy and hyperresponsive to his touch. Though I'm not going to let him win.

Why would my orgasm be a win for him? I can't explain it, but that's what it would be.

Fitz grins against my lips. "Jaymes, are you about to—"

"No." I grab his hands, removing them from my breasts while my heart thrashes around in my chest. I'm a hundred degrees and out of breath.

"Are you sure?" His lips brush my ear, hands gripping my hips while he shifts a fraction.

"St-stop."

He palms my ass.

I should have worn jeans. These leggings are useless. His erection might be buried under denim and cotton briefs, but I still feel it, and that's all it takes.

I bite my lip to suppress my moan or any other sound while remaining as still as possible. Does he know I'm holding my breath to hide the blinding orgasm ripping through my body? It's all I can do to keep from jerking my hips and mumbling a low "Oh god . . ."

This is a first. Never did I imagine the day would come when I'd feel the need to hide an orgasm. Fake one? Sure. But not hide it.

A fraction at a time, I release my breath. Nothing happened. Everything's normal.

"We"—I clear my throat—"better get home."

I lift my head from his shoulder and smile.

Fitz's gaze sweeps across my face, his expression nothing short of wonder. He swipes a finger along my forehead. My *sweaty* forehead.

"It's hot in here. You have the heat pretty high," I say with a nervous laugh.

"Do you need a cigarette?" A slow grin takes up residence on his smug face.

"You wish." I climb off his lap and plop into the passenger seat.

He laughs. It's great that one of us finds this amusing. He responds to everything I say with a chuckle.

"I'll get a hotel room. I assume you'll stay with your friend. Problem solved." He shifts his truck into drive.

I can think of a hundred places and ways we can have sex that don't involve sharing a bed or even the same hotel room. He extinguishes wildfires. How can he not see the danger in this situation?

"Yup. Problem solved," I mumble, staring out the window, feeling sweat between my cleavage and the warm, wet aftermath between my legs from dry humping Calvin Fitzgerald in the bowling alley parking lot.

Chapter Fifteen

I have no knowledge of TSA regulations. So I get my oversize shampoo and scissors confiscated, but only after I make the walk of shame to empty my water bottle, which disrupts the flow of the line and garners a few scowls.

"Thanks for the heads-up," I grumble while we mosey toward our gate, Fitz with his bag slung over his shoulder and me pulling my red suitcase behind me.

"Heads-up? How was I supposed to know you knew nothing about TSA? And if you wanted my help, you should have asked me to inspect the contents of your bag before we left home."

"Now I'm parched, with no water."

"We're past security. You can refill your bottle."

"The water won't taste right." I drag my feet behind him.

"Get something besides water."

"I don't want anything but water. I want the water from my bottle."

Several dozen feet from our gate, Fitz stops and pivots. I abruptly halt just short of bumping into him. "What's going on, Goldilocks?" he asks.

"What do you mean?"

"I mean, why are you so unruly today? So irritated and short tempered."

My teeth trap my bottom lip while my gaze shifts to the side for a few seconds. "I'm nervous about flying. And everything that's going on feels like a bad sign. And I overheard you talking with Maren and Will about this trip, and I know they think it's a bad idea, and they're probably right. So not only am I worried about dying, I'm worried that something's going to happen, and I *will* live to have to deal with the consequences."

His head pulls back like a winch in slow motion. It's as if he's following about 20 percent of what I'm saying. "You experienced minor hiccups going through security. It's not an omen. And Will and Maren thrive on worrying about unnecessary shit. And I don't know what you mean by something happening. It's going to be okay."

Is he serious? His idea of okay and mine are pretty different. Perhaps people who jump out of planes to put out wildfires are missing an essential connection in their brains. That connection allows normal people to have a healthy fear of dangerous situations.

"Fitz, I'm getting on an airplane for the first time. And I'm flying with a man who acts like I'm the bane of his existence one minute and the object of his affection the next. If we're lucky enough to land safely, my best friend will assume you're my boyfriend. And if we make it home in one piece, our roommates will not trust us, which is fair because they know you're not my biggest fan. Therefore, it makes no sense to them that you agreed to come to Miami with me. Nothing about any of this is 'okay.'"

His head slants to the side, eyes narrowed a fraction. "Death is the bane of my existence. Not you."

What?

Fitz's confession grips my heart and squeezes hard. Where the hell did that come from?

"You're an illusion." He messes with my backpack strap, giving his gaze a new place to focus. "A distraction. I can't stop looking at you. And I can't stop navigating closer to you, even though I know you're unreachable."

"Be—" I start to speak, but my thoughts trip over his words. I don't understand. "Because we live together?"

His lips bend into a sad smile when he returns his gaze to mine, and his knuckles brush my cheek. "Because death is the bane of my existence." He drops his hand and continues toward our gate.

My head spins a million thoughts into *my* existence—every possible explanation for his cryptic words. It's dizzying. Each thought breeds a new question. He can't touch me like that and walk away. He can't say that and not elaborate. My heart demands answers. It deserves to know why he will squash it to smithereens like Will did to Dr. Reichart's.

A woman's heart is woven from equal parts strength and vulnerability. Its love knows no boundaries. But it demands accountability. I'll never ask Fitz why he broke my heart. I'll simply insist upon him acknowledging *that* he did it.

When we board the plane, he nods for me to sit by the window. "There's no better view than forty thousand feet above the ground."

My nerves collide with giddy anticipation. This smile wouldn't be on my face if he weren't here with me. I sit and peer out the window at the workers on the ground. The butterflies in my stomach multiply by infinity when Fitz touches my leg while fastening my seat belt.

"In case we crash?" I toss him a toothy grin.

He winks. "In case we have a rocky takeoff or landing. Maybe for turbulence. If we crash, the seat belt's inconsequential."

"So we grab our parachutes and jump out before it crashes."

He laughs. "Not from more than seven miles up in the air."

"How far up are you in the air when you jump?"

"Three thousand feet."

"Do you get nervous? Or have you been doing it too long to get nervous?"

He eyes me for a few seconds.

Yes, I'm prying. I'm trying to peel back a few layers of Calvin Fitzgerald.

"I love it. The rush is always there. It's not a shit-your-pants adrenaline anymore. It's just an indescribable high. Not just the jumping. It's all of it. When I land on the ground and head toward the fire, I still feel it in my veins."

I love that. When Fitz talks about his job, he lights up. It's tangible. I can't help but feel a secondhand excitement, even if I can't imagine voluntarily jumping out of a perfectly good airplane and running *toward* a fire raging out of control.

When we taxi down the runway, I try to act like an adult, not a young child flying for the first time with my face plastered to the window. But I don't know if it's possible not to feel like a child now. At the heart of all "firsts" is a childlike innocence. I gasp as acceleration pins me to the back of my seat. And when we're wheels up, I feel it in my tummy. Fitz finds my hand, and I squeeze his like a woman pushing out a nine-pound baby.

We don't say a word; we just exchange grins. I feel that in my tummy too.

After we reach cruising altitude, Fitz leans back and closes his eyes.

Not me. I gawk out the window and take pictures and videos like no one has ever seen this view. I'm sure my never-before-seen footage from a commercial airplane will go viral. When we experience turbulence, Fitz reaches for me, resting his hand on mine without opening his eyes.

I'm fine. I'm more than fine. It's official—I love flying. But I don't tell him. He might deem it unnecessary to comfort me with his touch, and that would be more tragic than the plane crashing.

Chapter Sixteen

"Jamie!" Melissa squeals the second we exit the secure area. She hikes up her denim crop top and slides her phone into her baggy white linen pants.

I drop my carry-on next to Fitz and run into my best friend's arms.

"I've missed you *so* much!" I don't want to let her go, but I do.

She narrows her eyes, glancing over my shoulder. "Um . . . is he with you?"

I chose not to explain Fitz to her over the phone. My plan was to think of a solid explanation on the plane. That didn't happen.

With him at my back, I give her a tight smile and wide eyes. "Be cool. Okay?"

Her gaze remains glued to him. "*Pfft*. My middle name is Cool." She shoulders past me. "Hi. I'm Melissa, Jamie's BFF. You must be the gift she brought me."

Yep. She's *so* cool.

"Calvin, this is Melissa. Mel, this is my roommate, Calvin."

Her merlot-painted lips twist as she offers him her hand. "Sex Dream Calvin?"

Please, God. Just let me die.

His smile swells in increments, right along with his ego. I think he's two inches taller than he was just moments ago. "In the flesh," he says.

They laugh while my skin ignites into a bonfire of embarrassment.

"How was your first time flying?" Melissa loops her arm around mine, and we exit the airport.

"I don't want to jump out of the plane. I don't know who would do something like that. But I love flying." I glance over my shoulder at Fitz.

His gaze lifts from my ass to my face, and he winks. Fitz is not a winker. What's that wink all about? My ass? My comment about jumping out of planes?

"Fitz's hotel is not far from your apartment."

"What?" Melissa opens her convertible's trunk.

"He's staying at a hotel." I start to lift my roller bag in, but Fitz grabs it from me.

He's full of little surprises; each one makes a new crack in my heart.

"Nonsense." Melissa shakes her head as Fitz loads his bag.

"It's not nonsense. He's—"

"Shh." She holds out her hand before opening her door. "Not another word."

The second we step into Melissa's one-bedroom apartment, I focus on Fitz and his wide-eyed inspection. It's an oasis of white furniture, white paint, and white trim with hot-pink accent pillows, rugs, flowers, and washi tape, affixing black-and-white prints along one wall. Another wall displays a collection of hats in a gradient of pink shades.

"I like pink," she says with a shrug before gesturing to the sofa. "I put clean sheets on my bed. You two can have it, or—"

"I'll sleep with you. Fitz will sleep on the sofa."

Fitz clears his throat. "Or, I can sleep with Melissa, and you can sleep on the—"

"Stop!" I giggle. "Mel, you have to promise to ignore everything Fitz says. Bullshit is his native language."

She blots her brow. "What? Sorry. I didn't hear anything after Fitz suggested he sleep with me."

"Do you sleep on the right or left? Top or bottom?" he asks with a smirk.

Melissa bites her lower lip.

"Go." I push my roller bag in her direction. "I *just* said to ignore him. Take my bag to your bedroom while I have a word with my roomie." I give him a tight grin.

Melissa blows me a kiss and giggles before disappearing around the corner.

"Can you behave?" I cross my arms.

He wets his lips, barely hiding his grin. "I thought the point of coming here was so I didn't have to behave."

"I thought the whole point of you staying at a hotel was because you know you can't behave."

"No." He steps to the window and peers out at the busy street. "The hotel was for your benefit. You knew you couldn't keep from jumping me."

"Who's jumping who?" Melissa rejoins us.

"Nobody's jumping anyone." I clap once. "Let's grab dinner. I'm starving."

Melissa eyes me but just as quickly nods toward the door. "Tacos and margaritas across the street."

"Perfect." I toss Fitz an exaggerated smile. "Let's get a few drinks in you so you'll be too numb to feel the lumps in Melissa's sofa." I follow her out the door.

"If only my job involved *sleeping on the ground.*"

He wins. How does he always win?

Melissa dives into her interrogation the second we're seated at the restaurant. She peppers Fitz with every possible question about his job. And I realize I've asked him so little about it. Maybe it's because our relationship has been built on a solid foundation of banter. However, I have to give him credit for not only answering all her questions but doing it with a smile and not an ounce of the sarcasm he feeds me like slow-drip coffee.

Melissa decides to change the subject after thoroughly exhausting the smoke jumper Q&A. "Have you been on your skateboard yet?"

"A handful of times." I stir the last few ounces of my margarita.

"Jamie has broken three bones, sprained an ankle, cut open the back of her head, and needed stitches twice in her knees because she refuses to wear proper gear while riding her skateboard. And she's a *nurse*."

Eyeing Melissa, I shake my head. "It's restrictive."

"Or lifesaving." Melissa frowns.

"I'll get her a helmet and pads." Fitz wipes his mouth.

"I'm good."

"There's a reason your mom's nickname for you was Intrepid Little Girl."

Fitz chuckles. The look on his face melts me from the inside out.

The intensity of his gaze.

That sparkle in his eyes.

Every time Melissa reveals something from my childhood, he lights up a little brighter. I'm envious of him. I'd love to hear about his childhood, even if nothing would make me laugh or bring out the sparkle in my eyes.

"What's that look? You look like you spotted a ghost." Melissa's nose wrinkles. "I'm sorry. I shouldn't have mentioned your mom."

Fitz's gaze drops to his empty plate.

"It's fine. That wasn't it. I'm fine."

"I know you." Wrinkles fill her brow. "You're not fine. I've known you *for-evah*." Melissa downs the rest of her second margarita and jumps into the continuation of the Jaymes Lanette Andrews biography. "Jamie and I met when we were five. She and her mom moved into the apartment across from my parents. My family basically adopted Jamie and her mom since her mom was estranged from the rest of her family. So I know everything about her. Every boyfriend—she's had seven. Her first kiss—Riley Kirk, age eleven, Fourth of July on the beach. The loss of her virginity to Miguel, two floors down from our apartments.

"Jamie doesn't like pickles or broccoli. She's obsessed with the color yellow. She says she listens to all genres of music, but I guarantee her playlist is nothing but Imagine Dragons and Ed Sheeran. When she's tired, she gets cranky. And when she's excited, she nearly cries. If she says she loves dogs, she's lying. Jaymes is a total cat person. She hates to wear makeup. Never gets manicures or pedicures. And she was suspended from school for three weeks at the beginning of our senior year. But I'm not allowed to tell that story, so that's all I can say about that."

"I'm cutting you off." I take her empty glass and slide a cup of water toward her. "Why stop there? Perhaps Fitz wants to know when I got my first period or where I bought my first training bra." I press my palm to my head and shake it.

Melissa giggles, stirring her water with a straw. "Your first period was—"

"Oh my god. Stop!" I cover my face.

Melissa doesn't stop. She drank too much tequila. "It was toward the end of our seventh-grade year. You got it at Andie Olmen's house during her slumber party. Your mom was working, so my mom picked you up because you were so devastated. And you didn't buy your first bra. I gave you one of mine because your mom said you weren't ready for a bra, but you were the only one in our friend group who didn't wear one. And since you were homeschooled, you were also the lucky one who didn't have stupid boys snapping your bra strap."

"I'm never coming back here. Our friendship ends now."

Melissa bites her lower lip, but it doesn't contain her laughter.

"Let's go." I retrieve my credit card, but Fitz plucks the bill from the table and heads to the bar to pay it without a word. "Can you walk?" I ask Melissa.

"Of course I can walk." She stands on wobbly legs, adjusting her crop top before flashing unsuspecting patrons.

When I glance back at Fitz waiting at the bar, he signals for us to head toward the exit. We loop arms and start across the street. Fitz catches up by the time we reach her apartment building.

"Thanks for dinner. I would have paid," I say.

He holds open the door for us. "You're welcome."

I get Melissa to her room and in bed. She giggles, mumbles something, sighs, and falls asleep.

After I shower to wash off the day's travel germs, brush my teeth, and partially dry my hair, I pad on bare feet to the kitchen for water. "The bathroom's all yours."

Fitz hums his acknowledgment and slips into the bathroom for a shower. While he's in there, I search for an extra pillow and blankets. Just as I exit the bedroom, he opens the bathroom door in a pair of black gym shorts riding low on his hips, exposing the wide gray waistband of his briefs.

I stare at his bare chest for a few seconds before lifting my gaze to his. "The blankets are thin. Hope you don't get cold."

Fitz lets his eyes wander down my body, past my oversize yellow tee to my bare legs. "I'll be fine." He takes the blankets and pillow from me and tosses them on the sofa, plopping down next to them.

I stack the pink decorative pillows on the white velvet armchair. "Sorry she drank too much. I think she was nervous. She always drinks too much when she's nervous."

"Why was she nervous?" He fluffs the pillow and unfolds the blankets, spreading one over the sofa to sleep on.

I laugh, closing the living room blinds. "I'm pretty sure *you* make her nervous."

"Why would I make her nervous?"

I sit on the arm of the sofa. "If you're fishing for compliments, I'm not giving them out tonight."

"No? Why is that?" He stretches out on the sofa, lacing his hands behind his head. "Am I not Miguel?"

"Shut up." I laugh. "God. She had major diarrhea of the mouth tonight."

Fitz doesn't respond. After a pregnant pause, I realize I'm staring at his bare chest and maybe a little lower than that. My gaze shoots to his face.

He grins.

I clear my throat. "Are your scars from the same fire?"

"No."

"Is there a heroic story involved?"

He smirks. "No. But I could make one up if you want to fantasize about my scars."

I fight the impending eye roll. "You, uh . . . really should try my friend's burn salve."

"With the oil for my nuts?"

Pressing my lips together, I shake my head. "You're such an ass," I mumble while running my hands through my damp hair.

"Do you look like your mom?" he asks.

I still for a second before dropping my hands to my lap. "No. I look more like my dad, at least from the pictures I've seen of him. Do you look more like one of your parents?"

His brow wrinkles while drawing in an audible breath through his nose. "My mom."

"And your sister?"

Fitz's gaze drops to his lap. "My dad."

When he doesn't elaborate, I don't pry. Again, I feel that invisible line that I don't think he'll let me cross, at least not yet.

"I better let you get to sleep." I make it two steps before his hand snags my wrist.

He sits up.

I stare at his hand on my wrist, untethering every nerve.

"Jaymes," he whispers, pulling me between his spread knees. His hand drifts from my wrist to the back of my knee.

A shaky breath rattles my chest as his hands skate up my legs to the curve of my butt. "Fitz." His name falls from my lips in a breathy exhale.

He lifts his gaze to mine. It's mysterious, and his accompanying grin is a little mischievous. "How asleep is your friend?"

There's no room in my brain to calculate Melissa's sleep state while Fitz's fingers curl into the waist of my panties. "Passed out," I offer, an unsteady reply based on no facts.

His tongue makes a lazy swipe along his bottom lip as he drags my panties down my legs.

My spasming heart might wake Melissa. I can barely hear my breath past the rhythmic whooshing in my ears. We shouldn't do this.

We can't do this.

Fitz guides me into straddling his lap.

We can't do this.

An unavoidable gravity pulls me to him, and I fall into a sinkhole of need when his erection presses between my spread legs, the thin material of his shorts rubbing my sensitive flesh.

Here we are again.

My eyes briefly drift shut in a heavy blink, and I realize we can't *not* do this.

The second my eyes open, his lips press to mine, igniting everything.

One hand's in my hair. The other threads up my shirt.

I know a person's heart can't really explode, but I think mine might do precisely that as the pad of his thumb draws a slow circle over my nipple.

"I can't fucking think . . . ," he whispers, kissing along my neck. "And I blame you."

My hands crawl into his hair as my head lolls to the side. The buildup to this moment continues to stir inside me. My heart's sticky fingers won't be able to let go if he gets too close.

"Fitz." His name leaves my chest as a plea while I rub myself along his erection.

Again, he takes my mouth, tongue acquainting itself with mine while his hands grip my hips. I pull away to breathe, and we stare at each other, exchanging labored breaths. I curse the flimsy material between us. "This is a little wrong," I whisper with no conviction.

He lifts his hips again, drunken gaze, parted lips. "Jaymes, you're my favorite kind of wrong. And I want to watch you come again."

Dear god.

His throaty words could make that happen all on their own.

"Not *again*," I say, refusing to let him have anything over me. But I can't help but grin while discarding my shirt onto the floor behind me, leaving just the head of his erection beneath his shorts and briefs wedged between my legs.

"Again, and you know it." He takes the weight of my breasts in his hands and teases them with his soft lips and warm tongue.

My lungs draw in a breath, readying my next comeback, but it dies before reaching my lips when he whispers over my breasts, "You're so fucking beautiful."

Framing his face, I force his mouth back to mine, and I kiss him like he just called me *fucking beautiful*. Because surely Calvin Fitzgerald didn't say those words to me.

When I raise to my knees, kissing him deeper, Fitz slides two fingers between my legs, drawing another moan from my chest.

My fingertips trace the burn scar on his chest.

Fitz thrusts those two fingers inside me, and I gasp.

His intense gaze holds mine while my quickening breaths fall over his face in the dimly lit room. He's unequivocally the sexiest, most handsome man I've ever known. My heart and my head war over the physical and emotional sensations he evokes. I'm a discombobulated mess.

"Do you like when I'm inside of you?" He moves his fingers slowly in and out.

"Y-yes."

He adds a third finger.

"G-god . . . damn . . ." My nails dig into his shoulders while my abs tighten.

"How far are we taking this, Jaymes?"

He's controlled. Too controlled. His body commands mine in every way—the drunk lust in his eyes and his smoky tone.

It's not fair.

"All the way." I blink. It's slow and heavy, like the need he's building with his touch.

Keeping his steadfast gaze on mine, he withdraws his fingers and wipes them over my heaving chest. The hint of a grin quirks the corner of his mouth before that same mouth devours my breast, humming his pleasure while shimmying his shorts and briefs partway down his legs.

I lower myself, anxious to feel all of him, desperately hoping my heart doesn't do the feeling. He drags the warm head of his erection between my legs several times before bucking his hips and driving inside me.

It's too much. The fortress around my heart begins to crumble. He's an earthquake—a force of nature. And I don't stand a chance of surviving him.

Fitz grabs my butt with one hand and the blanket with his other and lays us on the sofa, kissing the life out of me. I think I could kiss him all night.

Unfortunately, I'm not supposed to kiss my roommate.

And I'm definitely not supposed to have sex with him.

"We're going to be homeless," I murmur while he kisses my neck.

Fitz chuckles, rocking his hips in a slow, firm rhythm. "Jaymes, it's called keeping a secret."

"What if—"

He cuts me off with another kiss, and I surrender my body and mind because Will and Maren are on the other side of the country, my BFF is passed out in the other room, and Calvin Fitzgerald is exactly where I've wanted him for weeks.

"This is your fault," he mumbles, kissing his way down my body, trapping my nipple between his teeth before flicking it with his tongue.

I arch my back. "W-what?" I'm unsure if I heard him correctly because his touch is all consuming and dizzying.

"Touching me all the damn time." He works his way back up my body.

"Goading me." He thrusts back into me, and my breath catches in my throat.

"Getting off on me in my truck." His hands tangle in my hair, and his mouth covers mine again before I can object to the blame he's placing on me.

My hands wander along his body, because Calvin Fitzgerald has irresistible, finely sculpted muscles that tense and relax under my fingers as he moves with me. And I want to feel every inch of him. I can't get enough.

After a deep, mind-bending kiss, my head jerks to the side so I can catch my breath for a second. "I'm com . . . I'm . . ." Each breath chases the next as I come undone beneath him.

"Of course you are," he says, just as the legs of Melissa's sofa decide to whine in protest of his vigorous movements.

My mind spins, my thoughts an aura of unhurried bliss. I'm boneless, euphoric, and so damn satisfied by the time he curses my name and stills inside me.

That. Happened.

It takes a moment for it to feel real. I wait for that brain worm of regret to extinguish every last flame of happiness. Except it doesn't. I don't regret it. If I could press rewind and do it again, I would.

"What took you so long?" I quip while he nestles his face into my neck, breath erratic, heavy body limp on mine.

"Fuck you." His body vibrates with his soft chuckle.

"Fitz?"

"Yeah?"

"I can't breathe."

He climbs off me, and I give him a shy grin while wrapping the blanket around my body, plucking my shirt and underwear from the floor, and hurrying toward the bathroom.

"Shit," I mumble to myself, sitting on the toilet, hunched forward, hands fisting my hair. "I had sex with Fitz. That was . . ." Stupid? Perhaps. But good. *So* good.

It's okay, I mouth, flushing the toilet and washing my hands. I give the messy-haired reflection in the mirror a toothy grin. "It was just sex," I whisper.

My heart laughs—a full-on bent-at-the-waist, gasping-for-its-next-breath sort of laugh.

When I return with the blanket, Fitz is back in his shorts and sitting on the sofa. We share a look. I can't read his. I'm unsure what mine means, either, so I sit beside him.

An uncomfortable silence settles around us.

"I'm on the pill, in case you were wondering."

"I've had a vasectomy, in case *you* were wondering."

My head pivots toward him. "Because you were tired of counting sperm?"

He smirks. "Exactly."

My lips twist for a few seconds. "But I do have genital herpes."

"I have crabs," he says, glancing at me with a serious expression.

I try not to react. If I react, he wins. And it's been well established that I'm not okay with him winning. Sadly, I can't hold it in. I snort, covering my mouth and shaking with silent laughter. I feel it in my belly—a deep contentment.

It cracks his stony facade, and he grins, snagging the blanket from my hold. "Go to bed."

"In the morning, will you pretend this never happened?"

Fitz straightens the wadded blankets. "Of course." He stretches out on the sofa, forcing me to scoot to the edge.

For a second, I frown, unable to hide my disappointment.

"Night, Fitz." I stand.

"Is Melissa waking up soon?"

I rest my chin on my shoulder. "No."

He holds up his blanket. "I'll have you in her bed by sunrise."

How did this happen? How did I fall so fast and hard for Calvin Fitzgerald?

I can hide my grin as I step back toward the sofa.

"I think your shirt will make us too hot," he says with a serious face that lasts two seconds before he breaks out his winning grin.

Losing the shirt first, I crawl up his body, and he covers as much of us as possible with the dinky blanket.

My face hovers over his. "You just like my breasts pressed to your chest."

"Fuck yeah, I do."

I rest my cheek high on his chest. "I'm going to listen to your heart until you feel the need to make me think you don't have one."

Fitz doesn't respond with words. He rests one hand on my back and the other on my butt.

My person.

Chapter Seventeen

CALVIN

She is . . .

Unexpected.

I find myself stretching my emotional capacity, giving her more than I think I have to give—which isn't much.

As the sun rises, I kiss her head. She's nestled herself between me and the back of the sofa. I'm barely on the edge. Hot and sweaty. Yet I feel something akin to contentment.

It can't be that. My life is unsettled with chaos, pain, and regret. I'm driven in one direction. Death chases me. I can't outrun it forever, but that sobering truth doesn't stop me from trying.

"You need to go to bed," I murmur next to her ear while resting my hand on her hip, giving it a gentle shake.

Her eyes flutter open. I can't help but grin. She's so beautiful. I have a handful of mental pictures that occupy a permanent spot in my memory. This one will join them.

"What time is it?" Her sleepy voice fills the intimate space between us.

"I don't know. But the sun's rising."

"'Mkay." Jamie maneuvers herself over me, standing and stretching before rubbing her eyes. When her tired gaze lands on me, her lips curl into an airy smile. "I dreamed we did something we weren't supposed to do." She pulls her nightshirt over her head and threads her arms through.

"You and your dreams. You're such a perv."

Her grin doubles. "Oh, Fitzy, you have no idea." She pads her way to the bedroom.

I know there's no way I'll get back to sleep. So I throw on a T-shirt and my tennis shoes and head out for a long run on the beach, inhaling as much ocean air as possible while the shifting sand makes every step a struggle.

I welcome the burn in my legs and lungs, the melting away of my thoughts.

Jamie and Melissa are still asleep when I get back, so I shower and stroll down the street for coffee and bagels. When I return, Melissa's in the kitchen, gulping down a tall glass of water. Her makeup's smeared into raccoon eyes, and her reddish-black hair is clumped in areas with a few strands glued to her face.

"Good morning." I place the coffee carrier and bagels on her round table by a watercooler and a fake fig tree.

She clanks the glass on the counter, out of breath from inhaling the water so quickly. "Can we talk before Jamie drags her ass out of bed?"

I sit and claim one of the coffee cups. "Of course."

"I think my friend has a crush on you." She eyes the other two cups of coffee, and I loosen one from the carrier and hand it to her.

"You're a god. Thank you." She peels off the lid and takes a cautious sip. "Jamie had a secluded life as a child. One parent. Homeschooled. Only a handful of friends in the neighborhood. When her mom died, she made one goal—to see all the places she never explored growing up. Hence becoming a travel nurse." Melissa glances toward the bedroom before taking a seat across from me. "Don't let her get stuck in Montana. She has a king-size romantic heart, and you're a shiny distraction. I'm asking you not to let her forget why she left here in the first place."

I nod slowly. My thoughts muddle, at odds with one another in many ways. I don't feel like I'm leading Jamie on. She's an adult, capable of making mature decisions. My ego likes that reasoning because it relieves me from accountability. The other voice in my head screams that I should do the right thing. But being with her feels right, even if it's not.

Why am I making this so complicated? I'll be the first to help her pack when it's time for her to leave Montana. That's what friends do.

"Well, you don't have to worry about that. I'm not boyfriend material. I'm not marriage material. I won't be anyone's husband or father." I take a sip of coffee. "And we're just roommates."

Ego wins.

"You helped her get on her first plane. I think you're more than roommates."

I set my coffee on the table and retrieve a bagel with cream cheese. "I was homeschooled too. We have that in common. We're . . . friends."

"Just friends?" Melissa narrows her eyes.

"Just friends."

As soon as those two words leave my mouth, said friend's bare feet scuff along the hard floor. "Morning," she mumbles, just as groggy as she was when I woke her hours earlier.

"Morning, babe." Melissa smiles.

Jamie squeezes her friend's shoulder. "God, that smells good. Who made a coffee run?"

"Your awesome roommate." Melissa holds up her cup like she's toasting my good deed.

"He's the best." Jamie claims the last cup in one hand while her other cradles my cheek. "Aren't you, Fitz?"

I try to remain physically neutral, as if my body doesn't react to her touch, or as though friends always touch each other this way. And I don't look at Melissa because I feel her gaze on me as Jamie sits in the chair between us. Her nightshirt barely covers the top of her legs—the same sexy legs that wrapped around my body last night.

Fuck, I'm getting hard.

"It was no big deal." I slide the bag of bagels closer to Melissa and Jamie. "I jogged on the beach and showered. But you two were still asleep, so I made myself useful."

"Fitz works out obsessively. Zero percent body fat. It's not fair." Jamie tosses a wry grin in my direction.

"So we hate him," Melissa says.

"We hate him so much." Jamie giggles, fishing out a bagel.

"Well, I'm going to jump in the shower. My brother and his wife planned a family luncheon before the official party tonight, so I hope you two can stay out of trouble while I'm gone this afternoon."

Jamie smiles over her mouthful of bagel. "We'll find something to do."

Melissa leaves us with a distrusting hum and disappears into the bathroom.

"Good morning, Calvin Fitzgerald." Jamie leans back in her chair, the cup of coffee hiding her grin while her foot rests on the edge of my chair between my spread legs.

I have no clue what to do or say. Reminding her that last night never happened feels like pissing in her coffee.

She sets her cup on the table and frowns. "You have at least a dozen worry lines on your forehead. Want to discuss them?"

"Speaking of worrying, Melissa is worried that you're going to get sidetracked in Montana and not travel to all the places you dreamed of traveling when you left here in January."

Her confidence slips briefly despite her quick recovery. "I like Montana, but perhaps it's only because I need other places to compare it to. I can assure you I'm not staying in Missoula."

I nod slowly. "She'll be relieved to hear that."

"Is she the only one who's relieved to hear that?"

"I don't know what you mean." I shove half the bagel into my mouth.

"Don't think I missed your subtle 'fuck you' to the idea of being in a committed relationship."

Chewing slowly, I mumble, "I'm not following."

"When a guy in his midthirties, who has never been married, reveals he's had a vasectomy, it's a flashing neon sign that he wants nothing to do with any sort of commitment."

"I'm committed to my job, and my job doesn't have a vagina or a biological clock. And while I'm not one of them, there are plenty of men who would be fine with a committed relationship; they just don't want kids. Not all humans have to procreate."

"True. However, biologically speaking, we are programmed to reproduce. It's in our hormones. Your desire to *fuck* is your human instinct to reproduce. If it weren't the case, you wouldn't have needed a vasectomy or to count sperm before that." She smirks, tearing off a piece of the cinnamon-sugar bagel. "You would simply not have sex because you wouldn't have the desire."

I shrug. "It's a choice."

She nods several times. "It is a choice, even if it goes against your biology. You're choosing to be single for the rest of your life. But it's not because you don't desire human connection, companionship, and a sense of belonging."

"No?" I fiddle with the lid of my cup to avoid eye contact for a few seconds. She's too good at studying me, seeing parts of me that aren't hers to see. "Then why?"

"That's a good question. One I've tried to figure out. I sense there's a line you've drawn, and I'm trying not to cross it. But that doesn't come naturally to me. I *am* a fixer. Empathetic. A good listener."

When I glance up, her lips bend into a melancholy smile.

"It's hard," she whispers, moving from her chair to my lap.

The vulnerability I feel when she looks at me like this is pure torture.

"I'm human." She messes with my hair. "And you're my person. I instinctually want to know everything about you." Her neck stretches, and she presses her lips to my forehead, depositing a kiss. And another. And another.

"And when you're inside me, I want to burrow my way under your skin, squeeze between your ribs, and hug that beating organ in your chest." Her lips brush along my scruffy jaw. "I want to feel your pain. And I want to take it away."

When her mouth finds mine, I can't control myself. My hands take their place in her hair. My lips part with hers. I taste her—devour her—while that hopeless, barely beating organ in my chest pumps harder. It's fucking angry at life.

It's angry that *she* is trying so hard to claim something that's not there. It's angry that all those places where she should fit are broken. They are nothing but unrecognizable pieces of rubble cemented together with eternal grief.

And maybe that's the true tragedy.

It's not that I've lost something. It's that I can never *have* anything or anyone. Grief isn't an anchor to the past; it's a thief of the future.

The bathroom door opens, and Jamie flies off my lap, eyes wide, while she backs farther into the kitchen, out of view.

Wrapped in a pink robe, Melissa strolls straight into the bedroom without glancing at us. Jamie's fingertips brush along her lips. Bowing my head, I rub the tension from my neck. What the hell am I doing?

"I'm going to shower now," she murmurs.

I nod without lifting my gaze.

Chapter Eighteen

JAYMES

I hide in the bedroom with Melissa while she does her hair and makeup. And I don't leave the room until she does. She's my buffer. I don't trust myself alone with Fitz. Yet that's precisely what's on the agenda for this afternoon.

"I'll be back by four to change my clothes for the party. What are you two going to do?" She hikes her purse strap onto her shoulder and eyes us while I sit on the opposite end of the sofa from Fitz.

"I'm thinking day drinking sounds like a solid plan." I press my lips together.

She laughs as though I'm not serious.

"Sounds like a plan to me," Fitz adds unexpectedly.

Melissa shakes her head and opens the door. "There will be plenty of alcohol at the party tonight. Maybe stay sober until I get back. Byeee."

The door clicks shut behind her.

We remain idle.

Silent.

Gazes pointed at our laps.

Finally, Fitz clears his throat. "If we stay here—"

"We're going to spend all day having sex."

"Pretty much. Were you serious about day drinking?" He glances over at me.

"Were you?"

"I'm not opposed to it."

"I'll get my purse."

The nearby bars are not open before noon, but we find a café that serves mimosas. Several drinks in, I start spilling more about my life than Melissa did the previous night. Sadly, no amount of alcohol makes Fitz share his past.

By noon, we're sitting in a booth at a sports bar, eating greasy burgers and drinking on-tap beer.

"Tell me more about Miguel," Fitz says, relaxed in the corner of the booth, one hand holding his beer, his other hand on the table, fingers drumming it.

It takes me a few seconds to remember Miguel while I stack my fries like a ladder next to my half-eaten burger. "He was older. His dad worked nights, and his mom was a waitress who always worked." My nose scrunches. "I don't know when she slept. Do you suppose she was a vampire?" I giggle, feeling a warm buzz.

He gives me several slow blinks. Is he considering my question? Or is he too drunk to know whether it's possible for Miguel's mom to be a vampire?

"We had to be quiet so we didn't wake his dad. And we had to be quick." I snort. "I think he jizzed himself before he wiggled out of his pants because it only went partway in." I hold up my finger and slowly bend it. "He was limp."

Fitz continues to blink slowly—a blank expression.

"But I gave him a second chance the following week, and he did better. Popped the cherry." I make a popping sound with my lips. "What about you? Did you have success on your first time?"

He narrows his eyes at my plate. "Wanna get out of here?"

"Where do you want to go? We shouldn't drive."

He stands and holds out his hand to me. "We don't have a car."

"That makes sense. I guess there will be no sobriety tests that involve you kissing me," I mumble, taking his hand after scooting out of the booth.

"Now, now . . . that was a scientifically proven method."

I giggle while we exit the sports bar. Fitz holds my hand as we stroll past shops and restaurants down the street. I'm gloriously buzzed, but I'm unsure if he's affected.

"Oh, look!" I tug on his hand to stop him and point at the window. "You know what we should do?"

He scowls at the neon sign. "You think?"

"I do." I pull him toward the door.

My phone chimes from somewhere in the room, rousing me from a deep sleep. When I sit up in bed, my stomach twists, squeezing its contents into the back of my throat. I lurch out of bed, sprinting to the toilet.

The souvenirs of my day drinking splatter into the toilet bowl. Then I collapse on my heels, wiping my mouth with the back of my hand. Day drinking might not have been the best idea.

"Oh god." I look down.

I'm topless and braless, and my jeans are unbuttoned and unzipped. Closing my eyes, I piece together the events that led me to worshipping the toilet. Everything plays in reverse order.

We were messing around on Melissa's bed. Then he started to nod off to sleep, and I did too. Before that, I remember laughing when we returned to the apartment. I don't know what we were laughing about, but I laughed so hard I cried. Then Fitz kissed me as only he does.

Hands claiming my face.

Tongue in my mouth.

All consuming.

"I want you," I shoved his shirt up his chest, kissing and licking his abs before he could close the door behind us.

"Fuck. What are you—" His back hit the open door, holding it open, as I dropped to my knees and released him from his jeans, eagerly sucking him into my mouth and humming my pleasure. *"Jesus Christ."* He panted, one hand pressed flat to the door, his other hand on the back of my head.

"Oh no, no, no . . ." I cover my face, remembering the elderly lady who crept past the door and gasped.

Climbing to my feet, I grip the edge of the vanity for a few seconds before washing my hands and face. Then I brush my teeth and comb my fingers through my hair. "Oh fuck . . ." My fingers graze the bandage over the sensitive area on the back of my neck, and I remember . . .

We got tattoos.

I return to the bedroom, where Fitz is asleep with one arm draped over his face, pants still open. No shirt. "Wake the hell up! Why did you let us get tattoos?"

I have three missed calls from Melissa and a handful of texts. While Fitz grumbles, slowly waking up, I exit the bedroom and return Melissa's missed calls.

"What the heck have you been doing?" she asks.

"Nothing. I mean"—I rub my forehead—"we . . . grabbed lunch and meandered around."

"Why didn't you answer your phone?"

"I was in the bathroom. Where are you?"

"We stopped by the marina to ensure everything was ready. I'm leaving now. But when I get there, I'll quickly change into my dress, and we'll have to go. Are you two ready?"

"Yes, uh . . . totally." I gather my shirt and bra from the floor and dart into the bedroom.

"Cool. I'll be there in twenty."

I end the call without a goodbye.

"Wake up! Melissa's on her way." I shake Fitz's leg. "Dammit, Fitz. *Wake up!*"

He grumbles and rubs his eyes before opening them.

"We. Got. Tattoos."

Fitz eases to sitting. "Yep." He winces. "We did. It was your idea."

"*Dude!* You had a say. We were not sober enough to get them. What irresponsible idiot gave us tattoos? Alcohol is a blood thinner. Guess what you shouldn't do before getting a tattoo?" My voice escalates with each word.

He chuckles, standing and arching his back in a long stretch. "Drink alcohol?"

"This won't end well. If we found someone that irresponsible, I can only imagine how irresponsible he probably is with keeping things sanitary and sterile." My stomach twists as I consider all the dangerous possibilities.

"We weren't that drunk. We were just enjoying life." He tips his chin and lifts his arm to inspect his tattoo.

"We have to be ready by the time Melissa gets here. Get dressed."

I'm never drinking a drop of alcohol again. When Fitz closes the bathroom door, I make the bed, throw on my dress, and apply makeup in the full-length mirror while my curling iron heats up.

Even though I can't see the back of my neck, I know what it says— more proof that I wasn't drunk enough to forget.

Mine says "He's mine," and his says "She's mine."

"One word, Fitz. You couldn't pitch in a little money for that extra word?" I ask when he stands in the doorway wearing the hell out of a black suit and crisp white shirt with a silver-and-blue geometric tie. I almost forget that I'm hell bent on blaming him for today's events.

"Pitch in?" He grunts a laugh. "I bet you make more money than I do. So the question is, why were you so cheap with something so permanent?"

"I was testing your level of generosity."

His lips twist, and he nods several times while inspecting my gold ruched dress with a cowl-neck and generous split up my thigh. "Let me guess. I failed?"

"Times infinity." I scowl at his reflection, even though it's hard because that suit does things to me. Things that get me into trouble.

"What's the big deal anyway?"

I twist the curling iron. "*He's my person* implies friendship. *He's mine* implies ownership. Something that's forever."

"It is what it is."

I unplug the curling iron and turn toward him, inhaling a massive breath and holding it for a few seconds. "It is what it is? How do we explain it?"

"Who's going to know?"

"What? Melissa will know. And Will and Maren will know. Basically, the three people we don't want to know will *know*."

"It's on the back of your neck, covered by your hair. And mine's on my torso, covered by my arm. Besides, you can always get 'he' changed to something else."

I think of words that end in *h-e*. I've got nothing. "What words end in *h-e*?" I brush past him to slip on my heels in the kitchen.

Fitz follows me while staring at his phone. "Well, there's *avalanche, heartache, toothache, unsheathe, mustache, guilloche—*"

"*Mustache*? Mustache's mine? That's ridiculous. And what the hell is *guilloche*?"

"It's, uh . . ." He squints at his phone's screen. "A decoration formed by two intersecting lines."

"I'm an idiot. No." I shake my head a half-dozen times. "You make me into an idiot."

His head juts back. "Whoa. Whoa. Whoa. If I make you into an idiot, then what do we say about the woman who suggested we get tattoos from a sketchy tattoo artist in the first place? *You* are the bad influence. And it's me who does idiotic things under your bad influence."

I wave him off. "Nonsense. I'll look into *guilloche*. And what will you change 'she' to?"

He chuckles. "I'm afraid my choices are fewer than yours. I'll probably go with *galoshes*."

"Galoshe's mine?" I grumble. "But seriously, you're older. Why did you let us get tattoos?"

Fitz slides his hands into his pants pockets. "Because you thought we should go day drinking, which made me more agreeable than usual. Need I remind you of the alternative plan?"

I zip my purse and look at him. "Day drinking didn't exactly stop *that* from happening."

A slow grin steals his lips. "You remember that, huh?"

I avert my gaze while setting my purse on the counter and filling a glass with water. "I woke up without my shirt and bra. *Something* happened. And yes, I remember!"

When he doesn't respond, I take a sip of water and turn toward him. Fitz grins. God! It's a huge grin. It breaks through my not-so-innocent facade. I have a waning desire to act unaffected by Calvin Fitzgerald. I know where he stands, even if I don't know why. And I accept it. Unfortunately, it doesn't change my growing feelings for him.

"I'm not doing anything to my tattoo." I shrug. "Someday, *he* will be mine."

The hint of a wince wrinkles his face, disappearing just as quickly as it appeared, but not before stealing his smile.

"But you'd better change yours to *galoshes*. It's the only thing that will make sense for you."

His cheeks puff for a few seconds before he slowly breathes. "But let's be honest, nothing about me makes sense."

"You need to stop listening to Will and Maren." I click my heels toward him, grabbing his lapels. "Can I just say you look incredibly sexy in this suit?"

A renewed smile slides up his face just as the door opens.

I step back.

"Late! I'm running so late. My brother has no sense of time." Melissa whizzes past us to the bedroom. "I'm going to need help zipping my dress!"

"That's all you." Fitz shakes his head.

"Coming."

Chapter Nineteen

CALVIN

Jaymes Andrews is the best mistake I've ever made. And if I had it to do over, I wouldn't change a thing.

In my rookie year, I turned around after we were told to evacuate, and I went back for the two guys who were seemingly trapped. I managed to save one. After countless surgeries, he's still unrecognizable, but he's alive. He's told me I made the wrong decision. And perhaps he's right. However, his wife and daughter have felt eternally indebted to me.

So, if I had it to do over, I'd make the same mistake, because not all mistakes are bad. Sometimes, a mistake is taking a wrong turn, an unplanned detour.

Tonight, I'm going to enjoy this detour because this is my first party at a yacht club. As soon as we arrive, Melissa excuses herself since she's one of the hosts.

We pass an impressive lineup of yachts and stroll over a wooden bridge to the clubhouse and its sprawling patio facing the water. Jamie clutches my arm to steady herself on the bridge.

Some guy in a fancy gray suit walks up behind her. "As I live and breathe."

She turns. "Noah!" Her arms wrap around his neck, and he lifts her off the ground, turning in a slow circle before returning her to her heels.

"Melissa said you took a job in Wyoming?"

"Montana."

"What the hell is that all about?"

"I needed a change. Oh"—she turns to the side—"Noah, this is my roommate, Calvin. Calvin, this is Noah. We attended nursing school together."

"Nursing school together?" Noah questions, eyeing her suspiciously. "To put it mildly." He chuckles.

He fucked her. I know that look. I had it two seconds before he arrived. But he's kind of an asshole for saying it that way in front of another guy.

"Calvin's a smoke jumper in Missoula."

Noah shifts his attention to me, stretching his neck and pulling his shoulders back as if he now has something to prove. I don't give a shit that he's a nurse and I'm part of an elite group of wildland firefighters. We don't need to compare dick sizes.

That's never been my game.

But for the record, my dick's twice the size of his. And Jamie knows it.

"I bet it takes a *different* kind of personality to do that kind of work," Noah says.

I nod slowly. "Yes. Smoke jumpers are intelligent problem solvers. We're focused. Brave. And then there's the physical part. We're in top physical condition all the time."

"Noah's looking into medical school," Jamie announces, shooting Noah a reassuring smile that he's not a loser.

He's not.

Nursing is a necessary and admirable profession, as is being a doctor.

"Well, that's great. Someone has to sign those prescription pads." I grin. It's not genuine. I must have misplaced the sincere smile.

Jamie frowns at me. Fine. I'm being a dick. The bigger dick. However, for argument's sake, let's say Jamie was my girlfriend. What kind of asshole picks up another guy's girl right in front of him and spins her in a circle while she's wearing a dinky dress that shows half her ass when she's lifted off her feet?

I take Jamie's hand as Noah opens his mouth to defend himself. "It was nice meeting you. Good luck with school, buddy."

Buddy. It's either a term of endearment for a guy who's actually your buddy, or it's what you say to a guy you never care to see again. And Noah's fake smile says he knows it.

"Find me later, we'll catch up," Jamie calls to Noah as I drag her toward the clubhouse, where there's music, food, and drinks. I don't need another drink today, but I could use one.

"What was that?" Jamie pinches my arm.

I smile at the waiter and reach for two glasses of champagne from his tray.

"No way." Jamie bats at my hand before I can secure the glasses. "We are not drinking."

"You suck," I grumble.

"What was that back there?" she repeats.

"What was what?" I head toward the food, since drinks are no longer an option.

"You were kind of a dick to Noah."

I take a plate and start piling food onto it. "You think?"

"Yes. I think."

"But would you say I was the bigger dick?"

"He wasn't—" She catches it a little too late, and her smile wins. "You're an idiot."

"You mean I have a bigger dick."

"I don't think you need to have a pissing contest with the first guy who crosses our path." She puts a few grapes and crackers on her plate.

"Jaymes, that wasn't a pissing contest. Nobody marked you. He wanted me to know he'd slept with you, and I shared the same sentiment."

"No. You don't want anyone to know what happened." She sets a serving spoon down and turns to me.

I feel her intense gaze on my face, but I focus on the buffet. We're not talking about this right now, so I finish filling my plate and meander toward the windows with the panoramic view of the water.

Over the next few hours, I meet everyone at the party. However, the only names I remember are John and Sadie. John's the chef responsible for the fantastic food, and Sadie's the tall blonde bartender running the open bar.

I'm five rum and Cokes (minus the rum) into the evening.

We stand next to Melissa and some guy from the hospital who she clearly likes. I tune out their conversation because I don't care about bowel reconstruction. "God, I love how that dress looks on you," I murmur in Jamie's ear because I'm bored and seeing her blush entertains me.

On cue, heat fills her cheeks.

"I also love how I feel between your legs."

Melissa and her friend halt their bowel-reconstruction conversation, focusing on Jamie. "Are you okay?"

She freezes. "He's drunk and saying incoherent things."

Melissa snorts. "Incoherent or inappropriate? You're blushing, babe."

"Stupid things," Jamie replies with a tight smile while stealing my Coke and setting it on the table. "Your liver's raising a white flag, Fitzigan. Let's go. We'll get a ride back to your apartment."

Fitzigan? Does she know her pet names for me only get me hard?

"Night, Jamie," Melissa says while Jamie takes my hand and pulls me toward the door.

"Tell your parents . . ." I slur my words. "T-tell them 'happy birthday.'"

"Anniversary," Jamie corrects me.

"My bad. I'm drunk."

"You're not drunk." She tugs me toward the boardwalk next to the lineup of yachts.

"I'm *so* drunk. I'm afraid we're going to have sex again or accidentally get another tattoo. But I'm glad you're sober to stop us from doing epically stupid things."

She halts, releasing my hand and facing me. "Having sex with me is *epically stupid*?" Her tone extinguishes every last spark of amusement.

With a heavy sigh, I rest my hands on my hips and glance at the sky for a beat. "Depends." I look at her. "Can it just be sex for you? Can the tattoos be nothing more than two people getting caught up in a moment of stupidity? Can it not be the end of the world *and* not be the beginning of anything? Can I not be the reason you don't travel from job to job, following your dream?"

She balls her hands, and her whole body vibrates while a storm of emotion fills her eyes. "Why do you have to come with a warning? Why can't you just kiss me like a normal person? Kiss me because you *want* to kiss me. Kiss me like—"

I kiss her, but not because I'm a normal person. I kiss her because she makes it impossible not to kiss her. Her bravery is commendable. But the problem with normal people like Jamie is they have normal reactions to things like kissing. Jamie has a gooey little heart that clings to things like hopes and dreams, kittens, the cycle of the moon, and late-night kisses.

It's not a fault. It's a gift that *normal* people possess.

I want to jump out of a plane. I want to put out fires. I want to run for miles. Work my body to the breaking point. Rinse and repeat.

I don't want to kiss this woman. I *need* to kiss her. It's my biggest weakness.

"I want you to be mine," I breathe over her lips while my fingers slide along her bare shoulder to the back of her neck and the bandage hidden beneath her hair. "Until you leave."

She draws in a shaky breath.

"But I can't be yours."

"Why?" She pinches her eyes shut.

"Because I never want you to feel that kind of loss. And you can't lose what you don't have."

Her eyes open. Jamie's mastered the contemplative look. She's unintentionally mysterious. One minute, I'm begging her for silence because she's oversharing, and the next minute, I want to crawl inside her head and get lost in her thoughts, live in her world.

Her fingers lace with mine, and she pulls me down a walkway between two rows of yachts.

"What are you doing?" I ask.

No reply.

Against my better judgment, I help her step onto a yacht. "I feel like we're going to get arrested."

"No." She smiles. "Bobby J's dad died and left him the yacht. But Bobby J hates boats. So the yacht never gets used."

"Who's Bobby J?"

"An old friend." After finding a key under a deck-seat pillow, she holds it up, proud of herself. It takes her several attempts to get the key in the hole because it's so dark. When the door unlocks, she reaches for the rail and descends the steps leading below deck.

As soon as I catch up to her, my fingers slide into her hair, and my forehead rests against hers. "You fuck up my head, Jaymes. You fuck it up so badly."

A tiny flicker of light from the yacht club flashes across her face through the porthole on our right. "So what?" Her hands remain limp at her sides. "You're not mine. But I'm yours, so the question is, What will you do with me?"

I cup the side of her face and kiss her neck. "Mine," I whisper.

She melts into me, kicking off her heels. "Lower," she says in a breathy voice, fingers knotted in my hair, tugging me in the direction she wants me to go.

I slide the dress straps down her shoulders, exposing her breasts. As I suck a nipple into my mouth, she hikes up her skirt so the whole dress is gathered around her waist.

"Kiss me lower . . ."

I kneel in front of her, peeling her black thong down her legs. The pads of my thumbs tease her inner thighs as I bury my face between her legs, spearing my tongue inside her as far as I can get it.

"Yesss . . ." She moans, tightening her grip on my hair with both hands to keep me where she wants me.

By the time she cries my name, I'm so hard that I can barely get my dick out of my pants fast enough. As soon as I do, I lift her to me and thrust into her. With my pants and briefs shackling my ankles, I shuffle us into the bedroom. The patient version of me would help her out of her dress instead of leaving it bunched at her waist, and I'd toe off my shoes to remove my pants and briefs. But I only go so far as to remove my jacket and shirt because I fucking love her breasts pressed to my chest. And I want her nails digging into my back while she chants, "Oh, god . . . yes."

She does too. She chants it so loudly I bet everyone left at the clubhouse knows she's getting close to having her second orgasm of the night.

This woman has me unhinged.

Both of her hands claim the sheet beneath us, jerking at the cotton while her heels dig into the mattress, and she grinds against me. "Y-yesss!"

My endgame should be my release, but it's not. With Jamie, it's watching her fall apart beneath me. It's the sexiest, most divine thing I have ever witnessed.

But the grim reality is that this is nothing more than an illusion.

Chapter Twenty

JAYMES

It's weird how little I remember from my childhood. And some of the things I think I remember don't make sense. So, I know those are memories of dreams, not reality.

However, one recurring dream from my childhood was of a couple. I never noticed their faces, just their backsides strolling down a wooden dock, hand in hand. She was in a peach floral sundress, a dainty white purse dangling from her other hand. In his other hand, he carried her high heels by their straps while she padded barefoot.

Even at a young age, I thought there was something special about a man carrying a woman's shoes, something tender about it.

This morning, I'm that woman with bare feet as Fitz and I stroll down the dock hand in hand before sunrise, and in Fitz's other hand are my high heels.

When we return to Missoula, he won't hold my hand or carry my high heels. And that's okay because I'm living the dream.

I dreamed of this moment long before I knew Calvin Fitzgerald. Dreams deserve recognition when they come true. So with the cold, damp wood under my feet, I recognize this moment as a dream come true.

Nevertheless, like all dreams, it is a mere moment in time. A moment that will come and go like the tide. Crashing at the surface one minute and getting lost at sea the next.

This weekend, we crashed. In a blink, I'll feel lost.

"Want to talk about it?" Melissa turns on the nightstand light when I ease the bedroom door shut. She sits up, rubbing her squinted eyes.

"Talk about what?" I step out of my dress and pull on leggings and a hoodie before repacking the rest.

"I'm not stupid. You spent the night alone with Fitz."

"Yeah, well, he was drunk. It was one night. When we get home, it will be as if it never happened." I hate lying to her, but I also hate the accountability that comes from her knowing that I'm in over my head. And maybe it's not a lie; maybe when we get home, it *will* be like it never happened. I'll hate that too.

"Look at me."

I ignore her.

"Jaymes." She slides out of bed and kneels beside my bag. "Look at me."

For three whole seconds, I'm brave. I hold it together. On the fourth second, I blink, and the tears accompany my quivering lower lip, and the captive breath in my aching chest releases.

"Your heart's too big for one night. It's the Pisces in you." She hugs me. "It's an unfortunate flaw you have."

I laugh through my tears. "Virgo. It's the Virgo in me."

"Whatever. It makes you one of the good ones, Jaymes."

I stiffen when her hand brushes my bandage.

"What's this?"

I lean away from her, straightening my back and wiping my tears. "Curling iron burn."

She reaches for my hair. Again, I jerk away from her.

Melissa's eyes widen. "What's going on?"

"Nothing." I shake her off. "What do you mean?"

"You're acting really jumpy over a curling iron burn." Her hand flies to her mouth. "Oh dear god! You have a hickey."

"Guilty." I offer a stiff smile and refocus on my clothes.

"Why would you bandage a hickey on the back of your neck that no one can see because your hair covers it? You get nasty reactions to adhesives. Take it off, goofy." She reaches for the back of my neck.

I slap my hand against it and wince at the sting. "It's not a hickey, okay?" I mumble. "It's a tattoo."

Her jaw plunges to the floor. "A tattoo? Are you kidding me?"

I deflate, shaking my head. "We were day drinking, and the next thing I knew, I was topless in your bed with bile climbing up my throat. After I vomited, I started to remember a few things, including the tattoo on my neck."

She snorts. "What tattoo did you get?"

"A butterfly."

"Let me see."

"I'll send you a picture. It's bandaged."

"It's a clear bandage, you goofball."

I cover my face with the shirt I just folded. "It's not a butterfly," I mumble.

Melissa walks on her knees and lifts the back of my hair. "Oh. My. God."

"I know," I squeak. "It's a long story. Can we not talk about it? Like . . . ever?"

"No. That's not an option. However, we need to get you two to the airport soon, so I'll give you a few days to get your story straight, and then we'll have a come-to-Jesus moment about this. Understood?"

"Understood." I drop the shirt from my face and add it to my bag.

By the time we exit the bedroom, Fitz is waiting at the door with his bag packed. He takes my suitcase, and with nothing more than a brief smile and a murmured "thanks," we follow Melissa to her car.

It's a bearable trip to the airport. Kudos to Melissa for yammering on about the party as if she knows Fitz and I need an out to not talk. At the terminal drop-off, Melissa and I share an emotional goodbye, then I navigate security—this time without any hiccups.

Fitz and I return to Missoula without exchanging more than a few words.

Without touching.

Without an ounce of recognition that something happened.

He breaks the silence when we pull into the driveway beside Will's Bronco. "Are we good?"

Good. What does that mean? All of a sudden, I'm pondering the meaning of *good*. I'm comparing it to *okay* and *great*.

We shared a great weekend.

I was good with the arrangement.

Now . . .

"Yep. I'm okay," I reply.

Good is a solid goal. Maybe I'll be there in a few weeks when Fitz jumps out of planes, I'm back in my work routine, and Will and Maren constantly remind me that Fitz has a challenging personality.

For now, I still feel him inside me like a deep breath I'm holding in my lungs for as long as I can. When it starts to burn, when I begin to feel like holding on to him is suffocating me, then I'll let him go.

"That's good," he murmurs as we climb out of his truck.

I didn't say "good," but he's into illusions, so I let him think what he wants.

"Hey, beach dwellers," Will greets us. He turns down the volume of the basketball game.

"I jogged along the beach. That was the extent of beach time," Fitz says.

"That sucks. You packed your tiny little Speedo for nothing." Will snags a beer from the fridge.

"Yeah." Fitz grabs a beer too. "But thanks for letting me borrow it." He smirks and taps his bottle to Will's.

"Have you seen Maren?" I wheel my bag to the back door.

"Not yet," Will says, sitting on the opposite end of the sofa from Fitz.

"When she gets home, tell her to grab a bottle of wine and come see me."

Will chuckles. "Jesus, Fitz. Sounds like you were an awesome travel companion."

I don't look at Fitz. I don't wait for his response. I can't.

◆ ◆ ◆

A little before ten, there are three knocks on my door. "Come in." I set my book aside and sit up, leaning against the headboard.

Fitz opens the door, holding a coffee mug. He's freshly showered, in sweats and a T-shirt. And, of course, he brought his clean, masculine scent with him. "Maren's not coming home tonight. There was a weather delay. I thought it was too late for wine, so I made chamomile tea." He shuts the door behind him.

"Where's Will?"

"Hospital. His chief collapsed. They think he's fine, but Will headed there to make sure." He hands me the tea and sits on the edge of the bed. "Can I ask what you planned to talk to Maren about?"

"You can, but I'm not going to tell you."

He runs a hand through his damp hair. "What do you need?"

"Need?" I sip my tea.

"If you tell Maren what happened, we might as well pack up our stuff. Is that what you want? It won't change what happened. It won't change the future. We're not going to ride off into the sunset together. Are you thinking we'll run our course for the next week or two? After that, I'll spend every minute I can at work. By midsummer, you'll move on to the next job. Is it worth finding a new place to live for a few months?"

"I love that you think this is about you. Maybe I have a lump in my breast. Maybe I want Maren to go shopping with me. Maybe I just want to catch up with her. Why does it have to be about you? Do you think my feminine heart is too fragile to handle a weekend between the sheets with you without picking out a wedding dress?"

"Why are you so angry?"

"I'm not angry!"

Fitz's eyes widen.

"I'm not angry." I slump, dropping my chin.

He rests his hand on my leg. "I'm not broken. I know that's what Will and Maren want you to believe. I'm built differently. I'm not like most of the other firefighters, who take the risk of having it all. A job. A family. I don't have a normal sense of self-preservation. I take risks without worrying about making someone a widow or leaving children without a father. It's how I do my job. It's the only way I can do my job."

I lift my head. "People who say they're 'built differently' are usually not built differently. They're afraid to *feel*. And they don't want to admit it. They don't want anyone thinking something's wrong with them. But not wanting to feel certain emotions only makes you human. It's basically the definition of self-preservation."

He doesn't offer a response. And I can't read his expression or his thoughts.

"But that's okay, Fitz." I rest my hand on his. "You're right. There's no reason to risk looking for new housing. I don't know why you're 'built differently,' and I don't need to know. I chose to be a travel nurse to spread my wings. In fact, I've already applied for a temporary opening in California. Missoula's just the beginning. And maybe *you're* just the beginning."

My mind does all the talking.

My heart? It's confused.

"Don't say that."

"Why?" I set my tea aside.

"It's easier to live the single life when I have regular reminders that women are needy, hopeless romantics."

He's too much. I press my lips together to keep from grinning. "Now you're being arrogant. It's not a good look."

"How am I being arrogant?"

"You're assuming my lack of tears means I'm not a hopeless romantic—that I don't need anyone. Maybe you should think of it like this . . . I *am* a hopeless romantic. I just don't need you." When the words leave my mouth, I want to dive into the air and take them back. In my head, it didn't sound so cruel.

Tension burrows into his brow as he stares at my hand on his. Then he removes his hand from my leg. "That's"—he stands, chest expanding on a deep inhale—"good."

Good.

It's not good. It's sad. A little tragic. And a lie.

"I'm still your person. Right?" I ask.

It takes him a moment to bring his gaze to mine. He looks lost, like he didn't hear what I said. "Yeah," he murmurs. "You're my best person."

When he says things like that, I can't help but want to fix him. Can he be like the old table someone sets at the end of their driveway? Free to a good home. Can I fix him and keep him?

Chapter Twenty-One

CALVIN

Training is in full swing—six weeks of rigorous PT, drills, and tests. When I get a day off, I help Will tear off the old deck and siding for much-needed renovations.

Today's a rare Sunday that all four of us are home and working on the house. It's the first time in weeks I've been with Jamie for more than a few minutes. I've found every excuse to avoid her in the evenings. It's not that hard since I'm exhausted every night.

"Jamie asked me about your parents the other day," Will says before cutting a new piece of siding.

I glance over at the women. Jamie's favorite pastime is riding her skateboard up and down the driveway and street. Maren's favorite pastime is "supervising" from her lawn chair. "What did she ask you?"

"She asked what I thought of them." He inspects the cut.

"What did you tell her?"

He chuckles. "That I haven't met them."

"Why did she ask you about them?" I hold up one end of the siding.

"She said she wanted to fix you before she moved out as a gift to Maren and me."

I study her while Will grabs the nail gun. She's laughing at whatever Maren says as she rides by Maren's lawn chair.

"What did she say when you said you hadn't met my parents?"

"She thought it was weird. Then she asked about your sister. And I looked like a fucking idiot because I had no clue that you had a sister. You're a vault, man. I think Maren and I have been generous with you. We've given you a wide perimeter. But you tell the new girl about your sister before telling us?"

"I haven't met your family." I shrug.

"My mom can't fly, dumbass. You've been invited to their house for Christmas. And you know *I* have a sister because you tried to stick your dick in her."

I grin. He's not wrong. Then she confessed I would be her first, and I bolted. Will gave me a good shiner the next day.

"And Maren thinks you don't have parents. She thinks they dropped you off in the woods, and wolves raised you. Yet you've met all of her family. In case you haven't figured it out, sharing personal information with your roommates is considered normal. Instead, we're left in the dark to speculate."

I mark the next board. "What have you speculated?"

"I would never tell you." Will carries the marked piece of siding to the saw.

"Why not?"

"Because if I'm right, you'll be pissed. And if I'm wrong, you'll be pissed."

"Just tell me."

"If I'm right, will you admit it?" He slips his protective glasses over his eyes.

"It would seem pointless not to admit it."

"You're right. Yet I somehow can imagine you not admitting it."

"Just say it."

Will frowns while making the cut. After he turns off the saw, he pushes his glasses onto his head. "I think you were abused. I think you ran away. And in light of recent revelations about you having a sister, I think you feel tortured every day because you left her behind."

I knew I wasn't going to be pissed either way, but I thought I'd have some reaction. Yet here I am, devoid of any physical or emotional reaction. "If it helps you sleep at night, I wasn't abused."

I only know how to interact with Will through unrelenting banter. So, I wait for a smart-ass reply. I need a smart-ass reply. He doesn't deliver.

"It will," he says.

No smirk.

No elaborate follow-up detailing his other theories about my past. He delivers those two words with sincerity.

"Aliens abducted me," I mumble as we align the siding.

Focusing on nailing it to the house, Will smirks. "They assured you Earth is as good as it gets, so you're determined to save it one fire at a time?"

"Exactly. But this stays between us."

Will chuckles. "Of course. I'll take it to my grave."

"Speaking of secrets, did Jamie ever talk to you about her boss?"

With a raised eyebrow, Will shoots me a look. "What about her boss?"

"Dr. Reichart."

"Yeah," he says slowly, setting the nail gun on the ground.

"Did you happen to take something of hers?"

"What are you talking about?" He crosses his arms while I grab my water bottle and take a few gulps.

"I'm talking about her virginity." I set the bottle on the bumper of my truck.

"*Who* told you about that?" He squints.

"Jamie."

"And she found out how?"

"Dr. Reichart, I believe."

His lips twist.

"There's a lot of standing around going on," Maren chirps before sipping her coffee.

"As opposed to sitting on one's ass like . . ." I clear my throat. "Some people?" I rest a hand on my hip.

Jamie hops off her skateboard and hands me her insulated mug of coffee. "You need some caffeine to soothe your mood."

"I don't want your germs." I shake my head.

She presses her lips together, taking back her mug. We have a silent exchange, and my dick gets hard remembering her saying *Kiss me lower.* We've swapped a few germs, but Maren and Will don't need to know I'd happily stick my tongue anywhere on her body.

"Jamie, did Everleigh tell you I took her virginity?" Will leans against my dirty truck.

Her eyes widen, gaze aimed at me.

I shrug. "I assumed you told him. It's been weeks."

"Yes. She told me. And she wanted me to tell you she'd like to get coffee sometime. It slipped my mind. Sorry."

"You . . . t-took Dr. Reichart's v-card?" Maren chokes on her coffee. "When was this? Last week? How old is she?"

Will frowns. "She was in medical school. I was in California for the summer."

"Was she legal?" Maren prods.

"She. Was. In. Medical school." Will huffs an exaggerated breath.

"I heard you." Maren claps her hands with each word. "Was. She. Legal?"

Jamie chews on the inside of her cheek, gaze ping-ponging between Maren and Will.

"Fuck," he mumbles. "I don't know. Who the hell gets into med school before they turn eighteen?"

"Everleigh Reichart." Jamie cringes when Will eyes her with a scowl. "And can I add that she thinks you broke her heart? So if you meet for coffee, just be careful."

"How did it get brought up? Did you two have a little extra time between patients and decide to compare notes and names about your first times having sex?" Will's failing miserably at containing his frustration.

"I can speak from experience—as a victim, that is—that Jamie talks about other people's sex lives a lot at work," I say.

"Fitz!" Jamie shakes her head. "That is not true."

"She tried to get me to raise one of the other nurses' kids as my own."

Maren and Will snort.

"I have to pee. I may or may not be back." Jamie's eyes shoot daggers at me before pivoting and stomping her sneakers toward the door.

"How did she not kill you in Florida?" Maren scolds me with a *tsk*ing noise.

"Luck," I mumble. "I'm grabbing coffee. Want any, Will?"

"No thanks. Maren, come hold this while I mark it."

I no sooner get my K-Cup in the machine than Jamie comes downstairs whistling.

"I need you to stop thinking you can fix me. I'm not broken." I retrieve a mug from the shelf.

Her jovial spirit dies, and she runs her hands through her hair, untangling it. "Where is this coming from?"

"From you asking Will about my family."

"Fine." She slips her hands into the pocket of her hoodie. "Then I'll ask you: Are you estranged from your family?"

"Yes. Satisfied now?" I focus on the coffee dripping into my mug. "Why?"

"You're not my therapist. You're not even *a* therapist."

"I'm not trying to give you therapy."

"Great. Then drop it." I sip my coffee and turn toward her.

She steps beside me with her hands on the counter's edge while watching Maren and Will cutting the siding by the garage. "Do you think about our weekend in Miami?"

"What are you doing?" I don't want to think about Miami. And I definitely don't want to talk about it.

"I do. And I think, for someone who keeps all used condoms and counts every sperm, you dropped the ball in Miami. What would you do if I were pregnant? Did you go to your follow-up appointment after your procedure to see if you're truly sterile? Would you *never* tell me about your family? Would our child *never* know his family?" She turns with her chin up and expectant wide eyes.

I face her and sip my coffee while weighing my words. There's no way to sugarcoat this. "I'd tell you to get rid of it."

She flinches.

"You think you know me, but you don't. I'm not an open book. I will *never* be an open book. Not for you. Not for Will or Maren. Not for anyone."

No tears escape, but I see them in her reddening eyes while she grits her teeth. And I'm sorry, really fucking sorry, but I won't mince words. I can't let her think some door to my past has been cracked open when it hasn't.

"I'm not trying to be cruel. I'm being direct and honest." I grip my coffee tighter and slip my other hand into my pocket to keep from touching her.

She swallows hard. "You said I'm your person. Your best person. You said I'm yours."

"You are."

Her whole body deflates.

"So you can imagine how personal and completely off limits this part of my life is when I won't share it with my best person, when I would tell my best person to get rid of a child if something like that happened. I will not let my existence, or lack thereof, be a significant part of another human's life." I glance out the window to ensure Maren and Will don't sneak in on us.

"What are you afraid of?"

"I'm not afraid of anything." I sip more coffee and set the mug on the counter.

"Then you have no reason to keep things from your friends."

"I'm not afraid. I simply don't want to share. Fear implies I feel threatened by the possible consequences. I don't. I just don't want to share. It's that simple. What are *you* afraid of?"

Her head jerks backward. "Nothing. Why would I be afraid of something? We're talking about you."

"No. We're talking about *your* need to know my business. Why are you afraid of not knowing?"

"You're deflecting, Fitz."

"You're prying."

"I'm not prying. You brought it up."

"You asked Will behind my back."

"You put your dick in me!" She stabs her hands into her hair. "And I'm not pregnant, but I could have been. And I wouldn't 'get rid' of it. I'd want your blood type, medical history, and every goddamn branch of your family tree. But all I need right now is not to see you. So fight your fucking fires. Go live your pathetically lonely life. I'm out of here in eight weeks. So, do me a favor. Don't talk to me. Don't look at me. Pretend I'm dead to you like you pretend everyone else is dead to you." She spins away from me and stomps toward the back door.

I grab her arm and drag her into the laundry room, shutting the door behind us.

"What are you doing?" Wriggling her whole body, she tries to escape my hold. "Stop manhandling me!" She flails, breaking free and pounding her fists into my chest. "You're a stubborn bully, Calvin Fitzgerald!" She lifts her chin and scowls before kicking my shin.

I wince.

She's. Fucking. Killing. Me.

I want to tell her, so she can fix the broken pieces of my life. That's what she does; she makes everything better. But not this. She won't understand my grief, my fears, my need to control what's left of my life.

When she reaches for the door handle, I hug her back to my chest, pinning her arms to her side. With my lips at her ear, I whisper, "I don't pretend they're dead. They are dead. They're *all* dead."

Chapter Twenty-Two

JAYMES

My anger dies.

Psych nurses are practical *and* empathetic. We feel deeply for the people in our care. Yet, we can make grounded decisions.

With him, I'm anything but grounded.

Fitz's chilling confession slays me. I think those words will haunt me forever.

I don't hide my tears. They're all for him, whether he wants them or not. The ache in my chest, the knot in my stomach—they're all for him.

His forehead rests on the top of my head. "Can you let it go now? Can this be enough for you?" His words are strained. I feel his desperation on a visceral level.

When his hold on me relaxes, I turn and face him while wiping my eyes. I nod slowly. He doesn't have to say any more. But I *do* want more.

"Enough?" My nod turns to a headshake. "I want your lips on mine." Lifting onto my toes, I brush my lips against his. "I want your hands all over my body." My fingertips ghost along his palms. "Under my skin," I whisper, dragging my lips down his neck. "Between my legs." I nip at his skin. "I want to feel you deep inside of me." I tease his skin just under the hem of his shirt. "And even then, it will never be enough for me."

"Jaymes," he whispers, brow tight. However, it doesn't keep his hands out of my hair. It doesn't keep his lips away from mine.

I exhale and melt into him, opening my mouth and sliding my tongue along his. In two months, I'm leaving Missoula.

For now, I'm here. I'm exactly where I want to be.

My hands grip his shirt to keep me upright while the intensity of our kiss grows, while dopamine floods my veins, rousing a deep need. He presses me to the wall, wedging his thick leg between mine.

Today is the day we will get kicked out of the house.

"I can't stop." He says each word in a strangled voice, his hand sliding up my shirt and yanking my bra down to expose my breast.

"Don't"—I pant so hard my chest hurts—"stop." My desperate fingers unbutton his jeans and fumble with his zipper.

He's inciting a riot in my head, and common sense is getting its ass kicked by lust. The need is feral and unrecognizable. I've never felt this lack of control over my body.

The creak and thunk of the back door closing send us apart. Fitz keeps a steady, drunk gaze on me while he buttons his jeans. I, on the other hand, suck in a sharp breath and hold it while I straighten my bra before my fingers race through my mussed hair.

Maren opens the laundry-room door before either one of us has a chance to speak. "Uh . . . what's going on?"

Shit. Shit. SHIT.

Fitz doesn't flinch. I've never seen such militant composure. I see the man who jumps out of planes and treks toward wildfires without much thought.

"Jaymes wanted to kiss me, but she didn't want you to see." He smirks.

Maren narrows her eyes for barely a second before laughing. "Seriously, what are you doing?"

"I *am* serious." He playfully tugs her ponytail while shouldering past her and waltzing out the back door, leaving me accountable to confess or lie.

Why would he do that?

I frown, hoping she assumes my flushed face is from him embarrassing me. "It's true. I just couldn't help myself." With a dramatic eye roll, I shake my head. "He hid in here and tried to scare me when I came down from the bathroom."

Even I don't believe my excuse. I'm not a good liar. She's going to know.

After a few seconds, she chuckles. "He's such an ass."

I nod a half-dozen times. "A hundred percent."

"Let's go grab sandwiches for lunch. Will said he's starving."

"Sounds good." I manage to speak without breathing.

When she turns toward the door, I exhale and nearly pass out from the stress.

"If you need anything else while we're out, text me," Maren calls to the guys as I follow her to her car.

Will cuts another piece of siding while Fitz eyes me, wetting his lips to hide his grin.

I'm angry because he's put me in an awful situation with Maren while I'm still reeling from the kiss. It was everything, yet not nearly enough.

And his confession (*they're all dead*) is lodged in my heart like a jagged shard of glass, making it hard to breathe and impossible to extricate.

"How are you and Will fine with not knowing more about Fitz's situation with his family? His past?" I ask Maren when we get a few blocks away from home.

"I met Fitz through my brother. He told me Fitz's past wasn't up for discussion. And when he said it, there wasn't any humor in his voice. I knew from the look on his face that there was a hard line. I think Brandon knew about Fitz's past. And I don't know anyone else who does. Perhaps Gary. But I think my brother took it to his grave. And Fitz is a vault."

"Why did he tell Brandon but not Will?"

"Brandon and Fitz were cut from the same cloth. Job first, everything else came second. Both loners. Both preferred books to people. Brandon was in the army before he became a firefighter. He never admitted it, but I think he had some PTSD. I think somewhere along the way, he shared things with Fitz that he never shared with me. And I think Fitz felt comfortable opening up to him as well."

"Aren't you curious about Fitz's past?"

"Of course." She shoots me a glance. "But we all have things we can't discuss or that trigger emotions we don't want to feel. So what's the point in forcing Fitz to talk about something he doesn't want to talk about? It's none of my business, and I respect that the way I had to respect my brother's refusal to open up about his experiences during the time he served in the army."

Not me. I have an overwhelming urge to dig and pry. I'm not the world's best friend right now. Maren hasn't had sex with Fitz. She's not invested the way I am. As that admission drifts to the forefront of my consciousness, I realize I'm *too* invested.

I knew I would be.

I tried to prepare my heart.

Still, here I am, unprepared for the inevitable.

After working four days of twelve-hour shifts, I get six hours of sleep and grab a late-morning coffee. Then I find myself headed toward the base. Pulling into the parking lot, I realize I should have made cookies. Instead, I'm showing up empty handed because I haven't found a second alone with Fitz since last week's laundry-room kiss.

To my surprise, Gary's at the front desk talking to Bailey.

"Jamie, what a pleasant surprise. Whatcha up to today?" Gary asks.

"I need to chat with Fitz. But if he's busy—"

"He's out back training the rookies. I'm headed that way. Come on."

I follow Gary past the plane to an open area where they're running drills.

"Yo, Fitz!"

Fitz supervises a group of men and women in full gear, dropping and rolling into a sawdust pit; he peers over his shoulder.

Gary waves him toward us.

My roommate looks sexy in his green cargo pants, brown boots, and smoke jumper–logo hoodie. He's also wearing an unreadable expression. I instantly second-guess my decision to come. I don't know why I assumed he'd be doing nothing and we'd find a private corner to discuss the kiss and other things.

"Jaymes." When he says my full name, it always sounds like I'm in trouble. I've never asked him why he doesn't call me Jamie. Not that I mind. Jaymes has never sounded better or made me feel sexier.

Gary heads toward the field, leaving us alone.

"Did you bring baked goods?"

I shake my head, pressing my lips together.

"Then what's up?" He crosses his arms.

Shit.

Why is he asking me that? I'm here because he kissed me, and I want to know if he'll do it again.

"I took that job in California. I don't start until mid-July, so I'll have time to decompress after moving before starting my new job."

There's a pause before he reacts. That is *not* why I came here. I haven't told anyone about the job. Fitz was going to be the last person I told, not the first.

Nevertheless, here we are.

Tiny lines crease his brow for a few seconds. "Congratulations."

"Thanks. It's just a job."

"A job in California. You get to add a new state to your travel map."

I fold my hands behind me and rock back and forth on my feet. "I don't have a travel map."

He chuckles, scratching the back of his neck. "You should."

I nod several times, but I've lost all momentum. "I miss you," I say under my breath, my gaze sinking to our feet.

"I'm right here."

"You've never been right here." With my emotions on full display, my heart can barely muster the bravery required to look him in the eye. It's a stifling vulnerability that makes it hard to breathe.

"What do you want from me?" he asks.

"I want everything, but I'll settle for your body."

The muscles along his jaw twitch, but that doesn't prevent a tiny smile from touching his lips. "Jaymes, I'm working. Did you show up for a booty call?"

"No." I bite the inside of my cheek. "Yes."

He scrubs his hands over his face, but no amount of scrubbing can erase his inflated grin.

"I'm kidding."

I'm 100 percent not kidding.

With a manufactured smile, I pull back my shoulders. "Maren's birthday is this weekend. She has to work but thinks she'll be home Sunday afternoon. I'm going to make her a German chocolate cake. Her favorite. Do you think we should do anything else for her?"

"What about sex?" he says.

I shake my head. "I don't think she wants that for her birthday. Or are you saying you and Maren should have sex for her birthday? Or all three of us? At that point, it seems unfair to leave Will out of it. Are you thinking of a full-on orgy?" I nod past him. "Maybe check with Gary and Evette. Oh Lord, you can't forget Mrs. Wilke."

Fitz rubs his fingers across his lips and glances over his shoulder toward Gary and the rookies running drills. "Jaymes?"

"Yeah?"

"Get the fuck out of here."

When he faces me again, we share identical grins. I step closer to him. I shouldn't. Anyone can see that I'm in his space in a way that a friend would not be.

"I will have a life, and it will be phenomenal. I will find *him*, and he will be mine. And to do that, I have to let you go." My gaze climbs up his chest to his face—his oh-so-heartbreaking face. "But I'm okay with you never letting *me* go. I hope you think back to this moment when your life feels lonely. And if you only remember one thing, let it be this. On a random Wednesday, the world's most fascinating woman stopped by your work and offered you sex. But you turned her down."

I could get lost in his expression. It's a new one. I'd say it's something between shock and awe. He reaches for my face, and for a moment, I think he will kiss me right here for everyone to see. I prepare my foolish heart for the explosion of joy from such a public declaration.

But he doesn't cup my cheek, the back of my neck, or my head.

"Ouch!" I flinch when he plucks a hair from my scalp.

He holds it between us. "For my scrapbook." His other hand unbuttons the pocket on the leg of his cargo pants, and he deposits my hair in it before securing the button and tossing me a smile that can only be described as wicked pride. "Now I'll never be lonely."

When the shock subsides, I reach into my purse without taking my eyes off Fitz. "Here. You don't need an appointment. We take walk-ins." I hand him Dr. Reichart's business card.

He reads it and grins. "Carrot."

"Carrot?"

Slipping the card into his back pocket, he glances around at nothing in particular. "Maren's favorite cake is carrot."

"I thought it was—"

He turns and saunters back toward the field. "German chocolate is my favorite cake. And I love that you want to please me on a subconscious level. Maybe you should talk to Dr. Reichart about *that*."

Chapter Twenty-Three

CALVIN

Chin and knee pads.

Kevlar jump jacket.

Jump pants.

Harness and parachute.

Reserve parachute.

Helmet, gloves, personal gear bag.

All this happens in two minutes, including a buddy jumper checking my gear.

"How much longer do you think you'll jump?" Gib, one of the rookies, asks when we're on the plane.

I squint out the window, holding my helmet in my lap. "Roughly until I die, give or take a few days."

Or lose my mind over some girl.

I shake my head at the thought.

I get intel on the fire. It's me and the rookie. As I survey the three thousand feet between me and the earth, I'm reminded that there's no better view.

Jump—thousand.
Look—thousand.
Reach—thousand.
Wait—thousand.
Pull—thousand.

The green handle releases the drag canopy, and the weight frees the rest of the main canopy.

And again . . . I think of Jamie baking in the kitchen with flour on her face, folding laundry while humming, skateboarding like a child with the wind tangled in her hair.

First fire of the season. It's going to be a long summer.

Over the next six weeks, I manage to stay alive, clock a shit ton of overtime, and avoid being alone with Jamie.

Tonight, however, my luck runs out. Will's on shift. Maren's in Arizona. And Jamie's done with her job in Missoula with a week left before she moves to California.

"You feeling good, Fitz?" she asks after I give her a quick "hey" and head up the stairs.

Stopping in my tracks, I press my lips together and exhale through my nose. "Feeling fine."

"Evette's been kind enough to let me know where you're at and when you leave a fire safely. It's just stuff that I figured *my person* might share with me. But he hasn't because he's busy distancing himself from me. So my question is . . . are you feeling good about the distance? Is it enough?"

Enough? When she moves to California, it won't be enough. If she moves back to Florida, it won't be enough. As long as she's on this earth, the distance between us will never be enough for me not to feel her, not to *want* her.

I take two more steps. There's nothing I can say to make her understand. So, everything that might come out of my mouth will feel like a lie. Offering *nothing* would be better than a lie, right?

And yet, I turn around and head down the stairs because Jamie causes a disconnect between my body and mind. When I lean my shoulder on the side of the fridge, she turns from the sink and dries her hands.

"Hello, Calvin Fitzgerald. It's lovely to see you." She tucks her hair behind her ear before folding her hands in front of her. Relaxed. Nonconfrontational. *Beautiful.*

I can be a dick and say nothing. Or I can be a dick and vomit an exhausting list of things I've been doing. Or I can pretend to be the man she deserves, even though I'm not that man.

"Evette told me you narrowly escaped a fire. She said a tree fell on a rookie jumper, and you carried him miles to the helispot. Gary thought you weren't going to make it."

Okay, her tone is a little confrontational.

I return a slow nod. "Well, I made it."

"Do you want to talk about it?"

"I'm good."

"Fitz," she whispers, blinking back the tears and clearing her throat.

I'm so fucking grateful that she's doing everything she can to compose herself. There's no need for tears. Nobody died. She's living her dream, and I'm *alive.*

"I'll check your Jeep's oil and other fluid levels in the morning. I'll check the tire pressure and tread and rotate them."

"Fitz." She shakes her head, eyes narrowed. "You can talk to me."

"I'm single because I don't want to check in with anyone. Will and Maren go about their lives without worrying about me, as I do with them. If one of us dies, it will feel tragic. It will *be* tragic. There will be mourning and a few tears. But then, life will go on as it should."

Jamie's face tenses, pink lips pressed together. "I lost my parents. It was tragic. There was mourning and tears. And heartbreak . . . so much heartbreak. At least for my mom. I don't remember a lot about my dad." Her eyes shift, her gaze finding mine as she slowly shakes her head. "But never did it occur to me that I shouldn't love them wholeheartedly. Are you even alive if you don't let your heart pursue its purpose in life?"

"What makes you think it's not pursuing its purpose?"

Her shoulders curl inward, a slow wilting of her body. I have this special effect on people.

She slides both hands into the pockets of her denim shorts, pivots, and makes her way to the back door. "Thank you for your service, Smoke Jumper Calvin Fitzgerald. It's been an honor knowing you."

I swallow her name before my stubborn heart can hurl it from my chest.

She shuts the door behind her, and I let her have the last word.

The next morning, on my one day off, I wake early, work out, and return home just as Jamie rolls into the driveway on her skateboard. Days like this, I feel every one of the ten years between us. She's youth personified.

A big dreamer.

Passionate.

Carefree.

I'll miss living vicariously through her. I'll miss watching her bake on Sundays, hearing her predictions of everyone's week based on their signs, and admiring how she folds fitted sheets into perfect squares.

Tiny grins.

Exaggerated eye rolls.

Her lips at my ear.

Her fingers clenching my shirt when we kiss.

I'll miss *her*.

"Where are your keys? I'll check over your Jeep now," I say, stepping out of my truck. I fully anticipate her "you don't have to" response.

Instead, she totes her skateboard to the shed and returns with her Jeep keys just as I open the garage door.

"Thank you," she murmurs without making eye contact.

"You're welcome." I take her keys and wait for her to look at me, but she doesn't.

She strides back to the shed, the wind catching her hair and exposing her tattoo. It fucking slays me.

I give up on her looking back at me, but at the last second, she does. I should look away, but I can't. I should say something, but I won't. The thread of stubbornness woven into my DNA is too strong. She turns first, disappearing into the shed. Does that make her the weak one? Or does it make me the weak one for being unable to look away or say anything?

Does it matter?

Chapter Twenty-Four

JAYMES

"I'm not going to cry," Maren says in a high-pitched voice like she's afraid to breathe.

"You are." Will snickers while loading my suitcase, skateboard, and box from my mom.

"Fine. I am." Maren hugs me.

I can't stop *my* tears but quickly wipe my cheeks when she releases me.

"You're welcome back here anytime, even if it's just on the sofa for a few nights." Will wraps me in his arms.

I nod several times, emotion clogging my throat.

"It sucks Fitz couldn't be here." Maren sticks out her pouty lip. "But he said he told you goodbye already."

He did not.

I return a reassuring smile. "I'm overjoyed that I managed to catch both of you at home on my last day here." I fan myself, feeling warm from the summer heat and my restrained emotions.

"What's that?" Maren's head cocks to the side, stepping closer to me while I absentmindedly pull my hair off my sweaty neck.

I quickly drop my hands to my sides and narrow my eyes. "What's what?"

Maren slides my hair away from my neck, sending my heart into a frenzy. "When did you get this tattoo? Have you had this ever since you've been here?"

I rub the back of my neck. "Yes." I force a laugh that I'm not sure sounds believable.

"How have I never noticed it?"

I shrug. "In all fairness, I rarely wear my hair up. I'm not sure why I even got a tattoo there. Oh, that's right . . ." I face-palm. "A drunken afternoon with my friend."

"What did you get?" Will tries to see my neck.

I reluctantly lift my hair again for two seconds.

"Who is *he*?" Maren's eyebrows form two perfect peaks. She and Will share the same look of excitement, like I'm on the verge of sharing some juicy details.

"Just a guy."

"You don't get a tattoo for 'just a guy.'" Distrust lines Maren's face. "You must have loved him a lot to ink yourself."

"I was intoxicated."

"Who in their right mind would tattoo someone who was intoxicated?" Will's head jerks backward.

I frown. "I thought the same thing. It's a miracle I didn't die."

"I think it's romantic." Maren smirks. "Risking it all to make a permanent statement about someone because you can't imagine not carrying a reminder of them with you forever."

Will bites his lips with a slow headshake.

Maren elbows him. "You wouldn't understand that level of romance."

"Getting drunk and making stupid decisions? I excel at that level of romance. And he's clearly not still hers, so can we really say it's romantic?"

I almost forget they're talking about me. I'll miss this banter with my roommates. The laughter. The camaraderie.

"It was stupid but not regrettable. If that makes sense," I interrupt.

"It makes perfect sense," Maren agrees.

Will rubs his chin, not as convinced as Maren.

I climb into my Jeep. "I'll check in. This is not goodbye; it's a see you later." I blow them a kiss and shut the door before Maren's next round of tears and before I let thoughts of Calvin Fitzgerald back into my consciousness.

It takes me three days to get to San Bernardino. Three soul-searching days of breathtaking scenery and summer heat mixed with refreshing dips in pristine lakes and delightful conversations with strangers along the way.

Idaho.

Utah.

Nevada.

California.

This girl who never left Florida is making great strides to rectify that regrettable situation.

As I keep track of fires, closures, and detours, I think of Calvin Fitzgerald jumping out of planes, cutting lines, sawing trees, and trekking through the wilderness with over a hundred pounds of gear in the stifling heat of summer.

A true warrior.

Does he think of me?

Will he miss me?

I know my heart will unavoidably carve time out to miss him every day for the foreseeable future. Maybe I should be angry, but I'm not. The emotions born from any kind of trauma are unique to everyone.

And how one person deals with it can be as personal as their DNA. I only have empathy toward him.

However, my heart is big. It can multitask. I can feel calm empathy while feeling hysterically heartbroken. I can want nothing but the best for him while selfishly wishing *I* were what's best for him.

A woman's heart isn't merely complicated; it's the reason humanity still exists. We are the nurturers, the peacemakers. We know when silence is more profound than any spoken word. And we know that pain is not love's enemy; it's the existential foundation that keeps humanity rooted in this world. It's the sole motivation to do better, get better, and be better.

"Okay, I didn't make it to Montana, but I've already started pricing flights to California." Melissa answers my FaceTime without a hello.

I laugh, surveying the new furniture in my dinky studio apartment. It's bigger than my shed, but not by much. "We'll have to sleep together in a twin bed." I flip the camera to show the space.

"Oh, Jamie, look at that wall of windows. You have great light. And I like your bed."

"I went with a daybed since I don't have room for a sofa."

"And a yellow quilt. Nice."

I grin. "Yes." I show her my white desk and chair facing the windows.

"Get some floating shelves for over the kitchen counter, and you'll be fine. Oh! And a shit ton of plants because you have *so* much light."

"Plants are a good idea"—I laugh—"since there's barely enough oxygen in the room for two people." I sit on the bed.

"That's because the air quality there is awful."

"Then why do you want to visit?"

"Because I'm worried you left your heart in Missoula."

I lean my phone against the desk lamp and continue unpacking. "Do you want to know what's most heartbreaking about Fitz?" I arrange my shoes below the hanging rod. "I think he doesn't feel capable of love because he refuses to say the words, but he shows love. He went above and beyond preparing my Jeep for the trip here. And I didn't ask him to do it. I think he's a true gentleman who tries to disguise his soft side with smart-ass remarks and a stiff upper lip."

"That is heartbreaking. Are you going to call or text him? Or do you feel like it's over, and there's nothing you can do? Can you salvage the friendship?"

"I would love that. But he's working all the time. And I'm not comfortable sending him messages. He likes not feeling accountable to anyone."

"It's a text, babe. That's the best part of messages. They're ready to be read whenever the recipient has the time to read them. Send. The. Damn. Message."

I grin. "I suppose it wouldn't hurt to thank him again for what he did with my Jeep and just let him know I'm here, and I hope he's safe. I can tell him I don't expect a reply."

"Or you can leave that part out. You're worthy of a reply."

"I love you, Mel." Eyeing my mom's box on the floor, I try to nudge it under the bed with my foot, but it's too tall, so I slide it into the corner by the stacked washer and dryer.

"Love you too, babe. I'll give you a few weeks to settle into your place before I book anything. Let me know how your first day goes."

"Perfect. Bye, Mel. Talk soon."

"Later, babe."

I gaze at my phone screen for over five minutes, composing the perfect message.

Me: I made it to San Bernardino. Thx for making sure my Jeep would get me here. I'm lucky to have u as my person. Hope ur kicking ass and staying safe.

I stare at the message for another few minutes. Then, I erase the "staying safe" part. It feels too motherly. It might put pressure on him to reply with the status of his safety.

Besides, Maren or Evette will let me know if anything happens to him.

After I unpack my suitcase and make a list of things I need to purchase, my phone chimes with a text from Fitz. My heart goes wild. It doesn't think; it just reacts.

Fitz: That's great. Ur welcome

I'm giddy that he replied so quickly. Hell, I'm delighted that he replied at all. Yet my greedy heart wants more.

I type numerous replies, trying to bait him into giving me more.

Tell Gary hi

If you're ever in my area, call me

Maybe I'll send a care package of cookies

I miss feeling you between my legs

Delete. Delete. Delete. Delete.

I grab my purse and head out to explore my new neighborhood and make a few purchases, perhaps some plants. "Let him go. He's not really mine."

Chapter Twenty-Five

CALVIN

Jamie's been gone less than a month, and Will's antsy to get a new roommate.

Sitting on her bed, I still smell her—a mix of flowers and sugar. I think about texting her. But why? I have nothing to offer her.

Locking the door to the shed, I vow to let her go, even though she's already gone. I pitch in, scrub the kitchen sink, and clean both bathrooms since I have a feeling I'll be headed to McCall tomorrow, and there's no telling how long I'll be gone. After dinner, I shower because there's also no telling how long I might go without one.

When I open the bathroom door, Maren ascends the last few stairs, carrying her boots in one hand and her purse in the other. "Hey! I'm surprised you're still here."

"I leave in the morning." I tighten the towel around my waist.

"Lucky." Her nose wrinkles. "I'm swapping out clothes and leaving in an hour."

"Have you seen Will lately?"

She shakes her head. "I always miss him. You?"

"No. But he messaged me, asking me if I knew anyone who might want to rent the shed before he posts it online."

"I don't know why he's so anxious to rent it. I might decide to move back out there." She grins. "Anyhoo, I have to get going. See you on the other side of the smoke." She starts to shuffle past me and holds out her hand.

I high-five her. "See you on the other side."

She halts. Her hand grabs my wrist and lifts my arm a few inches.

I narrow my eyes at her for a second before following her gaze along my bare chest.

The tattoo.

"Don't jump to any stupid conclusions," I say.

Her gaze inches up my body. Lips parted. Eyes unblinking. And I swear the blood's drained from her face.

"I lost a bet with the guys."

Maren still doesn't blink.

"So I had to get a tattoo of their choosing. Therefore, knowing I have no interest in ever being in a relationship, they chose this stupid thing to make it look like I have someone. I'm thinking of getting a female dog just to prove them wrong. How do you think Will would feel about a dog?"

If I didn't know better, I'd say she has tears in her eyes.

"Maren, what is it?"

"I think . . ." She swallows hard.

Not since her brother died have I seen her look this lost and disoriented.

"Maren, you're worrying me."

"I think Will is going to be angry."

"If I get a dog?"

Her gaze lowers to my tattoo again. "He's going to be angry that you broke the rules."

"What are you talking about?"

She knows. I don't know how, but she does. However, I'm not handing her one damn thing. If she does know, she'll have to say the words.

"I've never cared that you've been hell bent on living a bachelor's life for eternity. Marriage and babies aren't for everyone. And I honestly believed you were incapable of that kind of love." She blinks up at me. "But, Calvin Fitzgerald, you fell in love with Jamie. And she fell in love with you. And you . . ." Her eyes narrow as she slowly shakes her head. "You let her go. You found love. And. Let. Her. Go."

I can lie to Maren when I think the lie will do less harm than the truth. I no longer know if I have an accurate version of the truth. Is my truth the same as Jamie's? "We're friends. Close friends."

"Did you sleep with your *close friend*?" She doesn't blink, but I'm sure all the previous suspicious incidents (close calls) are replaying in her mind. She's known the answer without really *knowing* the answer.

"Yes," I whisper.

"Do you love her?"

"Yes."

Maren's lips part with a tiny gasp. She didn't expect that answer. Neither did I.

"Fitz, what are you doing?" Her voice is soft but laced with pain. "You were put on this earth to do more than fight fires. I'd give anything to find someone who made me want to risk losing my home. Losing my friends. Losing *everything*. That kind of love is a goddamn gift. You don't let her walk away."

I won't give Maren a knee-jerk reaction. Instead, I hold on to my words to ensure they're the right ones. I let her see the sincerity in my eyes. And then I hope . . . I *really* hope she understands enough to respect my decision. "You're right. She is a gift—just not mine." I rest my hand on her shoulder briefly before heading to my bedroom. "Have a safe flight, Mare."

"I'm not going to tell Will. What's the point?" she says.

I stop with my back to her.

"You're not the easiest guy to like. You're reserved and cut off from most other people. Jamie's not stupid. She's a beautiful, kind, and intelligent woman who could have her choice of men. Yet she fell in love with you. I do not doubt that you never led her to believe it would go anywhere. You're too broken."

I wince.

"So that means she likes you, Fitz. She likes you enough to take you any way she can get you. She didn't die. She moved to California. Be her friend. Reward her for leaving you by giving her whatever part of yourself you can. She doesn't actually have to be yours for you to love her."

◆ ◆ ◆

Fitz: Know of any good salves for burn scars?

I make an effort. It's foreign to me. I don't know what a genuine effort should look like. And I'm scared out of my fucking mind that I'm leading her to think we can be more than friends.

Fitz: Maybe something that can double as a testicle lube because it has nut oil

I grab my keys and head out before the sun rises. There's a good chance I won't return home for several weeks.

Just as I climb into my truck, my phone vibrates.

Jaymes: It's 4 am here. You're an asshole

I grin, and it feels like life. By the time I get to the base, there are two more texts from her.

Jaymes: I'll have it sent to u.

Jaymes: Venmo me $30

Fitz: U make more $

Fitz: U should gift it to me

"It's too damn early in the morning for any rational human to have that monstrous smile. Who sent you titty pics?" Todd asks when we reach the door at the same time.

"Your sister." I open the door for him.

"She sent them to me last night too. I had to rub one off just to get to sleep."

I shake my head. "You're a sick son of a bitch."

He shoots me a self-satisfied grin over his shoulder. "I'm an only child."

I pull my phone out of my pocket when it vibrates while heading back to the ready room.

Jaymes: Don't die today unless u specify in your will that u owe me $30

Gary plucks my phone from my hands. "Todd says you're rapturous today."

I snatch my phone back from him. "*Rapturous* isn't in Todd's vocabulary."

"He might have said perky."

"I'm perky every day."

"Jamie, huh? Why does she think you might die?"

"No idea."

"Tell her you have more lives than a cat."

"Let's get serious. We have a job to do," I manage to say with a straight face while collecting my gear.

Gary chuckles. "Yeah, but not a serious one."

Eight men and four women load up for the trip to McCall.

Chapter Twenty-Six

JAYMES

A bear killed Dwight Keane's wife.

He chased the bear but lost the hunt.

Until . . . he burned down thirty-two thousand acres of wildland to avenge his wife's death. If it weren't so tragic, it would be heroic. Dare I say romantic?

It's been years, and Dwight still talks about that bear—it's all he talks about. The doctors believe he's on track to spend the rest of his life in a California mental hospital. He's been released four times and recommitted each time.

"Dwight, it's vanilla yogurt and strawberries." My finger taps his gray fiberglass tray before running across the peeling surface of his dusty laminated desk. "Your favorite." I open his yellowed curtains the rest of the way. Light floods the room, illuminating the unmade single bed crammed into the corner of the dinky bare-walled space. The room reeks of bleach *and* urine. Today, the pungent urine wins with a full-on olfactory assault. Sometimes, Dwight enjoys marking his territory.

Beneath his bushy black-and-gray eyebrows, Dwight's vacant gaze points out the window overlooking a courtyard of weathered flagstone walking paths, decaying flower gardens, and a basketball court at the far end, with a few patients milling around. His full head of mostly gray hair, with a little dark brown still clinging to youth, could use a trim. It covers his ears in a style reminiscent of something from the seventies.

Some days he's Mr. Chatty. And some days, he doesn't have much to say. Instead, he narrows his brown eyes a fraction, like they are right now—pinpoints of concentration. When he's not focused on things that trigger memories of the bear chase, I find him poring over books about bears.

"Claire said you were waiting on me. Why don't you try some yogurt before it gets warm?" I drag a green vinyl upholstered chair next to him at a ninety-degree angle in the hope that he decides to focus on me.

After an eternity, he blinks, and his arm twitches.

I rest my hand over it and sit with him for a few minutes. Dwight relaxes with me because he occasionally thinks I'm his family. It assuages his anxiety.

"I heard you joined a book club."

He responds with a blink.

"Do you like working in the gardens?"

Dwight offers me the slowest nod. At first, I think he's dozing off, but he just as slowly lifts his head after his chin taps his chest. This has been his home for twenty-two years. Most people stay until they complete a competency evaluation to determine if they're mentally capable of standing trial. Others stay until they recover. And a few, like Dwight, become gravely disabled after being found not guilty by reason of insanity. It's heartbreaking.

A few hiccups have squashed his minimal progress. Tying up one of the nurses with her knee-highs and attempting to escape wearing her pink plaid trousers and blouse wasn't one of his finer moments. Neither was pissing on another patient, whom Dwight swore was on fire and spewing vitriol. That's when the marking started.

Stories have been passed down through the years, despite staff turnover since he was first admitted. Dwight's on his way to becoming a legend around here.

"I'm leaving now. It was nice spending time with you." I squeeze his fingers and stand.

"I'll eat," he mutters, pawing at my hand when it leaves his. "D-don't get all . . ." His pinched expression intensifies. "Don't get all rankled."

"I'm not rankled. Just busy." I chuckle, easing back into the chair and updating his chart while he slurps yogurt, eyeing me without reprieve.

He's quickly become my favorite patient. I'd say it's especially true on the days he thinks I'm his wife because he's incredibly sweet to me. However, it's more than that. Something deep in his eyes reminds me of a child crying for help. On the outside, he's a guilty man (even if he was found not guilty by reason of insanity), but on the inside, he's fragile and innocent.

"Annie, I dried between my toes and clipped my nails. And I didn't leave my towel on the floor," he says, surprising me with his sudden interest in chatting after showing little excitement to see me.

"Thank you. Annie would love that." I finish a few notes on my tablet and straighten the blanket on his bed. What wife wouldn't love her husband picking up after himself?

A dead one.

"Has the baby kicked?"

"You have a child?" I ask.

"Barbara."

"That's right. I think I heard that. On a scale of one to ten, what is your current level of depression?"

"Zero. We escaped the bear."

I nod. Some days, it's a ten because Annie didn't escape the bear.

"Do you have any suicidal thoughts?"

He chuckles, gaze still pointed out the window. "No. Annie would kill me if I tried to kill myself."

He's been here so long. I can't imagine a day he's in the present *and* emotionally well. Right now, it's one or the other but not both.

He glances over his shoulder. "You look as beautiful as you did the day I married you."

Aww . . .

I want Dwight to get better. I've never met his family or friends, but I like to imagine they are waiting for him. Maybe this is the year Barbara will visit him for the holidays. I've heard he's never had a visitor. Perhaps she'll come with her kids—little grandkids for Dwight. And it will trigger something that will allow him to heal faster and be whole again.

Is it likely? No. But the human mind has barely been touched by science. Even with all the advancements, so much remains a mystery.

"Let's go to the beach next time," he suggests.

I glance up from my tablet. "The beach? You like the beach?"

His tongue lazily swipes the yogurt from his top lip while he shakes his head.

"No? Well, I love the beach."

He winces as he always does when I say the wrong thing—when I say something his wife wouldn't have said.

After he finishes the yogurt and swallows his medications, I rest my hand on his shoulder. "I'll check in later."

"Watch out for bears," he mumbles, like it's a passive afterthought. His suddenly lifeless tone matches the rest of his gray, aging body— Dwight's fifty-five, going on eighty.

"I will," I promise.

There's something about him. I can't put my finger on it, but it's an unsettling feeling that resides beneath my skin and lingers for hours after being with him.

Four glorious days off.

I pick up groceries on my way home and then change into white jeans and a sleeveless yellow boho blouse for my dinner date tonight. Evette's in town visiting a friend, and she asked if we could have dinner. She's been the sweetest, keeping me updated on not only Gary's whereabouts but Fitz's too. That's how I know he hasn't been home to get the scar salve my friend sent to his house over three weeks ago.

I text Evette when I arrive at the crowded restaurant.

Me: I'm here

Evette: I'm at the back behind the bar

Shouldering through the crowd, I crane my neck to see past the bar. No Evette.

I look in every direction. She has a head of unmistakable red hair. How am I missing her? Turning for the third time, I catch sight of a man standing next to his chair. Dark jeans and a pristine white shirt. He looks a lot like . . .

"Oh my god." I cover my mouth.

Fitz grins.

I want to cry, but I'm not going to do that. Instead, my heart might explode, and I will likely die right here in this spot.

Someone bumps into me, bringing me out of my dazed state and propelling me forward a few feet. It's only been six weeks. But it's felt like six years.

"What are you doing here? Where is Evette?" I hug him and notice the petite, gray-haired woman sitting at his table smiling at us.

"Evette helped me surprise you. She's in Missoula. Hope you're not disappointed." He releases me.

Of course, I want to know who this woman is, but I can't stop gawking at him. And I kind of feel like he can't stop eyeing me.

"Jaymes, this is my grandma, Edith. She lives just a few blocks from here. Grandma, this is my friend Jaymes."

Grandma? Fitz has living family? What is happening?

"Nice to meet you." I hold out my shaky hand, trying to control my nerves.

She reaches out her left hand for an awkward shake. "Sorry, I suffered a stroke years ago. And my right hand still doesn't work properly."

I use both hands to hold her hand, giving it a gentle squeeze. "What a lovely surprise." I sit next to Fitz. "Did he tell you I had no idea he was coming? And did he tell you I didn't know he has a grandma who lives here?" I playfully narrow my eyes at Fitz.

"He said he wanted to surprise his roommate who recently moved here." She eyes him with an expression similar to mine. "But he didn't mention you were a beautiful young lady."

Edith manages to make me blush, just like her grandson.

"Calvin is full of surprises." I reach beneath the table and rest my hand on his leg for a brief second.

"I hope you don't mind; I already ordered for all of us," he says. "My grandma goes to bed early."

My nose wrinkles. "Sorry. I work long shifts. Had I known—"

"Please don't apologize, dear. How were you to know?" Edith comforts me with a smile.

"Well, thanks for ordering. Now tell me how it is that you're here when it's still fire season."

He rests his napkin on his leg. "After twenty-one days straight, they forced me to take two days off. I asked for four so I could visit my grandma and this nurse I met in January."

"I should thank you," Edith says. "Calvin only visits me over the holidays. He never takes breaks during the summer. So I know he's here for you more than me."

Fitz presses a flat hand to his heart. "Grandma! Your words wound me."

Her body gently bounces with a chuckle. "No, they don't."

My whole face aches from grinning. She's delightful and so unexpected. And Fitz? There are no words to describe him or his grand gesture.

"So you're a nurse?"

"Yes. I work in the psych ward."

"That must be interesting."

"It can be."

"How's your apartment?" Fitz asks.

"Dinky, but not quite as small as the shed. Has Will rented it out?"

"Not yet."

The waiter delivers our food, and we spend the next half hour eating and discussing Edith's boyfriend, who happens to be turning ninety next month. He's in a wheelchair and still lives on his own. They met when she was having physical therapy after her stroke.

I fade into the distance as much as possible and let Fitz and his grandma chat. He's here. That still blows my mind. His grandma lives here. How can he not see the ways the stars have aligned for us? This is bigger than coincidence.

"Would you like to meet for breakfast in the morning?" Fitz asks me as we exit the restaurant.

"Stop it," Edith says, holding on to Fitz's arm. "Just because I'm old and going to bed doesn't mean you must do the same. Drive me home, and then take Jaymes out on the town. Go dancing or to the movies or whatever you young people do."

We look at each other and grin. She's endearing.

I follow them to her apartment in an assisted living community and wait in the living room while he makes sure she gets into bed despite her repeatedly saying, "What do you think I do when you're not here?"

Calvin Fitzgerald is full of surprises. He thinks I'm all soft and gooey on the inside because I'm a "normal" woman who dreams of love and other ordinary things.

He's the soft and gooey one.

"So what's it going to be? Dancing or 'the movies'?" Fitz asks softly after he shuts her bedroom door while I inspect a few pictures on her sofa table.

I assume it's Fitz's family, but I'm afraid to ask. He's here. And I don't want to scare him away. If he wants to share his life with me, I need to let him do it in his own time, like inviting me to dinner with his grandma.

"Do you dance?" I turn toward him.

"No."

I grin. "Do Maren and Will know you're here?"

"Yes."

"Did you get the salve?"

"It's in my bag." He nods to the black bag on the floor by the sofa.

My heart's lodged so tightly in my throat I can barely breathe. "Is six weeks too soon to miss my person?"

"I'm pretty missable."

"Is *missable* a word?"

"*Missable* is absolutely a word. It's fuckable's cousin."

I cover my mouth to muffle my laugh.

His smile wanes. "Maren spotted my tattoo. And I'm guessing from her reaction, she found yours first because I watched her put two and two together in real time."

I nod, lips corkscrewed. I've talked to her nearly every week since I've been here, and she never mentioned seeing his tattoo. "Are you homeless?"

"No. But she said I needed to be your friend."

My heart leaves my throat, swan diving into the pit of my stomach. "So you're here because of Maren?" I grunt a laugh, running my hands through my hair and turning away from him. "That sounds like a more logical explanation."

"No. It doesn't."

I can't look at him yet. My feelings are pinned to my shirt like a gaudy nineties corsage.

"None of this makes sense," he says. "Not taking four days instead of the required two. Not booking a flight to San Bernardino while my fellow jumpers are managing fires. Not introducing you to my grandmother. Not this need to kiss you when I have nothing to offer but someone else's version of friendship. *None* of it makes sense." He blows out a long breath. "Yet here I am. Fumbling my words and wallowing around outside my comfort zone because I made you my person, and you don't fit in my life, but my life no longer fits me without you."

Oh, my heart . . .

I turn. Fitz has never looked this tortured. The tension in his face. The resignation in his eyes.

"Are you here for me or you?"

The lines along his brow dig deeper.

"It's not a trick question." I shake my head. "I don't even know how I want you to answer. Just honestly."

His gaze drops to the floor between us. "When I purchased the plane ticket, I was coming here for you." He lifts his gaze to mine. "When you entered the restaurant, I knew I was here for me."

I lied.

I wanted him to say *that*, but I didn't know it until two seconds ago. That's the thing with love; it's untimely, unannounced, and underestimated. It's not a choice. It's a state of being.

How do I tell Fitz that he loves me?

I don't.

He'll work it out on his own.

By then, I might be married to another man and pregnant with twins, but nonetheless, I'm overjoyed about Fitz and his wallowing heart. Better late than never.

I lift my shoulders and drop them into an exaggerated shrug. "We could kiss. And it could be our version of friendship. I don't want anyone else's version. Do you?"

His hand slides along my neck until his fingertips brush my tattoo. "No. I don't," he whispers before kissing me.

I close my eyes while he drags his lips from mine to my neck. "Come back to my place," I murmur.

"Yeah?"

I grin. "Yeah." I dig into my pocket and fish out my key fob. "You drive. I'm a little too intoxicated."

He takes it from me, eyes narrowed. "We didn't have alcohol at dinner."

"You." I turn and open the door. "I'm drunk on you, Fitz."

It's a ten-minute drive to my apartment. I still can't believe he never mentioned his grandma when I told him about my job here. She's *a ten-minute* drive from my apartment.

It's not a coincidence. It's fate. Right?

He parks my Jeep and leans over the console to kiss me. It takes several minutes to drag ourselves out of the vehicle. We meet at the back of the Jeep and kiss again. Fitz presses my backside against the spare tire. Our kiss grows into something that feels too intense to control.

Lifting me to him, he slowly treks toward my building.

"The . . . the key . . . ring . . . ," I pant as he kisses my neck.

My back hits the side of the building while he fumbles with my keys, finding the card to scan. The door buzzes, and he opens it with one hand while his other hand claims my ass.

I stop him before he heads up the stairs. "D-down the hall, last on the left."

We stumble into my tiny efficiency apartment and waste no time in discarding our clothes.

"Jaymes, you have a fucking twin bed," he mumbles over my lips when I push him back onto my single-size mattress.

I giggle. "I'm aware." I kiss his chest and abs, my fingers brushing his scars before my tongue makes a slow swipe up the length of his erection.

His head stretches back while a satisfied moan vibrates along his chest. I straddle him, guiding him between my legs. My heavy eyelids surrender when I sink onto him, hands flat on his chest.

When I open my eyes, he's watching me with an intoxicated gaze and soft lips that he occasionally wets with a lazy swipe of his tongue.

I lean forward, grinding against him, and he lifts his head, mouth on my breasts.

"God . . . Fitz . . . that feels . . ." I lose my words and mind.

His hands tangle in my hair while he kisses me deeply, slowly moving with me as the moonlight through my one-way windows washes over him, shadows flickering across his face when I sit up.

We are whispers of labored breaths and flesh colliding.

As my orgasm begins to course through my body slowly, he flips me onto my back and pumps into me harder, quickly finding his release.

I revel in this moment, mesmerized by him moving above me. Face tense, lips parted; it feels like a bonus orgasm—a compulsion I can't deny.

"Fuck you, Jaymes . . . god . . . just . . . fuck you . . . I never want . . . to stop." There is more to his words than the simple meaning behind each one. With Fitz, it's never what he says as much as how he says it.

I can't stop my grin as he fights his emotions. There's something gratifying about being the person who gives someone else strength. However, I'm thoroughly addicted to being Calvin Fitzgerald's greatest weakness.

He's not deficient in confidence. He's brave on a whole different level. Except with me, he's vulnerable. And I'm incredibly honored that he trusts me with the part of himself that he has yet to understand.

My sweaty *person* breathes heavily in my ear before kissing a trail down my chest to my abs, teasing my belly button with his tongue.

I giggle. "Stop! That tickles."

I feel his lips pull into a grin along my skin while he presses his hands into the mattress on either side of my body. He drags his tongue to my side and bites my skin just above my hip.

I jerk. "Fitz!" I wriggle beneath him.

He laughs, and it's an ecstatic sound.

I push at his chest. "I have to pee, and now I need a shower."

"Good idea." He lifts himself off the bed, grabs my hand, and pulls me to my feet.

"What's a good idea?"

He grips my shoulders and leads me around the corner into the bathroom. "Shower sex."

"I didn't say—OUCH!" I squeal when he smacks my bare ass.

"Just get the fuck in the shower."

Chapter Twenty-Seven

CALVIN

I've never wanted to share my past with someone as much as I do with Jamie. Also, I've never wanted to hide every miserable memory from someone as much as I do with Jamie. It's a ridiculous dichotomy, but it makes perfect sense to me.

So here I am, staring down the edge of a cliff, and I don't know whether I should run away or jump.

I do, however, know that I need to take a piss, but half her body is draped over mine in this tiny excuse for a bed. An inch at a time, I extricate myself from her clinging limbs and tangled sheets. By the time I step out of the bathroom, she's claimed the whole bed, hugging her pillow instead of lying on it.

I grin. My sister used to hug her pillow instead of lying on it.

It's nearly five o'clock in the morning, so I step into my jeans and pull on my shirt. When I kiss Jamie's cheek, she doesn't flinch, but she takes a longer breath and releases it in a contented sigh.

Thirty minutes later, I'm at my grandma's house, changing into running shorts and hitting the pavement toward the nearest trail and steepest inclines.

In true Grandma fashion, she has breakfast waiting for me when I return. "Go shower before you sit with me." She sips her coffee with a shaky left hand.

I inhale the sweet cinnamon from her streusel-topped coffee cake and grin. "Yes, ma'am."

After my shower, I check my phone. There are no messages.

"Jamie is lovely." Grandma eyes me intently when I sit beside her at the kitchen table.

"She lived in Florida her whole life until she moved to Montana last January. This year, she left Florida for the first time. Saw the mountains for the first time. Flew on a plane for the first time." I sip my coffee.

"What do you know about her family?"

"Not a lot. Her parents died."

"What else?"

I shrug. "I haven't asked anything else."

Her shaky hand sets the mug on the table. "Why?"

"I respect people's privacy."

"Perhaps asking her about her past would indicate that you're interested, not *prying* into her private life."

"Perhaps. But how can I know? So it's best to let her share those details if she wants to."

"I don't want to die before you find love."

"Then you'd better be immortal." I smirk before taking a bite of coffee cake.

"Calvin David Fitzgerald." She gives me the same scolding look she's been leveling in my direction since she took over raising me twenty-two years ago.

"You've always told me to follow my passion. That's what I'm doing. I love my job. And I love that I'm not accountable to anyone but you."

"Love *is* passion."

I make duck lips and shake my head. "Not always."

"You are a stubborn boy."

"I'm a stubborn man." I chuckle.

"If you don't converse any better than that with Jamie, then you're just a boy."

After last night, I'd say Jamie and I converse just fine. We simply use fewer words to communicate.

"She's in her twenties—ten years younger than me—seeing the world for the first time. The reason she's a travel nurse is because she doesn't want to stay in the same place right now. We're friends. And our friendship doesn't require that level of disclosure. Respecting the path she's on is something only a man would do."

"If she took a permanent job in Missoula, would you be more than friends?"

This is a losing battle. My grandma knows I don't want that life. She used to support and even encourage my choice to live alone. But her stroke took a lot of those memories. And that's not all bad because she lost the most tragic parts of her life too.

"Maybe." I lie because she's my grandma, and I don't know how much time she has left in this life. It seems pointless to disappoint her now.

She lights up. "You're going to be the best father and husband, just like your dad and his dad."

I nod slowly despite my knowing she will never live to see that day, and neither will I. "Thanks."

It's noon by the time I make it back to Jamie's. I'm surprised she hasn't called or texted me. I buzz her apartment.

She doesn't respond, but the door unlocks. As I make my way down the hallway, a couple screaming at each other from another apartment fills the space. Their bickering fades when I reach the end door. It opens slowly, like Jamie's lips curling into a dazzling grin. I take a second to admire her short yellow-and-green checked sundress.

"I wasn't sure I'd see you again."

I step inside, drop my bag, and remove my sneakers. "Why? I told you I took four days off."

"You didn't tell me they were all for me." She retreats backward until her butt hits the kitchen counter, and she reaches for the white rose I made her before I left this morning. "When I expect more from you, you give me less. Sometimes nothing. When I expect nothing, you give me more . . . so much more. You made a flower out of a tissue. You took something most people use to catch snot and made an origami rose." She twists the stem back and forth by her nose as if it smells like a rose, or maybe it's to hide her grin.

"The sex was good. I always make a rose if the sex is good."

She stops twisting the flower and flicks it at me.

I chuckle and catch it. "It's a compliment."

"I doubt it. What time did you leave?"

"Early."

"How's your grandma this morning?"

"Fine. Were you okay with me not coming back?" I sit at her desk, which is filled with plants and her laptop, and I set her rose next to a flowering succulent.

"Define 'okay,'" she says.

"Not mad."

"I was *okay* with you not coming back."

"You're the most spectacular friend ever."

She barks a laugh, crossing her arms. "Only with you, Fitz."

"What do you mean?"

"You're a rental."

I lift my eyebrows. "A rental?"

"Yeah. When someone rents a car, they don't feel responsible for it. They drive it and return it. But when you *buy* a car, you do your research. You want to know you're getting something with good ratings. Something dependable. It's a huge purchase, so you want to feel satisfied with your decision. And if it breaks down or something goes wrong, you have to invest to fix it. With a rental, you can just exchange it for a different one."

I think about her words. I'm not sure they make a lot of sense. "So if I hadn't returned, you would get a different rental?"

Jamie grins. "No. The goal isn't to rent."

"You want to own a man?"

She turns and lifts her hair off her neck.

He's mine.

Leaning back in the chair, I lace my fingers behind my head and exhale. "Well, what are your plans for this rental that you'll have to return in two days?"

Checking her watch, her nose scrunches. "I have a class in an hour."

"I thought you took four days off too."

"It's not for work. It's a jewelry-making class."

"Really?"

"Yes. One of the other nurses I work with suggested I learn new things. Explore my artistic side. She's been a nurse for nearly forty years. She said nurturing your creativity is the key to longevity in this field. It's a way to relieve stress while feeling a sense of accomplishment. Working in psych is rewarding in some ways but also a slow process. Mentally ill people heal at a much slower pace than someone recovering from surgery or something like a stroke or heart attack."

When I don't respond, she pushes off the counter and straddles my lap, hands resting on my shoulders. "The mind is complicated."

I hear everything she stops short of saying. "Can I watch you?"

Her grin swells. "You want to watch me? I'm not good at making jewelry."

"Well, I'm good at watching you, so one of us will feel successful today."

Her thumbs slide along my jaw. "It's only a five-minute drive. We have a little time. Maybe I can earn another rose."

This woman was made for me, just not in the right life.

I grin. "Let's see whatcha got."

Chapter Twenty-Eight

JAYMES

My person.

Calvin Fitzgerald is my dream—the kind that doesn't come true and ends with a pounding heart and an aching reality.

Our time together ends too quickly. He watches me create a copper-and-leather bracelet and matching earrings. We take his grandma for a walk, and I have the privilege of meeting Terry, her older man.

The following morning, Fitz jogs next to me while I ride my skateboard, and I'm the one who struggles to keep up.

"You're such a show-off!" I giggle, pumping around a turn into a headwind.

He runs faster.

After I'm exhausted and he's barely broken a sweat, we eat lunch at a rooftop café.

"Why do you suppose Maren never told me she saw your tattoo?" I ask, sipping my pink lemonade while watching him eat the rest of my lunch. Calvin consumes an enormous number of calories.

He chews, giving my question some thought. "I think she feels sorry for you, but she knows there's no changing the situation. So why bring it up?"

"Why does she feel sorry for me?"

He shrugs. "She thinks you have strong feelings for me and knows I will only disappoint you. I'm a disappointment to everyone who invests time in getting to know me."

He's not a disappointment. He breaks my heart, but not in a conventional way.

"I think the only person you should worry about disappointing is yourself."

He doesn't respond.

Not at lunch.

Not for the rest of the night.

We skip dinner and fall into bed early to earn more roses.

"Would Edith be okay with me visiting her?" I ask, dressing the following morning.

Fitz glances up from packing his bag. "She'd probably like that." He returns his attention to the bag, zipping it.

"I won't ask about her past."

About your past.

He shrugs. "She doesn't remember anyway."

"Does she ask about it?"

"Sometimes." He tosses his bag by the door.

I shove my feet into my ankle boots. "So she must know about some of it."

"She knows enough."

Tucking in the front of my white blouse, I narrow my eyes at him. "What do you mean?"

"She's been given a chance to live the rest of her life in peace. So I tell her things that are a little less awful."

"You lie?"

"I've softened the hard truth."

Does he know how badly I want to beg him for that hard truth? How difficult it is for me to bite my tongue? How much I want to nudge him for more? Staying on my side of the line is slowly killing me because he's unknowingly making me fall irrevocably in love with him.

"Fitz, you can tell me anything. Okay? I won't judge. I won't push for more. I can be an idle listener if you ever need to let go of anything."

"I let it go." He crosses his arms—the opposite of letting anything go.

"Here." I wrap the bracelet I made around his wrist. "It's not a tissue rose, but it's the best I can do." After threading the button through the loop, I glance at him.

Tension eases from his body, and he finds a smile for me. "I'm glad I came."

"You came a lot."

He shakes his head despite his grin. "Perv."

I laugh. "I'm glad you visited me. It was unexpected. Possibly the best surprise I've ever had."

"That's just sad for you."

Oh, Fitz . . . it's not sad at all.

I rest my hands on his chest. "Take care. Okay?"

He nods several times. And it would be easier to keep my shit together if he didn't slide his hand along my neck, fingers brushing my tattoo. My hand drifts from his chest to the side a few inches, over his tattoo.

We share a grin. I'd say a knowing grin, but I'm not sure I know anything anymore. Fitz took time away from what he loves the most to see me. He elicited help from Evette. Then he introduced me to his grandma. We've spent the better part of the past three days naked in my bed. And he seems obsessed with touching my tattoo.

I can't even begin to understand the look in his eyes. It's pure torture. I didn't put that look there, but I feel like I bring it to the surface.

Emotion works its way into my throat, making it hard to swallow and nearly impossible to speak, so I clear it and find something lighter to talk about than the reality that he's leaving. I don't know what this weekend has meant to him. "I bet Mrs. Wilke will be thrilled to see you."

"Yeah. Her nipples get pretty hard when I come home after being gone for so long."

I hum. "Are you going to tell her about us?"

"I'm not sure yet. She's never been that receptive to the suggestion of a threesome, so I don't know how she'd handle hearing about us."

We mirror each other's shit-eating grins, but mine fades first. "In a strictly friendly way, I will miss you."

"That's disappointing. I will miss you in a strictly sexual way."

With a dismissive smile, I open the door. "If you don't get going, the only thing you'll miss is your flight."

His hands slide around my waist, hugging my back to his chest. His forehead rests on the crown of my head. No words. Just slow breaths.

My skin prickles with a flood of emotions that I can't articulate. They have nowhere to go.

I wait.

And wait.

With each passing breath shared in silence, my heart cracks a little more. Aches a little deeper.

"I'm so sorry," I whisper.

"For what," he murmurs just before pressing his lips to my head.

"For whatever happened to your family."

He stiffens for a moment. I'm sure this seems out of the blue because he knows I don't know what happened. And that's okay. As much as I want to crawl into his heart and take away whatever keeps him from feeling worthy of love, I'm okay with offering blind compassion.

"Thank you," Fitz whispers, releasing me. He picks up his bag and struts to the exit without making eye contact again—a vanishing figure tugging my heartstrings.

"Calvin Fitzgerald?" I yell, wiping my tears before they escape.

He stops, but he doesn't turn.

"If you were normal and didn't have an awful past, do you think you could love me?" My fierce heart always trumps my controlled thoughts.

I'm not sure he heard me.

But then he continues toward the exit. "Jaymes, if I were normal, I'd love you enough. The problem is, I'm not normal, so I'd love you *too much*."

Not one look back.

The door closes behind him. Another apartment door opens, and a woman steps out, glancing in my direction. Then she does a double take.

"Are you okay?" she asks.

I nod despite the flood of tears trailing down my cheeks.

Chapter Twenty-Nine

CALVIN

"She's a goddess," Travis says, pausing the swing of his Pulaski to glance at the fire for a second.

I keep digging, but not without a slight chuckle. "You call every fire a goddess. I don't know if one this size deserves such a grand label."

"Fitz, you know she has potential. All the small ones have potential when there's no fucking humidity in the air, and it's eighty-five god-damn degrees in September."

By the following day, the six of us are ready to pack out, and Travis is trying to get a cell signal. "Laney's due any day. If I miss the birth, I think she's going to leave my sorry ass."

My back gives me a little protest when I slide well over a hundred pounds of equipment onto it. "You didn't plan that well. Sex in February. Babies in December."

"Sounds like a guy who doesn't have a wife or a girlfriend." Travis hikes his pack onto his back. "Some of us like to have sex during all the months of the year."

"You're a dumbass. You know that, right?"

"Speaking of getting your dick wet, I heard you visited Jamie in California."

"I visited my grandma. And I don't know what you do with your granny, but mine doesn't get my dick wet."

Travis laughs. "But does a certain nurse do it for you?"

Fuck yes.

Her hand sliding into the front of my briefs.

The grin she gives me, as if she's surprised I'm so hard for her.

Her nipples brushing my chest when she grinds against me.

Her hair in my face while she hovers above me, waiting for me to lift my head and steal her soft lips.

"Just keep your head in the game. If you spend too much time thinking about Laney at home, you'll fuck up and not make it home."

"What awaits you at home?"

I grunt. "Nothing. That's why I always make it home."

We scatter like quail for the pack out. The trek to the pickup spot is rarely a team activity. It's alone time for reflection. This is the life. It's easy to be with Jamie and think of the future I'm missing, but I feel at peace—at home—when I'm in this quietude, a mere speck among trees and fissured earth trails.

It's six miles to the lake, where a boat awaits us. When we return to the base, not only is Laney not in labor, she's there, waiting for Travis.

"I'm all dirty, baby," he says when she throws her arms around his neck, body angled to accommodate her baby belly.

"The doctor said he'll induce me in the morning if I don't go before then, so we don't have to worry about you missing the birth."

Travis hunches in front of her, resting grubby hands on her belly. "Did you hear that, Scooter? Tomorrow, you get to meet your dad."

"Stop!" Laney giggles. "We're not naming our child Scooter. Anyway, I think we're having a girl."

Travis kisses her belly. "Doesn't matter. We're naming her Scooter. Scooter Mooder."

I shake my head and grin, as does Gary and a few of the other guys.

"I remember when Evette used to greet me after a fire. There's nothing like returning to a woman who's dying to see you and so glad you're alive. Best sex of my life."

"What happened?" I drop my gear.

"She started fantasizing about my life insurance more than she fantasized about me."

"That's why I don't have one of those."

"Life insurance?"

I shrug off my shirt. "A wife."

"I'm not buying it. And you should text your girlfriend to let her know you're back and alive."

"I don't have—"

Gary's gone before I finish.

I'm not messaging anyone. I wasn't even gone for two days. No close calls. No need for anyone to worry.

Standing my ground, I make it home and finish half my dinner before I pick up my phone and stare at it. "I'm not telling her I'm safe and alive," I mumble to myself, since I'm alone tonight. "I'm just being a good friend. Seeing how she's doing."

Fitz: My scars haven't changed and my nuts are still chafed. I need a refund on that ointment

She doesn't text me right away. She's probably still working. It's almost midnight before my phone pings and wakes me up.

Jaymes: Thanks for letting me know you're okay. Night xo

"Dammit." I toss my phone back onto the nightstand and grin.

After a short night's sleep, I text her at four o'clock in the morning, her time, just to prove I'm still an asshole.

Fitz: Laney and Travis are having their baby today

It takes her five minutes to respond, just enough time to cuss me out. On cue, as I get in my truck, she texts me back.

Jaymes: If u die today I won't cry immediately because I'll be too sleep deprived

Jaymes: And I already sent a baby gift yesterday after Evette told me they were inducing today. Don't worry, the gift is from both of us

She can't be serious.

Fitz: We're not a couple

Jaymes: Love u 2. Have a great day!

"Fuck my life." I toss my phone into the passenger seat and back out of the driveway.

Chapter Thirty

JAYMES

"You look just like your mom. I knew you would," Dwight says after beckoning me into his room to show me he ate his breakfast and took his meds.

"Funny. I never thought I looked like her. She said I looked like my dad. But he died when I was five. He worked for NASA. That's pretty cool, huh?"

Dwight chuckles. It doesn't matter how often I try to bring him into reality; he laughs it off. Today's the first day I've been his daughter, not his wife. Maybe that's progress.

"I was a park ranger, not a NASA scientist." He slips on his cardigan.

"I know this." I help him get his other arm threaded through the sweater.

A park ranger who started a massive fire. The irony.

He slumps on the edge of the bed, head bowed. "I told her to stay close or take the bear spray. Always have bear spray."

I listen. What else can I say or do? His wife's dead. That's why I don't mind the days he thinks I'm her. She's not dead on those days.

"A nurse." He glances up at me. "She'd be proud, Barbara."

I smile.

"Do you miss her as much as I do?" he asks.

I nod. "I miss my mom so much."

"Yeah," he whispers, trying to pull off his cardigan.

"Aren't you going outside?"

"I'm tired. Those pills make me . . ." He gives up on taking off his cardigan, lying on his side with his cheek resting on his folded hands. "They make me tired. So I"—he closes his eyes—"stay out of trouble," he mumbles.

I frown. He doesn't need to be on such strong medications. He'll never get better if he's never given a chance to be himself again. No one in this ward is given the opportunity to be themselves or perhaps *find* themselves.

Midday, I take a lunch break and check my messages.

Evette: Laney had a little girl. Riley. 7 lbs, 4 oz. Both are doing great! I'll send pics when I have some

Jaymes: Great news!

It's unlikely that Fitz is on another fire so quickly, so I text him by copying and pasting Evette's message.

Jaymes: Laney had a little girl. Riley. 7 lbs, 4 oz. Both are doing great! I'll send pics when I have some

Fitz: Don't be like that. I'm embarrassed for u

He sends a photo of Travis, Laney, and Riley.

"Oh my gosh." I cover my mouth.

Jaymes: I'm proud of u

Fitz: I did nothing. I wasn't there

I giggle.

Jaymes: I'm proud of u for having friends who send u pictures of their baby

Fitz: I have friends

Jaymes: Yes. But ur friend is in San Bernardino

He doesn't respond. Either he's legitimately busy, or he's contemplating how to reply. I don't give him a chance.

Jaymes: Have to go. One of us has a real job

Fitz: Thx for letting me get back to it

I nearly spit out my water. Calvin Fitzgerald makes me laugh. He makes me cry. He makes me swoon. He makes me blush. He makes me *feel*.

◆ ◆ ◆

On my next day off, I visit Edith, bringing her flowers and a charcuterie box to share for lunch.

She lights up after taking forever to open her door. "What a surprise!"

"Hope I'm not interrupting you."

"Of course not. Come in."

"I brought flowers and food." I set them both on her kitchen table.

"The men in my life could learn a few things from you. Thank you, Jamie. What's the occasion?"

I remove the charcuterie-box lid. "No occasion. Well, I mean, it's my day off. That's always a reason to celebrate."

"That boy of mine is thirty-five, and you're the first girl he's introduced to me." She hands me a glass of lemonade and sits across from me. "That might not be true." With a tiny laugh, she shakes her head. "You're the first girl I remember. So if I met someone before my stroke, I either don't remember, or it didn't happen."

"If I were a betting person, I'd say it never happened. Fitz is content being single."

"Nobody's content being single. Are you?" She pops an olive into her mouth.

"For now, yes. But it's not part of my long-term goal like it is for Fitz."

Her lips twist, and she hums. "Why do you suppose that is?"

I open the sleeve of crackers. "I'm not sure. I think it's his job. He's worried about something happening to him and leaving a family behind. Honestly, I think it's more than that. Perhaps something that happened to him when he was younger." My gaze lifts to gauge her reaction, to see if I've crossed a line.

She has none. "I can't imagine what that would be. His parents died in a car accident. Sure, it was tragic, but that's life."

"What about his sister? Was she in the car too?"

Edith shoots me a funny look. "What do you mean? He doesn't have a sister."

"Oh." I focus on the cheese, carefully placing a square onto the cracker. "Sorry. I must have misunderstood him."

"He was thirteen when his parents were in a car accident. I raised him."

"In San Bernardino?"

"Yes." Her face tenses before she bites into a piece of sausage. "I don't know." She shakes her head. "I get confused by what I think I know and what Calvin has told me."

"What do you think you know?" I'm crossing a line, but in my defense, Fitz agreed I should visit Edith, and he didn't specify which topics I should avoid.

"Well"—she squints at the box of food—"it's hard to explain. This doesn't feel like home."

"I'm sure you probably lived in a house or apartment, not in assisted living."

"No," she says. "I mean San Bernardino. It doesn't feel like home. And I can't say why; it's just a feeling. You know?"

I'm at a huge disadvantage. It's like I'm talking to a patient giving me bits and pieces of their past, but I don't know if what they're telling me is true or an illusion.

And why is a car accident so off limits? Did he lie to me about his sister? That doesn't make sense. Did he lie to Edith? Was Fitz's sister in the car, and he didn't want to upset Edith more than necessary if she didn't remember his sister?

"Yes," I say. "I think I know what you mean. Home is a feeling. And I don't mean a house as much as a community. But I know that a stroke can leave you feeling lost and disconnected both physically and mentally. Perhaps it took away that feeling of home."

"Perhaps." She eyes me for a long moment. "When I met you at the restaurant, I thought you looked familiar. Maybe you've been my nurse."

"That's not possible. Sorry."

"Have you worked in the ER or the intensive care unit?"

"I worked in the ER in Miami. Have you been to Miami?"

She chuckles. "Not that I remember. But I'm old, and I've suffered a stroke, so it's possible. Do you like your job?"

"I do."

"I bet patients love you. You have a calmness about you. And a kind smile. I can see why my Calvin is so taken with you."

"Aw, thank you, Edith."

Again, her gaze lingers on me. "But it's going to bug me. I know I've seen you before."

I rarely forget a face, but I don't like being the reason for her distress. So I'm taking a page from Fitz's book and opting for a white lie.

"You should talk to Calvin. Maybe you have been to Miami. Maybe there was a minor incident that required a trip to the ER. I feel like I would remember you, but I've seen a lot of patients, so I may be the one who is not making the connection."

"I'll do that," she says, outwardly content to relax and try to figure it out later.

Chapter Thirty-One

I miss Fitz.

I miss Melissa.

Maren and Will.

Evette and Gary.

Living by myself seemed like a good idea. I thought I'd make friends at work. Instead, I have coworkers. Acquaintances. And Edith, who only makes me miss Fitz more. Maybe it's the monotony of my life. Whatever it is, I feel lonely. And that loneliness makes me think nonstop about Fitz.

"Have you seen Samantha?" Dwight asks while I wait for him to take his medication.

He's not eating today or interested in his meds. However, he's more lucid than I have ever seen him. Focused eyes. Clear speech. If he weren't assuming I'm his wife or daughter, I'd say he no longer belongs here.

I yawn. The couple down the hall from my apartment fought all night. "Who's Samantha?"

"My sister. Your aunt."

I guess I'm his daughter today. "I have not seen Samantha."

"She has the prettiest brown eyes." He points to the edge of one of his and draws a line down his face. "She has a scar from the corner of her eye to her jawbone."

I trace the same line from my eye to my cheek.

He nods.

I clear my throat. "Interesting. My mom had a scar there too. How did your sister get hers?"

He squints, confusion creeping into his whole face. "I'm not sure. She's older than me. I don't remember it happening." He rubs his temples.

"You've remembered a lot today. I wouldn't worry about that little detail. Maybe you don't remember because you were so young when it happened."

"Did she tell you?"

I hand him his yogurt, hoping he'll eat now. "No."

"You should ask her when you see her." He takes a bite of the yogurt as if on instinct. I've found he eats when he's not forced to focus on his food.

He grins while swallowing. "She used to stutter, so our mom made her take singing lessons. She had an awful voice, but Mom was right. It fixed her stutter."

What?

A wave of lightheadedness and nausea overtakes me. Did he really say that? "H-here. Take these." I hand him his pills.

"You're shaking." He squints, accepting the pills.

I fist my hand and slide it into the pocket of my pants. "I haven't eaten today. Can you just"—I nod toward his water—"take them for me, please?"

Dwight frowns but complies. "I'll take them for you. You'd better go."

I nod a half-dozen times. Without a goodbye, I stagger toward the bathroom.

"Jamie?" One of the other nurses tries to stop me, but I keep going.

When I reach the toilet, I retch, but nothing comes out. Sweat beads along my forehead. With clammy hands, I pull my hair away from my face.

"Jamie, are you okay?" She rests her hand on my back.

"No." I grit my teeth, hugging my stomach.

"I'll get someone to cover. Go home, hon. Do you need me to get you a ride?"

The room spins when I stand upright. My hands reach for the sides of the stall. It's a coincidence—an improbable coincidence—but not impossible.

"Jamie?"

I shake my head with each wobbly step toward the sink. Turning the cold water on to splash it onto my face.

She hands me a wad of paper towels.

"Thank you." I blot my face. "I can drive."

"You sure?"

I nod.

"Okay. Feel better."

When she leaves me alone, I stare at my reflection; all I see is my mom. I have her brown eyes. My finger slides along my face where she had her scar.

"It can't be," I whisper.

As soon as I get to my car, I call Melissa. She doesn't answer, so I text her.

Jaymes: Call me right away!!!!

Two blocks from the hospital, Melissa calls me.

"Mel—"

"Jesus, is everything all right?" Panic strangles her voice.

"No. I-I don't know. A patient said something." I grip the steering wheel tighter to stop my hands from shaking. "He's the bear guy." I press the heel of my hand to my chest. My heart won't stop racing. It doesn't feel right.

"The bear guy?"

"A bear killed his wife, and he started this huge fire, and he's thought I'm his wife. Then his daughter—"

"Jaymes, slow down, babe. Breathe."

I nod. "Breathe. Yes. Breathe." It's hard to breathe. I have to figure this out. It doesn't make sense.

"Where are you?" she asks.

"On my way home."

"Maybe you should pull over."

I shake my head. "I-I'm almost there."

"Why don't you call me back when you're at your apartment? Focus on getting there safely. Okay?"

"Yeah. O-okay."

Just as she disconnects, I slam on my brakes. My seat belt locks.

"Oh my god. Oh my god!" I cover my mouth, gaze affixed to the biker I nearly hit.

He flips me the bird as the car behind me honks. I drive slower than fifteen miles per hour the rest of the way. When I get to my apartment safely, I rest my head on the steering wheel and just breathe.

Dwight is confused. Maybe I didn't hear him correctly. I was focused on getting him to eat and take his meds. I grab my bag and head inside the building. The sweet smell of pot greets me, along with yelling. It has to be the couple down the hall from me who were fighting all night. How can they still be screaming at each other?

I need a long shower. Then I need to call Melissa back and calmly talk through everything. She will help it make sense. I'm tired, thanks to the couple whose door I'm approaching. When people are tired, their brains don't work as well. That's it. That has to be it.

"Shit." I bend down to pick up my keys after dropping them. As I stand straight, the door to my left opens (the bickering couple). I turn slightly, ready to ask them to please take it down a notch so I can think straight. In a panic, the young woman stumbles into me and trips, falling to the—

Whack!

Chapter Thirty-Two

CALVIN

It's a jaw-grinding day when someone makes a shitty decision to let a small fire burn when we could have dropped two to four men and snuffed it out. The "let burn" is now a vast conflagration we're flying past on our way to a smaller fire that no one will know about if we get to it soon.

That's the point. We put out fires in remote areas that rarely make the news *because* we put them out quickly and efficiently.

We bank left and get a good look at the fire, an angry dragon seeping a slow-rising column of smoke.

I'm out of the plane once I get the slap on my shoulder. The wind has its way with me for several seconds, a dizzying blur of tilting landscape at ninety miles per hour.

The sky.

The plane.

The horizon.

The ground.

I go through the count, and then it's peace. A serenity like nothing else. And in this moment, I tell myself *this* is the reason I do it.

But who am I kidding? I think the same thing when I'm on the ground cutting a line, sawing trees, or crawling around on my fucking hands and knees, feeling for hot spots.

What bugs me is this constant need to remind myself just how much I love my job.

Beyond the ominous clouds, there's something off about the day. A sudden shift in the wind adds an unplanned hundred-or-more yards of drift. Trees. I'm headed for the trees. By some miracle beyond my experience steering my ass out of a bad situation, I find a tiny clearing and manage to land without snagging my chute on a tree or body slamming a boulder the size of a small car.

Alan, a rookie, doesn't fare as well; he finds a tree—thankfully a shorter one.

"Fuck!" His displeasure echoes.

When the other two land, I remove my gear and radio for the supply boxes.

While making my way to Alan, I check my phone. There's a message from a number I don't recognize.

Hi Calvin, it's Melissa. Jamie's fine. There was an incident. I flew in this afternoon. I'm at the hospital. She was accidentally attacked yesterday. A concussion and a broken nose. She'll go home tomorrow. She didn't want me to tell u, but I thought u might want to know

My hand drops to my side, clenching the phone as I watch the plane drop boxes of supplies. *What the hell?* How does one get "accidentally" attacked? Was it a patient?

"Alan!" Erin screams.

My gaze shoots to the tree, and I sprint toward his body, dangling five feet from the ground. He's red in the face, clawing at the suspension line that's a noose around his neck. Todd and I lift the weight of his body while Erin climbs the tree to help him untangle the line.

We lower him to the ground, and he stares at the sky with shallow, rapid breaths and probably visions of God descending from heaven to take his dumb ass to the pearly gates. We've all done something stupid that's given us a glimpse of the afterlife.

I wouldn't be a good leader if I didn't state the obvious and make this a learning opportunity for everyone gathered in a circle around Alan. "Always check for lines before you release your harness attachments," I scold (teach), when I know he will live another day.

He rubs his neck without looking at me. "I was pissed that I didn't steer clear of the tree, and—"

"Welp, no time to be pissed. There's still a dozen ways you can die today; let's focus on avoiding those and put the goddamn fire out."

After we unload the supply boxes and trek to the fire, I bark orders, feeling out of sorts and on edge, trying to forget about the message on my phone and the member of my crew who tried to be a piñata. "Right here, dig a cup trench."

"Up either side and tie it off at the top?" Todd finishes for me.

I nod.

Three hours later, we have a completed line, and we break for food. I update dispatch and recheck my phone. No new messages, but I also don't have any bars.

"You good?" Erin asks. She's a second-year rookie. A true talent. She's also the most emotionally in tune with everyone, which isn't always a good thing in a male-dominated profession of blowhards who pride themselves on not showing emotion. Most of the women keep that shit locked up, too, but not Erin. She can relentlessly tear into the earth with her Pulaski one minute and rock a baby to sleep the next.

"Yup." I nod several times, but I don't make eye contact.

Everyone chuckles when I pull out my favorite snack, a frozen bean-and-rice burrito. It's good and warm by the time I get a chance to eat it.

I find a believable smile to give them before getting back to business. "We need to get the burning snag down. Todd and I have the crosscut. You two make the bed."

As soon as our break ends, we return to work, felling the burning snag, throwing dirt on it, and tearing it apart.

"Dispatch said we'll be picked up at oh seven hundred. Grab dinner, and get some sleep. We'll be up early for another check, gearing up, and a four-mile hike to the helispot."

Todd, Alan, and Erin share stories during dinner. I stare at my phone and play every scenario in my head. Where was Jaymes attacked? Why? And why wouldn't she want me to know?

By 0500, we're grabbing food and checking for hot spots.

"You good?" Todd asks.

"Jesus, I'm fine. Should I make a public announcement?" I pack the tools.

"So you're not good. That's all you need to say."

I feel his gaze on me, but I don't have the time or patience to make him feel okay about asking me anything.

After we get picked up, I muster as much professionalism as possible to discuss everyone's performance, which was good. If there is such a thing as textbook, this was it.

An hour later, we're back at the base for a shower, and all personnel gather for a debrief.

"Go." Gary grabs my arm before I take a seat.

I narrow my eyes.

"Do you know about Jamie? Her friend messaged Evette this morning."

After a beat, I nod.

"Then go. Take whatever time you need."

"I'm fine. I'll text her after we finish." I pull away from his hold.

Again, he grabs my arm. We have a silent standoff.

I glance at the door. "I need you to let me do this my way."

Gary frowns, but he releases me.

This is my life. And when I read the message from Melissa, I was reminded why *this* is my life.

The debrief is quick. I finish my day like it's any other day. And I do it under the scrutiny of Gary's watchful eye.

I go home.

I make dinner.

I wash my dishes.

Will arrives home from his tai chi just as I head up the stairs.

"Hey." He tosses his keys on the table.

"Hey," I say, making it halfway up the stairs before stopping. "Listen." I turn. "Melissa, Jamie's friend, messaged me. Two days ago, Jamie was *accidentally* attacked—"

"What the hell?!"

I shake my head. "She's fine. It was a concussion and a broken nose. I haven't had a chance to get back with her, so that's all I know."

"Well, how long have you been home? What do you mean you haven't had a chance to get back with her? When did you get the message?"

"Yesterday."

"What the fuck, Fitz?" Will pulls his phone out of his pocket. "Does Maren know?"

"I was on a call. I couldn't exactly leave or send out a group text."

"Hopefully, Maren will see my text and reply." Will lifts his gaze and eyes me with disapproval. "She'll go see her, or I could take a few days off to go see her." He heads toward the kitchen.

I run a hand through my hair and follow him. "I'm going to go," I say.

Will pulls his empty water bottle from his bag. "I'm sure she'd rather see Maren, no offense."

"No, she wouldn't," I counter with slow, calculated words.

Will eyes me. "What do you mean by that?" He pulls his phone from his pocket. "It's Maren. Hey." He answers it on speaker.

"Jesus Christ, what do you mean Jamie was attacked? What the hell? Are you with Fitz? God, I hope he's already with her."

Will squints at me. "Why would *he* already be with her?"

The line goes silent.

"I'm here, Maren. Will and I were just starting to discuss why I'm going to visit her. It's a broken nose and concussion. I'll let you know when I find out any more information."

"Okay. Well, I'm sorry, Fitz. But it's time," Maren says.

"Time for what?" Will narrows his eyes.

"I'll be home tomorrow. Give her my love." Maren ends the call.

"Did you *fuck* our roommate?" Will's words cut through the tense air as he slides his phone onto the counter with one hand and parks his other hand on his hip.

Slowly, I nod.

With a deep inhale, Will looks at the ceiling.

"But for what it's worth, it never happened here."

Will grunts. "That's a relief, because that's what the rule meant—don't screw fellow roommates *in* the house."

"Are you done?"

Will crosses his arms. "Why? You don't want a girlfriend or a wife. You don't want kids. So why risk having Maren and I pissed at you? Why risk getting kicked out of the house? Why take advantage of *our friend* who is ten years younger than you?"

All great questions. I don't have the answers, but I won't show Will that side of my messed-up psyche. "I'm thirty-five, not fifteen. I can navigate sex with a woman without it turning into a total debacle. It's about setting expectations and boundaries. And stop making it sound like it wasn't consensual or that I took advantage of someone who just turned eighteen."

Will returns a blank stare. "She wears friendship bracelets and gets excited when there's a full moon. She reads her horoscope. I bet she cries while watching Disney movies. There's no way you two hooked up without her *feeling* more than your amateur attempt to make her orgasm."

"Fuck you."

He slowly shakes his head and walks toward me, resting his hand on my shoulder. "No, Fitz. Fuck you for standing here talking to me when someone attacked her *days* ago."

Chapter Thirty-Three

JAYMES

"Hey." Melissa's lips pull into a shaky smile while she slides from my desk chair to the edge of my bed. "Do you need more for your pain?"

"N-no." I clear the frog from my throat. "I hate how it makes me feel."

She hands me a glass of water and holds the straw while I sip. "I think the point is for you *not* to feel the pain."

I wince, trying to sit upright. "My head."

"It's a miracle you only have a concussion and a broken nose. No missing teeth. No fractured skull. And you have one eye that's not swollen shut, so there's that."

"I don't feel miraculous. I feel like I've been asleep for days."

"You've slept a lot. And they caught your neighbor late last night. I called to check this morning. His girlfriend is beside herself. She feels responsible. That baseball bat was meant for her, but she said she tripped, and you were just there."

"Right place. Right time," I mumble.

"Well"—Melissa's nose wrinkles—"let's not go that far."

I gingerly touch my broken nose. "Let me see a mirror."

"I think we should wait on that." Melissa rolls her lips over her teeth.

"It's still awful, isn't it?"

"You're a nurse. Do I really have to review the stages of bruising with you?"

"This is exactly why I didn't want you to notify anyone."

"And by anyone, you meant Calvin."

"I meant *anyone*."

She nods slowly. Too slowly.

"If you called him—"

"I didn't call him." She cringes. "I texted him."

"Mel!"

"Don't 'Mel' me. Do you have any idea how freaked out I was when you didn't call me back? And the next thing I knew, the hospital was calling me because I'm your emergency contact. I thought for sure you'd been in a car accident."

"What did he say?"

"What?"

"Calvin. Did he respond to your text?"

"He's probably on a fire," Melissa says, but it does little to ease the ache in my chest.

That's code for *he hasn't responded*. It's been three days since the incident.

"Jamie, you have to tell me about the bear guy. You were in a panic the day you called me. You said he thought you're his wife or daughter?"

"Dwight," I murmur before inhaling and sorting through the events of the past few days. "He asked me about his sister, whom he called my aunt. After I said I hadn't seen her, he proceeded to tell me about a scar on her face going from her eye to her jawbone." I wait for Melissa to react.

She squints before returning a cautious nod.

"My mom had that same scar."

"I know. But I don't think she was the only person with a scar from her eye to her jaw."

"He said his sister stuttered when she was younger, and their mom made her take singing lessons to help. And it cured the stutter."

"Did your mom stutter when she was younger?" she asks, slightly laughing, like it's impossible.

"Yes."

Melissa's smile dissolves. "That's . . . freaky." She taps the pads of her fingers on her lips. "Did your mom have siblings?"

"No."

"Well, there you go. It's a freakish coincidence, and that's where it ends. Again, people share similar scars. Some people stutter. And I bet singing is a common treatment for stuttering."

"Stuttering is four times as common in men," I counter.

"But clearly, women can stutter."

"He said, despite the singing lessons, his sister was a terrible singer. My mom said the same thing about herself."

Melissa drums her fingers on her legs. "Most people are terrible singers."

"His sister's name was Samantha."

"Your mom's name was Lauren."

I relinquish a slow nod. "Her middle name was Samantha."

"That's—"

"Stop," I say. "Just stop trying to pretend it's impossible or highly improbable when the truth is . . ." Swallowing hard, I look around the room. "I don't know the truth. And I don't know why my mom would have lied to me—no. Not just lied to me. It's possible she made up a whole new story. And she changed her name. That makes no sense. But it also doesn't make sense that everything Dwight said is just a coincidence. He knows virtually nothing about me, so he wasn't intentionally doing it to freak me out. Which only leaves one logical explanation."

"Nothing about this is logical, Jamie."

"Was she so embarrassed that her brother did something so awful that she wanted to completely cut herself off from him and the rest of the family, if there was other family? And what about my dad? Did he know? I would have been . . ." I try to remember how long Dwight has been in the psych ward. "I would have been two? Three? And my dad died when I was five."

"What do you remember about your dad?"

I shrug. "He worked for NASA. And after he died, my mom moved us to Miami."

"You remember that?"

"No. She told me that."

"I don't know, Jamie. Maybe you should show him a picture of your mom."

I don't relish the idea of sharing any personal information with him for many reasons. I just never thought one reason would be that I'm possibly related to him.

"What if he recognizes the picture?"

Pressing her lips together, Melissa's eyes widen until she blows a lengthy breath out her nose in a *whoosh*. "I don't know. Does he have family? Maybe you could get something from them."

"No one's ever met any of his family."

"Shit."

"The only person who knows the truth is mentally unwell. Confused. And often delusional."

"What is his full name? I'm going to see what I can find on him."

"I feel like I've already said too much. I'm going to get fired."

"Yeah, Jamie. You should be more concerned about your job than knowing who your mom was."

I pick at a stray feather from one of my pillows. "Dwight Keane. A bear killed his wife. He chased the bear but lost the hunt. Until . . . he burned down thirty-two thousand acres of wildland to avenge her death."

"That's . . ." Her nose wrinkles.

"Tragic."

She nods.

My phone vibrates.

Fitz: I'm here. Are u able to open the doors for me? Or can Melissa do it?

"Oh my god. No!" I show my screen to Melissa.

She smiles. "I knew he'd do the right thing."

"What? No! He can't see me like this. Please don't let him in. I'm begging you." Before I finish my desperate plea, she's pressing the button to let him into the building.

"You're not that vain. I'm sure he's seen worse."

I want to cry. It's not vanity. I'm not worried about not wearing makeup or having a stain on my shirt. My nose is broken. I have two black eyes, and one is swollen shut. I'm nearly unrecognizable in the worst way.

Melissa opens my apartment door, and I throw a blanket over my body.

"Hey, you didn't have to come, but I'm sure Jamie is thrilled to see you."

She's a liar. We are no longer friends.

"Hi, where is—" Fitz stops midsentence.

It's quiet.

It's hard to breathe because he's here. Because I have a broken nose. Because I have a blanket over my head. If I die, so be it.

"Yeah, um . . ." Melissa hums. "I might run a few errands since you're here now. Bye, Jamie. See you after a while."

I don't respond. Maybe Fitz will leave, too, even though I'm dying to see him. Unfortunately, my desire not to be seen is more intense, so I stay hidden.

The door clicks shut.

It's eerily quiet except for the air exchange.

"I should have been here sooner, but Melissa messaged me right after I jumped. And I didn't have a good signal."

I don't respond.

"Who did this to you? Melissa said it was an accident."

"Fitz, I know you took time off and bought a plane ticket to come see me. If I reimburse you, will you turn around and go home?"

"No."

I deflate. Tears burn my eyes when I didn't think my face could hurt more. "Fitz," I murmur, "my neighbor's boyfriend tried to take her out with a baseball bat, and I passed their door as she was running from him. She tripped, and he missed her and hit me. I look like a boxer who went twenty rounds."

"Jaymes, boxing doesn't go twenty rounds." The edge of my bed dips.

"Please go."

His hand slides under the blanket and rests on my foot. The first tear breaks free.

"If your neighbor's boyfriend isn't behind bars, I'm going to end him."

"He's in jail."

"Then why are you hiding?"

"Because"—drawing in a shaky breath, I slowly pull the blanket away from my head—"I look like this."

Fitz doesn't flinch. Not a single muscle twitch. "Your freckles hide most of the bruising. And that eye isn't anything that can't be dressed up with a pirate's patch."

"Stop," I say with a half laugh and a half sob.

He grins, pulling stray hair away from my face. "You've never looked worse, Jaymes."

Laughter wins, but I still manage a few more tears.

Fitz's smile wanes. "I'm just *so* fucking sorry this happened to you."

"You're not. Gary and Evette will finally think you're hotter."

When his smile returns tenfold, it feeds my soul, filling it until it runs over. "*Still*, Jaymes. They'll *still* think I'm hotter. Not *finally*."

If he backed down one inch, it would break me. I need our banter.

"Do Maren and Will know?"

"Yes."

"Does Will—"

"Will knows you can't keep your clothes on when you're around me. He knows you've violated me on countless occasions. And for that, he's threatened to demote me to the shed. Hope you're proud of yourself."

Again, he makes me laugh—more of what I need. Yet, it's more than that. I think it's what he needs. Fitz doesn't know how to deal with emotions.

I lie on my side. "Can I have your arms around me?"

After removing his shoes, he spoons my back to his chest and kisses my head. "I'm so glad you're okay," he whispers.

No sarcasm.

No banter.

Nothing made up.

Just his truth in its rawest form.

"I'm so glad you're here, but I know this isn't what you want."

"A baseball bat to your face? No. It's not what I want."

"I mean this *feeling* like you have to be here for me. You don't. I don't expect Maren or Will to come running if something happens to me. Hell, I feel bad that Melissa jumped on a plane to come see me, and we've been friends forever."

"So, who would be here if it weren't Melissa or me? Maren or Will?"

"I can walk. In a few days, I'll be fine driving. It could have been so much worse. Someone from work would have helped out."

"Okay. I'll take off then." He releases me and stands.

I roll over. Speechless.

He slides his feet into his boots. "Tell Melissa it was nice seeing her."

I can't open my mouth, let alone turn a coherent thought into actual words, before he slides his bag over his shoulder and exits my apartment.

My heart shoves a flood of emotion into my throat. Trepidation propels my body out of bed, wincing once standing upright. Panic crawls to the end of my tongue, ready to scream as I open the door.

Fitz is propped against the doorframe, one ankle crossed over the other.

"You're an awful person," I mumble.

"Is that your way of apologizing for kicking me out?"

"I didn't kick you out. You left. And the difference between us is I came after you. When I left—"

Shit.

I can't say it. The emotions are too raw. Everything about my feelings for this man is too raw. Too much. Too real.

"When you left, I didn't come after you," he whispers.

I turn, returning to bed and sitting on the edge. "I think my mom lied to me," I murmur, keeping my head bowed. "I think one of my patients is my uncle. My mom never wanted to talk about her family. All I knew was they weren't part of her life, part of my life. But now I think she was embarrassed by her brother's actions, or maybe she wanted to protect me. I don't know." I lift my gaze. "But I'm twenty-five, and I've lost my parents. My past feels like a lie. My best friend lives on the other side of the country. And I've fallen in love with a man who can never be mine."

His brow furrows.

"So you'll have to excuse me if I'm trying really hard not to need anyone. You, of all people, should understand that. However, I'm not like you. I'm not good at it. Because deep down, I do need people in my life who worry about me, who check in on me, who would feel a little empty inside if I died."

Fitz deflates. "I worry about you." He takes a step closer. "I'm checking in on you." He squats in front of me, resting his hands on my legs. "And if you died"—he swallows hard—"it would fucking *gut* me."

I don't know if my head can take much more, but here I am, bleeding tears. Breathless in a choke hold.

"And I can deal with that. I just can't handle the idea of *you* grieving me," he murmurs.

I press my hand to his cheek, and he leans into my touch. "Too late," I whisper. "Whether you choose to love me or not, whether I'm with you or find someone else who wants my heart, if I'm alive when you leave this earth, I will grieve you. Your smile. Your laughter. Your touch." I sniffle through my stuffy broken nose with shaky breath. "But I won't regret anything. This love is worth the pain."

Fitz bows his head, resting his cheek on my leg, and I stroke his hair.

"Your patient is your uncle?" he asks in a soft tone, once again leaving my heart unacknowledged and bleeding out.

"I don't know. But he shook me the other day when he told me about his sister. Everything he said described my mom. A scar on her face. A childhood stutter. And her name. His sister's name was my mom's middle name. Same eye color. Too many things to be a coincidence. Melissa's going to do some research. Maybe it's something. Maybe it's nothing."

Fitz blinks with a faraway expression.

"What?"

He shakes his head. "I think about my sister too. And how she didn't want to go, but I didn't want her to stay. I wanted my grandparents to take me to an arcade, and if she had stayed, we would have gone to a movie of her choosing instead. So she went with my parents, and my grandparents took me to the arcade. They died. All three of them just . . . gone."

My knuckles brush his cheek, and he closes his eyes briefly before lifting his head. "You should rest."

"Thank you for telling me that." I control my response. I have a million follow-up questions that I hold captive on my tongue. Go where? Died how? Who else knows?

"Don't thank me." He fluffs my pillow and straightens my bedding. "It's really fucking depressing, and nobody should have to hear about something so tragic."

I don't have a response, so I lie down and take a nap, where dreams can shape reality into something different. I hope it's something better.

Chapter Thirty-Four

CALVIN

I spend the night with my grandma and let Melissa stay with Jamie.

The next morning, I wake to the fruity aroma of light roast coffee.

"Quick trip?" Grandma asks, pouring me a cup.

"My flight's in four hours." I sip the coffee. "Yeah, quick trip. I wanted to make sure she's okay."

"Because my boy's in love." She grins behind her mug.

"Because I'm her—"

"Calvin, so help me; if you lie, I will wash your mouth out with soap."

I shake my head with a chuckle. "I tried not to love her."

"You failed." She eyes me much like my mother did—all knowing. A not-so-subtle gloat.

"Miserably."

She holds up her crooked finger. "It's time." Bending forward, she grabs the table's edge and stands, making her way into the bedroom. A few minutes later, she returns. "I found this a while back. I think it was your mother's. She must not have been wearing it that day, or perhaps the hospital returned it to the family. I don't remember."

I stare at my mom's diamond wedding ring on the table before me. The hospital didn't return it. There's no way she was wearing it. "Grandma—"

"She'd want you to give it to the woman you'll marry."

After she eases back into her chair, I reach across the table and rest my hand on hers. "I'm not getting married." I could continue to feed her lies, but I don't want her saying anything to Jamie. There's no need to break both of their hearts with my truth.

"Well, maybe not today. But perhaps someday."

I pick up the ring, holding it between my thumb and index fingers. "I think I love her too much to marry her."

She scoffs. "Nonsense. What could you possibly mean by that?"

My grandma doesn't remember her grief. She doesn't remember the depression. She doesn't remember the suicide attempts. She doesn't know how many times she told me never to get married. Never to put my heart in that position. Never to have children.

No family to abandon.

No emotional accountability.

Just a life of service and good deeds.

I don't know my count on good deeds, but I've been serving as a firefighter my whole adult life.

"I have a high-risk job. Jamie deserves to sleep at night without wondering if I'm coming home in one piece or at all."

"Is that what she said or your decision for her?"

I set the ring on the table and slide it toward her. "It's the decision I made for myself years ago. Abandonment sucks."

"You weren't abandoned." She's right. That was her term. After my grandfather died, she said her family "abandoned" her.

"Orphaned."

Grandma winces.

Glancing at my watch, I take another sip of coffee before standing. "If I'm going to spend a little more time with Jamie before I leave, I'd better get going." I bend over and hug her. "Love you."

"Love you too." She reaches for my hand and places the ring into it. "It's yours, Calvin. Whether you give it to anyone or not, it's yours."

With a pained smile, I slide it into my pocket and nod. "Thank you."

◆ ◆ ◆

Jamie buzzes me in and waits for me at her door. She's in leggings and a T-shirt. Big smile. Wet freshly showered hair. And her black eyes are slightly more violet than blue today. Still, she shines, making my aching, regretful heart rattle.

"Good morning." I kiss her on the cheek.

She clutches my shirt as I begin to stand straight and pulls me back to her for a kiss on the mouth.

"Morning," she says, grinning against my lips. "Is your flight on time?"

"So far." I shut the door behind me. "Where's Melissa?"

"The library or a coffee shop. She's researching my patient to see if there's any connection to my mom."

"What's wrong with your computer?" I nod toward her desk.

"She wanted to give us some time alone since you're leaving today."

"That was generous of her. How are you feeling?"

"No headache today. And I'm less groggy. My nose is still stuffy. But my eye doesn't hurt as much. I messaged work this morning. I think it's time to go back. I'm doing half a shift tomorrow." She sits in her desk chair, so I sit on her bed.

"Progress is good."

"Yes. I feel bad that you made such a quick trip for nothing."

"I got to see you. That's *something*."

She frowns. "I'm not exactly a pleasant sight to see."

"I disagree, but if you want to see me with both eyes, you should come to Missoula when you're all healed."

"That sounds like an invitation I can't refuse." She bites her bottom lip and smiles.

"Will and Maren would love to see you. Gary and Evette too. Hell, they'd love an excuse to have a party." I glance around the room. There's a container and a white envelope on the kitchen counter. "What's that?"

She follows my gaze. "Oh, it's, uh . . . a cupcake and a card."

"For who?"

Jamie clears her throat and smiles. "For me."

"From who?" I stand and grab the card next to the empty envelope.

> Happy birthday to the world's best friend.
> Love you! Mel

"It's"—I slowly turn—"your birthday?"

"It, uh . . . yes. But it's just another day. I nearly forgot it until Melissa gave me the cupcake and card."

Reason number seven hundred and sixty-three why I don't do relationships: they require remembering important dates.

I'm an asshole. No matter how she tries to spin it or downplay it, I'm an asshole.

Her phone chimes, and she glances at the screen and smiles. I steal it from her.

"Fitz!"

It's a text from Evette.

> Happy birthday, Jamie! Hope you're recovering well. Love from me and Gary!

I swipe out of that message and discover messages from Will and Maren as well. Both wishing her a speedy recovery and a happy birthday.

"It's no big deal," she murmurs when I return her phone.

"You could have mentioned it."

"That's uncool. You don't remind people that it's your birthday." She crawls into her bed, leaning on her pillows against the wall.

"What can I do for you?"

"You being here is everything."

I run my hands through my hair. "I'm such a dick."

"Yes. But you're the bigger dick. Or at least you were at the anniversary party." She grins—my girl's poor face. I want to break into the jail and beat the life out of her neighbor.

She nods toward the box of tissues on her desk. "Make me a dozen roses."

"I'll go buy you a dozen roses."

"That's just lazy. I want Calvin Fitzgerald originals."

With not much time before I have to leave for the airport, I sit at the desk and construct a dozen tissue roses, placing them in a blue glass.

"I love watching you do that. It's crack. You're patient and meticulous. What else is in your origami repertoire?"

I return an uneven smile. "This is it. I'm a one-trick pony. My mom taught me."

Jamie smiles with a little emotion in her eyes. "They're beautiful. Come here." She pats the bed beside her.

I sit on the end and lie back with my head on her legs. She fists my shirt in her hand and pulls it up my torso, then traces her finger over my tattoo.

"I wasn't that drunk."

Her finger pauses. "You wanted the tattoo?"

Blowing a long breath out of my nose, I close my eyes without answering her.

"Am I yours?" she murmurs.

It's unfair of her to ask me that on her birthday with my head in her lap and her soft hand stroking my skin. "You're mine."

She brings my hand to the back of her neck. "Are you mine?"

The wall I built many years ago begins to crack. There's another man out there, probably many men, who would love her until the day they die, who would give her the life she wants.

Marriage.

Babies.

Security.

Home by five.

Help with dinner dishes.

Men who would sure as fuck know and remember her birthday.

She should want those men.

Jamie traces the outline of my lips with the pads of her fingers. "If you want to wait and see how my nose heals before you answer, I understand."

God, I fucking love her.

I kiss her palm and wrist. "I'm yours."

Chapter
Thirty-Five

JAYMES

Melissa's online research confirms everything Dwight told me. He has a daughter named Barbara Keane and a sister, Samantha Keane, although she can't find an address for either. But if what I suspect is true, Samantha (my mom) is dead. Melissa also doesn't find records of his parents' deaths or, if they're living, their whereabouts. Sadly, the trail runs cold quickly for Mel because details on Dwight and his family are confined to reports about the fire.

I don't have direct patient contact on my half day back at work. Supposedly not because of my face, but who are they kidding? I look scary. I research Dwight, but his medical records don't shed new light on his past or mine. It's possible I'm missing something, since digging into his past records is not part of my job, and I don't relish the idea of getting caught snooping around.

As my swelling decreases over the following days and my eye begins to look normal again, I manage to use enough makeup to soften the bruising. The only patient to notice anything is Dwight.

"Is someone abusing you?" he asks as I pick up the book at the end of his bed. *California Grizzly.* "I haven't seen you in a while, and nobody would tell me why."

"No one's abusing me. It was an accident. I'm fine."

"A car accident?"

I lift my gaze and take the excuse he's offering me. "Yeah. The airbag got the best of me."

He glowers for a moment. "I'm glad you're okay. I was really worried."

"Thanks." I step back and pull my phone out of my pocket. "Can I show you a picture of someone you might know?"

His brow tightens before he relinquishes a tiny nod.

I'm not sure I'm ready for this. If he doesn't recognize her, all will be right in my world again. If he does . . . well, I don't know what I will feel. I've tried to imagine it, but I can't.

I hold up the picture of my mom.

Dwight doesn't have an immediate reaction. He studies it, taking the phone from me. "She looks so blissful."

The photo was taken on the day I graduated from nursing school.

"Do you recognize her?"

After inspecting the photo for a few more seconds, he glances up at me. "Of course. It's Samantha. Did you talk to her? Is she coming to visit me?"

I think I knew, but it still didn't prepare me for this moment. The noose tightens around my neck. Swallowing past the suffocation, I clear my throat. "Are you sure it's her?"

He scoffs, returning my phone. "She's my sister. Of course I know it's her." He curls his lips and taps his front tooth. "She has a crown on that tooth. Broke it in half when she fell off her bike."

Jesus Christ . . .

"Yeah, s-she told me that."

He stands and heads to the door. "Tell her to come see me."

◆ ◆ ◆

Just as I enter my apartment building after work, Fitz calls me.

"Hey." I make my way down the hall, eyeing the door where the incident happened as I pass it.

"Halloween party at Gary and Evette's on the thirty-first. Can you make it?"

"Uh . . ." I switch to speaker and peek at my schedule. "I work the thirtieth, but I could try to get a flight late that night or early the next morning. The question is, Can *you* make it—or Gary, for that matter?"

"All we can do is try. We might get an early snow."

I open my apartment door and lob my bag on the counter.

"You still there?" he asks.

"Yeah. Do you remember what I told you about the patient I thought could be my uncle?"

"Yes."

I toss my phone onto the bed and retrieve *the box* beside the washer and dryer. "Well, I think it was confirmed today that he is, in fact, my uncle. I showed him a photo of my mom, and he recognized her. He even knew about her crown on the tooth that broke when she fell off her bike." I rip the tape off the box. "But now I wonder, Why did she lie to me?"

"Jaymes, speaking from experience, people lie about their past to prevent pain. Pain to themselves or pain to other people." Fitz leaks his past to me one morsel at a time.

I sit on the bed next to the box and deflate. "I know. She was probably embarrassed that her brother was in a mental hospital. Still, changing her name? That seems a little excessive. He's in California. We were in Florida. Wasn't distance enough?"

"Did he commit a crime?"

"Yes."

"Then perhaps she didn't want to be part of the publicity. What did he do?"

"I'd rather not say yet. I think I've already crossed a line by giving Melissa so much information about him."

"That's fair. How are you feeling?"

I can't help but smile. "Physically? I'm feeling so much better. No surgery is needed for my nose. The swelling is gone. And I can hide most of the residual bruising with makeup."

And my uncle started a fire . . . the kind you must risk your life to extinguish.

"And the asshole who did it?"

I retrieve folders and manila envelopes from the box. "He's been charged with aggravated assault."

"You seem preoccupied. I'll let you go. I have some things to finish up before I can head home."

"Sorry. I'm looking through a box of random documents that belonged to my mom. Trying to find . . ." I blow out a breath. "I don't know." I set a stack of large envelopes on my lap. "I miss you, Fitz. And I'm not saying that to guilt you, I just—"

"I miss you too."

His words wrap around my heart, giving it just what it needs after I showed that photo to Dwight. *Uncle Dwight.*

I open my mouth to say *I love you*, but I stop short of those three words. He knows I love him. We've come too far. I don't want to spook him. I want him to feel my love but not feel suffocated by it.

"I'll book a flight for the end of October."

"Sounds good."

"Bye," I murmur before ending the call.

Just as I suspected when I threw these papers in the box, they're a bunch of tax returns, old rental agreements, and car-loan documents. Another envelope has my father's death and birth certificates.

Karl Hayden Andrews

He was thirty-seven when he died—a computer engineer for NASA.

I don't remember much about him, but I remember watching a shuttle launch from Kennedy Space Center. I remember being on his shoulders. At least, I think I remember. Maybe my mom showed me a picture, and I'm remembering that.

Her death certificate is in its envelope, which I shoved into the box before moving to Missoula. I sift through the papers to see if her birth certificate is there, but I come across mine first and set it aside to put it in a spot where I can find it easily.

I continue searching for her birth certificate and find it folded between her high school and college diplomas.

My chest grows heavier with each passing minute. Both her diplomas and her birth certificate say *Samantha Grace Keane*. Nothing has the name Lauren.

Why did she change her name?

I call Melissa.

"Hey. How are you doing?"

"Good," I say, without sounding believable. "I need to find Barbara Keane, Dwight's daughter. Today, I showed him a picture of my mom, and he knew . . . he knew right away that she was his sister."

"Damn."

"I know. Right? I think I knew before I showed it to him, but I was still taken aback when he confirmed it. So I've been digging through this box of stuff I kept after cleaning out my mom's place. I found her birth certificate and her high school and college diplomas. Her name was Samantha Grace *Keane*. Not Lauren Samantha Mendes, which she told me was her maiden name. The truth's been right here all along."

"Shit, Jamie. That's . . ."

"I know. Trust me. I know. So before I announce a reunion with my uncle Dwight, I need to find Barbara, *if* she can be found. Something tells me she's the only one who can help me make sense of this."

"You need a private investigator. When I searched for Barbara Keane, my head was spinning because I couldn't find any mention of her beyond the articles about the fire. And if she's married, she'll have a different name. But that's beyond me. I'm not an investigator."

"Is that crazy? Getting a private investigator?"

"Crazy is trying to figure this out yourself."

Chapter Thirty-Six

The private investigator I hired is backed up, but he promised to start looking into Barbara Keane as soon as possible. On the one hand, I'm relieved because I'm still struggling to come to grips with the idea that my mom lied to me. On the other hand, I just want it over, the mystery solved, so I can move on with my life.

This trip to Missoula for the weekend is exactly what I need to keep my mind off the debacle of my past.

A few phone calls and daily texts are not enough.

I'm dying to see Fitz. Will and Maren too.

"Oh my god! That face says everything." Maren gives me a mock-pouty expression when I exit the airport in Missoula.

"Hey!" I park my roller bag and hug her. "What look are you referring to? What face?"

She releases me. "I told Fitz and Will I wanted to pick you up. I said you'd be most excited to see me." She takes my roller bag and pulls it toward the parking lot. "But your face dropped the second you spied me."

"That is not true." I clasp her free hand and squeeze it. "I have missed you something fierce."

"But have you missed me as much as say . . . Will?"

I giggle.

"Or, uh . . . who's that other guy you lived with? Oh, Calvin. Surely you didn't miss that asshole." She unlocks her car and deposits my bag in the back before turning with a sly grin.

I bite my lips together. Eyes wide.

"Matching tattoos."

I nod slowly, knowing I must look like a mammoth pile of guilt.

"What's it like to fall in love with grumpy Calvin Fitzgerald? Better yet, how is that possible?"

I shrug. "Why didn't you say anything? We texted so many times after you saw his tattoo. Why didn't you tell me?"

"I didn't know if he'd tell you. And I wanted *you* to tell me. I wanted *you* to trust me with it. I don't expect that of him, but I expected it of you."

I sag.

"No. I'm not mad at all." She gives me a crestfallen smile. "How are you? When I heard about your attack, my heart broke hard. I couldn't imagine who would do such a thing to my friend."

"I'm good." I rotate my face around. "See? You can't even tell, other than that my nose is a little crooked, but it will stay that way."

"It's not crooked. Get in. Will's dying to see you."

I love her game. She's not wrong. I was slightly disappointed when I saw it wasn't Fitz, but this anticipation is incredibly rewarding—a massive adrenaline rush.

"I can't get anything out of Fitz," Maren confesses, pulling out of the parking lot. "He hasn't made a single friendship bracelet with your name. He's not checking his horoscope. And when I ask about his girlfriend, he says, 'Who's that?'"

I laugh. "Well, I'm not sure I'm his girlfriend. I'm not sure he's the girlfriend type."

"So it's just friends with benefits? I don't buy that. That look back there at the airport was the look of a woman getting ready to run into her lover's arms. That was the look that said you were going to have at least one orgasm before making it back to the house." She snickers, not even taking herself seriously.

"I can't talk about this with you. It's too weird. It's like you're his sister." I cover my face and shake my head.

She rests her hand on my leg for a second. "Full disclosure?"

I nod, hands sliding down my face.

"When I spied Fitz's tattoo, I couldn't breathe. I stood right in front of him and put myself in your shoes. And, oh man, did my heart ache. Two of my favorite humans fell in love but weren't together. And if you ever tell Fitz I called him one of my favorite humans, I will deny it."

I grin.

"But it shook me. It shook me because I asked him if he slept with you, and he said yes. Then I asked if he loved you, and he didn't hesitate. Not one damn second, not a tiny breath of hesitation. He said yes so resolutely it felt like a punch to my gut."

My eyes burn with emotion. I can't believe he said that to her. I need to see him. I need to see him *now*. It's hard to sit still. Why doesn't Maren drive faster? She can't tell me how *resolutely* he loves me, and then drive five miles under the speed limit.

I'm dying!

My heart flips like an acrobat when Maren pulls into the driveway behind Will's Bronco.

Will steps onto the porch first, with Fitz behind him, while Maren opens the back. I reach for my suitcase, shaking uncontrollably.

She glances over at me. "Oh my god," she whispers, pressing her hand to her chest. "You're so excited to see him that you're shaking."

I grip the suitcase. "I am not."

Maren laughs. "I love this so much."

"There's our girl. All in one piece, just like we like her." Will holds out his arms as soon as I turn.

I hug him. "Missed you so much."

"Gah! I knew it. I knew it was me who you missed."

Maren laughs.

Will releases me and turns. "Oh, this is Calvin. Our soon-to-be ex-roommate because he breaks the rules."

Fitz eyes me with complete mischief, hands tucked into the front pockets of his charcoal cargo pants. "Jaymes," he says, and his husky voice is so seductive. Or maybe I'm just needing him in a bad way. It's only been five weeks, but that's an eternity without Fitz.

I take several steps and throw myself into his arms.

"Oof!" He chuckles.

"Jesus, I thought you two would play it cool for a bit," Will grumbles.

"How soon can you be inside me?" I murmur in Fitz's ear.

He grabs my legs and lifts me off the ground, guiding them around his waist. "Later," he says to Will and Maren, carrying me around the house to the backyard.

I kiss his neck, nibble his ear, and slide my cheek against his scruffy face. As soon as the shed door closes behind us, he kisses me with so much passion it makes me dizzy. Between kisses, our clothes scatter in a mess on the floor.

When I'm down to just my panties, I kiss his chest and unbutton his pants. "I've missed you . . . missed this," I murmur over his abs.

Before I can slide his pants down his legs, he guides me back, crawling over my body, kissing me, and palming my breast. His hand then slides down my stomach, dipping into the front of my panties.

I grab his face. "Don't make me wait." My words are breathy and impatient.

Fitz grins. "Wait for what?" He kisses his way down my body, kneeling on the floor at the end of the bed while peeling off my panties.

"I n-need you." I try to sit up, desperate to pull him on top of me.

Instead, he rests his hands on my knees, spreading my legs and dipping his head between them.

"Oh god." I flop back onto the bed, one hand finding his hair, my other claiming a fistful of sheets at my side.

Something between a hum and a moan escapes him while he licks and sucks me intimately with complete abandon and unhinged seduction.

I want this, but I want him inside me when it happens. My need for him to fill me outweighs my need for a release.

I moan. Yes, a *moan*. Who am I kidding? He's always made me moan.

My body wriggles and twists to get him to stop because I haven't felt this level of hunger from him, and it's unraveling me too quickly. "C-Calvin Fitzgerald?"

I manage to get him to lift his head.

Hungry eyes.

Wet lips.

He slides off his pants and briefs, keeping his gaze on me the whole time, while I creep on my knees toward him.

"What do you need, baby?" He nibbles at my neck, his hands on my ass, then my breasts, and in my hair like he wants to touch me everywhere at once.

I take his erection in my hand. "I need you *inside* me."

The second my back contacts the mattress, he grabs my thighs and thrusts into me.

"Oh god!" I grip his ass, taking a second to acclimate. "Don't rush it," I say just before he sucks on my bottom lip.

With a strained laugh, he releases it. "I'll see what I can do."

I grin, and he kisses me.

Everything about us feels right. We fit. The Capricorn and the Virgo. Does he feel it? Did he feel this—whatever invisible thing *this* is—from the day we met? I did.

Does he know I've never felt so loved? Yet, he's never said those words directly to me. He thinks he's broken, but he's not. He's molded, sculpted, and perfectly created just for me.

He's mine.

"Jaymes . . ." He runs out of breath, hand on my ass, guiding me so that we fit as close as possible while pumping into me at a quickening pace.

I curl my fingers into the thick muscles along his backside as my lips part in a silent cry.

His face tenses, neck stretched, body ridged: a beautiful masterpiece—the finest specimen.

He lowers his body to lie flush to mine, and we breathe together. I know I'll run out of oxygen soon from his weight. But for now, I'm content stroking his hair while his fingers ghost along my hip and leg.

◆ ◆ ◆

It's the ultimate walk of shame.

We enter the house's back door to find Will and Maren waiting for us in the living room. Will's watching football, and Maren's scrolling on her phone.

Fitz doesn't skip a beat. He acts like he just got home from work, heading straight to the coffee machine and tossing in a K-cup. I, on the other hand, shoot Will and Maren a cringey smile while making a beeline upstairs for the bathroom to clean up.

After *handling* things in the cleanup department, I make what feels like a second walk of shame back down the stairs.

Maren spies me first and smiles. "How was it?"

Fitz, parked at the counter with his back to Maren, coughs on his coffee.

I shrug a shoulder. "It was fine."

Will snorts while I pass Fitz to get a glass of water.

"What's everyone wearing to the party tonight?" I ask.

"Will and I are going as Jack Skellington and Sally," Maren says enthusiastically.

"The Nightmare Before Christmas?" I laugh. "Very cool." I inspect Fitz.

"Don't look at him," Will says. "He never dresses up. *Ever.*"

I can't help the sour expression on my face. "You invited me to a Halloween party, but you're not dressing up?"

He pauses his coffee mug at his lips and inspects me like he's still thinking about what happened in the shed. "Correct."

"That's not okay, Fitz."

He grins. "Do you have a costume?"

"Absolutely. Wicked Kitty."

"Come again?" He scrutinizes me.

"Black leather teddy. Black thigh-high boots. Ears. Mask. Whip."

"That sounds hot," Maren says.

Fitz shoots her a look, but I don't think it's a kind one.

"I was thinking you could dress up as a smoke jumper." He gives me a tight grin.

My forearms rest on the counter, so we're face to face. "I'll go as a smoke jumper if you go as the wicked kitty. Someone's wearing the wicked-kitty costume."

"I'll pay you a hundred dollars if you go as the wicked kitty," Will offers.

"I'll add an extra hundred," Maren chimes in with a laugh.

"Want me to call Gary and Evette to see if they want in on this?" I ask. "You could make some good money tonight."

"Do you think the leather teddy would fit me?" Fitz scratches his chin.

"No." I mirror his chin scratching. "Perhaps I should be the one to wear it."

"And I'll go as a smoke jumper."

"Come on." I grab his arm. "Let's scrounge you a costume at the eleventh hour."

"This is a terrible idea," he grumbles while I pull him toward the door.

"Grab your keys," I say. "We'll be back."

Maren and Will laugh. "Good luck."

Chapter Thirty-Seven

CALVIN

"Don't give me that look," Jamie says.

I'm not sure what look she's referencing. Is it the there's-no-fucking-way-I'm-letting-you-wear-that-leather-teddy-out-in-public look? Or is it the I-can't-believe-I-let-you-talk-me-into-this-mouse-costume look? The same look works for both. Either way, I'm rethinking this party idea.

I don't know if my long tail, pink nose, and whiskers do it for her, but I've never wanted to fuck a pussy so bad in my life. This woman looks more like a dominatrix than a cat.

"If you would have planned ahead of time, there would have been a bigger selection of costumes." She practices whipping my pillow while I sulk in front of the mirror on my wall.

Her leather teddy barely covers her boobs. And the bottom of it doesn't fully cover her ass.

"But let's be honest, had there been a bigger selection, I still would have bought you the mouse costume. You have a few wrongs to right in the mouse community. Think of this as community service or a form of rehabilitation." Again, she whips my pillow.

I adjust my erection so I don't look like a mouse with a tumor. And yes, she bought the costume because I refused.

"Let's go so we can hurry and leave the party." I head toward the stairs just as Will opens his bedroom door dressed in his Jack Skellington costume.

He presses a fist to his mouth and sniggers. "Jesus, what the fuck, man?"

Before I can knock out his teeth, the wicked kitty steps out of my room. Will's eyebrows crawl up his forehead as he drops his fist.

"Will! I love your Jack Skellington," she squeals, jumping up and down.

"You look . . ." He whistles and shakes his head.

"Don't look at her," I warn just as she spins in a circle. "And don't spin around." I grab her shoulders and lead her down the stairs.

As soon as we get to the party, I fetch a drink from the cooler in the backyard. Alcohol is my best friend tonight. It will take the edge off the snickering behind my back.

Gary, Captain America, rests his elbow on my shoulder. Leaning against me like a pillar, he nods toward Jamie, her usual life-of-the-party self, with a group of women, including Evette. She certainly garners a lot of attention for someone who claims not to be a people person.

"As if showing up to my party in this mouse onesie didn't already scream 'pussy whipped.' You actually brought a pussy with a whip."

I don't want to laugh, but I can't help my grin. "Shut the fuck up."

Gary cackles. "Seriously, man. I know she thinks she's a cat, but she's—"

"Don't say it."

A wet dream.

"Is she coming back to Missoula after her assignment in California?"

"I doubt it. She wants to travel the country. Why would she come back here?"

Gary stops using me as a post and turns toward me. "You. Ya dickhead."

"She's here now, but she's not living here." I take a long swig of my beer.

"Don't you want to *be* with her?"

I nod toward her. "Here we are. See how easy that was?"

He shakes his head. "She's in California. What happens when she's someplace like Maine, working nights, less time off, longer and more expensive flights, and you're in the middle of a long fire season? What kind of relationship is that?"

After staring at her for a few seconds, I shrug. "It is what it is."

"Dang, Fitz. Whatever you do, don't say those words to her. Women don't like aloofness. Todd, what the hell are you supposed to be?" Gary heads toward the garage door, where Todd's gesturing to his chest, but I'm not sure why.

Wicked Kitty, with her painted face, makes eye contact with me and worms her way in my direction from the opposite end of the porch. "Cheese?" She holds out her plate.

"You think that's funny?"

She pops a cube into her mouth. "It's not *not* funny."

"What are your plans after you're done in San Bernardino?"

"Don't know yet. Why?"

"Just wondering."

A tiny vein along her forehead pushes to the surface. "You're a locked vault with some things, and with other things, you're so transparent it's cringeworthy."

"What's that supposed to mean?" I steal a spiderweb pretzel from her plate.

"You're scared to death that I'm going to move back to Missoula, and you'll have to make a real decision to commit." She turns.

I ogle her scantily clad body as it distances itself from me, getting lost in the sea of costumes. Am I supposed to go after her? I don't know how this works.

Pinching my lips, the mouse chases the cat to the porch and into the house.

"What did you do?" Maren eyes me while I shoulder my way through the kitchen.

I brush her off with a quick headshake.

As I start up the stairs, a scarecrow grabs me. I'm pretty sure it's Evette. She points to the front door.

"Thanks," I mumble, changing directions.

A few late arrivals make their way up the drive, illuminated with LED pumpkins. My cat is walking down the sidewalk.

I chase after her. "We're two miles from the house. It's cold. Are you really walking all the way in that getup?"

"I know I don't pack out of fires with a hundred and fifty pounds on my back, but I'm capable of walking two miles in fifty-degree weather."

"Can we talk?" I keep several steps behind her.

She whips around. "I don't know, Fitz. Can we talk?"

I hold up my hands. "Is this just about what I asked you? How did we go from what happened in the shed earlier today to this?"

"Exactly!" She throws her arms in the air and nearly takes out my eye with her whip. "How can we have that kind of sex, that kind of passion, and hours later, you ask me that question? The tattoos. The surprise visit. The trip after I was assaulted. The invitation to come for this party." She shakes her head. "How can all that lead to you worrying that I might want to be with you? Really *be with you.*"

My lips part to respond, and she holds up a hand.

"Before you say one word, I need you to know that I'm not saying I'm planning to move back here immediately. I do, in fact, have career goals. I do want to travel and make money to buy a house. I'm twenty-six and in no hurry to settle down into a life of marriage and family. However, it would be really fucking nice if the guy I love would at least pretend to want to be with me." She shoves my chest.

"Goddammit! I do want to be with you. And I want my awful fucking past to disappear from my mind forever. I want a different life with a different set of circumstances. But I don't want to pretend with you." I rake my fingers through my hair and lace them behind my neck. "I don't know what kind of cruel god would bring you into my life. Even if I deserve to see what I can never truly have, even if I deserve to suffer, *you* don't deserve anything short of . . ." Shaking my head repeatedly, I tear at my stupid costume until I manage to escape its confines. "Everything." My shoulders curl inward, ripped costume in one hand, my other hand balled into a fist. "You deserve everything, Jaymes. You deserve *everything* beautiful in this world. You deserve *everything* I want to give you but can't."

She wipes tears from her painted face, smearing it everywhere. "You're right. I deserve everything," she seethes. "So do the right fucking thing, and give it to me."

Stepping closer, she bravely lifts her chin despite her trembling lips. "It was a car accident. It was tragic, but *so* many things are tragic. I don't understand. You're too strong. It doesn't make sense. My dad suffered a stroke. That's tragic. My mom died of cancer. Tragic. *Life* is tragic." She wipes more tears. "Give me *everything*." Her hand covers her mouth, and she swallows hard, swallows her sob, swallows the pain.

I'm her pain.

"Don't love me like a martyr," she whispers thickly, strangled with emotion. "Love me like a hero. Jump without looking back." Her eyes pinch shut, releasing more tears while she inhales shakily. "Fight for me. Save *us*."

Chapter Thirty-Eight

JAYMES

Fitz has no idea how much I need him right now. I have an uncle I never knew about. A whole life I never knew existed. Lies that don't make sense. The void I've felt for years, growing up without a father figure. So I desperately need something true in my life. Something—someone—I can call my safe place in this confusing world.

He's already taken my heart; now I need him to do right by it.

"Let's go home," he murmurs, finding my hand and leading me back to the truck.

My heart's hemorrhaging. Is this it? Are we at an impasse?

"I'm going to shower," he says as we enter the dark house.

"Me too." I follow him up the stairs.

He heads straight into his bathroom and shuts the door with no invitation to join him. It feels like the beginning of the end.

After my shower, I dry my hair and stare at my reflection in the mirror. Will I regret this? Why can't I be like Maren and Will and respect Fitz's need not to talk about his painful past?

"In here," he says as I step toward the stairs. He's sitting on the end of his bed, arms on his knees, hands folded.

With a shaky breath, I pad my way into his room and sit on an old metal chest by the window.

We remain idle in silence for a minute, maybe two.

"I fight fires because that's where I see them." His words are ominous, imparting a sense of foreboding.

And for a second, I consider asking him to stop. I second-guess my need to know because I'm terrified this could be more than I'm ready to hear.

"It's an awful way to die. The smoke. The heat. The panic." He rests his head in his hands. "All because a crazy man started a fire to kill a fucking bear."

My.

Heart.

Stops.

What is he doing? Why is he saying this?

"It engulfed thirty-two thousand acres. Seventeen people died, including five firefighters. My mom. My dad. My sister."

The room spins just like my mind. I'm not hearing this. It's impossible.

I slowly shake my head.

This is not right. That's not what happened. Edith told me . . . *Fitz* said . . .

Didn't he?

He lifts his head with pain etched into his face. "I see my sister the most." He swallows hard, eyes reddening. "She's screaming. She's telling me to stop the fire. And she looks behind her, like she's looking for our parents. Then she cries." He pinches the bridge of his nose. "And sometimes I hear her whisper 'Thank you' when the fire's out."

Jesus . . .

Words don't exist. I'm afraid to speak. I'm so scared to take a breath or even blink. I'm gutted, decimated—a hollow shell of flesh and bones.

Fitz waits between slow blinks. He waits for me to say something.

Something sympathetic.

Something soothing.

Something that one lover would say to another.

Is this it? Is this the guilt and embarrassment from which my mom tried to protect me? The crushing feeling that accountability has been transferred to me?

"I don't know what happiness looks like," he says, as if that's all there is to say—as if that explains everything. And perhaps it does. He's no longer an enigma. Calvin Fitzgerald is a survivor of unspeakable life circumstances.

He can't give me *everything* because he has nothing left to give.

Tears sting my eyes.

"But I know what grief looks like," he continues. "And I know how it feels. I wouldn't wish that upon anyone. One day"—he bows his head and runs his hands through his hair—"I'm afraid I'll fall from the air *just* to trek into the fire. No tools. No lines to dig. I'll follow my sister because it wasn't fair that I lived, and she . . ." He presses his lips together, slowly shaking his head and closing his eyes.

She died.

I stand with weak knees, trudging through a cruel fate to reach him. He spreads his legs and hugs me. My cheek rests on the top of his head.

"What happened to the man who started the fire?" I ask. It's an awful question, but I have to know for certain. Maybe Dwight Keane isn't the only man in history to have started a fire to kill a bear.

Fitz draws a deep breath and releases it with his forehead pressed to my chest. "He was found not guilty for reason of insanity. I'm sure he's drugged up and strapped to a bed somewhere. Or dead. I hope he's dead."

I stiffen for a few seconds before releasing a controlled breath. "I'm sure he never intended for so many people to die."

Fitz lifts his head. "What?" His face contorts.

"I'm sure he wasn't thinking clearly. How could you be?"

"Don't fucking do that. I know you work with the mentally ill, but *don't* try to defend him to me. Why would you do that?"

257

"I . . . I'm not trying to do that."

One look.

With one look, I know this will end us if I let it—if I tell him the truth.

He never needs to know. I wish *I* didn't know. When I get home, I will call the private investigator and tell him to forget it. I don't need to find Barbara. If she doesn't care about her father, why should I? I won't be in San Bernardino forever. I can treat Dwight like any other patient. This will all fade away. I don't need an uncle.

"I'm sorry. I shouldn't have said that." I press my hands to his cheeks. "What you've been through is unimaginable." I kiss him slowly before resting my forehead on his. "But don't march into that fire, Fitz. They're not waiting for you to die; they're waiting for you to live."

He pulls me onto the bed and shuts off the nightstand light. Then he hugs me like a security blanket until his breaths slow and his body relaxes.

I can't relax. There is no security for me. I'm still awake when Maren and Will come home from the party. Their hushed chatter lasts for a while before their bedroom doors click shut.

And still, I can't sleep. Fitz's confession plays in my mind, and I question everything in the universe. I question the meaning of life. Is it really just a random chain of events? A ping-ponging set of circumstances? If destiny is nothing more than a cliché used to sell books and movies, then how did I find my uncle? Is that a coincidence? And how have I fallen in love with a man so intimately connected to my newfound family?

It doesn't make sense. It's not destiny. It's a nightmare.

I worm my way out of bed without waking Fitz, and I tiptoe down the stairs, feeling thirsty, anxious, and on the verge of hyperventilating. This won't work. I'm not a good liar. I can't pretend I'm not hiding this massive secret from Fitz.

I gulp a glass of water and stand at the sliding door overlooking the shed in the soft glow of the adjacent streetlight. I was so drawn to this place when I saw the pictures. It *felt* right. It felt like my destiny.

The floor creaks behind me, and I startle.

"What are you doing?" Fitz's groggy voice ghosts along my ear with his lips. His hands slide around my waist.

I continue to stare out the window while his touch brings a rush of tears to my eyes. I rub them like I'm tired, the wet emotion smearing across my cheeks. "Couldn't sleep," I murmur.

"No?" He gathers my nightshirt in one hand while his other hand slips down the front of my panties.

I close my eyes and rest the back of my head against him, hoping for a reprieve from the leaky emotions. I need this.

The distraction.

The escape.

The connection to the person I fear losing the most.

I press one hand flat to the window while my other guides one of his to my breast. Yes. I need this, to get lost in how he makes me feel so alive, so wanted and needed.

"Baby, spread your legs for me."

"Fitz," I moan. "Say that again."

He could turn me on with nothing more than his lips at my ear, whispering dirty words. They're an electrical charge in my veins, dizzying and powerful.

"Baby." He slides his leg between mine, nudging them apart. "Spread your legs for me."

With my arousal coating his middle two fingers, he works them inside me, drawing a sharp gasp from my open mouth—the heel of his hand rubbing my clit. His other hand squeezes my breast and tugs at my nipple until it's hard between his fingers.

"Give me your mouth," he says just before his tongue draws a line from my shoulder to my jaw.

I turn my head as far as I can, and he covers my mouth with his. Our tongues collide, making deep strokes together. I gasp for a breath and drop my chin to my chest, both hands pressed to the glass.

He removes his briefs and slides my panties down my legs. Guiding his warm, wet erection between my legs, he whispers in my ear, "Shh . . ."

I grunt, biting my lips together when he drives into me. My knees lock, and my nails scrape along the window. His hands take the weight of my breasts, pulling my back a little straighter as we fall into a rhythm. Each of his breaths grows louder and harsher. And I lose myself in him and the life I want with him.

I fall first.

Muscles spasming. Knees buckling. My jaw slacks in a silent scream while my heart thrashes around in my chest.

"Oh fuckfuckfuck . . ." Both of his hands move to my hips as he grinds into me, stills, and collapses forward so his hands are pressed to the window above mine. He pants at my ear, body relaxed and replete.

When we catch our breath, I turn into him, and he wraps me in his arms. His hand ghosts up my back, beneath my hair, and his fingers stroke my neck.

He's mine.

Fitz says he loves me in silent but humongous, heart-wrenching ways.

Chapter Thirty-Nine

Last week, Fitz drove me to the airport and kissed me goodbye. We parted with the promise of spending Thanksgiving together in Missoula, including Edith, while Maren and Will are with their families.

I've left two messages with the private investigator, asking him to abort his search, but he hasn't returned my call.

It's hard to be around Dwight without feeling different. Whether his ramblings seem coherent or complete gibberish, they are impossible for me to ignore. More than that, it's difficult not to ask him more questions.

In fact, it's impossible.

"Did Samantha have children?" I ask.

Today, he's not well. The last shift reported him vomiting during the night. His skin is paler than usual, and he hasn't been out of bed today. But he's trying to eat some fruit for me.

Deep lines spread across his forehead. "No. She couldn't have kids."

"No?" I sit on the edge of his bed.

"No." He sets his partially eaten food aside and scoots down, pulling the blanket over him.

"Do you know why?"

"I . . . I don't remember."

"That's okay. You rest." I gather his uneaten food. "I'll check in on you later."

He closes his eyes and mumbles something.

After work, I heat a can of chili—a chili that doesn't compare to the Fitzgerald family recipe—and video message Fitz.

"Yes?" he answers. I don't see him, just an open book hiding his face, but at a weird angle that makes it hard to read the title. He's at the kitchen counter with his phone, most likely propped against a beer bottle.

"Whatcha reading? Maybe I can tell you how the story ends."

He eyes me over the top of the book with a single peaked brow.

"Is it a mystery?"

"No."

"Fantasy?"

"No."

"Romance?"

"No."

I sigh. "I give up."

He lowers the book. "Have you read a lot of books about World War II generals? What are the chances of you being able to spoil the ending?"

"I've read zero books about World War II generals. Nice to see you too."

Fitz slides a receipt into his book and sets it aside. "Did you have a good day?" He laces his fingers together on the counter and offers a goofy, toothy grin.

"It was good. Thanks for asking. Yours?"

"Prescribed burning. It was all mind-blowingly titillating."

"You're a little frisky tonight. Frisky Fitz. Why is that? Does reading about World War II generals get you hard?"

"What makes you think I'm hard?"

I set down my soup spoon and shrug off my shirt.

"Jesus. What are you . . ." He picks up his phone and heads up the stairs. "Will could have been on the sofa. Or young children could have been watching."

I giggle, returning to my chili in my soft pink bra and black pants. "Whose children?"

"Sometimes I mentor young firefighters."

"Liar."

He shuts his bedroom door. "And I bring them to the house for my special chili instead of that crap out of a can you're eating. And why is that? How is it that you make sourdough bread from scratch but eat chili out of a can?"

"We're not done talking about your imaginary mentoring, but if you must know, I'm not a cook. I'm a baker, like my mom was a baker, not a cook. That's what makes us a good match. I bake, and you cook."

He hums, but I'm unsure if he's agreeing with me or giving me the hum that's his verbal eye roll.

"Speaking of my mom. Today, I came across some information that makes me wonder if I was adopted."

"Sorry, you're going to have to put your shirt back on, and I'm going to have to stop stroking my dick if we're going to have a serious conversation."

I spit out my chili the second the spoon reaches my lips. "Stop." Wiping my mouth, I laugh. And I also thread my arms through my shirt and pull it over my head.

He brushes his hand on his shirt like he's wiping it off.

I shake my head. "Only the king of SPAM would masturbate to a can of soup."

Fitz chuckles. "As you were saying. You think you were adopted?"

I hate this line. I want to share my life with Fitz, but there is a hard line that I'm scared out of my mind to cross. If he knew about Dwight, what would he do? My chest aches as I try to imagine it.

"Since my parents are dead, does it matter? However, the familial health history might be important if I have kids someday." Instant regret punches me the second I put a period in that sentence.

Fitz's crestfallen face says it all.

I sigh, setting my spoon in my half-empty bowl of soup. "I can't keep pretending that I don't want to leave that door open. Tiptoeing around you on this subject is exhausting."

He rubs the back of his neck, face tense. "Jaymes—"

"No. I don't want to hear it. You're ten years older. So what? You're afraid of dying. So what? That makes you human. You got a vasectomy. So what? That can be reversed. Or we could use a sperm donor. Or—"

"Jaymes, we're either a day at a time or nothing. I won't ask you to tiptoe and pretend if you don't ask it of me. You know where I stand. And if my grandma hadn't had a stroke, she would fully support me, because she was the one who told me to stay single. Never have kids. No one to miss you so much they try to take their own life the way she did after losing my parents, my sister, and my grandpa. Want to know why I was homeschooled? My family died. And it was so devastating, I couldn't go back to school."

I deflate. At every turn, I learn something new, something tragic.

Will I ever see Fitz with all the puzzle pieces in place?

"I'm sorry." I lift my gaze to the screen. "Still, you could change your mind," I murmur.

He doesn't argue, but the resistance remains etched into his handsome face. With a heavy sigh, he nods slowly. "Sure," he whispers. "Anything's possible, even if it's *highly* improbable."

I'll take a 1 percent chance. He can hold on to his ninety-nine. Fitz has been the object of my affection since the day we met. I know the parts of him that he's too afraid to see. We wouldn't be us. We wouldn't fit like we do if he weren't meant to live—really *live*—this life with me.

"Maybe we both need to let go of the past," I say, with a tone of surrender. "And maybe that won't change the future, change who we are. But if we stay tethered to the past, how will we know if, in the future, we can fly?"

"Baby, I already know I can fly." The beautiful hint of a smile steals his lips, and I know we're good. For now, we're good.

I remove my shirt again, and my bra.

His eyebrows slide up his forehead as I continue eating my soup.

"We're done with the serious talk for tonight. Why don't you rub one out while I finish my chili and make my online chess move? Melissa and I have been stuck on this game for a week."

"Sucks being homeschooled," he says.

I hear a noise while I stir my chili. "Is your hand back down your pants again?"

"Fuck yeah."

I laugh. "I love you, Calvin Fitzgerald."

He tips his head back, eyes closed. "I know you do."

Chapter Forty

During my jewelry-making class, my phone vibrates with a call. It's the private investigator I hired. Since I no longer care to pursue my search for Barbara, I don't bother to answer and disturb the class. Afterward, I return his call.

"Nathan Moore," he answers.

"Hi, Mr. Moore. This is Jaymes Andrews. Sorry I missed your call. I was in a class. Did you get my messages? I'm no longer interested in finding—"

"Yes," he interrupts. "My apologies. I had a family emergency. I meant to contact you earlier with an update."

"It's fine. As I said in my messages, I no longer want to pursue this."

"I understand. However, I think you need to know what I found," he says with gravity to his words.

I sigh. "Okay. What did you find?"

"Can you come by my office?"

"Can't you just tell me over the phone?" I glance at the time on my dashboard. I want to get in a workout and grab some groceries.

"I'd rather not."

"If Barbara's dead, you can tell me. I've never met her. I can take the news."

"She's alive. That's why we need to talk."

I massage my neck, regretting calling him in the first place. "I can come now."

◆ ◆ ◆

Nathan's musty-smelling office feels more like the workplace of an NFL general manager. It's jammed wall to wall with sports memorabilia: photos, jerseys in glass cases, and two signed footballs atop a bookshelf.

"Thanks for coming, Ms. Andrews."

"Jamie." I smile, shaking his hand.

"Please, have a seat. Can I get you something to drink? Coffee? Water? Whiskey?" He offers a veneered smile while stroking his hand along his nearly bald head like it's a nervous habit.

"I'm good. Thanks." I sit in a worn leather chair on the opposite side of his scratched oak desk while he closes his laptop and pulls a legal-size envelope from a desktop file sorter.

"I must say, once I started digging into this for you, it was impossible to stop. I'm used to looking into cheating spouses, identity theft, doing background checks . . . things of that nature. But this was quite the plot twist. So I did some extra work in case you need help connecting the dots."

"Can I just interrupt you for a minute?" I lean forward, resting my hands on his desk and drumming my fingers. "I've decided the revelation of discovering Dwight Keane is my uncle is more than enough. In fact, I wish I didn't know it. I wish I would not have taken this job in San Bernardino. I'm sure Barbara Keane, if that's still her last name, has good reasons for cutting all ties with her father. I can think of a big one. But I'm done. That's between her and Dwight. My mother went out of her way to protect me from this whole situation. I think I should trust her judgment and let sleeping dogs lie."

"Ms. Andrews—" Nathan shakes his head. *"Jamie."* He offers an apologetic smile. "I'm not sure what has changed your mind since you hired me, but given Dwight Keane's history, I understand why you might want to distance yourself from the tragic situation. However, since you're twenty-six, I think full disclosure of your past would probably be the wisest decision, should you ever need to know more about your family for health reasons."

"She's sick," I say with a cautious undertone. "Barbara's sick. Isn't she?"

Nathan's forehead wrinkles. "No. Well, I don't believe so." When he leans forward, bringing a slight tobacco stench with him, I sit back in my chair.

Something feels *heavy*. It's just a feeling that I can't shake.

"Jamie, after Dwight was committed, his sister took custody of Barbara."

I shake my head. "Did he have more than one sister?"

"No."

"Well . . ." My head spins. "I don't know—I don't understand. That would have been my mom. How long did she have custody?"

He slides a stack of papers from the envelope. "Samantha Grace Keane changed her name to Lauren Samantha Mendes. She married Karl Hayden Andrews."

"My dad."

Nathan glances up at me. "After Samantha married, a judge also granted her request to change Barbara's name." He doesn't take his eyes off me. "Barbara Keane is now Jaymes Lanette Andrews."

My lips part to speak.

Nothing.

"Samantha, or *Lauren*, was your aunt. Karl was the man she married. But they weren't your biological parents. You are the only child of Dwight and Annie Keane."

I stare at copies of birth certificates, social security cards, and court documents. It makes no sense. He missed something. He messed up.

Every time I open my mouth to speak, the words die. I'm too numb to think, let alone say anything. This isn't real. I'm not hearing him correctly. He's wrong.

"Annie's parents died before the accident. She has two brothers. Kalen is fifty-two. He lives in Idaho with his wife. They have three adult children. Ryan is the other brother. He's forty-seven and lives in Wyoming—no wife or kids. Dwight's parents are still alive. Waylon and Aubrey live in Flagstaff, Arizona."

No. My mom said her parents were dead.

She said a lot of things that weren't true.

Nathan hands me a tissue. I stare at it for several seconds before I realize my face is wet with tears. I'm silently bleeding out in front of a stranger, but it doesn't hurt. I feel *nothing*.

"What happened to your family was a horrific tragedy. But from everything I've pieced together, I can only guess your well-being was a priority. Your aunt gave you the life you deserved. She took on a huge responsibility. Living a lie is a painful existence."

Stripped of confidence, all coherent thought, and my identity, I find my legs. His words carry measurable weight, and it's hard to stand beneath such a heavy reality.

Nathans stands, too, sliding the papers back into the envelope. "Do you have any questions?"

Everything feels lethargic; even my gaze takes forever to find his face. "I have *many* questions." I blink several times. "But the person who can answer them is dead."

His expression wilts. "I'm sorry," he whispers.

Sorry. I let the word bounce around in my head. Sorry for what?

A bear eating my mother?

My father starting a fire that killed people, including Fitz's family?

Living a lie?

Falling in love with a man I can never have?

Losing the woman who I thought was my mother?

He hands me the envelope. It takes me a few seconds to reach for it. I don't want it. But what I want doesn't matter anymore. My life is simply *what is*.

Chapter Forty-One

We don't choose our family.

I conjure a dozen ways to make sense of this and another dozen excuses to let the past go and pretend it's not real.

The previous shift said Dwight was agitated during the night. This morning, he's medicated and barely responsive. I pull up a chair next to his bed. He cracks open his eyes, and they're lifeless. My heart climbs up my throat, swelling, aching, *suffocating*.

Maybe yesterday's revelation shouldn't matter. I'd reconciled with the idea that he was my uncle. Somehow, I'd managed to distance myself from him.

Uncles rarely nurture or raise their nieces. Memories made with uncles might include holiday gatherings, perhaps a shared vacation with cousins.

But fathers, at least in my dreams, they create life. They blow raspberries on little tummies because they love the sound of giggling. They hold tiny hands when they cross the street. They carry miniature versions of themselves on their shoulders—with love and pride.

Fathers read bedtime stories and chase away monsters.

They dry tears and kiss boo-boos.

Fathers are guardians of hearts and protectors of innocence.

I rest my hand on my father's cheek.

"Barbara," he murmurs while his eyes drift shut.

Tears spill down my face, and I choke on a sob.

"Watch out . . . f-for bears." His froggy voice carries so much agony that my heart can barely take it.

I imagine the intense level of *mad* love he possessed for my mom to have lost his mind, all sense of self-preservation, and all touch with reality to do something so egregious.

"I will," I breathe, stroking my thumb along his cheek. My head rests on the edge of his bed. "I w-will." Everything blurs behind unrelenting tears as I shake with silent sobs.

By Saturday, I have four missed calls from Fitz and a string of unanswered texts.

After half a glass of wine, my hand stops shaking enough to press his name on my phone.

"What is going on?" he asks. No "hi" or "how are you?"

Living a lie is a painful existence.

So is losing the person you love most in the world. I've lost Fitz; I just can't bring myself to tell him yet. Every day, I wake up hoping it is nothing more than a bad dream.

"I've had a cold. Sorry. I've been sleeping and working. How are you?"

"Good. Hope you're feeling better."

"Yeah. I'm getting there."

"Are you still okay with flying with my grandma to Missoula for Thanksgiving?"

I pour a second glass of wine. Fuck, this hurts.

"She's never been to Missoula to visit me. No pressure, but she's really excited."

I bat away a few tears and take an ample gulp of wine before humming, "Mm-hmm. I've got it."

"You sure everything's okay? I know I screwed up Halloween with my attitude and by dumping the entirety of my past onto you. I have no clue how to navigate this. There's a hundred percent chance I'll fuck this up."

Swallowing a sob, I bite my lips together and fight for an even breath and a brave, steady voice. "You won't. Have you"—I wipe the last few tears—"been putting out any fires?"

"I've only jumped once since Halloween."

"How are Maren and Will?"

"Annoying."

I find something to pass off as a tiny laugh. "And Evette and Gary?"

"Old and boring."

Again, I laugh, but this time it's real. It also pulls more tears from me. Fitz has finally decided to give us a chance. A true chance. He's opened up to me. We're spending a holiday together with his grandma. And all I can think about is the family I have. The ones who let me go. The ones who have died. The *one* who is living with demons. When I redirect my thoughts to Fitz again, I search for the words.

I contemplate the right time.

The right place.

There's never the right place or time to destroy something beautiful. I'm sure that's how Fitz felt when Dwight started the fire that killed his family.

"Tell Edith I'll call her after I purchase the tickets. I need to make sure my time off is approved."

"I'll tell her."

Taking one of his tissue flowers from the blue glass, I twirl it between my fingers. "I need to shower and wash a load of laundry."

"No phone sex tonight?"

Emotion hits me again, and it takes a few seconds to regain my composure. "Do something special for Mrs. Wilke. I bet she's felt pretty neglected." Pinching the bridge of my nose, I close my eyes. Everything hurts. I know life isn't easy. Bad things happen to good people. Not everything has a rhyme or reason.

Still, I feel like I'm being punished. Was I an awful person in another life? Or is this a sins-of-the-father kind of fate?

"Mrs. Wilke it is." Fitz chuckles.

This is where I say something more. A jab. A snarky comment. Something inappropriate. Yet I have nothing.

He begins to speak, but my phone cuts out for a second. I glance at the screen. "Sorry. Melissa's calling me. Talk later?"

"Sure," he says.

"Bye." I switch over to Melissa. "Hey."

"Why have you been ignoring my calls?" she asks.

"I've been ignoring all calls and texts."

"Why? What's wrong?"

"Wrong," I echo her, playing with that word. *Is* something wrong?

"Jamie, you're acting weird. What's wrong? You're scaring me. Did something happen to Calvin?"

"No," I mutter. "Well, sort of."

"What?"

I set the tissue rose back in the blue glass. "His parents and sister died in the fire that Dwight started."

"Oh my god," she breathes. "Does he know Dwight's your uncle?"

I laugh a little. A new round of tears burns my eyes, and I laugh a little more—a little maniacally. "Oh, Melissa, if only it were that. It's not *that*."

"Jaymes, what's going on? You seem—"

"Like I should admit myself to the hospital where I work? Like I fell in love with the perfect man for me? Like I did the impossible, and I convinced him to fall in love with me? Or like the private investigator found Barbara Keane?"

"Jaymes—"

"Because he did!" I boom, stabbing my fingers through my hair while my other hand grips the phone tighter. "He found Barbara fucking

Keane. But it wasn't easy because her name was changed. Wanna know what to? Do you?" I pace my tiny apartment.

"Stop. Breathe, Jamie—" Melissa begs in a nervous tone.

"Jaymes. Lanette. Andrews. *I* am Barbara Keane. Dwight is *my* father." My whole body shakes, hijacked with uncontrolled emotions. I pace faster, a storm of blinding, angry tears flooding my eyes. "FUCK!" I grab the blue glass of tissue flowers and hurl it across the room. It shatters against the wall. I fall to my knees, bending at the waist. "A-and . . . ," I sob, "Fitz will never understand. And I-I d-don't know how to t-tell him he fell in l-love with me for n-nothing."

"Jaymes . . . ," Melissa whispers. Though she's on the other side of the country, I *feel* her voice. I feel her arms around me. I see the tears in her eyes. And I know how badly she wants to make this better for me. However, her silence says it all.

Nothing can make this better.

Chapter Forty-Two

CALVIN

In two days, Jamie's arriving in Missoula with my grandma. And I'm pretty sure she's still upset about Halloween because we haven't talked more than a handful of times in the past few weeks. She's been busy or tired or any number of other excuses that haven't sat right with me.

It's time to jump. Go big. Show her my whole fucking heart. She needs to know that the only thing I fear now is not being with her.

But first, I need a little moral support.

While Maren and Will dig into their Chinese takeout, I set my phone on the counter between them. I've pulled up an old article about the fire that took my family's lives.

"What are we looking at?" Maren asks, wiping her mouth.

Taking a deep breath, I push past the tightness in my chest. Opening up has never been easy, but Maren and Will are family to me. It's time I trust them. "I wasn't raised by wolves. And I wasn't abused. I was orphaned after my parents and my sister died in this fire. It's why I became a firefighter. It's why I've avoided close relationships."

Will's eyes narrow at the article briefly before glancing up at me. "I'm sorry, man."

I shrug. "I don't need anyone to feel sorry for me."

"Can I ask why you're showing this to us now?" Maren asks.

"Because Jamie knows."

Maren returns a sad smile, or maybe it's a sincere one. "What are you going to do, Fitz?"

I pull the ring from my pocket and slide it onto the counter.

Maren's eyes widen as she gasps and covers her mouth. It only takes one blink for her to cry. One blink for her to stand and throw her arms around me. "I love you, Calvin Fitzgerald. I'm thrilled for you."

Will smirks. He's not crying, but I imagine the expression on his face is the same as my father's would have been if he were still alive.

Pride.

Love.

And maybe a little relief that I am, in fact, not broken.

Will shakes his head at Maren when she releases me and plops back into her chair.

"What? You are a heartless, emotionless man, William Landry."

He bear-hugs her until she wriggles out of his hold. "I'm emotionally stable. That's all."

"*Pfft*. When are you proposing, Fitz?"

I tuck the ring back into my pocket. "On Thanksgiving, in front of my grandma. I'm not expecting Jamie to abandon her dreams of traveling. And I'm not going to stop jumping out of planes. But at some point, when she's ready to put down real roots, I want them to be with me."

"Do you think she'll say yes?" Will scratches his chin.

"Shut up, Will." Maren elbows him; he bobbles his chopsticks. "Of course she'll say yes. But seriously, Fitz, you better have a long spiel of romantic things to say first. And don't think getting down on one knee is too cliché. It's timeless. In her heart, every girl wants her man to get down on one knee."

"It's symbolic of the rest of your life, buddy. She will break you like a horse. And you will be brought to your knees."

I chuckle at Will. Jaymes has already brought me to my knees. She's broken me. But she's also put me back together. She *is* the best I've ever had—the best there ever will be. And I'm clueless about what this means.

Marriage.

Commitment.

Accountability.

Yet I'm not nervous. No second thoughts. I trust her. Wherever she leads, I will follow.

◆ ◆ ◆

My two favorite ladies.

I grin.

Grandma putters her way toward me at the airport with Jaymes several steps behind, pulling both roller bags. "Calvin."

I hug my grandma and kiss her cheek. "Did you have a good flight?"

"It was fine, dear."

I release her, and Jamie smiles, zipping her white jacket. She's painfully reserved. My hand slides along her neck until my fingers graze her tattoo.

She flinches.

I narrow my eyes for a second before bending to kiss her. When our lips touch, she stiffens. I've sorely underestimated how upset she was on Halloween. I'd hoped she'd be over it by now. Maybe it will make the proposal even more meaningful. It will be the ultimate apology.

"You good?" I narrow my eyes.

"Mm-hmm." A smile has never looked so fabricated. She averts her gaze.

I bite my tongue because this isn't the place to push her on it. So I take the suitcases and lead the way to the parking lot.

When we arrive at the house, I help my grandma out of the truck while Jamie retrieves the suitcases.

"I'll get those, Jaymes."

"I've got them." She wheels them toward the front door.

Grandma holds my proffered arm while I escort her into the house. "I never thought I'd get to see your place."

"It's Will's place, but it feels like mine with him and Maren gone for the holiday." By the time I shut the door and help Grandma out of her jacket, Jamie's at the top of the stairs. "Maren washed her sheets, so my grandma will be in that room."

Without looking back, Jamie nods and turns right.

"Can I get you something to eat?" I ask.

"You know what I need?" Grandma straightens her blue paisley blouse.

"What's that?"

"The bathroom. Then a nap."

I chuckle. "Understandable. Sorry for the stairs."

"It's fine." Again, she takes my arm, and we navigate the stairs like two sloths.

By the time we reach the top, Jamie's waiting for us.

"Need any help?" Jamie asks, sliding her hands into her jeans pockets.

"I'll take it from here, dear. You've already done too much." Grandma pats Jamie's arm before disappearing into the bathroom.

I stand two steps from the top and pull Jamie into my arms so that my head rests on her chest over her heart. "I've missed you."

After a few seconds, she teases her fingers through my hair, and her body vibrates when she inhales a shaky breath.

I lift my head, eyes squinting. "I wasn't going to push this, but I can't ignore it. Are you still upset about Halloween?"

Her eyes are a million miles away, eerily dislocated from me, this moment, and everything around us.

I've never seen anyone appear so lost.

"No," she whispers.

The bathroom door opens. "Don't mind me. I'll be napping." Grandma heads toward Maren's room. "I'm a heavy sleeper."

Her overly obvious hint would typically pull a chuckle from me, but I can't find the slightest smile.

"I'm having my period," Jamie says, sliding past me to descend the stairs.

Admittedly, I'm not an expert on women's hormones and the mood swings that accompany them. Maren either hides the emotional elements of her cycle, or I've totally missed them.

I follow her down the stairs and into the kitchen.

"I should start on the pies. Did you get the ingredients?" She opens the fridge door.

I close it and stand in front of it, arms crossed. "I don't think you've been on your period for a whole month. You have to spell this out for me. And I'm sorry if that makes me an asshole for not knowing or not reading your mind or the stars, the moon—whatever. What did I do wrong?"

Her forehead wrinkles while she stares at my chest. "I'm so"— she pauses, pressing her lips together for a beat—"*sorry* that you've felt unworthy of love. Of family. Of a full and beautiful life." She lifts her gaze to mine. "You've done nothing wrong—just the opposite. You've done everything right. Never forget that you are *worthy* of everyone who chooses to love you."

"Jaymes." I frame her face, not expecting her tears. But in a single blink, they escape, and I wipe them away one by one. "Baby, no. Don't cry."

It's not just tears. She sobs.

"No." I deposit endless kisses all over her face. "I love you. I love you. I love you. And I should have just said it a long time ago."

"D-don't say that," she manages to blurt out, losing all control. "I-I t-thought I could w-wait."

I hug her, wrapping my arms so tightly around her that I fear I'll squeeze her to death because I need her to *feel* my love. "Wait for what?"

Panicking is not my thing. I don't panic. But I can't help but wonder what happened. Christ, did she fall in love with another man?

She couldn't wait for what? Me?

"I can't hold it in any longer." Her words cut through the nonexistent space between us—a gut-wrenching confession.

Then it all comes out at once. A long sentence with no pauses, no breaths. "The patient who thought I was his daughter and then I thought was my uncle is not my uncle. My mom was not my mom. She was my aunt who tried to protect me from my father, Dwight Keane—the man who started the fire that killed your family. And I'm so sorry, Fitz."

With a gasping inhale, she steps away from me and cups a hand over her mouth. Eyes painfully red and filled with endless tears. "I'm *so* very sorry," she whispers past her held breath.

I hear her, but the words haven't fallen into place yet. They're still jostling in my head, like in the Boggle game I used to play with my grandma. Some of the letter cubes are on their sides, waiting to be shaken into their respective slots. Then I can see everything and connect the pieces.

Slowly shaking my head, I murmur, "That's impossible."

She presses the back of her hand to her runny nose and sniffles. "I wish it were."

I continue to shake my head. "You're from Florida. You've lived there your whole life. He was a park ranger in California."

She hiccups and sniffles again. "My mom—my aunt—lied to protect me." She wipes her face, but her eyes are far from dry. "She changed her name. She changed my name. And she did it all for me." Wringing her hands in front of her, she stares at the floor between us. "And I . . . ," she whispers. "I'm trying to figure out what kind of cruel god would let me move here, of all the places in the world. And of all the men in the world, I meet you."

Her face scrunches. "And fall in love with you. Then, out of all the jobs I could have taken, I ended up at the hospital where my father's a patient." She laughs with a painful grunt. "But not just anyone's patient. *My* patient."

Not since the day I found out my parents and sister died have I felt this numb.

This speechless.

This confused.

This angry at the world.

"Say something," she whispers, lifting her gaze to mine.

I have *no* idea what she expects me to say. Was there a question in that mind fuck of a confession? But she's waiting for my response, bleeding desperation. So I respond without thinking. I say the only thing that I feel right now.

"I hate that he's still alive. I hope he dies an awful death. I hope he tries to kill himself a hundred times and fails each time with maximum suffering until his miserable fucking soul leaves his body to *burn* in hell for eternity."

Jamie swallows hard, releasing a new round of tears, lips quivering until she hides them behind her shaky hand as if I've offended her. I don't think there's anything more offensive than murder. Surely she has to see that.

Something in her eyes dies, as if a part of her has left her body, leaving a vacant hole. And she pivots, taking even, unhurried steps to the stairway. Seconds later, she descends the stairs with her suitcase in hand, dons her jacket and boots, and opens the door.

I open my mouth to stop her, but nothing comes out.

Click.

I stare at the door and the space she's left on this side of it. The space she's left in my heart.

Chapter Forty-Three

Another white lie.

Another holiday filled with forced smiles and small talk.

Grandma accepts my excuse for Jamie's sudden absence—that they were short staffed at the hospital due to several nurses being sick. And I fly with her back to San Bernardino on Saturday, then return home on Sunday.

"Where have you been?" Maren asks when I enter the house with my overnight bag. "And why didn't you send pictures? I've messaged Jamie a hundred times to see if she'll spill the beans or send me a photo of her diamond ring. But she's not responding." Maren stands from the sofa, stretching. "Spill, Fitz. I want all the details."

I head up the stairs. "There's nothing to share."

I barely reach my bedroom threshold before she's on my tail. "What happened? Did she say no?" she asks with incredulity.

Tossing my bag on the bed, I then unzip it and remove my dirty clothes. "I didn't propose."

"Why not?"

"Maren." I pause my hands and close my eyes. "Can we not discuss it now?"

"Fine. I'll call Jamie until she answers." She pivots and exits my room.

"Stop," I say, pinching the bridge of my nose. I don't face her, but I can hear her feet padding back in my direction. "She recently discovered that her mom lied to her. Her mom wasn't her mom. She was her aunt. Her biological mom died in conjunction with the fire that killed my parents."

"Oh my god. That's awful."

"No." I turn. "The awful part is that her father started the fire."

Maren's jaw slowly unhinges. "How . . . what . . . wh—"

"Don't. Just don't ask me anything else. I don't know anything else. I don't care. It doesn't matter."

"Poor Jamie," Maren murmurs.

"What?" I flinch. "Poor *Jamie*? Are you fucking kidding me?"

Maren jumps. "Fitz, I . . . I didn't mean it like that. I just meant that your family's death is not her fault. I'm not trying to downplay the seriousness of what happened to your family. The whole thing was a tragedy for so many people. But she was just a child when it happened. She lost her biological mom. She lost the woman who raised her. She lost the man she thought was her father. And now she's dealing with the revelation that everything was a lie, *and* her birth father is responsible for so many lost lives? I'm sorry, but that is horrific."

"So what? Am I supposed to overlook everything? Get down on one knee and ask her to be my wife, so for the rest of my life, I have an in-person reminder of the man who murdered my family?"

Maren takes several steps and wraps her arms around my waist, resting her cheek against my chest. "I'm sorry, Fitz. No. I don't mean that at all. I shouldn't have said that. It was terrible timing. Jamie's not here. You are. My reaction was insensitive. I know you must be hurting." She releases me, retreating several steps toward the door. "I honestly don't know what I would do if I were in your shoes. I know you love her. And I understand if that's not enough."

Love her.

My heart can't make sense of its feelings for Jamie. Something was severed that day. And maybe I don't know how I feel about Jamie because I *can't* feel. Or maybe there's nothing left to feel.

Maren starts to pull my door shut behind her but stops. "I'm here for you the way you were there for me when Brandon died. Okay?"

I nod slowly. After she shuts the door, I finish unpacking my bag and slide it under my bed. I pick up my mom's diamond ring from the top of the dresser and stare at it. I was ready to stop looking back at my tragic past because Jamie was worth taking a risk, for a life I never dared to imagine. And when I was with her, I didn't think about my parents and sister. She was the ultimate distraction.

Now she's the ultimate reminder.

My light became my darkness.

"How the fuck did this happen?" I mumble, opening the top drawer and depositing the ring next to a few watchbands and spare buttons.

Chapter Forty-Four

JAYMES

I always try to advocate for my patients, but I have a vested interest in Dwight Keane that I won't share with his doctors or other nurses. And I'm advocating for fewer meds, more lucid days, fresh air, healthier food, and sunshine.

I'm desperate to fix things in my life, even if I know in my gut they are beyond repair.

Dwight is beyond repair.

My relationship with Fitz is beyond repair.

My shattered dreams . . . beyond repair.

"Did you have a good session with Dr. Lin?" I ask Dwight while he eats his dinner.

"I did. I told her about you."

I lift my eyebrows. "Oh yeah? What did you say?"

"I said I'm the luckiest one here because my daughter is my nurse."

I chuckle, knowing Dr. Lin doesn't know or believe I'm Dwight's daughter. If I thought telling her the truth would help resolve his issues and get him out of this facility, I'd do it. Instead, I think it would lead to me leaving my position earlier than planned. Then who would look out for his best interests?

"Well, I'm a travel nurse. I won't be here forever. In fact, I might be done after Christmas, unless I get my contract extended, which I'm hoping will happen."

"How's your family?" It's the first time he's asked me about *my* family.

"I'm not married. No kids." I barely get the words out of my mouth with my composure intact. And my hand instinctively goes to the tattoo on my neck every time I think of Fitz, which is often. Clearing my throat, I smile. "However, I have three days off starting tomorrow, and I'm taking a flight to go visit your parents."

He stops midchew, brow tense. "Their graves?"

"They're alive."

Dwight shakes his head, brushing off my reply. "If they were alive, they would have visited me."

My chest constricts. "Yeah," I mumble. "You're probably right."

Nathan gave me an address for my grandparents, but there's no guarantee they'll be here because the landline is disconnected. The cell phone number is questionable because I can't get an answer, and there is no voicemail set up. However, since I've never seen the Grand Canyon, it won't be a wasted trip, even if they're not here.

I park the rental car on the tree-lined street and inspect the gray ranch house.

"This is a bad idea," I mumble, combing my fingers through my hair while checking my teeth in the rearview mirror. They abandoned Dwight. They abandoned me and their daughter. Why do I feel this aching need to meet them?

I check my phone. I've checked it every five minutes since the day I walked out of Fitz's house on Thanksgiving.

Nothing.

I know we're done, but my heart loves living in denial, so I let it cling to irrational hope just to keep from crying twenty-four seven.

With a brave inhale, I step out of the car and trek up their driveway. After three quick knocks on their door, there's a long pause—so long that I turn around to leave. And part of me is relieved they're not home. My nerves are knotted in my stomach.

"Hello?" a stout, gray-haired man says upon opening the door.

I turn. "Hi. Are you Waylon? I'm, uh—"

"Barbara," he whispers, sliding his thick round glasses up his nose and closer to his brown eyes.

It takes a moment for the sound of my untold name from his lips to sink in. It's not a guess. He knows it's my name with certainty. "H-how did you know?"

He opens the creaky door a few more feet. "You look just like your mom."

My smile falters, tripping over unexpected emotion, but I nod and take a deep breath. "So I've been told." I step inside.

We stare at each other for a few awkward seconds. What do I say now? Everything I sorted out on the way here is nothing but a jumbled mess, like the inside of a suitcase that's been handled roughly.

I glance around the room, wringing my hands. It's a modest home with outdated walls covered in wood paneling and light-blue floral wall-paper. Water stains on the popcorn ceiling. Dusty rose carpet.

"Can I hug you?"

My gaze flicks back to him and his hopeful expression. It's endearing and one more thing that knocks me off kilter.

I chuckle and nod, fighting a wave of emotion.

He hugs me. "We were at Samantha's funeral," he says before releasing me. His voice breaks when he says her name.

"Why didn't you introduce yourselves?"

Waylon returns a sad smile. "We weren't supposed to exist in your life any longer."

"Oh my goodness."

I turn toward the woman's fluttery voice.

Her trembling hand covers her mouth, eyes a blue-gray, face blotched with age spots and creased with wrinkles, white hair matted on the side like she's been napping. "How?" she asks as if it takes all the oxygen in the room to say that one word.

Before I can answer, she throws her bony arms around me. "You're such a beautiful young woman."

"You must be Aubrey." Keeping my arms around her, I lift my hand to wipe away a stray tear.

"Please, sit down." Waylon gestures to the living room. "We don't mean to overwhelm you. It's just—"

Aubrey releases me and pulls a wadded tissue from her pocket to blot her teary eyes.

I shake my head before sitting on the sofa while they sit in rocking chairs on the opposite side of a faded wood coffee table. "Don't apologize. I can't believe I'm here either." I nervously rub my hands over my jeans. "I'm still processing recent revelations. I thought Samantha was my mom."

They nod slowly with sympathetic smiles.

"And I thought my father worked at NASA and died when I was really young."

Again, they nod.

This is harder than I thought it would be. Am I angry that, even now, they're not sharing everything with me? Or do I admire them for keeping some vow to protect me at all costs? "I haven't decided if it's fate or life just being *life*. But I'm a travel psych nurse, and I took an assignment at a hospital in San Bernardino." I pause for their reactions.

The change in their expressions tells me everything—they know where their son's staying.

"I stumbled upon the truth. He—my father—knew me before I knew him." After another pause, I open my mouth to say more, to tell them exactly how I figured it out. But those details don't matter. They aren't necessary anymore. Only one thing matters to me now. "Can I ask why you've never visited him?"

Aubrey frowns, again blotting the corners of her eyes while looking at Waylon.

He leans forward, hands folded between his spread legs. "We did, shortly after the trial." Reaching for Aubrey's hand, he squeezes it. "He was unrecognizable. When we looked into his eyes, there was nothing there. That's when we realized we didn't only lose Annie and the baby that day; we lost our son too. Reporters were harassing us. Our car was vandalized. Bricks were thrown into three windows of our house, and our front tree was set on fire. So we moved. We didn't change our names like Samantha and you, but we also weren't protecting an innocent child."

Swallowing hard, I clear my throat. "You said you lost Annie and *the baby*. What baby?"

They eye each other for a beat. "Annie was six months pregnant." Aubrey sniffles.

After the past two weeks, I'm not sure I have any tears left to cry, but my body tries anyhow.

"How is he?" Aubrey asks.

I press my fingers to the corners of my eyes. "He has good days and bad days. I don't know if he'll ever live on his own again, but he's kind, charming, and smart on the good days. He reads so many books when he's not too heavily medicated." As the words leave my mouth, I think of Fitz and his voracious consumption of books. "He likes to garden too. I don't remember him. I barely remember the man I thought was my father. But Dwight is a gentle soul who experienced something unimaginable. Before the connection between us was made, I was drawn to him. And if I don't get an extension on my time at his facility, it will be hard to leave."

"Will you visit him when you're no longer there? Do you think of him as your father?" Waylon asks.

"Do you still think of him as your son?"

Tension pulls at his eyes. "We haven't seen him in over twenty years."

"I know. But do you still think of him as your son?"

Again, a look is exchanged. Then they nod.

I smile. "I think of him as my father, even if I still don't know how I feel about it. And he knows I'm his daughter. He knew it way before I did."

Aubrey wipes more tears. "Would he recognize us?"

"He thinks you died."

She flinches. "Why?"

I lift a shoulder into a tiny shrug. "You said it yourselves. You haven't seen him in over twenty years. I don't mean to upset you, but the truth matters."

She leans into Waylon and softly cries.

"I think you should visit him. Help him piece together a reality."

After two days with my grandparents, including a trip to the Grand Canyon, I fly home only to find out that I won't be getting an extension at the hospital in San Bernardino.

"I'm heartbroken," I say to Melissa while eating salad and a side of cauliflower wings at a sports bar near my apartment after work.

All by myself, surrounded by Christmas decorations. And Sinatra in the background suggests I have myself a merry little Christmas.

She cuts out for a second.

"What?" I push my earbud tighter into my ear.

"I said you've experienced too much heartbreak lately."

"Agreed."

"Have you heard from Maren or Will?"

"Maren called me while I was in Flagstaff. She apologized for waiting so long to contact me but didn't know what to say." I take a bite of salad and chew several times before mumbling, "There's nothing to say."

"Did she say how Fitz is doing?"

"I didn't ask. And she didn't say."

"Why didn't you ask?"

"Because I'm not emotionally ready for the answer. If he's doing fine, it makes me feel inconsequential. If he's miserable, it makes me feel like an awful person for ruining us."

"You didn't ruin anything. It's not your fault. It's nobody's fault."

I nod to myself, sliding my bowl away from me. This conversation has robbed me of my appetite. "She was pregnant," I murmur.

"Who?"

"Annie. My mom. She was six months pregnant the day she died."

"Oh my god."

"Yeah. Dwight has never mentioned it. Well, maybe he did. He talked about a baby, but then he said Barbara's name in the next breath. I can only imagine how repressed the memory is in his mind. And I don't want to imagine how he would handle that memory surfacing. He's already so sad, Mel. He reminds me of Fitz's grandma in a way. Fitz never reminded her that his parents died in a fire instead of a car accident. And he's never told her that he had a sister. I bet he hopes she never remembers. Well, I hope Dwight never remembers the baby."

She hums. "How are you doing, hon?"

"I'm fine," I mumble, handing the waiter my credit card.

"No. How are you *really* doing? I know you're not fine."

With a nervous titter, I sign the credit card slip and hand the copy and pen to the waiter. "I'm in a restaurant. You can't ask me for that level of honesty when I'm in public." I snag my purse and zip my lightweight hoodie before exiting the restaurant.

"Oh, Jamie. I wish I were there to hug you."

"Me too." I unlock my car. "But then I'd be crying all the time. And my eyes can't take much more crying. My heart is buried under a pile of sadness and grief. This isn't sustainable." I fasten my seat belt. "Maybe leaving San Bernardino is a good thing. I can visit Dwight. And his parents are coming for Christmas to see him. They're renting a house and staying through New Year's. Part of me hopes they'll decide to move here to visit him more often. But I think it's doubtful."

"Hey, it never hurts to put that out in the universe. Maybe it will happen."

I hum. "Perhaps."

"How did you end things with Maren? Was it a nice-knowing-ya goodbye, or do you think you'll ever see her or Will again?"

"She said she'd fly to San Bernardino for a girls' weekend after the holidays, but I don't know if she was serious or if it was the easiest way to say goodbye without too many tears."

"Sorry, hon."

"I'm heading home, so I should get off the phone. I'll call you tomorrow and talk solely about your love life. Okay?"

Melissa laughs. "It will be a thirty-second conversation."

"Then we'll strategize and review your dating app profiles and pictures."

She giggles, and it's exactly what I need. "Night, Jamie."

"Night, Mel."

Chapter Forty-Five

CALVIN

"Want to talk?" Gary pulls out the chair next to my sewing machine and straddles it backward.

"About?" I stay focused on the zipper.

"Jamie."

"What about her?"

"It's a week before Christmas, and I'm just now finding out that your life imploded over Thanksgiving."

"*Implode* is a strong word. Who couldn't keep their mouth shut?"

"Maren talked to Evette."

Figures.

"You finally shared your past," he says.

Gary's one of a handful of people who have known for years how my family died. He knows his fires. He reads as much, if not more, than I do. He's also been a good friend who has never breathed a word to anyone else. Maren's brother was that kind of friend too.

"Jesus Christ, man . . . Dwight Keane is Jamie's father." He shakes his head and whistles. "That's some fucked-up shit."

I return an easy nod without looking at him.

"Maren said you were going to propose to her. Fitz, if you don't want to talk to me, that's fine. But you need to talk to someone. You have *never* wanted a wife or a family. Hell, you even made sure you can't get a woman pregnant. Yet you were going to fucking *propose* with your mother's ring. You don't just sleep that shit off."

I stop the machine and glance up at him. "You think I need what? Therapy?"

"I think you need to talk about it with someone."

The legs of my chair screech along the floor as I scoot it back a few inches and cross my arms. "Let's talk."

Gary's eyebrows lift a fraction before he clears his throat. "Okay. How are you holding up?"

"Fine."

"Are you sleeping well?"

"Yes."

"Suicidal thoughts?"

"No."

"Depression?"

"No."

"Are you sure? Because if I were in your shoes, I'd hate the world."

"I hate her father. He's not my world. So I don't hate the world."

"She was your world."

My lips part to give a response, but I don't have one.

Gary gets a slight smile as if he's proud of making a point.

"I don't hate her."

He nods several times. "That's good. She's the sweetest, kindest young woman I've met since I met my wife. She doesn't deserve hate from anyone. She was three years old when tragedy struck her family. Like you, she was a victim of something horrible. Just a child."

"I'm aware."

Gary has a stare-off with me. He twists his lips for a few seconds. I don't know where he thinks he's going with this informal therapy session, but it's not far. "Maren and Evette understand why you can't be with her."

I return a slow nod.

"But I don't."

"Then you're fucking blind."

"I think you're the one who's blind. If you look at that woman and see your past, then you're not only blind, you never saw her in the first place. And that means you don't deserve her. She's infinitely too good for your sorry ass."

"What did you say to me?" I stand, sending my chair crashing into the table behind me.

Gary stands, but he doesn't stand as tall as me. And I've been itching to ram my fist into something. It might just be his face today.

He smirks, taking a few steps backward as I inch closer. "You're right. You don't hate her. You hate that you love her more than you've ever loved anyone. You hate that some other guy's going to take what's yours. The girl. Her love. *Your life.*"

I ball my hands into tight fists. "She dropped this all on me on Thanksgiving and walked out the door while my grandmother napped upstairs. The same grandmother who tried to take her own life a few weeks before I turned eighteen because she couldn't deal with the grief of losing my parents, my sister, and her husband. She didn't condemn a thing he did and had this horrified look when I spoke about him. She probably left me to be with him. And *I'm* the asshole in this scenario?"

"What did you say to her?"

I shake my head. "What are you talking about? Nothing."

"She confessed that Dwight was her father, and then she followed it up with 'I choose him'? I don't buy it. What was your response?"

"I told her I wished he was dead."

"I one hundred percent understand why you would feel that. I would feel the same way. But that's her father."

"He's a fucking murderer!" I grab Gary's shirt and shove him against the wall.

"Whoa! What the hell?" Two other guys run into the room and pull me off Gary.

"His wife died," Gary says without raising his voice. He says it so matter of factly that it makes me nauseous.

"You don't kill innocent people because a bear attacks your wife." I struggle in the grip of the two guys holding me, but they don't release me.

"Love makes us crazy." He nods toward me. "Look at you. And she's still alive."

"This isn't about her. It's about my family." Again, I try to yank myself free.

Gary straightens his shirt. "Of course it's about her. Your family's dead. Nothing will ever be about them again. And I know that makes me an asshole for pointing out the obvious. But you need to stop being the victim. The sooner you accept that, the sooner you can have your own goddamn life."

Chapter Forty-Six

Maren skips into the kitchen wearing her Santa hat. "We're caroling tonight. Get ready."

Will and I don't take our attention away from Sunday-night football.

"Do you want peppermint marshmallows or regular marshmallows in your canteens of cocoa?"

We don't respond until she steals the remote and shuts off the game.

"What the hell, Mare?" Will dives toward her to retrieve the remote.

"No. I promised Evette we'd *all* go caroling with them tonight. So get your asses off the sofa, and be ready in five." She slides the remote down her shirt and into her bra.

"I love that you think that's going to stop me. I've seen plenty of tits. Your tiny ones won't even faze me." Will smirks.

Maren flips him the bird before strolling into the kitchen.

I haven't spoken with Gary since our incident at work. We've managed to stay out of each other's way. It's best if I stay home.

"I'm not feeling well. Headache." I rub my temples.

Maren opens the drawer by the fridge and pulls out a bottle of pain-relief pills. "Take two, and get your ass ready." She tosses me the bottle.

I shoot her a scowl and slap the bottle onto the counter.

She winks. "Good boy."

Fifteen minutes later, Maren's driving our grumpy asses to Gary and Evette's. There are at least a dozen people gathered in their front yard.

"Merry Christmas, my lovelies," Evette chimes, in her long white coat and red Santa hat, handing us LED candles.

Someone bumps my shoulder, so I glance left.

Gary holds out his gloved hand. "Truce? I handled everything like a dick. You're my guy, and I just want you to be happy. And I so badly wanted that happiness to be her. I'm sorry."

I stare at his proffered hand.

Maren kicks the back of my knee. "What would Jesus do *three days before Christmas*?" she mumbles. Of course she knows about our fight. Nothing's a secret around here.

I shake his hand. "Truce."

"Grab cookies if you need them or hot drinks if you don't already have one. Let's go," Evette announces.

I feign Christmas cheer and mutter a few lyrics as we stroll through the neighborhood. Three songs into this delightful gig, my phone vibrates in my pocket. It's my grandma. I fly to California tomorrow. She probably has her days mixed up and is wondering why I'm not there yet. "Hello?"

"Calvin?" She sounds weak.

I stiffen, and panic sets in before I can utter a word. "Grandma, what is it? Are you okay?"

"They . . . they took Terry to the hospital. He wasn't . . . I-I shook him. He didn't respond. They were shocking h-his heart. He wasn't—"

"Okay. Just sit down, and try to breathe. Are you alone?" I hand Will my canteen. He narrows his eyes.

I cross the street so I can hear better. Maybe *I'm* the dick tonight, but I'm relieved it's Terry and not her. I don't know Terry that well, so my emotional investment in him is close to nil. However, I don't like that she's panicked and I'm so far away.

"They wouldn't let me go in the ambulance." Her voice quakes.

"There's nothing you can do. Do you have a neighbor who can be with you? My flight is in the morning."

"I-I don't know. I can't breathe. What if he's not okay?"

I grip my phone tighter and yank my beanie from my head. She needs to calm down. She's survived so much worse; she just doesn't remember. "Just hold tight, and stay by your phone. I'm going to see if Jamie can wait for news with you. And I'll call you right back. Okay?"

"O-okay."

"Everything all right?" Will asks, having abandoned the other carolers too.

"No. My grandma's guy friend was hauled off in an ambulance. He's probably dead. And she's alone and in a panic. She's going to have another fucking stroke if she doesn't calm down." I hold my phone to my ear, waiting for Jamie to answer.

"Fitz?" She sounds surprised.

"I'm sorry. I wouldn't bother you if I had another choice, but my grandma just called. They took Terry to the hospital. He was unresponsive. She's panicking. I'm flying out in the morning, but—"

"I'll take care of her," Jamie interrupts. Her words aren't panicked like my grandma's or tight with frustration like mine. She's calm and grounded.

"Thanks," I sigh.

She ends the call with a clipped "yep," and it takes me a minute to shake off the sound of her voice and its effect on me.

After a delayed flight and a long line at the rental counter, I finally reach my grandma's place and park next to Jamie's Jeep.

I'm not ready to see her. I don't know if I'll ever be prepared to see her again. The emotions are too raw. And a month apart has only intensified them. I can't think of her without hearing Gary's speech replaying in my head.

I open the front door.

"Shh . . ." Jamie holds a finger to her lips while easing the bedroom door shut behind her. "She finally fell asleep an hour ago." She frowns, eyes red like she's been crying. "Terry didn't make it. It's hit her hard. I caved and gave her something to help her sleep."

I nod slowly. This fucking hurts. But I don't know the exact source of the pain. I just know that standing feet from her is almost unbearable. "Um . . ." I clear my throat. "Thank you. I didn't know who else to call."

She brushes past me. I curl my fingers into fists, resisting the urge to touch her.

"I'm glad I could be here for her." She pulls on her gray ankle boots. "I felt bad that it took me so long to get here. I've been spending the holidays with"—she lifts her gaze to mine while sliding on her jacket—"friends. And it's about an hour away. But with holiday traffic, it took me just under two hours."

Friends.

She stressed *friends*, and her downcast gaze reeks of guilt or regret. Does she mean *friend*? Singular? A guy?

I press my lips together, biting my tongue. It's none of my business. *"You hate that some other guy's going to take what's yours. The girl. Her love. Your life."*

It seems early to move on. Maybe she's just numbing the pain. Perhaps I need to do the same.

"I'm an asshole for calling you. I should have figured out something else to do days before Christmas. And you had plans that I screwed up. Not to mention the drive. And staying the night." I pull a wad of folded cash from my pocket and hand her two fifties. "At least let me pay for your gas. And please give my apologies to *your friend*."

She stares at the cash in my hand. "Fitz, I don't want your money. I care about Edith. I'm glad you called me." When she lifts her gaze to mine, pain twists her beautiful features, as if the money is an insult.

"She's not your responsibility." I inch the money closer to her.

She ignores it, bending down to grab her purse from the floor. "Yeah, well, put your money away, because I'm not your responsibility." She opens the door. "Let her sleep for several hours before checking on her. She needs to rest." She pulls the door shut.

I'm flat-out nauseous, and my chest aches like I'm having my own health crisis. I open the door and step outside. "Are you upset with me?"

Jamie stops, slowly turning. She grabs her purse strap and sighs. "No."

I rest a hand on my hip and drop my head. "I'm trying to figure out how to move on without regretting everything that happened before Thanksgiving weekend."

"Does it matter?" Her gaze drifts to the side; she stares off into the distance before she continues. "It's over. If you need to regret ever meeting me, then do it. Nothing changes where we are now. I wasn't your future. I wasn't really yours. And you were most certainly never really mine."

"That's not true." A pang of anger swells in my chest.

She shakes her head and turns, continuing to her Jeep. "I'll be your scapegoat, but I won't be your punching bag. My feelings might not matter to you, but they matter to me."

"Feelings?" I follow her. "Are you serious? Do you have any idea how I felt when you dropped that shit on me and then just left? Huh? Did my feelings even cross your mind? Talk about treating someone like a punching bag."

She stops at her door and whips around. "You wished a hundred miserable deaths upon my father before hoping he'd burn in hell! He didn't hunt down your family and kill them. He listened to my mother scream as a bear attacked her and their unborn child while I was home—a three-year-old child. And I never asked you to forgive him. I never asked you to forgive me. I flew Edith to you. And I told you the truth. Then I quietly left. You didn't stop me. And I get it. You needed space. And I didn't know what else to say. So I left. But don't stand here and act like you weren't fucking relieved that I was no longer a choice you needed to make."

"I MADE MY CHOICE!" My words explode as I take a step closer.

She falls back against the driver's side door, eyes wide.

"I chose *you*." The words grind out of my chest. I'm breathless and so damn miserable. "I had my mother's ring and the two most important people with me for Thanksgiving. I told Maren and Will that I chose *you*. This huge weight was lifted off my shoulders because I knew that you would say yes. And you would consume my whole fucking body and soul, and nothing and no one would ever matter as much as you."

I won't blink and let her see me cry, but watching her fall apart under the weight of my words is killing me.

The tears streaking down her cheeks.

The redness in her eyes.

The quivering of her lips.

The soft sobs vibrating her whole body.

My voice loses its drive; the anger simmers into pain. "Then you took it all away—*he* took it all away. Just like that, I hated Dwight Keane all over again."

I don't touch her but can't tear my gaze away.

She furiously wipes her face and sniffles. "If you hate my father, then I can't imagine how you'll ever love me." When she turns, I take a step back.

I watch her get into her Jeep. Then I let her drive away.

Chapter Forty-Seven

JAYMES

Six months later . . .

Love is a jagged knife. If it's not lethal, it leaves, at the very least, a deep scar, an unshakable feeling, a recurring memory . . . a cheap tattoo.

"Are you nervous?" Melissa asks.

I adjust my AirPods to hear her better. "It's fire season. I'm not going to run into him." The rideshare pulls into the parking lot in downtown Missoula. "Thank you," I say while climbing out and fixing my dress.

"You're braver than I am."

"I never thought I'd see Betty O'Neil get married. I'm not missing this for anything."

Melissa laughs. "You're a good friend, Jaymes Andrews."

I grin. "Thank you." I stop before the entrance to the church. "I'm here. I'll call you later."

"Have fun."

I slip my earbuds into my clutch and silence my phone. It's a beautiful church, with lovely frescos and stained glass windows. There's an organ on the balcony and a much larger gathering than I anticipated.

Her groom is much older, a kind and patient soul to welcome Betty and her three dozen kids into his life. When he wipes away tears as she walks down the aisle, I leak some of my emotion. It's a beautiful ceremony.

As I exit the church, a calloused hand slides around my arm, and I turn. "Oh my god." I hug Will.

"I wondered if you'd be here." He releases me and grins.

"There was no way I was going to miss this wedding." I nod toward him. "You look so dapper in a suit."

He tugs at his tie. "It's too damn hot for this."

"I know, right?" I use the program to fan myself.

He eyes my airy, light-blue strapless dress and scoffs at my comparison. "Not even close."

"Are you going to the reception?" I ask.

"Her parents own a vineyard. I'm not a wine guy, but an open bar is an open bar."

I giggle, and we turn as the happy couple emerges from the church. When they're tucked into the old Rolls-Royce, I smile at Will. "I'll see you there, then."

"Where are you parked?" he asks.

"I'm not." I hold up my phone with my rideshare app.

"No. You're not riding with a stranger when I'm headed to the same place."

With a sheepish smile, I shrug. "Are you sure?"

"I'm offended you even have to ask." He offers his arm, and I take it. "Where are you staying?"

"A hotel."

"Dammit, woman. No. That's not okay." He opens the passenger door and helps me up into his Bronco.

"It's a nice hotel."

"No." He shakes his head, shuts my door, and removes his tie on his way to the driver's side door. "Fitz is on a fire. I don't know when we'll see him. Maren's gone too. We can have that torrid affair we always planned on having."

I snort. "So it wasn't just me?"

He smirks, backing out of the parking spot. "I've missed you. And I'm a shitty friend for not staying in touch after what went down. But Fitz is—"

"He's your friend too. Please don't feel the need to explain. I think I would have been disappointed had you and Maren not stood by your guy. Fitz needed you, but he never would have admitted it."

Will gives me a quick sidelong glance with a melancholy smile and a tiny nod. "It hasn't been easy. He distanced himself from everyone. I think I saw him on less than five different occasions all winter. He spent most of his time down south. And he hasn't let me rent out the shed, so the dumb motherfucker's paying double rent."

My heart jolts, but I try to hide my physical reaction. Instead, I clear my throat, and with a weak attempt, I try to laugh it off. "That makes no sense."

"Maren thinks what happened with you is Fitz's new trauma, his new excuse to be an asshole and reject all opportunities to have a normal life. He's stopped going to Gary and Evette's parties. No dating. Just nonstop work. Well, he still visits his grandma over the holidays."

I manage a slow nod. Everything inside my chest aches. I did this. "Where are you working now?"

My gaze remains affixed to the view out the window.

"Jamie?"

"Huh? Yeah?"

Will chuckles. "Where'd you go? I asked where you're working now?"

"Oh, I'm between jobs. After San Bernardino, I took a position in Denver for a maternity leave, then I had a short stint in Bismarck. But for the past month, I've been hiking. Spending some much-needed time in nature."

"Really? Where?"

With a nervous laugh, I slowly shake my head. "I'm afraid to say."

"Why?" He stops at the light and glances at me.

"I'm hiking the area where my mother—my biological mother—died. Where Fitz's family died," I whisper.

Will's eyebrows shoot up his forehead.

My nose wrinkles. "I know. It sounds weird. My father's been diagnosed with colon cancer. Most days, I don't think he understands or acknowledges his diagnosis, even with his parents visiting when they can and trying to explain things to him. He's just not comprehending it. And maybe that's a blessing for him. Anyway, he asked me to find my mother and tell her how sorry he is."

Ever so slowly, Will returns his gaze to the road and follows the car in front of us when the light turns green. "So you're what? Searching for a body?"

"No. He's not consistently of sound mind. Sometimes he thinks she's alive, and sometimes he knows she's dead." I smile, fiddling with my sand dollar pendant. "But I take pictures of the sunrises and sunsets. I take pictures of the new trees and wildlife and share them with him. I show him life after death. And for me, it's been a form of closure. I need it. I've released so many emotions. And I know when I take my last hike to release his ashes"—I turn away and blink back the tears—"it will be the beginning of something new that I won't share with my past." I quickly blot the corners of my eyes and release a tiny but joyous laugh. "I'll *fly*."

Will rests his hand on mine and gives it a gentle squeeze.

Then, for the next three hours, we drink wine, dance, laugh, and celebrate love.

"Are you good to drive?" I ask him as he helps me to the Bronco.

"I cut myself off an hour into the night. You're safe with me."

I slip off my heels before climbing into the passenger seat. "You're such a good man, William Landry. You should find yourself a good woman. Maybe a psychiatrist."

He chuckles, shaking his head. "Nice try, matchmaker, but I'm good." Before I can continue making my case for Dr. Reichart, he closes my door, and I fall asleep before we get out of the parking lot.

"Hey, do you need me to carry you?" Will gently shakes my arm.

I peel open my eyes and wait for everything to stop spinning. "This isn't my hotel?"

He unfastens my seat belt. "I'll take you to your hotel in the morning. Friends don't leave friends drunk and alone."

"Drunk is a strong word," I mumble, sliding out of the seat.

"Whoa!" Will catches me when my feet fail to do their job.

"I'm good." I right myself. "I can walk."

"If you say so." Will heads toward the door, carrying my purse and heels.

I stop at the bottom of the porch steps, feeling numb but not numb enough to forget everything.

"You okay?" Will asks after opening the door.

"He carried my shoes." I slowly blink and gaze at my shoes in Will's hand.

"Who carried your shoes?"

"Fitz," I whisper, rubbing the heel of my hand over my chest. There it goes again, that jagged knife called love. "After the anniversary party," I murmur. "We made love on a boat. And he held my hand at sunrise, walking me down the boardwalk with my heels in his other hand." It hurts to smile, but I can't help it. "I never told him I used to dream of that." I chuckle, shaking my head. "It was a silly dream. I don't know why my mind created it. I just knew that it wasn't the shoes. It was him." I ease my gaze to Will's face, barely visible in the dark. "Thank you."

"For what?"

I take one step, then another. "Thank you for showing me that it was just a dream. Anyone can carry my shoes." I step into the house.

Will turns on a light. "You can sleep in the shed or Maren's bed to be closer to the bathroom."

I continue up the stairs and take a left into Fitz's bedroom, gently closing the door behind me. Unzipping my dress, I then step out of it and crawl into bed, hugging his pillow and drifting off to sleep.

The following day, I slide into my dress, use the bathroom, and find Will in the kitchen with a cup of coffee waiting for me.

"Good morning." He leans against the counter and grins behind his mug.

"Morning." I inhale the dreamy steam before taking a sip.

"I didn't hear you get up in the night. Did you get sick?"

"No. I wasn't that intoxicated." I glance around. "But I need to get back to my hotel. A shower and clean clothes are calling my name. Where'd I set my purse and shoes?"

He nods to the sofa. "I'm not sure where you put your shoes."

"You had them, didn't you?"

He shakes his head. "I thought I handed them to you when you walked up the stairs."

I set my coffee on the counter and retrace my steps, even getting on my hands and knees to look under Fitz's bed. "Where could they be?" I scratch my head as Will watches me from the doorway.

"That's weird. I'll check again in my Bronco. But for now, I'll grab you a pair of Maren's flip-flops and let you know when I find them. I can always ship them to you."

I continue to shake my head. "They didn't just vanish."

Will meets me at the top of the stairs and hands me Maren's shoes. "It was probably a mouse."

"Shut up." I laugh, descending the stairs.

He transfers my coffee into a canteen. "Coffee to go."

"You're the best."

"Tell me about it." He grins, grabbing his keys. "It's like you slept with the wrong housemate."

I open the door and giggle. "I think that's been well established."

Chapter Forty-Eight

CALVIN

Will gives me a suspicious look when I pull into the driveway. He sets aside his can of deck stain and wipes his hands on a rag hanging from his back pocket. "Didn't expect to see you so soon."

"Yeah, well, sometimes things go as planned." I head toward the back door.

"Those are called damn good days."

"Amen," I mumble.

He follows me into the house, pulling two beers from the fridge and handing me one.

"Thanks," I say. "You have the whole weekend off?"

Will takes a long swig and then nods. "I attended a wedding yesterday."

"Open bar?"

He chuckles. "Vineyard reception."

"Wine." My face sours while I set my beer on the counter. "Well, I need a nap."

"Okey dokey." Will gives me another weird expression.

But I don't have the energy to give a shit, so I head upstairs and straight into the bedroom, where there's a pair of silver heels on my bed.

I turn to have a word with my dumbass roommate for getting drunk and screwing some girl in the wrong damn room. But as soon as I turn, I find him leaned against my doorway, arms crossed over his gray T-shirt splattered with dark stains.

"Ran into our old roomie at the wedding yesterday."

My jaw stiffens; just the mention of her unearths unwelcome pain.

"She's been hiking the trails where it all happened over twenty years ago. Her dad's dying of cancer. She's as innocent and beautiful as the day she walked through our door. And she was a little too tipsy to be left alone after the reception, so I brought her here. But she wasn't wearing her shoes by then, so I carried them inside, and she barely made it up the porch steps because I showed her that any guy could carry her shoes. When all this time, she dreamed of *you* carrying her shoes down some boardwalk after spending the night with her on a boat."

Will glances at the floor, scraping his teeth over his bottom lip several times before shaking his head. "I love my job. I value my freedom. I thought there was nothing better than casual sex, breaking gaming records, watching football, and drinking good beer." He lifts his gaze, eyes slightly narrowed. "But last night, I caught a tiny glimpse of what you let go. I didn't see my old roommate. I saw a woman who loves you. And all I could think was how I'd give my whole fucking life to find my own Jaymes Andrews. I'd give my whole fucking life to be *the guy* who carries her shoes and makes all her dreams come true."

He nods to the bed. "I wrote the hotel address on the bottom of her shoe."

I take two steps before glancing at the bottom of her shoes. He also wrote the date. I peer back at him, eyes narrowed.

Will grins. "I knew she'd want to remember the date she lost her shoes just to find you." He turns and struts toward the stairs. "It's time, buddy. Go bring our girl home, or else I will burn down the shed, kick your ass to the curb, and put a ring on her finger myself."

It takes me forty-seven minutes to step out of my truck. And when I do, it scares me more than any jump I've ever made from a plane. She's the fire I will never control. If I let her burn, she can bring new life.

I knock twice on her hotel-room door and wipe my hand across my forehead while swallowing past the lump of doubt in my throat. It's been six months. She shouldn't be here. I should have found her first. This is a terrible idea. She'll expect answers that I don't have. So I turn, but it's too late. She's opening the door.

Her wide eyes blink several times before they shift to the heels in my hand. "Will is a liar," she murmurs.

I don't know what she means. All I know is my heart wants to throat punch me. It's livid that I've kept it from her for six months. Every breath drops to the pit of my stomach—it feels like the first time I jumped. My body's disconnected from everything else. I must remind myself to breathe.

She's the breathtaking horizon.

The canopy that slows my fall.

The perfect place to land.

She's the quietude after the last flame dies.

"Can we talk?" I manage past the boulder in my throat.

Her gaze returns to mine, and she smiles and steps aside.

I hand her the heels and make my way to the far side of the room, next to the window.

"Who wrote in permanent marker on the bottom of my shoes?"

"I'll get to that." I sit on the window ledge.

She frowns at the writing on her shoes for a few more seconds before dropping them onto her bag and giving me her full attention. She's the best sight in the world, even in frayed denim shorts and a wrinkled white T-shirt. Not being with her has felt like a long trip from home.

"Is it . . ." My cowardly gaze drifts to my feet, and my voice loses momentum. "Is it okay if I need you? Or is it too late?"

She doesn't answer, so I'm forced to look at her.

Shaking her head, she sits on the end of the bed. "No. I'm not what you need."

God, she fucking slays me. "Why?"

"Because I require more than you have to give. And I know this because it's been six months, and Will stole my shoes to get us in the same room. That's not fate. It's manipulation."

"Maybe it's fate."

She scoffs. "You don't believe in fate."

"You don't know what I believe. And I know this because *I* don't know what I believe anymore. But I know sometimes you need to step back and distance yourself from the situation. Sometimes, you need to walk away to gain perspective and see things clearly."

"Are you telling me you've had a recent moment of clarity?"

"Yes," I say with unwavering confidence.

Her expression bleeds with uncertainty.

I shrug. "What do you need?" I'm dying. My *need* to touch her has me in knots, a suffocating rope around my neck while the ground beneath me begins to crumble. I rub my hands along my jeans.

She eyes my fidgety hands. "Everything," she whispers.

"Everything," I echo, nodding several times before standing. "Okay."

She shakes her head as I take a step toward her. "If you touch me . . ."

I stop. "Then what?"

Her head continues to shake while emotion builds in her eyes. "Then you'd better be ready to accept all of me."

Again, I echo her, "All of you." Then I take another step.

She swallows hard and bats away the first tear. "You'd better be ready to give me *everything*."

"Everything."

"No. You can't just repeat my words. You have to know what *every-thing* is."

I shrug. "It's everything."

She tips up her chin, so brave and strong—so beautiful. And she's everything I've convinced myself I don't deserve.

But dammit, I want her anyway.

"*Everything* is a wedding where you cry when you see me in my dress for the first time. And it's supporting my career as much as I support yours. It's digging my car out of the snow and doing all the dishes when I bake for you. It's not outrunning me on my skateboard."

I can't hide my grin as I take another step.

She holds out a flat hand and shakes her head. "It's a trip to the urologist to reverse your vasectomy."

I don't move. Not a blink. Not a breath.

"It's rubbing my back and feet while I grow our babies. It's sending me texts to let me know you're alive. It's only taking carefully calcu-lated risks with your life because it's no longer just yours. It's football games and trips to the beach. It's being a part-time homeschool teacher because we both know our kids will do weird but awesome shit, like studying the moon cycles and poring over books about world wars and sinking ships."

Just when I think she can't stretch her neck any further or set her jaw any firmer, she does. She waits patiently (and guardedly) for me to disappoint her again.

"Can you do that, Fitz? *All* of that?"

Again, I open my mouth and start to take the final step.

And again, she stops me. But she can't stop her tears. "And my f-father is dying." Her lower lip quivers. "And I know that makes you h-happy." She sniffles and wipes her face. "But it's *crushing* me." She bites her lips together and gulps more emotion. "And I need you *never to* say anything hurtful about h-him again." She holds her breath and shakes her head, voice barely audible. "I'm *truly* sorry. I know he's responsible for your family dying. And I *hate* that he caused you that kind of loss and pain. And I hate that he won't live long enough to be of sound mind, because I believe if he really understood what he did, his remorse would be so heavy that his heart would sink to the bottom of the ocean. I hate everything about that fire he started. I hate that he did it. But I don't hate *him*."

She sniffles, lower lip still trembling. "I've grown to love him in a complicated way, but Fitz . . . I love you more. So. Much. More."

I kneel before her, wedging my torso between her legs. First, I wipe her tears. Then, I rest the pads of my fingers on the back of her neck. "Everything," I whisper, brushing my lips against hers.

All the tension drains from her body, and she leans in, wrapping her arms around my neck and kissing me. Jaymes isn't the girl of my dreams. I never allowed myself that luxury.

She's the girl who has taught me how to dream.

I don't know what to say about her father. Fear of saying the wrong thing has a choke hold on me.

Her delicate hands frame my face; residual tears cling to her eyelashes. "Why is the date and hotel address on the bottom of my shoes?"

The rapid subject change draws a laugh from me. I glance over my shoulder at said shoes. "Will thought you'd want something to commemorate the day you lost your shoes so you could find me. He's an idiot."

"That's so romantic."

I roll my eyes.

"Do you think Mrs. Wilke will be my matron of honor?"

This. Woman.

How does she do it?

How does she open her heart so wide it can encompass the grief of losing her father *and* my need to breathe—my need to escape the gravity of the moment?

Not much brings me to tears, but Jaymes Andrews owns my emotions. She knows me better than anyone, including myself. And it has nothing to do with "getting to know me." She simply *gets* me.

"I haven't asked you to marry me. You're getting ahead of yourself." She remains statuesque, silently calling my bluff.

"I don't have the ring," I say, knowing that I'm going down. I know it. She knows it. But I think she'd be disappointed if I rolled over too easily.

She blinks. That's it—a single blink.

I grin.

Her soft lips twitch into their own tiny smile, and her thumb slides along my cheekbone.

"For the record," I continue, "I was coming to get you before I knew you were in town for the weekend. I didn't consciously know it, but that beating thing behind my rib cage knew it. So we're not giving Will credit for everything."

The sparkle in her eyes shines a little brighter the longer I hold out. All she's giving me is a knowing grin.

I can't let her win. I'll propose when I'm ready.

"I don't know the moon cycles. I'm going to mess things up. I think I'll be a good father, but we don't even know if my testicles can be fixed." Now I'm just grasping.

She breaks form just to give me a slow, reassuring nod.

"But I'm him." My fingertips stroke the back of her neck. "When the world's most fascinating woman stops by my work on a random Wednesday and offers me sex, I'm *him*. I'm the guy who will drop everything to have sex with her."

My confession threatens her composure as she rolls her lips between her teeth to hide her smile.

I turn my head so her palm brushes my lips, and I close my eyes and kiss it. Fuck it. She wins.

"Be my wife, Jaymes Barbara Keane Lanette Andrews."

When I open my eyes, more emotion fills hers.

I ghost my lips over her mouth and whisper, "I will love you like a hero. Jump without looking back. I will fight for you. I will save *us*."

Her soft laugh comes out as a tiny sob. "You're him." She kisses me. "You will always be *him*."

Epilogue

JAYMES

Ten days ago, Dwight Keane left this earth to reunite with his wife and the unborn child he never met. I believe he's making amends for his mistakes.

I believe there's life after death.

Today, I'm letting him go in a graveyard of burned trees—thousands of skewers pointed toward the blue sky, memorializing a tragedy while slowly fading into the lush green forest floor.

"You're not an easy person to find."

I startle, glancing over my shoulder. "What are you doing here?" I barely have a voice. "You're supposed to be at the Kinney Park fire."

Fitz retrieves a water bottle from his backpack and takes a long swig. "I heard your father died. Why didn't you text me?"

Staring at the jar of ashes in my hands, I murmur, "I thought it was good timing. You were busy. Nothing needed to be awkward. I could do what I needed, and that would be that."

He surveys the area, and I can't help but wonder what's going through his mind while he squints at the sun slicing through the tree skeletons. "Did you know"—he grins, waiting for me to recognize that he's using my line—"that the cones of certain species of trees need extreme heat to release their seeds? A resin has to be melted for the seeds to be set free. And these seeds grow best in burned soil. Sometimes, for something beautiful to take to life and grow, everything around it has to be sacrificed. All we see is the destruction, but if you wait long enough—if you're patient—*magic* happens." Sticks and crushed rocks crunch beneath his boots while he approaches me.

"I can't believe you're here," I whisper.

"Six weeks ago, you said *everything*. You also said yes." He takes my hand, fiddling with his mother's ring on my finger that means more than a promise. It's a symbol of forgiveness and trust.

All I can do is blink. No one loves as big as Calvin Fitzgerald.

He removes the lid from the jar. "Letting go is hard." He steps behind me, places his hands over mine, and we scatter the remains together. Emotion stings my eyes.

He presses his lips to my neck and kisses me. "Scattering human remains without a permit can result in a five-hundred-dollar fine and up to six months in jail."

I laugh, despite the tears. "I have a permit."

"Liar." He nips at my earlobe.

"You're such a rule follower."

Fitz's whole face nuzzles into my neck while his arms squeeze me tighter, and I giggle.

"Did you get the job in San Antonio?"

I slide in his arms to face him. "I think so. I have one more interview next week. And if that goes well, I'll be heading to Texas by the end of the month."

Fitz grins. "For how long?"

"Two months."

He hums and nods. "You'll like Texas."

I like Calvin Fitzgerald. And if I'd let my heart trump my brain, I'd be looking for a full-time position in Missoula. But Fitz wants me to fly for a bit so I never regret not traveling before having a family. So I plan on finding jobs that coincide with fire season and taking the winters off to hibernate with him in Missoula. And the rest will happen in the right time.

I ground him.

And he makes me soar.

When he releases me, he slides the jar into my backpack before hiking it over his shoulder next to his. Then he offers me his hand, and I take it. "Come on."

"Where are we going?" I ask.

"I don't know. We'll figure it out."

"I love you, Fitzy."

I only see the side of his face, half his ginormous grin. "I know you do."

I don't know why I expect any other answer. "And you love me."

"Too much."

Our love is magic.

Acknowledgments

Nina Grinstead, I love our friendship and the safe space you give me to work through the emotions that come with this writing gig. I'm blessed to have you by my side, opening doors and helping me chase my dreams.

Jenn Beach, thank you for doing all the hard work so that I can do what I love. You've accepted way more roles than I know either one of us ever imagined. We are a true team. Don't ever leave me!

Lauren Plude, I'm beyond grateful to you for giving me this chance and walking me through every step with kind and encouraging words. You were the first to say yes, and I'll never forget it.

Mackenzie Walton and Megan Westberg, thank you for making this story shine while being mindful of my voice on every page. You have challenged me to be a better writer. It's been a privilege to learn from you.

My readers, thank you for letting me live a dream life, welcoming me into your world, and allowing me to share mine with you.

Thank you to my family for being my favorite love story.

ABOUT THE AUTHOR

Photo © 2016 Anna Jones

Jewel E. Ann is a *Wall Street Journal* and *USA Today* bestselling author. She's written over thirty novels, including *Look the Part*, a contemporary romance; the Jack & Jill trilogy, a romantic suspense series; and *Before Us*, an emotional women's fiction story.

Ann is a free-spirited romance junkie with a quirky sense of humor. After her best friend of nearly thirty years suggested a few books from the contemporary romance genre, she was hooked. With ten years of flossing lectures under her belt, she took an early retirement from her dental hygiene career to stay home with her three awesome boys, manage the family business, and write mind-bending love stories. When she's not donning her cape to save the planet one tree at a time, Jewel enjoys yoga with friends, good food with family, rock climbing with her kids, and of course . . . heart-wrenching, tear-jerking, panty-scorching novels. She's living her best life in Iowa with her husband, three sons, and a goldendoodle.